BORN OF
BETRAYAL

SHERRILYN
KENYON

piatkus

PIATKUS

First published in the US in 2015 by St Martin's Press, New York
First published in Great Britain in 2015 by Piatkus

1 3 5 7 9 10 8 6 4 2

Copyright © 2015 by Sherrilyn Kenyon

The moral right of the author has been asserted.

*All characters and events in this publication, other than those
clearly in the public domain, are fictitious and any resemblance
to real persons, living or dead, is purely coincidental.*

All rights reserved.
No part of this publication may be reproduced, stored in a
retrieval system, or transmitted in any form or by any means, without
the prior permission in writing of the publisher, nor be otherwise circulated
in any form of binding or cover other than that in which it is published
and without a similar condition including this condition being
imposed on the subsequent purchaser.

A CIP catalogue record for this book
is available from the British Library.

ISBN {TPB} 978-0-349-40277-2

Printed and bound in Great Britain by
Clays Ltd, St Ives plc

Papers used by Piatkus are from well-managed forests
and other responsible sources.

MIX
Paper from
responsible sources
FSC® C104740

Piatkus
An imprint of
Little, Brown Book Group
Carmelite House
50 Victoria Embankment
London EC4Y 0DZ

An Hachette UK Company
www.hachette.co.uk

www.piatkus.co.uk

Since 2004, internationally bestselling author **Sherrilyn Kenyon** has placed over sixty novels on the *New York Times* bestseller list; in the past three years alone, she has claimed the No.1 spot seventeen times. This extraord̶ ̶ ̶ ̶ ̶ ̶ ̶ ̶ continu̶ ̶ ̶ ̶ ̶ ̶ ̶ ̶ ̶ ̶ ̶ ̶ ̶ ̶ ̶ ̶ ̶ she ̶rites ̶ ̶thin.

F̶ ̶ ̶ ̶ ̶ ̶ ̶ ̶ ̶ ̶ ̶ ̶ ̶ ̶ ̶ he p̶ ̶e-eminent voice in pa̶ranormal fiction ̶by critics, Kenyo̶ ̶ ̶ ̶ ̶ ̶ ̶ ̶ ̶elped pioneer – and define – the current para̶ ̶ ̶ ̶ ̶ ̶ ̶al trend that has ̶aptivated the world and continues to blaze new tra̶ ̶ ̶ ̶ tha̶ blur traditional genre lines.

With more than 25 million copies of her books in print in over 100 countries, her current series include: The Dark-Hunters, League, Lords of Avalon, Chronicles of Nick, and Belador Code.

Visit Sherrilyn Kenyon online:

www.darkhunter.com
www.sherrilynkenyon.co.uk
www.facebook.com/AuthorSherrilynKenyon
www.twitter.com/KenyonSherrilyn

Praise for Sherrilyn Kenyon:

'A publishing phenomenon . . . [Sherrilyn Kenyon] is the reigning queen of the wildly successful paranormal scene'
Publishers Weekly

'Kenyon's writing is brisk, ironic and relentlessly imaginative. These are not your mother's vampire novels'
Boston Globe

'Whether writing as Sherrilyn Kenyon or Kinley MacGregor, this author delivers great romantic fantasy!'
New York Times bestselling author Elizabeth Lowell

Sherrilyn Kenyon's
Dark-Hunter World Series:
(in reading order)

Fantasy Lover
Night Pleasures
Night Embrace
Dance with the Devil
Kiss of the Night
Night Play
Seize the Night
Sins of the Night
Unleash the Night
Dark Side of the Moon
The Dream-Hunter
Devil May Cry
Upon the Midnight Clear
Dream Chaser
Acheron
One Silent Night
Dream Warrior
Bad Moon Rising
No Mercy
Retribution
The Guardian
Time Untime
Styxx
Dark Bites
Son of No One
Dragonbane

The Dark-Hunter Companion

Dark Bites

Also by Sherrilyn Kenyon:

League Series

Born of Night
Born of Fire
Born of Ice
Born of Shadows
Born of Silence
Born of Fury
Born of Defiance
Born of Betrayal

The Belador Code

Blood Trinity
Alterant
The Curse
Rise of the Gryphon

Chronicles of Nick

Infinity
Invincible
Infamous
Inferno
Illusion

By Sherrilyn Kenyon writing
as Kinley MacGregor:

Lords of Avalon Series
Sword of Darkness
Knight of Darkness

For all the dreamers of the world who never give up, no matter how hard life tries to knock you down. You are the bravest of the brave and stand as heroes for us all.

To my readers, who are ever my source of comfort and joy. Thank you so much for all the smiles you've given me. And to my friends and family who understand my weird, quirky ways and are willing to share me with the voices in my head.

To my agent and editor, and the staff at St. Martin's (and my copyeditor), who work so very hard on our behalf to make each book the best it can be. You, too, are our silent, unsung heroes. You take a lot of fire in the background and yet march ever onward into the face of opposing forces to make sure we have the books we all cherish every month. Thank you for all you do.

May we never see a day where we live without our imaginary worlds and people to transport us away for our escape on those hours when we need it most.

BORN OF
BETRAYAL

PROLOGUE

Where are my clothes? And what did you do with my towel?"

Furious and defiant, Galene Batur lifted her chin with a dignity she definitely didn't feel as she faced Fain Hauk in the male locker room of their school.

Her worst enemy. Lying bastard.

Faithless dog!

Seething, she raked a glare over his perfect naked body. A body that earlier this day would have left her breathless with heat.

But now . . .

Now she wanted every inch of that lush, caramel skin flayed off his bones. Most of all, she wanted his betraying heart in her fist.

"It's true, isn't it?" she asked breathlessly.

Fain scowled at her. "Is what true?"

"Are you in love with a human?"

"Excuse me?"

"Don't you dare deny it! Merrell Anatole just told me that he saw you and Omira Antaxas having sex yesterday! Yesterday! After I left you and went to get ready for the party! How could you?"

The color faded from his face, confirming her worst fear as he stammered, no doubt searching for a believable lie.

For a full minute, she thought she'd be sick. Tears filled her eyes as she struggled to breathe. No wonder Fain had asked her to leave a few minutes ago when she'd been trying to give him what she stupidly thought was joyous news. He no longer loved her. Merrell had been right. Fain didn't care. She'd lost him completely.

To a human!

"You're pledged to *me*, Fain!"

A tic started in his jaw. "By our parents. Before we even started school. Neither of us had a say in it."

As if that mattered? A pledge was a pledge. To an Andarion, it was as binding as marriage. And he was supposed to honor his word.

Honor *her*. No wonder he'd refused to touch her again all these weeks since his birthday. He'd barely come near her after she'd given him everything she had of herself. Her heart and body.

Her very soul.

Now she knew why. And here she'd stupidly thought he might have gone stralen. That, she could have lived with. But this . . . *this* she would have never believed. Not of her precious Fain. He'd promised to love her forever.

There's only you for me, Stormy.

Apparently *not*.

Agony choked her. "You've betrayed me!"

He looked away. "I'm sorry, Galene."

Furious, she snatched her pledge ring from her finger and threw it in his face. He didn't react at all as it struck his chest and bounced away. Damn her bad aim! The least she could have done was put out his eye!

How could he do this to her after all these years? Tears choked her even harder as his words shattered her heart.

Worse, they shattered her dreams. She'd come here to share with him the most blessed news. This was supposed to be the happiest day of her life.

Instead, it was the most miserable.

No, *he* was the most miserable!

Since their parents had pledged them over a decade ago, she'd lived only for the day when they'd marry. Had dreamed only of a life partnered with Fain Hauk.

Now he'd not only dishonored her, he'd done it with a human. A *human*!

"Where are my clothes?" he demanded again. "What did you do with the towels?"

She'd hidden them both, but damned if she'd tell him that. "Why don't you ask your *woman*?" She started for the doors.

Fain caught her. "Galene! This isn't funny."

She snatched her arm from his grasp and bared her fangs

at him. "No, it isn't. At all! You have shamed me and I curse you for it, Fain Hauk. I hope you spend eternity in utter agony!"

Before he could recover, she shoved his naked ass through the doors, into an auditorium full of sentient beings—parents, students, and teachers—and locked the doors behind him.

This was their graduation.

In more ways than one.

A tiny bit of regret went through her over what she'd just done to him, but she refused to let it take root. He deserved it, and more.

This is about payback.

After this, everyone would laugh at her, just as they were laughing at Fain right now. Once word got out that Fain had chosen a human over her, she would be tainted for the rest of her life. No decent family would ever accept a pledge from hers again.

With his actions, he'd damned them both.

So be it. She didn't need a husband. She damn sure didn't need one whose heart belonged to some *human* female.

And still the agony of losing him was there. An agony that would only worsen once her parents learned of this. They would be so disappointed in her.

Galene pulled her ornate veil from her hair and let it fall free. Forget graduation. There was nothing here for her, except more humiliation, and she'd had enough of that in her life. She would not go out there and be laughed at or pitied.

Fain wanted a human. She wanted dignity.

And by the gods, she would have it. From this day forward, she would never again trust in anyone. She knew better.

Human. Andarion. It didn't matter. Sentient creatures used and they lied. And she was done with them all.

"You better hope I never lay eyes on you again, Fain Hauk." Because the next time she did, she *would* kill him.

CHAPTER 1

It was all-out war.

Prime Commander Galene Batur stared at the report of the League attack on an Andarion outpost where almost two hundred civilians had been mercilessly slaughtered.

And for what?

Human vanity? How she hated their inferior species. Humans had never brought her anything but utter misery. Now they had brought her a whole new bloody war that would cost the lives of countless Andarions. Cost her the lives of her loyal soldiers who would be forced to protect their repugnant species.

How she wished she could bomb the entire human race into oblivion.

"Commander?"

She looked over her shoulder at her lieutenant commander's call. Dressed in the standard red and black Andarion command uniform, Talyn wasn't just her second-in-command

and adjutant, he was the only male she'd ever trust at her back.

At twenty-nine, he stood head and shoulders above her, and most everyone else. Muscular and unbelievably handsome, he wore his long black hair in typical Andarion warrior fashion—tiny braids that were held away from his face by a red band. Her only complaint with him was the well-trimmed moustache and goatee he'd started wearing lately. It was a current fashion trend she didn't care for. At all. But he thought it made him look more masculine and sexy.

As if he needed help in either of those departments.

Still, his presence caused her heart to soften. It took everything she had not to reach out and cup his beloved cheek and kiss it tenderly. But he wouldn't approve of such open affection before the rest of their troops.

Her Talyn was always prim and proper. Always circumspect. Respectful.

"Yes?"

Talyn saluted her. "I have an urgent message for you from the royal house."

Galene forced herself not to wince. It must be the tadara wanting information she had yet to gather about the attack.

Sighing that she didn't have more to offer, she headed for the secured line. She placed the link in her ear before she opened the channel.

Instead of Tadara Cairistiona eton Anatole, it was Tahrs Nykyrian who showed on her monitor. Unlike his fraternal twin brother who'd been removed from succession, Nykyrian appeared human with his white-blond hair and green eyes. The only part of him that betrayed his Andarion roots was his set of fangs . . . along with his height and military prowess. While she might not appreciate his human half, she definitely respected his exemplary war record and battle skills.

She gave him a curt bow. "Your Highness, to what do I owe this honor?"

"I know you're busy, Commander, and I hate to take your attention away from our troops for even a second, but I have serious business to discuss with you. The Alliance has decided that we need a single military leader we can trust to oversee our joint forces and armies as we fight against The League. Your name was the first one to come to our minds, and we are all in agreement. We'd like to offer the position to you."

Stunned, she stared at him, amazed by the offer. "I'm honored, Highness."

"If you need time to think it over . . ."

Was he serious? Who in their right mind would turn this down? This was a dream appointment anyone would kill to possess. A once-in-a-lifetime opportunity.

Galene would command the single largest military movement in the entire history of their United System of Planets.

"No, Highness. I would love to lead Alliance forces. I only have one concern. I know that part of our forces are Phrixian and Caronese." Misogynistic troops and armies that would balk heavily at taking orders from a female commander.

"You'll be assigned a male adjutant for handling them . . . a well-respected Tavali commander. Likewise, you'll be responsible for dealing with the Qillaq directly, since they won't take orders from a male."

That was certainly true.

It was rare for any army to be as integrated with both sexes as the Andarions were. Male or female didn't matter. Only competence and lethal skill did.

"When would you like for me to start?" she asked.

"Immediately. The Tavali are on their way to you right now with a transport and your new adjutant. The two of you will be flown to their northernmost base, where The League has been making their heaviest strikes. All we'll need is for you to name your successor for the Andarion armada, until the war is over."

Galene gestured to Talyn. "We will see it done."

Nykyrian inclined his head to her. "Welcome aboard, Commander. May the gods smile upon you. Always."

"Thank you, Your Highness. I promise, I will do you, your mother, and Andaria proud."

"I know you will." He cut the transmission.

Galene stared at the blank screen as she considered this latest twist of fate.

Wow. She, the daughter her parents had callously thrown out from their house when she was just a girl, was going to lead their combined forces in the war against The League. If they won, she'd be eternally famous. Revered and renowned. A celebrated war hero equal to the beloved War Hauks who'd once saved their race from conquest and slavery.

If they lost, she'd be executed for treason.

One hell of a gamble. But then, as the Andarion armada's prime commander she'd die if they lost, anyway. At least as their military leader, it would all be in her hands, and if they failed, she alone would be to blame.

Thrilled and a little scared, she turned toward Talyn.

His beautiful white eyes glowed with loving pride. "Congratulations, Commander."

She smiled at him. "I shall name you the new prime commander of the armada."

He shook his head. "I will go with you to The Tavali."

"No . . . you belong here."

"I belong at your back, Commander. Protecting you. Always."

"Talyn—"

"Mom," he stressed the word, making her realize that she'd dropped their strict military behavior first, by using his given name. "I will not stay here while you interact with others who could betray you. You will need a support staff you know is loyal to you and above reproach. Now more than ever. If you think for one moment that I will stay behind while you risk your life for all of us, you don't know me at all." His gaze burned into hers. "You go. I go."

She wanted to beat him. But how could she? "You are ever my pride."

"And you are ever my cherished mother."

Smiling, she pulled his head down so that she could press her cheek to his. "I love you, *mi tana*."

"I love you, too."

She fisted her hand in his hair. "I should order you to stay."

"Only if you wish to see me court-martialed."

She tugged at his hair. "Don't tempt me, scamp." Releasing him, she stepped away with a frown. "Call Commander Ilkin. We can promote him."

"Yes, ma'am. And I'll personally assemble an Andarion security detail for you."

Galene rolled her eyes at his paranoia—as if she couldn't protect herself. She would argue that with him, too, but he was far more stubborn than she was when it came to such things. Years of fighting his steel will had taught her that.

"See it done quickly."

He saluted her. "Yes, ma'am."

Her heart swelling with love and pride, Galene watched him leave to carry out his orders. In all the universe, he was the only family she had. The only family she needed.

You should have been a surgeon, Talyn. It was what she'd drilled into him from the cradle. But her ever-defiant boy had refused, and followed her into the military as soon as he graduated primary school.

Evil little booger. Stubborn and headstrong . . .

Just like his father.

No one could ever tell him what to do. The gods knew she had tried. Many times.

Now he would follow her into war. It was the last thing she'd ever wanted for Talyn. But there was no way to keep him out of it. The time had come for all of them to choose a side.

At least this way I can keep an eye on him.

And she would tear apart anyone who threatened her baby.

Sighing, Galene took a moment to look around the Andarion command center that had been her home since Cairistiona had overthrown her own mother and assumed the throne. Talyn had been here, at her side, almost the entire time she'd led their armada. It would be weird to adjust to a new army. A new way of doing things.

But she was nothing if not adaptable.

Okay, not really. She hated change passionately. But she liked to lie to herself about her inflexible flexibility.

Still, a whole new chapter was about to begin for both her and Talyn. She didn't know what it would hold, but she couldn't wait to see where it led her.

Good wind blows to all ill things.

A chill went down her spine as she remembered her father's old saying. She only prayed that this time, he was wrong.

CHAPTER 2

F ain felt his stomach shrink with dread as they dropped tether and called for the Andarion contingency they were here to pick up.

I fucking hate you, Jayne. This was why he didn't have friends. Why he didn't want them. Because they invariably did shit like this to him.

His brother, Dancer, and Dancer's friend Jayne thought it was funny to volunteer him to be the adjutant for a female who hated his guts with the fire of a million suns.

It wasn't.

The last time he'd seen Galene Batur, she'd shoved his ass into a public arena with all his business hanging out, and had locked the door behind him. Something he'd been beaten for, and not just by his parents who'd been horrified by the indecent display.

He couldn't wait to see what Galene would do to him this time.

Probably shoot me.

If he was lucky.

If he was really lucky, it wouldn't be in his balls.

Sighing irritably, he stood up to get it over with. There was no need in delaying the inevitable. He might be a lot of things, but a coward had never been one of them.

And it wasn't like he hadn't been shot before. At least this time he had on battle armor. As long as she didn't shoot him in the head or groin, he would survive the encounter.

Physically, anyway.

Dignity . . . might be a problem. They were oh for seven on that one.

He hesitated by the door and pulled down a helmet so that he could add an extra layer of protection between his groin and whatever might go flying at a part of his anatomy he'd like to preserve. Though, to be honest, he wasn't sure why at this point. Not like he had many chances to use it anymore.

Don't go there.

Chayden clapped him on the back. "You all right, Hauk? You look like you're about to hurl."

Fain cut a glare toward his friend. *Hurl? No . . .*

Kill. Definitely.

"I'm fine."

Fain's little brother came out of the holding area to stand next to him. "I'm with Chay. You look a little green, *drey.*"

Fain dodged Dancer's hand as his brother reached to touch his forehead, and barely resisted the urge to slap him. "I know you were just a kid when I ran off with Omira. But do you remember the fact that I was pledged to an Andarion female before I married her?"

Dancer's jaw dropped. "No. I have no memory of that at all. Who were you pledged to?"

Fain faced the ramp that was lowering in front of them. "Prime Commander Galene Batur."

Dancer's curses rang in his ears as Fain headed down the ramp toward the one female he was sure would gut him on the spot. As he scanned the gathered Andarion soldiers, he kept the helmet carefully positioned.

Just in case.

His gaze went straight to her, as if it was drawn there by magic. *Damn,* was the first thought that went through his head. As with all Andarion females, Galene had been a gorgeous teen. But the adult warrior waiting on them had to be one of the sexiest, most beautiful of her kind. Because Andarions aged much slower than their human counterparts, she didn't appear any older than thirty.

Tall, lithe, and exquisite, she was dressed in a standard red and black Andarion battlesuit. One that hugged a body made to be privately worshiped by hours of leisurely naked activities.

And often.

He sucked his breath in sharply as an involuntary image went through his mind of her wrapping those long legs around him. He hadn't been this attracted to a female in a long time. Not since the last time he'd seen her.

Every part of him was alert and panting.

And he was twice as glad now for the helmet at his crotch.

I should have worn looser pants. God help him if he had to sit down with a hard-on this fierce. That pain alone might kill him.

Focus.

Something much easier said than done.

What the hell had I been thinking or drinking when I walked away from that?

Young and stupid didn't quite cover it. But then, there'd been extenuating circumstances that had forced his hand. Things that had made staying with her completely out of the question. *Maybe I should have fought harder to stay.*

Yeah, right. It hadn't been that simple.

A fight, he could have won. What they held over his head had been totally out of his control and beyond his young abilities to stop.

She looked up and met his gaze. His throat went dry as his body hardened even more and he remembered the way she used to look at him.

Like he was her cherished hero.

And I fucked her over. Badly.

Yeah, he'd earned the hell that had been his life. How he wished things could have been different. Especially between the two of them. While he'd been enamored of Omira, it was nothing compared to what he'd felt for Galene when they were kids. This was his first and only real love.

The one who'd gotten away and had haunted him every minute of his life.

His one true regret.

The worst decisions in life are always the ones we make out of fear.

He hated to admit how right his father had been whenever the old bastard had quoted that. But life had shown him just how wise his father was.

At first, her gaze swept past him, to the other Tavali trailing in his wake. She had no idea who he was.

Not until he pulled his Tavali mask down and exposed his face.

Galene was impressed by the military formation and discipline of the Tavali crew—something she'd never expected from outlaw pirates who were as famed for their blatant disregard of rules and social conventions as they were for their savagery. While they each wore different uniforms and styles of battlesuits, they conducted themselves like any disciplined army.

She'd been told that they had their own set of laws they strictly adhered to, but she hadn't believed it.

Until now.

This was impressive. And the one leading them was a huge, massive warrior. One equal in size to Talyn, which was quite a feat for any species. Tall and broad-shouldered with braided hair laced with bleached blond stripes, he was even more muscular than an average Andarion male.

And that swagger . . .

It was masculine and mouthwatering. Confident. She had no idea of his species, but whatever it was, he did credit to it.

That was her thought until he stopped and stood with all of his weight on his left leg. She almost smiled at a commanding stance that was identical to one Talyn preferred, especially whenever he was uncomfortable with his surroundings.

The Tavali's gaze held hers hostage as he slowly reached up with one hand to lower the black and red mask that concealed his war-painted face.

Andarion. That explained his white eyes.

Just as she was sucking her breath in, in appreciation of his rugged handsomeness, recognition slammed into her. Yes, he was older and now sported three days' growth of his beard, but she knew that proud jawline. Knew those perfect, gorgeous features and caramel skin that had once set her on fire.

Actually, they still did. Only instead of lust, they filled her with raw, unmitigated rage.

Reacting on pure instinct, she pulled her blaster out and fired. The shot landed straight in his chest where his missing heart should have been.

Total chaos erupted as he fell to the ground and the other Tavali pulled their blasters out and took aim. As did the Andarion soldiers with her.

Throwing himself in front of her, Talyn pulled the weapon from her hand. He and the ten Andarions he'd chosen as her personal guard formed a wall between her and the others.

"Medic!" a human Tavali called out in Andarion.

"Arrest them!" a Sentella soldier demanded.

Galene looked past Talyn's shoulder to see Dancer Hauk, Fain's younger brother, calling out for the soldiers to secure her and her team.

Talyn moved in closer, to protect her.

"No!" She grabbed her son's arm to keep him from doing something even more rash than *her* stupidity. "Stand down!"

Talyn did, until a soldier went to cuff her wrists. "Get your hands off her!"

Before she could catch him again, Talyn had eight Tavali and two of their own bleeding on the ground at his feet. With a blaster in each hand, Talyn held the others at bay as he kept himself in front of her. "Anyone else want a free trip to the hospital and paid leave?"

"Talyn!" she snapped, placing her hand on his shoulder. "Enough! Everyone calm down."

Dancer held his blaster angled at Talyn's head. "I believe *you* started this, Commander, when you shot my brother."

"And now I'm ending it. Everyone, arms down!"

They all hesitated.

"Dancer!" Fain growled as he rose to his feet. "Drop your weapon." Biting his lip, he grimaced and glared a hole through her. "I deserved it."

Only then did Dancer lower his blaster.

"Talyn," she said gently as she ran her hand down his arm and pushed his aim toward the floor. "It's all right."

She felt his muscles flexing in debate before he glanced to her and let his weapons fall to the ground. The Tavali surged forward to handcuff him. Something he didn't protest until they went to cuff her again.

Faster than anyone could blink, Talyn knocked the two guards closest to him away and used his foot to kick his blaster back into his hand. He put himself between her and the others.

"One hand to the commander and so help me, I'll fucking kill every one of you bitches!"

Fain's gaze darkened as Talyn's weapon went back to Dancer, who was inching toward them. With unbelievable speed, Fain attacked Talyn.

Galene's head spun as cold terror consumed her. Both Fain and Talyn were former titled Andarion Ring fighters. And right now, they fought with death in their eyes. If she didn't do something fast, they'd tear each other apart.

Dodging their blows, she forced herself between them, and pushed them to opposite sides.

"Enough!" she roared.

Dancer moved forward to take Fain by his arm.

Holding his chest where she'd shot him, Fain spat the blood on his lips to the ground. He glared his hatred at Talyn. "Aim at my brother again, and I'll rip your fucking spine out, punk!"

Talyn didn't flinch at the threat. "One hand to the commander again, and I'll rip apart every ass here, including yours *and* his, *old man.*"

She sucked her breath in sharply at the double-edged insult. Not just that Fain was older, but to insinuate he wasn't Andarion . . . it was the worst sort of slap in the face for their kind.

Fain licked at his busted lip as he watched Galene place her hand over the heart of the soldier in front of him.

"It's all right, *mi courani,*" she said in a gentle tone, using an endearment that called the male soldier her precious heart. "Stand down."

The soldier's eyes softened as he glanced at her and covered her hand with his. Lowering his head, he brought her hand to his lips, and kissed it before he stepped back.

But not so far that he couldn't shield her with his body again if he needed to.

Disgusted, Fain met Dancer's gaze and shook his head. Galene had chosen quite the boy toy for herself. The kid was large, even for an Andarion. And as much as Fain hated to admit it, the bastard could fight. It was actually impressive what he'd done.

And the ease with which he'd accomplished it.

"Isn't he a little young for you?" Fain asked her snidely.

Galene pinned him with a sneer. "I don't think it's any of your business who I live with."

Fain's jaw went slack that she'd openly admit such a scandalous relationship in front of everyone. While it wasn't unheard of for unmarried commanders to sleep with their staff, they were usually highly discreet about it. Rarely did they flaunt it.

He scowled at her. "Well, aren't you full of surprises?"

She raked him with a scathing grimace. "I learned early . . . from the best."

He took a step forward.

So did Talyn.

Galene pushed them apart again. "Boys! Enough!"

Fain curled his lip before he dropped a potent verbal bomb on them. "You do realize that you both just attacked a member of the Andarion royal family?"

Galene gaped. "Excuse me?"

Dancer quirked a smug grin. "The tadara adopted my brother."

Fain expected that to take some of the fire out of her boy toy's eyes. It didn't. Defiant and reckless, he snorted disdainfully at the news.

"Talyn!" Galene snapped before the child could speak. "Not another word. I mean it!"

He inclined his head respectfully. "Yes, Commander." But his gaze said that he was struggling to hold back his opinion.

And it wasn't a happy one.

Fain returned his sneer with one of his own. "I should have you both arrested."

"Try it," the male said with an arrogant, taunting grin. "You'll be dead before they cuff me. . . . If I'm going to jail again, old man, I'm going to make it count."

"Talyn!"

A tic started in his jaw as Galene reached up, buried her hand in his braids, and forced the boy to meet her gaze. Only then did the fire in his eyes go out.

She pressed her cheek to his and whispered in his ear before she kissed his forehead. Her hand lingered on his goatee as her gaze held his a moment longer.

Finally quelled, the soldier took a step back.

Fain swept his gaze around the other Andarions here. The fact that none of their soldiers found this display odd said it all about Galene's open affair with her second-in-command.

Normally, Andarions never touched each other in public. Not even married couples. Unless they were fighting, it was their custom to keep a respectful distance from each other at all times.

A fierce, unwarranted hatred for the boy consumed him. He had no idea why he'd care or feel the jealousy inside his heart, but he did. And it wanted that kid's head on a pike.

While Fain's entire life had gone straight to hell after their last encounter, it was obvious Galene had been living quite the dream with her child-lover.

Galene stepped back as the medics arrived to tend Fain's injuries.

She met Dancer's glare. "We shall withdraw to my office, where I will contact Tadara Cairistiona immediately and inform her what has happened. If she still wants my arrest, I'll surrender myself to her authority. Until then . . ." She turned her curled lip toward Fain. "I hope you die painfully of your wounds."

And with that, she walked away.

Talyn passed one more hate-filled glare at him before he followed after her. Like a dutiful puppy.

Little fucking bastard.

Yeah, okay, huge fucking bastard, but still . . .

The medic let out a low, evil laugh as she saw Fain's wounds. And especially the one at his eye that was already swelling, and burning like a mother. "I see you met the commander's bodyguard. What'd you do? Speak to her in the wrong tone of voice?"

Fain gave the Andarion female an arched brow. "Does he do this kind of thing a lot?"

She snorted as she examined his eye. "Actually, he must like you."

"How so?"

"You're still breathing. He normally kills anyone who so much as grimaces in the commander's general direction."

Dancer sighed as Fain sat down on the stretcher and allowed them to remove his chest plate to inspect the blast wound. "I'm sorry, Fain. When you said she was a nasty piece of work, I should have listened to you. I had no idea she'd hate you *this* much. I thought I was the only one you motivated to this level of violence."

Fain looked down at the bleeding wound in the center of his chest. Had he been wearing anything other than his Tavali armor, that shot would have killed him instantly. As it was, it hurt like hell and he'd be bruised for a few days, but he'd live. "I figured she wouldn't be happy to see me again. However, I did underestimate her exact degree of hatred for me."

"What did you do to her?" Chayden picked up the helmet Fain had been holding against his groin.

Fain swallowed hard as he met Dancer's gaze before he answered Chay's question. "I broke off our engagement to marry a human."

The medic sucked her breath in sharply at his words.

As a human, Chayden had no idea what a slap that was, and what it would have cost Galene in their society. "Yeah? So?"

The medic snorted. "She must have really loved you at one time."

"Why?"

"She didn't shoot you between the eyes."

Galene swallowed hard as the door to her office closed, and she moved to call the tadara. She'd no more than reached for the controls when Talyn finally spoke to her.

"So that's my father."

"Excuse me?"

He sighed heavily. "There's no other male you'd attack like that, for no reason. Only Fain Hauk."

Tears choked her at his emotionless tone. "If you knew, why did you attack him?"

"He came at my mother. No one does that. I don't care who or what you are."

She could kill Talyn for his own recklessness . . . which he'd inherited from Fain. "You shouldn't have endangered yourself for me. You know better."

He shrugged nonchalantly. "You didn't hesitate to protect me."

"I'm your mother."

"And I'm your son . . . as you raised me."

She was torn between the desire to hug him for that, and spank his bottom like she'd done when he was a boy. "I told you to be a doctor, didn't I?"

He gave her an impertinent grin. "You raised me to be fierce. Like you. Not to don a medic's robe and serve others."

"Careful," she warned him, "you're not so big or old that I can't still take you over my knee."

He snorted derisively at her threat. "I'd like to see you try."

She popped his butt. "Impudent boy."

The light in his eyes faded as her link buzzed. "Is that the tadara?"

"Most likely."

Talyn gave her a sincere look that said he would be more than willing to die for her. "I won't let them harm you, Matarra. Not for that worthless piece of shit."

"He's your father, Talyn. I won't have you insult him."

The tic returned to his jaw as he looked away.

She moved to answer her link. As predicted, it was Tadara Cairistiona.

"What happened?" she asked without preamble.

Galene bowed her head respectfully. "Forgive me, *mu tadara*. I was caught off guard and allowed my emotions to get the better of me. I had no idea that you had adopted a new son. You should have told me we had a new royal family member to protect, and that he would be arriving with The Tavali."

The look on the queen's face was stern and lethal. "It's just us, Galene. I want your side of this matter before I render verdict. And I want the whole story."

Galene's gaze went to Talyn. "Before His Highness was disowned by his Hauk birth mother, I was pledged to him."

Cairistiona sucked her breath in sharply. "Fain left you for the human he married?"

She nodded. "Because of his actions, I was abandoned by my own family and turned out in disgrace."

"Say no more, Commander. I understand. I would have shot him myself, in your place."

Thank the gods the tadara was so understanding. But then they had decades of history together. And an unbreakable loyalty to one another.

"I am sorry, Tadara. Had I some warning about Fain's identity, I would have handled it better. But this is the first time I've seen him since the day he told me I failed to please him."

Cairistiona's speculative gaze went past Galene, to Talyn. "Is he Talyn's father?"

Galene clenched her teeth. Only two living beings besides her knew the identity of Talyn's father. Talyn and his great-grandmother, who'd taken her in years ago when Galene had been living on the street, pregnant with him.

But it was a death sentence to lie to her queen. "Yes, Majesty."

"Does he know?"

"I've never kept such secrets from my son. Talyn knows. His father does not."

Cairistiona let out a bitter laugh. "Talyn?"

He cast a concerned glance to his mother before he stepped forward and bowed to her. *"Mu tadara?"*

"It appears you are now of royal vestiture, child. My grandson. A tiziran of Andaria."

His jaw went slack. Until now, he'd lacked full lineage. As such, he'd been ineligible for many Andarion benefits, including marriage. It was something they'd both accepted a long time ago as a very bitter fact.

Now . . .

"What have you to say, Tiziran Talyn?"

He swallowed hard before he spoke. "I know not, Majesty."

"Yaya," Cairistiona corrected playfully, using the Andarion term for grandmother. She laughed at the stunned expression on his handsome face. "Breathe, child. Remember, you once sat in my lap to color and draw on paper, and do your homework for school. . . . I know it'll take some getting used to. Your father is having the same trouble acclimating to the title. But you will in time."

She returned her attention to Galene. "It appears I cannot punish my grandson for protecting his birth mother. Even from his birth father. And while I would normally have your head for this assault, the circumstances were extenuating. As such, and given the fact that Fain will live and is remarkably understanding of your motivation, I'll let this event pass un-punished. But let's not repeat it, shall we?"

"Never, Majesty."

"Cairistiona or Matarra, Galene. You are the mother of my grandson, after all. As such, I will send a contingency of royal guards for you both. And while Talyn, as tiziran, can be excused from military service, I'm going to assume that he has no inten-tion of leaving your side while we're at war." She passed a ques-tioning look to him.

"My place is with my mother."

Cairistiona smiled proudly. "Spoken like a true Andarion."

Her gaze returned to Galene. "If you can refrain from slaughtering the father of your child, we shall proceed as if none of this has happened. Is that acceptable?"

"Yes, Majesty."

"Cairistiona."

Galene hesitated before she spoke again. "Cairistiona . . . I'm assuming you'll want me to step down as——"

"No. I'd like to see you continue on as the commander of our combined forces. You are still the most qualified to lead us. And I'd feel much more confident with you at the helm than a commander from one of the other nations."

"It will be my honor, Ma . . . Matarra?"

Cairistiona smiled in approval. "Very good. And have no fear that I will tell Fain about his child. That is your place." She sighed heavily. "For now, I will say that the additional guard is to make sure the two of you don't attack him. However, there are certain advantages our precious little lorina will have as a tiziran. I'm sure both of you will want them for him. When you're both ready, let me know and I will make a public announcement for Talyn."

Galene inclined her head to her. "Thank you. For everything."

"Don't thank me yet, Lena. This has all the earmarks for disaster. We are at war with The League. If we lose, all of us will pay with our lives. We have committed treason against the organization that has reigned over all our worlds for the last five hundred years. May the gods be with us all." Then, she cut her transmission.

Indeed. Galene turned toward her son. "Funny, this was not how I saw the day going in my mind when I woke up this morning."

Talyn laughed. "Nor I."

Her gaze softened as she digested his new place in their world. It was more than deserved and she couldn't have wished better for him. "Tiziran Talyn. It has a beautiful ring to it."

He scoffed at her words. "I'm not a tiziran, Matarra. This changes nothing."

"It changes everything. It silences all those bastards who have mocked you for being a lack-Vest. All those spiteful bitches who have turned their noses up whenever you've glanced their way and they learned you held only my lineage. I can't wait to see them choke on their own bile when they hear this news."

And still he shook his head with blatant disregard. "I've never cared what they thought of me."

That was sadly true and she knew it. But he had cared what they thought of her. She'd mopped too many tears from his beautiful face when he'd been a small child. Had tended too many bloody noses from the fights he'd been in with those who had called her whore and worse.

And she'd seen the silent hurt in his teenaged eyes when females had viciously spurned him because he had no paternal lineage. Only his mother's broken one. They had been so incredibly cruel to him.

Even his military rank had been viciously stripped from him at one time because of Fain and his family's feud with the Anatoles.

He'd suffered so much as a direct result of what his father had done. For Fain abandoning them. That, more than anything, was what she hated Fain for. She could handle her own humiliation. She'd chosen her path with her own free will.

It was what had been unjustly given to Talyn that burned bitterest.

What her son had been forced to endure that made her crave vengeance from his father. Her proud, precious baby had deserved none of it.

Tears choked her. "You have ever been my brave champion." When everyone else had abandoned her, Talyn had stayed by her side. Ever the dutiful son.

Maybe not verbally. He did have his father's limited fuse, and a smart mouth capable of lethal sarcasm that had tested her temper and restraint on many occasions.

But his heart had always been loyal. Always loving.

Always ferocious. Her fierce little lorina.

"You deserve to be a tiziran."

"Titles mean nothing to me. You know that."

Only his rank as her adjutant had ever mattered to him. He'd worked insanely hard to achieve his rank as fast as possible so that he could be with her and watch over her. Something that had been twice as hard for him since he'd lacked his father's prestigious military lineage and had been under the direct command of his father's childhood enemies.

It was why he'd been forced to become a prizefighter for the Andarion Ring as a mere boy. With every title he'd earned, his military rank was supposed to advance to match his proven martial skills. Yet he'd had so many boulders hurled at him that unlike other Andarions, it hadn't happened the way it should have.

But even without his father's lineage, even with her being harder on him than she was on her other soldiers, he'd risen to become one of the youngest officers in the Andarion military. Had attained his current rank at an age when most were only beginning their obligatory service. Had risked literally life and limb to keep them all safe.

He had done her proud.

"You may think nothing of those things, Talyn. However, that's not true of others, and I know how much you want to marry and start your own family."

He looked away, but not before she saw the bitter yearning that lived inside him for something he'd been denied all these years.

"Exactly. I do know *you,* my son. As tiziran, you will have your choice now of any female who meets your fancy."

He scoffed at her words. "If I wasn't good enough for them without a royal title, I damn sure don't want them because of it. Besides, I love my Felicia. I'm grateful and lucky to have her in my life."

Galene bit back a scoff at his words. While she adored Felicia for taking care of Talyn whenever he was allowed liberty, she knew the truth.

Felicia was still a paid companion—a contracted mistress who lacked full lineage, too. One Talyn had been forced to pay top dollar to keep in a style that was unheard of for others of Felicia's birth standing. And the unfair terms of Felicia's original contract still sickened Galene. No other Andarion male would have been forced to sign such a travesty, or spend the credits Talyn did for her services.

Or to buy out her contract from her agency, as he'd been forced to do. Galene flinched as she remembered *that* particular nightmare, and what it'd cost Talyn.

But because of her and Fain, Talyn's social standing ranked below even that of a slave's. It didn't matter how many fighting titles he'd earned. How many citations and awards he gained as a military hero. He was still unable to legally marry.

Even a paid companion.

Worse? Only one companion brokerage in all of Andaria had been willing to contract with him at all. The rest had rudely slammed their doors in his face, leaving him with no other options for a female in his life.

Title and lineage were all that mattered to their race. The purer the lineage, the better, and the more choices an Andarion had.

Had Fain married her as he was supposed to, Talyn would have had all the pride and dignity of a military prince. Instead, Fain had abandoned them and taken his lineage with him.

But now that Fain had a new family lineage, Talyn might be able to salvage the rest of *his* future. "Your father's blood gives you everything I never could."

"You've given me the only things that matter."

Cupping his cheek, she shook her head. "You should have married long ago. We should be planning the Endurance for your eldest child by now."

He rolled his eyes at her. "I don't need a wife nagging me. I have a viciously overprotective mother for that."

Before she could respond, her office door pulsed open. She glanced past Talyn's shoulder to see the arrogant beast himself entering without being announced. Her lips curled involuntarily.

Talyn pulled her against his chest and held her so that she couldn't attack Fain again. "Don't kill him," he whispered in her ear. "Cairistiona won't forgive you that."

Laughing, she hugged him close. "All right." She kissed his cheek before she let go.

"I'll be just outside." Talyn passed a threatening glare to Fain. "Call me if you need anything, Commander."

"I will, Talyn. Thank you." Forcing herself to remain calm, she faced Fain. "What are you doing here?"

Grimacing in distaste, Fain watched Talyn until the door was closed behind him. "You just can't keep your hands off him, can you?"

Galene arched a brow at the jealousy she heard in that deep, sexy tone of his, and couldn't resist egging it on. "You should have been in here a few minutes ago when I was physically spanking his little ass. I think you would have enjoyed it. I know I did."

He twisted his lips up in disgust. "You really live with him?"

"Yes. I have for years."

"And what? Do you have to burp him after you feed him, too?"

"I've been known to."

Fain gaped. Even though he tried not to judge others, he was nauseated by her and her lifestyle choices. How could she be so flagrant with a boy almost half her age? Did she have no dignity whatsoever?

"What happened to you, Galene?"

"I was stripped of my family and forced to live homeless on the street. You?"

That took some of the fire out of him. "I never meant to hurt you."

She gave him an arch stare. "Wow. If the damage you did me was without effort, I shudder at what you could do if you actually applied yourself. What did you think would happen when you left me for a human? That my parents would throw me a parade? Send flowers and celebrate the shame of it?"

"I assumed you'd pledge another male. Merrell or Chrisen Anatole. Actually."

Shivering at two names that revolted her, Galene looked away as old memories flared. Had she not been pregnant . . . had Fain not been disowned over a human . . . she might have survived the scandal. But once her pregnancy showed and after his mother had publicly disavowed him as a traitor to their race, no family would accept her. Not while she carried a lack-Vest baby of an Outcast father.

And no matter how much better *her* life would have been, she couldn't bring herself to destroy her child. Nor could she have given him up. Not with what happened to abandoned Andarion children. She'd refused to save herself by sacrificing Talyn. His conception had been *her* stupid mistake.

Not his.

While she regretted every minute she'd ever known Fain Hauk, she'd never once regretted Talyn in her life. No matter how hard or awful it'd been, one look at his precious face had made everything worth it.

"Well?" Fain asked. "Why didn't you marry Merrell?"

"Aside from the fact he was psychotic and cruel, Merrell wanted nothing socially acceptable to do with me after you left. I was a pariah to everyone, Fain. So deformed, they all claimed, that I drove the high-caste male I was pledged to into the arms of a pathetic human female. . . . Instead of shoving you into that auditorium, I should have killed you where you stood. That would have saved my social status, and *that* is my sole regret in life."

"Really? That's all you regret?"

She laughed bitterly. "You're right. I do have one more."

"And that is?"

"That I didn't aim at your head on your arrival."

CHAPTER 3

Talyn drew up short as he left his mother's office to find his "uncle" waiting in the secretary's lounge. A few inches shorter than him, Dancer looked a lot like his father. Enough that it made him want to punch the bastard out where he stood.

But unlike his father, his uncle had red, glowing eyes, instead of the typical Andarion white.

It was a rare genetic defect that caused Dancer's eyes to glow red like that. One that meant his uncle was overly possessive and loyal to his female and family. A trait that was inside Talyn, too. Ironic, really, as that was a genetic mutation most Andarion females would sell their souls to have in their males.

And here all but Felicia had rudely turned him away.

If they only knew his true heritage. . . .

Dancer raked him with a less than complimentary stare. One that turned into a stern frown as he finally focused on Talyn's features, which were very similar to both his own and Fain's.

Just as Dancer opened his mouth to speak, a tall Hyshian female swept into the office with a bright smile.

One Talyn returned immediately as she grabbed him into a fierce bear hug. At least she made his day better since she was like a second mother to him. "Jaynie? What are you doing here?"

Her back to Dancer, she cupped his face in her hands. "I heard Lena shot Fain on his arrival and had to tel-ass immediately to see for myself." She frowned as she saw the bruise on his eye and split lip, courtesy of his father. "What happened to my sexy baby?"

Talyn shrugged nonchalantly. "Same as ever. I bumped into a fist."

Tsking, she continued to examine his face. "I thought you retired from Ring fighting?"

"I did. But not from asshole fighting. . . . So how's Hadrian and the kids?"

She snorted. "All good. Sway's been nagging me to let him go camping with you again. I don't know what the two of you did last time, but he really enjoyed it."

"Traded porn mostly. You know . . . typical guy stuff. Kid gets tired of swimming in the mostly estrogen pool."

Chucking him on the arm, she laughed.

"You two know each other?"

Turning around, Jayne finally realized Dancer was in the room. "Hey, sweetie! I didn't see you there. Why you hiding in a corner?"

He jerked his chin at Talyn. "Keeping my eye on him."

She laughed. "I must have missed one hell of a party."

"That you did," Hauk said drily. "Fain failed to explain to us exactly what a powder keg the commander would be. We were extremely ill prepared for her hot reception."

She turned back toward Talyn. "So, I have to know. Fain refused to tell me. What is this prank your mother supposedly pulled on him in school?"

"Mother?" Dancer asked incredulously.

Talyn ignored him. "On their graduation day, she shoved him naked into an auditorium full of witnesses."

She covered her mouth with her hand. "No, she didn't."

He nodded.

"Why does she hate him so much?"

"They were pledged," Dancer answered. "She's the one Fain left for Omira."

Jayne sucked her breath in. "Damn, Hauk. Why didn't you tell me that before I stuck them back together?"

"I had no idea until Fain opened the door on our arrival here. I was just a kid when he was disinherited. I didn't know anything about a previous pledge . . . but, in retrospect, his embarrassing a Batur and breaking pledge with that prestigious lineage explains a lot about my mother's unforgiving hostility toward him." Dancer narrowed his suspicious gaze on Talyn. "I'm surprised your father married your mother, given that."

Talyn had to force himself not to roll his eyes at his uncle's dense stupidity.

"Lena's not married," Jayne said before Talyn could stop her. "She's never been married that I know of."

Dancer went pale as he mentally did the math and realized who Talyn's father had to be.

"Yeah," Talyn said drily. "So glad I inherited my intelligence from my mother's side of the family."

Seeing the look on Dancer's face, Jayne scowled. "What?"

Dancer looked sick as he struggled to accept the bitter truth. "Why didn't she say something?"

"To whom?" Talyn asked defensively. "Who in your family would have given a single shit?"

Dancer raked a hand through his braids. "Does my mother know?"

"Know what?" Jayne asked. "What do you two know that I don't?"

Crossing his arms over his chest, Dancer jerked his chin at Talyn. "That he's my nephew."

She snorted derisively. "Impossible. Keris would have been . . ." Her voice trailed off as she finally put it together. "Oh my God, no wonder she shot him. I'm just surprised she didn't go for his head."

Talyn scoffed. "I'm surprised she didn't go for his crotch. It explains why he was holding a helmet there when he came off the ship. She must not have changed much since her youth."

Dancer approached him slowly. "I knew you looked like Fain. But damn . . . I just thought that was why she'd picked you for a lover."

He screwed his face up in painful distaste. "That's my mother you're talking about. Do you mind?"

Dancer laughed. "No. No wonder you attacked us like you did. You were protecting your mother." He tried to pull him into a hug, but Talyn shoved him back.

His uncle took the rejection in stride. "Fain's going to shit when he finds out. I can't believe he has a son."

Jayne's evil laughter joined his. "Who's going to tell him?"

Stepping back, Dancer shook his head. "Not me." He reached to cup Talyn's cheek in his hand so that he could examine his features.

Talyn slapped his hand away. "I'm not your whore, *giakon*. Get your hands off me."

Again, Dancer shrugged his insult away. "The guilt from this is going to destroy Fain."

"Good." Talyn stepped out of his uncle's reach. "I hope he chokes on it."

"Careful. That's my brother you're talking about, and he's a good male. He's stood by me when no one else has."

"Nice to know he can be loyal to someone. The gods know, he never showed that side of his character to my mother."

Jayne came between them. "Whoa, guys. Breathe and stop before you say something you're going to regret. You both are entitled to your feelings. But Dancer, you don't know how hard their lives have been. I love every one of you. You're my family. That being said, Fain hurt them. Badly. And Talyn . . . you've no idea what your father's been through. Trust me. Fate got him back. With interest. He hasn't lived a fairy tale, either. There's a reason he's in a Tavali uniform."

"And I don't really give a shit, Aunt Jayne."

The door to his mother's office opened. His father came storming out.

Fain curled his lip at Talyn, then turned his attention to Jayne and Dancer. "I cannot work with that . . ." His voice trailed off into a choked sound as he gestured at the door. "She's impossible!"

Talyn grabbed him. "Did you hurt her feelings? What did you say to her?"

As his father went to punch him, Dancer came between them. "Stop it! Both of you!"

"Talyn!"

He froze at his mother's sharp tone and withdrew from the fight.

"Yeah, you better keep walking, *whelp.*"

"Fain!" Dancer snapped through gritted teeth. "Bite it!"

He held his hands up in surrender. "Call Nyk. I'm out of this." With long, furious strides, he quit the office.

Dancer let out an elongated breath as he locked gazes with Galene. "I know you hate my brother and I'm sure you're entitled to it. But you should both know that while you had each other, he had absolutely no one. He didn't even have a country to call home."

Galene curled her lip. "What about his *human?*"

Dancer's gaze turned sharp and biting. "Let's just say that out of the two years they were together, his happiest memory is probably you shoving him naked into an auditorium full of family and friends, and locking the door behind him." And with that, he followed after Fain.

Galene couldn't breathe as those words echoed in her ears.

Two years?

What?

She looked at Jayne for an explanation. "What happened to his wife?"

"Before or after he caught her screwing a human male in their bed?"

Bile rose in her throat. "You're serious?"

Jayne nodded, then pulled her into a comforting hug. "I had no idea Fain was the one who left you."

"I had no idea you were such close friends with his brother." Because of her less-than-legal activities and associates, Jayne never talked about her friends or family in anything more than the most abstract of terms or nicknames. She never mentioned anyone, other than her husband and children, by their real names. And only if you were really close to Jayne did you get that much.

Without commenting, Jayne glanced to Talyn. "How are you holding up, sport?"

He shrugged. "I'm Andarion."

"That's really not an answer."

"For him, it is." Galene rubbed his arm. "Notify the team that we'll try this again tomorrow with The Tavali. I need the day to mentally regroup."

"Yes, ma'am." He gave her a sharp salute before making an about face and leaving them to carry out his orders.

Jayne snorted. "I'm so used to him as a civ that I forget how military our boy really is when he dons that uniform."

Galene smiled proudly. "I'm far more likely to break protocol than he is."

Jayne let out an elongated breath. "I'm really sorry about this, Lena. I'm the one who suggested you for the position. I had no idea what I was getting you into."

Sadness choked her as she thought back to the day she'd first learned she was pregnant with Fain's child. It had been one of the tiny handful of perfect moments in her life. They had been pledged on his sixth birthday. Only two days apart in age, they'd been raised together and had gone to the same schools. Since he was to be her husband, she hadn't even looked at other males.

Back then, Fain had been her entire world. A renowned and regaled athlete and champion, he had been destined to become a war hero like his father, and she'd planned on med school like her parents. Their wedding had been set for the fall following their graduation.

And Talyn had been conceived on Fain's birthday. Her virginity a gift to her beloved fiancé.

Instead of becoming a delighted father and devoted husband as she'd expected, Fain had shattered her heart and thrown her love away as if it were meaningless. She'd never recovered from his betrayal.

He was her one and only.

And she was nothing to him . . . just discarded garbage he'd left in the past and never looked back for.

"I hate him so much," she whispered. "But he did give me the greatest gift of my life. I couldn't ask for a better son."

"He's just like his father."

Galene quirked her brow at Jayne's comment.

"He is," Jayne said defensively, with a nervous laugh. "Now that I know, I see it clearly. I don't know how I could have missed it all these years. Talyn's not Fain's son so much as he's his clone. Driven. Fierce. Solitary. Intense. Stubborn. Loyal."

"I will argue that last bit."

Jayne shook her head in disagreement. "Something happened, Lena. Something really bad. I know Fain and have for years. If he broke pledge with you and you don't know why, it was something foul. He wouldn't have just walked away for no reason. That's not the male I've known. There is no one more honorable or loyal than Fain Hauk."

"He was in love," she spat the word.

With a human.

Jayne screwed her face up. "Maybe, but here's a question for you, and you're from a medical family so you'd know the answer better than I. Keris, Dancer, and Talyn are permanently stralen. What are the odds that gene missed Fain entirely?"

She shrugged. "Genes are strange things."

"Yes, they are. And it is an extremely rare trait, but . . . think about it." Jayne walked away.

"It's possible Fain never loved either of us," she whispered under her breath. However, if that was true, why would he have left his Andarion heritage behind to marry a human?

He wasn't quite *that* stupid.

As much as it pained her to admit it, Fain's life must have sucked as much as hers did without his prestigious lineage. He'd been military royalty before the scandal. One of the original twelve warrior clans of Andaria.

The first of the warrior clans. His family of War Hauks had established and set the standard for every warrior who had followed after them. It'd been his direct ancestor and older brother's namesake who'd founded The League they were currently fighting.

In the blink of an eye, like her, Fain had lost everything. And Jayne was right. As rare as the stralen gene was, for two brothers, Talyn, and other direct family members to have it, it would be extremely unlikely for it not to be in Fain, too.

Of course, there was one way to know for sure.

Tell him he has a son.

Regardless of his feelings for her, his body chemistry would kick that gene into overdrive if he thought his son was threatened.

Not that it mattered. She wouldn't risk Talyn's life to find out. Fain wasn't worth it.

Still . . . it did give her something to think about.

CHAPTER 4

W e need *you* to do this."

Fain cursed at Nykyrian Quiakides—royal Andarion prince and pain in his ass—who sat behind an ornate black desk on the screen in front of him. "Ryn is the Tavali ambassador—"

"Whose mother is in charge of the Wasturnum—twelfth generation to rule that branch—and his beloved little brother is the Caronese emperor. The UTC won't see him as impartial, and you know it."

Still, Fain argued against his appointment to serve with Galene. "I'm now an Andarion tiziran. Won't they have issues with *that*?"

"It's not the same, and you know it. You weren't raised by my mother and have no real loyalty to her. You're not blood related to the throne and can't inherit. End of the day, you're still one of the pirates. Just like them. Disinherited. Disowned. A freed slave. Someone who has no use for the laws and traditions of any known nation. *You,* the Universal Tavali Council will trust."

In that moment, Fain seriously hated the UTC.

"What about Chayden?" he asked Nykyrian. "Can't he do it?"

"Qillaq prince by birth whose beloved, full-blooded sister is the next queen of the Exeterian Empire and whose father was a Gondarion prince and commander. Yeah . . . it's a no-go, too." Nyk sat forward to pin him with an intense glare. "*You* have no real political ties to any throne and no blood loyalty to any single Tavali Nation or group. You don't even run your own crew. Your only blood tie is to The Sentella, and that, The Tavali trusts. Best of all, *we* trust you. Because you're an Andarion male with strong military ties and heritage, the Phrixians will follow you. There's no one else who can do this, Fain. You're in a unique position for it."

Bloody effing awesome.

The irony of it disgusted him. The very things that had ruined his life were now the very things that locked him into a position of power he'd never craved. While he wasn't a follower, and had always adamantly refused to be one, he wasn't a leader, either.

Both positions sucked. It was why he didn't run his own crew.

He just wanted to be left alone to live what was left of his miserable life.

"I can't work with her. She hates my guts, every individual one of them." Fain gestured to the blast mark on his battlesuit. "She shot me, Nyk. Point blank. No warning. In the heart!"

"Well . . . we've all had the urge to shoot you, Fain. She just had the fun of it."

He childishly mocked Nykyrian's misplaced humor. "And you want *her* to lead *your* army?"

Nykyrian nodded. "I'm told you're the only one she hates to this degree. Everyone else should be safe from her aim."

"You're not funny."

"I'm a little funny."

Fain growled at him. "You're an asshole."

"Is that the worst insult you can toss at me? Really? You're slipping in your old age."

Fain fanged him. But because they were such old friends, it didn't faze the bastard at all. "Is she willing to work with me? Or do I need to buy thicker armor?"

"I've been assured that she won't shoot you again."

"What about cutting my throat?"

"We didn't get that specific. Would you like me to draw up a contract, with her listing any and all possible ways she could end you and saying she won't?"

"I hate you." Fain sighed heavily. "Fine. I'll go get her and take them to the Porturnum. But if I die doing this, I plan to haunt you every day of eternity."

"Good. I won't miss you, then."

Fain knocked on the door of Galene's condo. Only a block from the palace, it was one of the nicest buildings in the bustling metropolis of Eris—the Andarion capital city. The doorman had

49

been a little skittish on his arrival, but since Fain had come in with an Andarion royal guard, he'd let Fain pass with nothing more than an irritated grimace.

So what the hell was taking her so long to answer the door, anyway? Her condo couldn't be *that* big.

She's doing it strictly to piss you off.

Most likely.

He knocked again.

The door slid open to show her boy toy in nothing but a simple white towel. He had a blaster in one hand while he eyed them warily.

Anger boiled inside Fain at the sight, especially given all the scars on the little bastard's body, including marks on his shoulders that appeared to be those of a disinherited male. But the one that truly chafed his ass was the tat on the kid's throat that marked him as an Andarion felon who'd spent time in one of their top-sec prisons. Given all that, Galene must have seriously called in favors to keep the little bastard in the military with a commander's rank.

Worse, she hadn't been lying. They really did live together. And she must dearly love the boy to overlook that degree of scarring. In their culture, those marks were considered a deformity, and explained why such a high-ranking male in the Andarion armada remained unmarried.

No female, other than Galene, would be able to look at Talyn with anything except scorn and disdain.

This day keeps getting better and better.

Fain curled his lip. "I'm here for the commander."

Her boy toy sneered at him. "You should have called first."

"She was told to expect me."

"Not first thing in the morning." Grimacing at the group, the boy toy allowed Fain into the elegant condo, but not the others. He closed the door in their faces, and headed toward the kitchen, where he had a bowl of hot cereal set on the counter-top. He placed his blaster beside it before he sat on a barstool and returned to eating.

"You have company, Commander."

At his disgruntled words, Galene leaned over the counter to see Fain. Dressed in a short, lacy nightgown, she gaped then pulled her robe closed and belted it. But not before an image of her lithe, athletic body and those lush, full breasts was firmly implanted in his mind. "What are you doing here?"

Dying of horniness, apparently.

And unspent rage.

Fain ground his teeth at the violent reaction of his treacher-ous body. Dammit! Why couldn't he be near her without get-ting the hard-on from hell?

"I'm supposed to escort you to the Porturnum's HQ. Re-member?"

"In an hour," she growled.

"What can I say? I couldn't wait to see you again."

She rolled her eyes at his sarcasm.

Her boy toy stood up and leaned over the counter to place his bowl in the sink. He met her gaze and arched a quizzical brow. "You want *me* to shoot him this time?"

She had the nerve to smile. "Don't tempt me, scamp." She

moved his blaster away from his hand. "You should finish dressing."

"Yes, ma'am." He headed for the hallway. For the first time, Fain realized he had a pronounced limp as he walked.

"And don't leave your damp towel on the floor again. Hang it up."

Without a word, the boy toy jerked the towel off his hips and tossed it at her. Completely naked, he passed a smug, taunting grin at Fain before he headed to the rear of the condo.

Disgusted by his flagrant display and the wealth of hideous scars over the boy's back, Fain wanted blood. It took everything he had not to go after the punk and teach him a valuable lesson in manners.

Laughing at the boy's impudence, Galene took the towel into what must be the laundry room. She came out to add her own glare at Fain. "I wish you wouldn't antagonize him."

"*I* antagonize *him*? Are you serious?"

"Yes. I would think you're old enough to know better."

"But not him, huh?" Fain curled his lip. "Maybe you should sleep with someone closer to your own age."

She didn't respond as she headed for the hallway. "We'll be out in a minute."

Biting his lip, Fain had never been so furious in his entire life. It was actually painful.

As he waited and contemplated murdering them both, he drifted into the spacious living room that held an incredible view of the city. Something he would have appreciated more if he'd been in a better mood.

But right then, only bloodshed would placate him.

Trying to put it out of his mind, he swept his gaze over the contemporary furniture and noted the number of pictures in the place. More than that, he realized that the photos were *all* of her pet.

Little effing bastard . . .

He paused at one of her with the boy toy when the kid was a lot younger. . . .

A *lot* younger. Like around six or seven, and dressed in a yellow and black lorina costume for a play. How sickening was that?

Scowling, Fain stepped closer to the frames that held the boy's graduation certificate, and an article from a sports magazine about him. His frown turned into a gape as he saw the kid's name on the cover and he realized who the boy was.

Talyn *Batur.*

Oh dear gods, he's her son.

Shit! Talyn Batur.

Talyn B-a-t-u-r, *the* Ring fighter of the century, was her only son. Her kid was an Andarion legend. That little bastard had also beaten every record Fain had set in the Ring. *Every* one of them. Records that no one had ever thought would be beaten by another fighter.

And that *is her son. Effing figures.* She'd probably had him beat Fain's records just for spite.

Feeling like an idiot, he rubbed at his sore jaw. No wonder they called the kid the Iron Hammer. He definitely hit like one.

Disgusted with himself for how he'd behaved toward them, he sighed at his own childishness. He should have recognized the Hammer. How could he have been so stupid as to not realize who Talyn was?

But that thought ended as he noticed the date on the boy's graduation certificate.

If that was correct . . .

Carefully, he scanned the document more closely. It was only partially filled out because it was missing Talyn's paternal lineage.

All of his father's heritage.

For that matter, Batur was *her* family name. And now that he looked closer at the photos of Talyn as a boy, Fain realized how much Talyn favored his nephew Darice. How much Talyn looked like him and Dancer.

Then his gaze went to Talyn's caste code that was listed on his certificates. ✕-12-6. *The bastard son of a disinherited male. That* slammed into him like a cheap kick to his stones.

Ah, shit.

He stiffened as he sensed a presence behind him. Turning, he saw Talyn there in his Andarion battlesuit. Talyn, who was the same exact height and build he was.

The boy's gaze went past Fain to the diploma before he called out. "Hey, Ma! Dad just figured out how to do the math to calculate my age and date of conception. He's having some kind of apoplexy over it. I think you need to come in here before he pisses on your floor. And if he does, I did not do it, so don't yell at me for it. And I will *not* clean it up."

Fain couldn't breathe as Talyn confirmed his fears.

I have a son.

A beautiful, strong, grown son.

Stunned and awed, and feeling like a total asshole, he reached to touch the bruise he'd given Talyn yesterday during their fight.

His white eyes filled with hatred, Talyn pulled back and licked at the scab on his lip from another blow Fain had gifted him with. "Don't touch me."

Dressed in her uniform, Galene hesitated in the doorway. No wonder she'd shot him. It all made even more sense now.

Completely aghast, Fain stared at her. "Why didn't you tell me?"

"I tried, and you told me to shush . . . that you didn't have time for me. You were busy."

Fain winced at the memory of her hurt expression that day in the locker room before she'd stormed out, only to return a few minutes later to confront him with Merrell's lies.

"That was what you came to tell me?" he asked her.

"Yeah. Congratulations, Fain. You're a father."

And how had he thanked her for her precious gift? He'd allowed her to believe that he was in love with another female. That he'd shamed her with a human lover. "No wonder you shoved me into that auditorium." He shook his head. "You still should have told me."

"Why? So that I'd be forced to marry a male in love with someone else? A human, no less. Call me provincial, but I wanted better than that."

Fain twisted the ring on his pinkie around with his thumb. Fate had seriously fucked him over.

No, fate had fucked all of them over.

"I'm so sorry, Galene."

"I'm not the one you need to apologize to." Her gaze went to Talyn.

His features were absolute stone.

Fain wanted to embrace him. It was a physical ache inside him to touch a son he'd never thought to have, but it was painfully obvious that Talyn wanted him to die on the spot. "I'm sorry, Talyn."

"There are some things sorry doesn't fix, old man. This is definitely one of them."

"I know. Believe me, I know." His heart shattering, Fain blinked against the tears that choked him as he thought about everything they'd all been deprived of. The years that the three of them should have been a family.

I have a son. . . .

A child he'd never been able to hold and soothe. A son he'd never taught to fight or protect himself. One he knew absolutely nothing about. Bitter, aching regret choked him hard.

Talyn met his mother's gaze. "I'll give you two the room."

As he started past her, Galene touched his arm. "Are you okay, baby?"

"I'm fine, Matarra."

Galene winced. That wasn't true and she knew it. But it was the best she'd get out of him. Talyn never showed anyone his emotions. His childhood had been too brutal for that.

Without another word, her son headed for his room.

Her heart hammering, she watched as Fain scanned the other photos of Talyn over the years. Their son had been a beautiful child. Overachiever to the extreme.

But then, Talyn had been forced to be three times better at everything he did to be seen as half as good as others.

Fain met her gaze again. "I don't know what upsets me more. The number of times I made money off Talyn's wins, or the times I lost money betting someone would gut him in the Ring."

"Don't even talk to me about that, Fain. Or I *will* kill you where you stand. You've no idea how much I hated him fighting for a prestige that should have been his at birth. How many times I've paced a waiting room floor, praying he'd live through the injuries he'd sustained because he had no future without battling for it. And even then, he was never given his due, because he never had a fully Vested lineage backing him." She clenched her teeth and glared at him. "Damn you for that."

Fain choked on the pain inside his heart. As a boy, he'd thought to trade his own life and future to save Dancer's. Instead, that "noble" action had cost his son his.

Galene's and Talyn's futures were not supposed to have been part of the bargain he'd made with Chrisen and Merrell Anatole to keep Dancer and Keris safe. Nothing had turned out the way it should have.

And never had he hated himself more.

"I can imagine what you've been through."

"No, Fain. You can't. Not really. You were always so popular. Everyone loved and adored you. Worshiped the ground the mighty War Hauk tread upon . . . Our son has never known that. Most decent, self-respecting Andarions won't socialize with him. At all. Even as an officer, he wasn't allowed to shower in the same barracks area as any Vested soldier. The only female who will have anything to do with him is a paid companion he has set up in his condo, across town. I had to send him to school with Hyshians because our race wouldn't allow him to attend an Andarion school with a broken lineage. Every door he reached for was brutally slammed, not in his face, but on his little hands."

He winced in response, and well he should.

"The Hyshian and human children weren't allowed to play with him because he was Andarion. And the Andarion children weren't allowed to talk to him because he was the bastard of an Outcast father. Do you know he was even too humiliated to tell me that he'd finally broken down and paid for a mistress? Had he not been coldly shot down by his own commander— who hated *you*—and almost killed, I'd have never known he had that much in his life."

She jerked her chin toward his awards and articles. "Even though he was and is the most celebrated fighter in Ring history, her agency still refused to allow Talyn to have a full contract with her. He had to take on more fights to buy it out or lose her to a fully Vested male. And you *never* want to know what the cost of that contract was. It still boggles my mind and fills me with fury."

Fain ground his teeth. Every Andarion mistress and her agency that he'd ever heard of, or known, would have sold their souls to make a lifelong pact with a military officer. Especially one who held the second highest rank in their armada, and wasn't fifty years old with it. Not to mention the fact that, as Galene had said, Talyn Batur was an intergalactic champion regaled by every known world who followed the Andarion Ring sport.

It sickened him to think of what his child had gone through because of him.

"If I'd had any inkling, Stormy, I would have busted hell wide open to provide for both of you."

She let out a weary sigh. "It doesn't matter now, does it? We can't go back. And we both had a guilty hand in ruining our son's life."

"I don't know." He gestured at the trophies and awards on the shelves and wall. "You look like you've done an amazing job with him."

Galene looked away. Tears filled her eyes as she tried not to remember the past. "Every day, I ask myself if I could have done more. If I *should* have done more."

Fain gave her a hard, harsh stare. "You're a much better mother than I ever had. At least you loved him. Protected him. You didn't eject him from your house and make him an Outcast who didn't dare step foot in any Andarion territory without a death sentence hanging over his head."

Galene swallowed at those words. Funny, she'd never thought of Fain that way. For all these years, he'd been a target for her hatred. She had never really considered how hard it'd been for him to be alone, without lineage.

Mostly because she hadn't cared. She'd wanted his life to be lived in total misery. Wanted him to pay brutally for leaving her.

For leaving Talyn, and causing her baby harm.

Now that she knew he had, it didn't make her feel better as she'd thought it would.

It, too, made her sad.

"Having raised Talyn, I will never understand how my parents did me the way they did. Or what yours did to you. There's no way I could ever hurt him. Not intentionally."

"As I said, you're a much better mother than any I know. He was lucky to have you. The only thing he got shafted in was the father department, and for that I am *so* incredibly sorry."

"Commander?"

They both turned as Talyn rejoined them.

He handed a link to his mother. "There's been another attack."

Flinching, she took the link from him and left the room to answer the call.

Awkward silence filled the air between them as Talyn stared a brittle hole through him.

What did someone say to a grown child they'd never known they had?

All of a sudden, Fain had a whole new respect for Nykyrian, who'd been faced with this when his ex had dropped Thia on him, out of the blue.

Uncomfortable, he cleared his throat. "Your mom said that you have a female?"

Talyn continued to stare at him, without comment.

"Does she have a name?"

"Yes."

Fain winced at the fact that Talyn had no intention of making this any easier on him. "And it is . . . ?"

A full and very slow minute went by before he answered. "Felicia."

"It's a beautiful name."

And still he glared at him. Damn. Forget Talyn's martial skills. That cold stare alone could let blood.

"How long have the two of you—"

"I don't talk about my personal life with strangers."

Wounded and hurt, Fain nodded as he remembered reading that in a few different articles over the years. It was something the media had beaten Talyn up over. The Iron Hammer didn't show his face in the Ring, or out of it. Nor did he speak of anything other than his matches. He kept everyone at arm's length. The most the media had dragged out of him was that he liked to rock climb and camp on weekends. And that was *if* they could ever get an interview with him at all.

"Is there anything I can say to you that would end with us at least on friendly terms?"

"You're dying with a painful, terminal disease and only have a few hours to live *might* work."

Fain let out a tired "heh" with that. "Aren't you at least curious about me?"

Talyn snorted. "Not really."

"You've no questions whatsoever?"

"He's never asked any questions about you or your family," Galene said as she rejoined them. "Not even your name."

Fain didn't know why, but that hurt more than anything. "I see. We'll keep this strictly military, then. I'll stay out of both your ways, and you can contact me whenever you need me to relay orders to the Phrixians. Darling Cruel—the Caronese emperor—you can deal with directly. He has no problem taking orders from a female, as Jayne has bossed him around for years, and broke him in when he was young. If you need to contact one of his commanders, you can text me and I'll forward the orders. Most of the Tavali shouldn't have any problem with you. If they do give you any trouble, forward their names and I'll tell you who they answer to. You can easily deal with their four primary commanders, and if it helps, Ryn Cruel— Darling's older brother—is the son of Hermione Dane. She's the leader of the Wasturnum, and she sits at the head of the UTC."

Galene arched a brow. "UTC?"

"Universal Tavali Council. She goes by Kirren, and you will need that name to get through to her. It's her call sign, reserved only for those closest to her. All the Tavali operate that way. It's how we keep outsiders and spies from knowing anything about us."

Talyn narrowed his gaze on him. "What name do you use? Faithless?"

Fain let the insult go. "I don't. Nor do I answer to anyone. I'm what's called a Rogue."

"And that is?"

He returned Talyn's glare with an equally cold look. "Some-one with no family or individual National allegiance. What Andarions affectionately call an Outcast, only the Tavali don't try to kill us on sight. They just use us when they need cannon fodder or decoys, and we pay a yearly fee directly to the UTC, instead of a tithing fee to a National Presidium."

Galene glanced away as she caught the pain that flashed into Fain's eyes. She shouldn't care.

At all. And yet she did.

Because I used to love him.

Maybe. And maybe it was because Talyn favored him so much that it was her love of her son that made her more sym-pathetic to the man he took after.

Yeah, she'd go with that, for now.

Fain tapped at his ear. "Hauk, go," he said to whomever was calling. He waited several seconds before he spoke again. "We'll be right there." He met her gaze. "Your guard is on board and waiting with my crew. If you two are ready, we can be on our way."

As they started for the door, Talyn tapped his ear. "Hey, is something wrong?" He placed his finger against the link and frowned as he listened intently. He led them out to the hall-way. "You need me to call for you?"

Fain duplicated Talyn's frown in a disturbingly similar manner. "Is he okay?"

Galene nodded as they headed for the lifts. "He's talking to Felicia."

"How do you know?"

"The warm concern in his voice and the amount of concentration he's giving the caller. The gentleness of his tone. He only talks to her like that." She led them into the lift.

Talyn checked the time.

Fain was stunned by the difference in Talyn's demeanor while he spoke to his Felicia. Everything about Talyn was different now. For the first time, he seemed vulnerable.

"Honey, listen, if you need me to, I don't mind. I've still got a few before we're hit the bay." Talyn completely ignored everyone else as he followed them into the lift. "Yeah, okay. But if they give you any more lip at all, you let me know and I'll deal with them. I mean it. No one disregards you like that. Ever. I will totally bust their asses for it."

His features softened and he closed his eyes as if he was savoring whatever she was saying to him. "Yeah, me, too. I'll check in when I can. Stay safe. Love you." He lowered his hand and turned instantly stern again.

"Is everything all right?" Galene asked.

Talyn gave a curt military nod before he elaborated. "The pool monitors went out and the new company I hired was harassing Lish because her name isn't on the account. She just wanted to make sure it was okay to add herself to it." A fierce tic started in his jaw.

Rigid and pissed, Talyn headed out of the lift and toward their transports as if he wanted to commit murder.

Fain pulled Galene aside in the lobby while the others followed Talyn. "Why's he so angry about a pool company?"

She gave him a dry stare. "Why do you think, Fain? He

can't legally pledge marriage to the female he loves more than his life. So he, who is the second highest ranking member of the Andarion military, is forced to be bound by curfew and barracks restrictions that won't allow them to live together. The only way to keep him out of a barracks is if he lives with the commander he serves . . . his own mother. Meanwhile, the mistress he's contracted with is left to tend his home with companies that don't want to deal with either of them because neither of them is fully Vested and their contract isn't through a traditional agency." She barely whispered the next words to him. "Rather it's one that could get them both arrested if anyone ever investigated it fully."

"Why doesn't he get out of the military, then?"

"And do what? He's the bastard son of a disinherited War Hauk. Who would hire him or deal with him in the private sector? He's a lack-Vest, Fain. The fighting schools won't even allow *him,* the Iron Hammer, to train other fighters. Can you imagine how humiliating *that* is?"

"Then allow me to adopt him. I know Cairistiona would approve it for us. As his father, I can give him full protection of the royal house. He'd be an eton Anatole and a Winged Batur then, and no one would dare to look him in the eye, never mind say anything unkind to him."

"I will gladly allow it. But it's not up to me, is it? And it won't undo all the humiliation he's been put through since birth. You were raised with two of the most prestigious bloodlines on all of Andaria flowing through your veins. Andarions gravitated toward you in school. Everyone wanted to be *your* friend."

She jerked her chin toward Talyn, who was waiting for them on the curb. "With my family lineage and yours, he should have been a higher caste than even you were growing up. Instead, he was spat on and laughed at. Denied and degraded by those who aren't even fit to be speaking directly to him. I'm not the one you need to win over, Fain. He is."

Fain ground his teeth as Galene left him to join their son. She was right. He could see the way the other Andarions looked at Talyn. Even though he was a titled champion and their commander, they still showed their smug contempt for him. Something they would have never dared to do to a War Hauk or a fully Vested Batur.

That was what made Talyn so stern and reserved around everyone. Why he showed no emotion whatsoever.

"You okay?"

Fain nodded as Dancer joined him. Then he shook his head. "I can't believe I screwed over my own son."

"You didn't know."

"It doesn't change anything, does it?"

Dancer sighed. "I'm sorry, Fain."

So was he. "Can you do me a favor, little brother?"

"Anything."

"Find out who this Felicia is that he's contracted with." Maybe she could give him some insight into Talyn.

The one thing he'd learned over the years was that any male's weakness was always the female he loved. Especially when that male was a War Hauk.

Talyn might hate *him*, but his son would listen to his Felicia.

If Fain could win her over, he might be able to start building a relationship with Talyn. It was at least worth a try.

"Do you have her full name?" Dancer asked.

"No. She's living in Talyn's condo. That's all I know about her."

"Oh, well, by all means, make it easy on me, why don't you?"

He gave his brother an irritated smirk. "If I knew more about her, I wouldn't be asking you for information. I'd find it myself."

Dancer fanged him. "You really suck as a brother."

"Yeah, well, you should have to deal with mine. He's a stellar asshole."

Rolling his eyes, Dancer left Fain and got into the transport behind Talyn, who sat beside his mother.

Fain sat across from them.

While they rode, he noted the way Talyn kept checking his link and biting back a smile while he covertly texted with his female.

Yeah, his son loved her. Dearly. She was the way to his heart.

And sadly, both Galene and Talyn—the two beings who hated him most—were the keys to his.

While he'd regretted much of his life, there was nothing he regretted more than having walked away from them. But he'd had no choice. Had he stayed, Dancer, like their brother Keris, would have been mercilessly killed.

His little brother still bore those scars that had ultimately forced Fain's hand.

Now . . .

I will *make this right*. He had no idea how, but he would find a way to save them all. Even if it killed him.

CHAPTER 5

Fain watched as Galene and Talyn boarded his ship. They had no idea that this had been his primary home for the majority of Talyn's life.

And his own, for that matter.

A strange sensation went through him as he watched his "family" heading toward the flight deck to strap in while the rest of the Andarions that came onboard with them gathered in the cargo area. All that was missing was Dancer's pregnant wife and two kids, and everything Fain loved would be contained within these metal walls.

Everything.

He pulled Dancer to the side. "Can I ask a huge favor?"

Dancer scowled. "What?"

"You know where we're headed. Find Talyn's female and bring her to the Porturnum station to stay with him. I think he'll like that."

Dancer's gaze softened. "You sure?"

He nodded. "Families shouldn't be separated. And while you're at it, why don't you bring Sumi and the kids, too? I know you don't want to be away from them, either."

A strange shadow appeared in Dancer's red eyes. "Who are you and what have you done with my I-don't-give-a-shit-about-anything brother?"

Fain snorted at his mock sarcasm. "Shut the fuck up and do what I said."

"Now there's the familiar asshole I know so well and love for reasons still unknown."

Fain made an obscene gesture before he shoved his equally gargantuan brother down the ramp. He turned to catch Talyn staring at him with an arched brow.

"What?" Fain asked irritably.

Before he could respond, Chayden let out an obnoxious, "H-a-m-m-e-r! Be damned if it's not an honor to work with *you*!"

Talyn turned his scowl toward the Qillaq Tavali pirate. A light of familiarity darkened his eyes. "Chayden Aniwaya?"

Chayden drew up short. "Ah crap . . . Do I owe you money?"

Talyn snorted at his reaction. "I'm an old friend of Morra and Qorach. Qory talks about you all the time."

Recognition brightened Chayden's entire face as he laughed and clapped Talyn on the back, then realized he probably shouldn't have been quite that forward with someone who could put him through the titanium walls with a sneeze. He placed a little more distance between them as he continued to grin at Talyn. "So you're Sexy Baby T! I should have known. Though to be honest, the way they talk about you, I thought you'd be about three years old."

Talyn visibly winced. "Morra swore she'd keep that between us. I'm going to kill her next time I see her."

Laughing harder, Chayden held his arm out toward Talyn. "Then it's twice an honor to meet you. Any friend of Qory's or Morra's is a brother to me. And I know better than to threaten their Sexy Baby T."

With a sound of irritation that would have scared anyone with half a brain—which meant Chayden ignored it entirely—Talyn shook his hand.

Chayden let out a low whistle over Talyn's grip. His face a comical mask of awe, he grabbed at Talyn's biceps with a loving intimacy that would have had most men searching the floor for their teeth over *that* groping audacity. Even Fain doubted he'd have been so tolerant of being pawed like that from the Qill. And for an Andarion, that kind of touching was strictly forbidden from anyone other than family or lovers, and reserved for extremely private time. "Whoa! You're so much more massive than you looked on the monitors whenever I saw you fighting in the Ring. I can't imagine anyone dumb enough to think they could *ever* take you on and win. Damn, boy. You are ripped!" Gaping even wider, he gave one more squeeze to Talyn's massive biceps.

Fain bristled at Chayden's impressed tone. "He's the same size I am."

Chayden finally quit molesting Talyn's arm and snorted disdainfully at Fain. "Yeah, but he's a *lot* scarier than you are, Hauk."

Talyn cracked a cocky grin that really didn't help Fain's foul mood, as Galene laughed.

While Fain didn't appreciate being the brunt of Chayden's screwy humor, he'd take it to see the way her eyes lightened with humor. Damn, she was beautiful. That look made his stomach flutter and all the blood leave his brain faster than he could breathe.

And to think, she should have been his all these years. . . .

Bitter regret ripped through him as he drifted back in his mind to the last dance they'd attended together, the week before graduation. Knowing their time was limited—that he'd have to let her go and move on without her in his life—he'd treasured it with everything he had and committed every second of it to his memory. He could still hear the strains of the slow song that had played while he held her in his arms and swayed with her. Dressed in Batur blue, she'd looked up at him with eyes that radiated love and acceptance. Adoration.

Total happiness to be with him.

That had been the last perfect memory of his life.

He'd sell his worthless soul if he could go back and stay there with her, forever. If he could just freeze that one moment and hang on to her.

How he hated those memories that tortured him worse than anything.

As Fain headed for his pilot's chair, one of the Andarions they'd brought with them came to the flight deck to speak in a whisper to Talyn. A few inches shorter than them, he appeared around Talyn's age and had the bearing of someone bred from one of the highest-caste bloodlines. His immaculate battlesuit bore the military badges of a decorated major, but didn't list his name, which also said he ranked high enough that it was omitted for safety reasons.

Listening intently to the major, Talyn stroked his goatee with his thumb. "What do *you* want to do?" he asked in Andarion.

The major scoffed in a most undisciplined way. "Like you have to ask?"

Fain arched a brow at the disrespectful tone Talyn took in stride.

With a similar snort, Talyn pushed the major back like Fain used to do to Dancer when they were kids and Dancer irritated him. "I'll deal with your paka. Go hug a seat."

The major struck his heart with his fist, then opened his hand in a gesture of brotherhood and devotion before he headed to the back to fasten in with the others.

Fain passed a curious stare to Galene.

"He's Talyn's adjutant."

That only confused him more. "And the two of you allow him to talk to his CO like that?"

Neither of them answered his question.

Fine. Whatever. The Andarion armada was a hell of a lot more lax now than it'd been when Fain was in it. His former CO would have had him court-martialed for such a thing.

Or splintered against the nearest wall.

Trying not to let it bother him, he went to his seat.

Dressed in the red and white battlesuit that marked the Porturnum Tavali, Captain Kareem Venik got up from the con.

He saluted Fain as he surrendered the ship's controls. "Returning the lady to her owner, Commander Hauk. Preflight's complete. The *Storm Dancer*'s all ready for your loving touch."

Fain cringed as Kareem spoke the ship's name out of formal Tavali tradition. "Thanks, Captain Venik."

He inclined his head to Fain and moved to take the gunner's chair.

Galene scowled at Fain as she heard those words. "This is *your* ship?"

Logging into the controls and firing the engines, Fain nodded.

"*Storm Dancer?*"

While he fastened himself in, Fain let out a tired breath at her tone. He brought up the launch sequence and made sure he quelled the AI for the trip. "I'd lie and say I named her for my brother, but you'd know better." Storm Dancer and Stormy were the nicknames he'd teased Galene with when they were kids. For some reason, she'd loved to run through the rain, and laugh and dance while it soaked her to the bone. Her parents had thought her insane.

He'd always found it fascinating and adorable. And had often chased after her through the rain until he was as wet as she was. It'd been just such a chase that had led to her stripping his clothes from him on his birthday. . . .

And to the conception of Talyn.

Gods, to have that innocence and joy again. He could still feel her bashful hands on his bare skin while she explored every inch of his bare body with her inquisitive touch. Hear her laughter in his ears as he tasted her and she whispered to him how much she loved him.

That memory punched like a fist to the stones.

Refusing to look at her and see the hatred that was there for him now, he forced himself to put the past out of his thoughts. "As soon as everyone's secure, we'll launch."

Galene clicked her harness into place while she glanced around the ship, impressed with the quality and beauty of the metal beast he'd named after her.

But why? It made no sense that he would do that after he'd abandoned her and everything else he'd ever known. She couldn't understand what had possessed him. Yes, they'd been young.

Still . . .

In spite of what Jayne said, Omira must have meant as much to him as Felicia meant to Talyn. It was the only thing that made sense. Why else give up his life and family for her? Fain had literally thrown away his entire future for Omira.

No one did something like that lightly. Not even when they were young and stupid.

"How long have you owned this?" she asked quietly, trying to distract herself away from how gorgeous he was as he took control of the ship.

Fain double-checked their settings without looking at her. "About twenty years."

Odd. He'd have taken ownership just a handful of years after he'd broken her heart. Why would he have done such when he'd always hated these things? Even in the armada before he'd left her, he'd never really liked flying or piloting. He'd always preferred palace assignments or infantry. As far back as she could remember, he'd told her that he wanted nothing to do with space travel.

Give me solid ground under my feet, and fresh air to breathe. I want real sun on my skin, not the fake holos that pass for it.

"What made you buy it?" she asked him.

A becoming blush covered his handsome features, making him all the sexier.

Before Fain could comment, Captain Venik answered. "My father liberated the lady from her previous, undeserving owner. Since Hauk was part of the original manifest take, my father offered her and a small crew to Hauk to run until Hauk earned the price of the ship and his freedom."

Did Kareem mean what she thought he did? "Manifest? As in part of the cargo?"

She didn't miss the pain in Fain's eyes as he ran over his settings. "I was conscripted, for a while."

Her stomach shrank with a sympathetic pain she didn't want to feel. "Conscripted how?"

Had he been a slave?

Finally, Fain turned toward her. His hard, fierce stare was so similar to one Talyn used whenever he was hot about something that it sent a shiver down her spine. "I don't talk about my past."

Father and son.

Jayne was right. They were far more similar than they should be, given that they'd never known each other.

Before she could respond, Talyn passed a fierce grimace at the ship's markings, and in particular Fain's individual Tavali flag, or Canting as The Tavali called it, that was unique to him and his ship. "You make a lot of raids into Andarion territory, Hauk?"

"A few over the years."

A familiar tic started in Talyn's jaw. "You have a black Zi-class fighter with the same serial and Canting on it?"

"Yeah, why?"

"Just curious." Talyn strapped himself in.

Fain turned back around to stare at him as a really, really bad feeling of dread went through him. There was only one reason he could think of that Talyn would know his ship's Canting and fighter's serial numbers off the top of his head.

Please tell me I didn't . . .

"Why are you asking?"

Talyn still didn't answer. He merely cut a covert glance to his mother. One that warned Fain to leave the topic alone.

Bile rose in his throat. Before his common sense could intervene, Fain asked the one question that bothered him most. "Please tell me I've never run against my own son."

The fury returned to Galene's eyes as her head snapped in Talyn's direction.

Wincing, Talyn cursed him under his breath as he cradled his forehead with his hand.

"Is he the rat bastard who shot you down during your last dogfight?" There was no missing the hatred and fury in her tone.

"No, Mum," he said quickly. "I swear to the gods, he's not

the one who brought me down. That wasn't a single ship or fighter. It was a mass attack of many."

Fain's frown deepened at their exchange. There was something more to all of this. "What she's talking about?"

"Nothing," Talyn said firmly.

Galene wasn't quite ready to let it go. "Answer me, Commander. Have you ever fought him in battle?"

Talyn cut a gimlet stare to Kareem and Chayden before he returned it to his mother. "Do I need to get Vari up here to verify my account, since my word obviously isn't good enough for Her High Holiness? Believe me, he knows who fought us that day. And who shot me down. It wasn't Hauk." Talyn raked him with a sneer. "Trust me, *he's* not that good a pilot."

Offended to the core of his being, Fain swallowed hard as he met Galene's hate-filled grimace. "I would never have fired on my son . . . had I known."

Chayden sucked his breath in sharply. "Whoa . . . whoa . . . wait a minute. The Iron Hammer's your kid? No shit?" He turned in his seat to look at Talyn. "You're Hauk's son? Seriously?"

Talyn gave Fain a harsh stare. "Through basic biology only."

Chayden let out a low whistle as he took over navigation. "Can someone say *awkward*? We could cut this tension with a knife, but the hostility's so thick here, I think it's a bad idea to introduce sharp objects into it."

Wisely remaining silent, Kareem nodded his agreement.

Fain didn't speak while guilt gnawed at him. Like Galene, he had a bad feeling that Talyn was withholding vital information. Though why the boy would protect him when he hated him so much was beyond his best comprehension.

Trying not to think about something he couldn't change, he settled the mic in his ear and launched.

Once they were leaving the Andarion atmosphere, he made the mistake of glancing toward Galene. The hatred in her white eyes shrank both his testicles and made him physically ill. Shit, at this rate, they were practically crawling back into his stomach—and if she didn't stop that glaring hatred soon, he'd be female by lunch.

Never once had he considered the fact that while he'd made Tavali runs for Venik against his former homeworld that he might be fighting his own kid.

Or Galene. She was supposed to have gone to med school, like her parents. He had no idea what had sent her into the military instead. Especially given her family history with the Andarion armada and the Purging that the former tadara had done against the entire Batur lineage to brutally wipe them out. Why would Galene risk military service given that the former queen had wanted her entire bloodline exterminated?

Something must have gone seriously wrong to put her on that course. Something he couldn't begin to fathom.

Kareem inclined his head to Talyn. "How long you been in uniform, Batur?"

"Fourteen years."

Fain cringed at a number that definitely would have put them head-to-head under Tadara Eriadne's reign.

"How many as a pilot?"

He held his breath, terrified of hearing his son's answer.

"Almost seven, total."

Kareem scowled. "First or last?"

"First."

Double shit.

Yeah, that was right in the thick of when Fain would have been making his heaviest attacks in Andarion territory. There was no telling how many times he'd engaged Talyn in battle.

Probably Galene, too.

"What made you stop?"

Before Talyn could answer, his nose and ear began pouring blood. Cursing, he leaned forward and pulled a cloth from his pocket to hold against them.

Galene gasped. "Talyn?"

He sighed at his mother's worried tone. "I'm fine, Commander. It's nothing." He glanced toward Kareem. "To answer your question, I was medically grounded after my last near-death experience. While I can still fly, the doctors don't like what the sudden changes in pressure and escape velocity do to my body. In space, I'm fine. It's the *reaching* space part that gets bloody for me." He glanced at the blood on his hands. "Literally."

Galene glared at Fain with a searing hatred that shriveled his innards.

He glared back. Just as Fain started to defend himself, Talyn placed his hand over hers.

"Let it go, Mum. The past is done. Lay it to rest." Talyn returned to his conversation with Kareem. "What about you? How long you been Tavali?"

"I took my Canting and oath at eighteen. But my birth father's Braxen Venik. Leader of the Porturnum Nation." He jerked his chin toward Fain. "He's also Fain's father."

Talyn arched a brow at that.

"Tavali father," Fain explained. "You have to be adopted to wear our uniform. You can't just raise the banner and proclaim yourself Tavali. Anyone that stupid is taken out of our gene pool immediately. Unlike other nationalities, Tavali is a citizenship that comes with obligation. It's a privilege you earn and maintain, not a birthright."

Galene snorted. "My God, Fain, how many times have you been adopted in your lifetime?"

Fain ground his teeth at her snotty tone.

Kareem stiffened. "You need to show him some respect. There aren't many slaves who'd take the blast for their owners that Hauk took for my father. Trust me, he more than earned his place in our family."

Galene's jaw went slack. "So, you weren't conscripted? You really were enslaved?"

Fain winced at something he didn't like thinking about or remembering. And he damn sure didn't want to talk about it, especially not in front of Venik's kid as Venik had been one of his owners, and it still stuck in his craw. "It was a long time ago. . . . Venik fostered me after I saved his life, only because he felt he could trust me. Cairie, a few weeks back, after I helped rescue her granddaughter. Honestly though, her adoption was nothing more than an FU to my real mother."

Talyn wiped the blood at his ear. "How so?"

Fain started to answer that it came from when his father had broken his pledge with Cairistiona by sleeping with Fain's mother the night before they were to legally finalize it. But self-preservation stopped that particular brand of stupid from spilling out of his mouth. Talyn would be the first to point out the irony and that faithless acts of treachery must run in the blood of all male Hauks. "Personal grudge from when they were kids."

Galene cocked her head. "So *you're* The Tavali who saved Tizirah Thia?"

"You don't have to sound so surprised. I have been known to battle from time to time. And I didn't do it alone."

She bristled at that. "You'll have to forgive me if I don't automatically associate acts of heroism and altruism with *your* name . . . given *our* past."

Fain shook his head at the contempt he heard in her voice. Contempt that cut him deeper than anything else. There was no way he'd ever be able to redeem himself with the very female he should have died to protect.

How can I ever make this right? It just didn't seem possible.

Kareem turned in his seat to face Galene and Talyn while Fain headed them out toward deep space. "Look, I know there's some bad history here, but Fain is my brother and the Tavali are nothing if not loyal to our own. So let me warn you now, if you want to stay healthy and happy in your new assignment, you'll stow the disdain for Commander Hauk before we land. Any shit-talk against Hauk is shit-talk against a Venik, and you don't want to say anything negative about my family in our HQ. It won't go well for you."

Galene scoffed. "Tavali don't scare me. Ever. But don't worry. Your beloved *brother* is safe from any further harm where I'm concerned. I intend to avoid him as any sentient creature would a contagious STD."

Great. Just what he'd always wanted to be. An STD to the only female who'd ever owned his heart. *Mom and Dad would be so proud.*

But there was one thing he needed to make clear. "And I need to warn you, Kareem. While they are here, the Baturs are under *my* protection and are to be left alone. Any Tavali who fucks with them will get the worst end of me. That includes your father."

As soon as they docked at the Tavali station, Fain saw Braxen Venik waiting to greet them, with an entire squadron of Hadean Corps soldiers as his escort. The Hadean Corps were the Tavali enforcers and their version of a highly trained tactical police unit. They had to be since The Tavali were an extremely rough and well-trained group who lived to fight and play hard.

Tall and fierce, Brax was half Andarion, but looked mostly human with his dark eyes—just like Kareem. Only his elongated canines betrayed his Andarion heritage, and that tiny bit of Andarion biology had cost the male dearly in his life, and left Brax with a bitter resentment toward the entire Andarion race. It was why Brax had hated Fain the first time they'd met.

Why, even though Fain had been a bound slave kept by humans, Venik had dragged him off the ship—which was then called the *Cerulean Escapades*—by his hair, and shot out both kneecaps while he'd been chained and unable to protect himself.

Venik would have done more, but the fire and venom in Fain that refused to beg or be dominated by anyone or anything had given the Tavali pause.

Fain's only response to the assault had been to look Venik in the eye and laugh. "Pain I can take, old man. Do your fucking worst, and you better make sure I die. 'Cause if I get loose, I'm going to rip out your guts and strangle you with them. I promise you."

Those growled, hostile words had finally won the pirate over and made him respect the fact that Fain was every bit the warrior Venik was.

However, the expression on Brax's face today said something bad was brewing. And that the male was highly pissed off and out for blood.

Curious about what had him in such a foul mood, Fain left the ship first.

As soon as Fain was close enough, Brax hugged him like a brother before he narrowed his dark gaze at the twenty-two Andarions with them. "I heard you were shot on your arrival. Should we return the favor to them?"

"No!" Fain said quickly. "Two of them are my family."

Brax quirked a brow. "As I recall, your *family* disowned you. Left you for dead."

"Not these two. And it's complicated. I'd just rather they be treated with respect."

Brax nodded slowly. "I'll let the others know, then." He moved toward Galene. "Commander Batur?"

She hesitated at the flash of his fangs. "You're part Andarion?"

"My father. My mother was a Qill warrior, as is my wife." He frowned as he saw Talyn approaching them. A knowing glance at Fain let him know that Brax had already deduced who Fain was related to and why it was complicated. "Another Commander Batur in the mix." He took a moment to study Talyn. "You're not *the* Talyn Batur, are you?"

"I am."

He held his hand out in friendship. "Nice to meet you, Hammer."

"You, too, Captain Venik." There was an underlying crisp chill to Talyn's voice.

His friendliness vaporizing, Brax curled his lip the moment he saw Chayden disembark and head in their direction. Without a word of greeting, he spun and led his men away.

Chayden grinned widely as he joined them. "Look at me, making friends everywhere I go." Lifting his nose, he sniffed at the air. "You can just smell the happy welcome . . . oh wait, someone needs a bath." He clapped Fain on the back. "Oh yeah, that's me, too!"

Galene passed a quizzical stare to Fain.

"Chayden has major brain trauma. I think his sister must have slapped him too hard in childhood."

Laughing good-naturedly, Chayden winked at her. "Venik hates my Tavali father, Gadgehe Hinto. It's an old blood feud between them. Which means I get to irritate the grand

85

Porturnum leader with impunity. It's awesome." He glanced to Fain and grinned before he spoke to Galene. "And if you want me to rattle *his* cage, just holler at your boy and I'll do it. I live to make beautiful females happy."

Galene smiled. "Thank you, Chayden. I just might take you up on that."

Flashing his dimples, Chayden clicked his teeth. "By the way, we should probably let you know that Venik isn't a captain. His rank is technically high admiral and Tavali presidium."

Talyn gave him an emotionless stare. "I know. I did it to piss him off."

Chayden let out a low, insidious laugh as he clapped Talyn on the arm. "You and me, Hammer, we're going to be *good* friends. I can tell."

From across the bay, Brax motioned Fain away to speak to him while a small group of Tavali women came forward to show Galene, Talyn, and their soldiers where to bunk.

Talyn carried his mother's gear through their impressively clean and modern hallways toward their rooms.

After what seemed like miles of hiking, the Tavali women finally showed them the bunk corridor where their rooms were lined up like prison cells.

With a smirk, the shortest woman opened the closest door. "For you, Prime Commander."

Galene screwed her face up at the small, cramped quarters they'd reserved for her group. They really did look like prison cells. It wasn't just the hallway. They even held that peculiar antiseptic, institutional smell. "Is there nothing better than this?" she asked the female Tavali closest to her.

She shrugged. "It's where we always put our special guests. Sorry it's not up to Your Majesty's high standards."

Talyn caught Galene as she started for the woman. "It's fine, Commander. I'll take the smallest one." He cut a fierce glare at the woman who'd led them here. "Give our females the larger rooms. If there are any to be had."

The woman stepped back to let Talyn enter his "closet."

Galene wanted to weep at the paltry quarters. She knew The Tavali had better accommodations than this—there was no way they'd bunk their crew in something so horrible—but The Tavali and Andaria had a long and ugly history of war between them.

Obviously, this was their petty way of getting back at their former enemies, even though they were here to help them and be allies.

Something that proved to be more than apparent when she entered her hot, stifling room. Without another word, she set her duffle on the small cot. Sadly, it was better than what Talyn was dealing with. At least she could turn around without bumping into anything.

Disgusted, she picked up her link to call him. "Hey, *mi tana*. You want to exchange rooms? Mine's a little larger and you're a lot bigger than me."

"It's fine, Mum. I had a smaller bed in gen-barr. At least it has its own bathroom. I can manage."

I can manage. Her heart broke at his most common phrase to her after the word "fine." "Ever my brave soldier. Love you, Talyn."

"You, too."

Galene hung up and started to unpack, only to learn that there was nowhere to store her gear. Not even a closet or nightstand. Infuriated, she'd just set her duffel on the narrow desk when Fain texted over a map of the facilities and instructions on where their command center was located, as well as her office.

Disgusted with all of The Tavali in general and Fain in particular, she refused to text him back. Effing bastard. He was probably the reason they were being housed here.

Trying not to think about it, she went to the bathroom to freshen up.

Fain frowned as he waited and waited for a text from Galene. When she didn't respond, he traced her location.

No . . . *that* had to be a mistake.

Someone's screwing with me.

Assuming they were being toured and not actually placed on that side of the base, he finished up his reports for Nyk and logs for Brax before heading to the room numbers assigned to Galene and her team.

The moment he opened the door and saw the cramped closet-sized hole that was her room, he wanted blood.

This was utter bullshit!

He stepped back to leave at the same time the bathroom door opened.

It wasn't Galene.

Dressed in only a towel while drying his hair with another, Talyn came out to glare at him. "Don't you fucking knock?"

"I thought this was your mother's room."

Lowering the towel in his hand, Talyn arched a brow at that and gave him a withering glower. "Are you trying to piss me off? Or is this a natural talent you possess?"

"Apparently, it's an innate skill where you're concerned."

That piss-poor attempt at humor didn't resolve any of the tension in the room. If anything, it made it worse.

Fain sighed at his other raw talent—making bad situations fatal. He'd never been good at diffusing things. Only blowing them up. "Since I have you alone for a minute, can I ask you something?"

"Yes. You're an asshole. I took a survey and everyone agrees." Talyn didn't lose a beat or crack the slightest trace of a smile. His delivery was totally deadpan.

Fain would have been more ticked off had it not been some thing he would have said to someone he hated, had he ever thought of it.

Talyn hung the towel around his neck and held it with both hands as he leaned against the bathroom door to watch him. "Are you going to ask it, or stand there staring at me like a perv?"

Damn, the kid had way too much of him in his DNA. Poor

Galene that she had to put up with him. "That look you gave Venik earlier. What was behind it?"

"He was so cute and fluffy, I couldn't help noticing."

Fain rolled his eyes. Damn, that level of bad attitude must be hardwired into all Hauk DNA.

"You two have history. Since we're supposed to be working together and I'm the lucky moron assigned to this disaster, I don't want to get blindsided by bad blood. What's the deal between you two?"

Talyn let out a long, annoyed breath before he answered. "I merely found it amusing that the bastard didn't remember meeting me nine years ago when he held a blaster to my head and threatened to pull the trigger."

Nine years ago . . .

Fain's eyes widened as he remembered the one and only time Andarions had infiltrated this station and infuriated Venik to the point of murder. The Tavali had been sheltering Eriadne eton Anatole during the Andarion civil war that had only ended when Cairistiona was crowned and her mother deposed. "You were part of the Andarion strike force that came here to retrieve the former tadara?"

"I was the commander of it." Talyn moved to the cot to pull out his clothes.

"Why didn't you tell your mother about that?"

He glared at Fain. "To what purpose? She needs her head clear to lead. It's my baggage to carry. Not hers. She has enough to deal with. She doesn't need to know Venik almost killed me. Especially since he can't even remember it."

As Fain watched him digging through his duffel, he noticed something else peculiar about his son.

Without a word, he took Talyn's hand into his and scowled at the tattoo Talyn had in a band around his unification finger. Written in Andarion were the words "Forever Felicia's."

Because Talyn couldn't legally marry or even buy or wear a wedding ring, or bear Felicia's family crest in any way, Talyn must have done that as a way of publicly honoring his female. Of showing the universe he was committed to her.

Laws be damned.

Ever defiant. That particular tattoo was a bold move on Andaria, where Talyn could be arrested for it if the wrong official happened to see it, and was in a particularly shitty mood.

Growling at him, Talyn jerked his hand out of Fain's grasp.

Fain stepped back, his gaze falling to the photo on the bed of a beautiful Andarion female, sitting at a white desk with her chin resting on her hand as she smiled sweetly at the photographer. "Felicia?"

"It's none of your business, old man." Talyn tucked the picture in the bag, but Fain didn't miss the care he took to protect it from harm.

Realizing anything he said or did would only piss his son off more, Fain opened the door to leave. But as he did so, he felt the twenty-degree difference between the hallway and the stifling temperature in Talyn's room. "Why's it so hot in here?"

"Air's broken."

"You report it?"

Talyn gave him a droll stare. "No. I live for sweltering heat. At home, I'd have to pay good credits for a sauna this extreme."

He ignored the dripping sarcasm. "What did they say?"

"I'm on the list. They'll get to it when they have time. Now, if you don't mind, I've already given you one free show. That's my limit and there's not enough room in here to dress with you standing on top of me."

No, there wasn't.

Furious with his Tavali comrades, Fain left and pulled out his link. He called the Station Support Center to ask about the *lovely* Andarion accommodations, and was greeted with proud laughter.

"Yeah, we put the bastards in the slag block quarters."

Fain's vision darkened. "I want them moved," he growled. "Immediately. They're here to help us, not be hazed."

"You're serious, Hauk?"

"More than serious. I want them out of here faster than you can tel-ass, and the Baturs are to be given family accommodations, with *all* working facilities. If not, I'm making a personal visit up there, shoving my foot up your collective asses, and none of you are going to be walking out of that room tonight. You understand me?"

"Yes, sir."

"Good. You have twenty minutes. Run, assholes. Fast." Fain hung up and almost walked into Galene as she was headed for Talyn's room.

For the merest instant, he saw the way she used to look at him . . . like he was her hero. "You didn't have to do that."

Fain's body reacted instantly to her presence. Dammit. All he wanted was to hold her again. To kiss those perfect lips . . .

But she'd viciously attack him if he tried. He could feel her slap already.

Clearing his throat, he tried to ignore how much he still loved her. But it was even harder than his body was. "I didn't bring you here to be abused. And I'm not about to leave Talyn sweltering in a cell so small he doesn't have enough room to change his mind."

She inclined her head to him. "Thank you for taking care of my baby."

Fain choked on his grief at the fact that she refused him the honor of claiming Talyn as his. But then, what could he really expect?

Talyn was right. All he'd done was donate some DNA. He'd never once been there for either of them.

And that hurt most of all.

"If you want, I can show you to your new quarters. Help you carry your things?" He gestured toward Talyn's room. "He was dressing when I left him a second ago."

She pulled out her link and texted Talyn. After a brief pause, a blush stained her cheeks. "He's checking in with Felicia. They have so little time together that I try not to intrude on it." Biting her lip like she'd done as a girl, she put her link away and headed back toward her room with the sexiest military swagger any soldier had ever possessed.

Now *that* was the sweetest ass he'd ever laid eyes on or hands to. And it set fire to every part of him. But then Galene had always made him salivate. Always made him appreciate the cut of her body . . .

Knowing better than to pursue *any* of those thoughts, Fain had to quicken his stride to catch up to her. His Stormy had always moved forward, at full speed. With purpose.

He searched his mind for something to distract himself from the hard-on that was killing him. "So . . . do you approve of Talyn's female?"

She paused to open the door to her quarters. "Would it matter if I didn't?"

With Talyn's defiant attitude, not really.

Fain cursed as he glanced past her and saw the paltry cell she'd been assigned. While her room was slightly larger than Talyn's, it was still a dive-hole. This was ridiculous and it made him want to beat the shit out of everyone who'd had a hand in it. So much for Tavali hospitality, and it didn't help that it reminded him of his early days with their order when he'd been a slave, or what The Tavali snidely referred to as a slag—the lowest order of their society that was The Tavali equivalent of an Andarion lack-Vest.

Yeah, those were memories he'd rather not have. The Tavali could be as cruel and nasty as anyone else in the universe. Especially to Andarions.

"I'm really sorry about this." Fain reached for her duffle on the small desk. "Is this everything?"

"Yes."

He lifted her gear. "Then follow me."

Galene tried her best not to notice how incredibly sexy Fain moved as she reluctantly obeyed. Honestly, he was huge and devastating, and she hated how badly her body reacted to his presence. How much she still ached for him in spite of what he'd done to her.

I so want to hate you.

No, she *needed* to hate him. But he didn't make it easy on her, especially when he was being kind. Just like when they were kids. It was what had made her love him to begin with. Unlike his older brother, Fain had never bragged about his heritage or used it to belittle those around him.

Ever respectful of others, he'd even given his school jacket away to a fellow student who'd torn the only one his parents had been able to afford for him. Because he was a War Hauk and more was expected of him than others, Fain had been severely punished by school officials for not having his uniform jacket. He'd taken it in stride and never breathed a word to anyone what he'd done or why. He'd simply said he misplaced it and couldn't remember where he put it.

She only knew what he'd really done because she'd witnessed him doing it from a distance.

And he'd borne far worse than that from his father who'd expected him to be a fierce military officer in their proud family tradition. His mother who had constantly berated him for any act of kindness or charity.

You're a War Hauk, Fain! For the love of the gods, remember that. Only the tahrs himself stands above you in caste!

But Fain had never cared about that. His heart had been one of honor and decency. And while he'd been as fierce a fighter as any Andarion male she'd ever known, he was always respectful and sweet to her. He'd rip anyone else apart, but the moment he laid eyes to her, he'd calm down to a quiet peacefulness.

Like a tamed battle-lorina.

As they walked on and on, she slowed. "Should I be worried? Where exactly are you taking me?"

He cracked a charming grin. "To the side of the station where we put creatures we actually like. You and your guard were assigned slag quarters."

"By your *father's* orders?"

His smile fading, he opened a door and sighed. "I'd like to say no, but given what I know of Venik, it wouldn't surprise me. He's not exactly fond of Andarions. The last time any were here, they blew up half his station."

"Yet he adopted you?"

"What can I say? I'm irresistibly fluffy."

She snorted at that as she swept past him, then froze at the opulent suite of rooms. "Is this . . . correct?"

He nodded as he set her bag on the floor near a leather sofa. "It is, indeed. If you don't like it—"

"No," she said quickly, afraid he'd return her to the crappy side they'd just come from. "It's very nice. Thank you."

He inclined his head to her. "I'll have Talyn put in the room that's adjacent to this one." He gestured toward a door on his right. "You can open the door between your quarters. That should keep him in line with his barracks restriction."

Sadness bit her hard at the reminder. "Thank you. The last thing I want is for him to lose his rank. Again. He's worked and suffered enough already."

Fain opened his mouth to speak an instant before a blaring alarm sounded.

Galene scowled at the highly unpleasant shrieking noise. "What's that?"

"We're under attack."

All the color faded from her face. For a moment, Fain thought she might pass out as she placed her hand against the wall to catch her balance.

Worried about her, he closed the distance between them. "Stormy?"

She didn't even react to his old nickname for her. Instead, she grabbed the front of his battlesuit in two desperate fists. Tears swam in her pale eyes as she stared up at him. "Don't let my Talyn fly. Ground him!"

He scowled at her uncharacteristic behavior. "I'll try."

"No," she choked, shaking her head as she tightened her grip on him. Her breathing was labored and panicked in a way he couldn't fathom. He'd never seen her like this before. "You can't . . . I-I-I can't . . . Talyn has to stay here! On the ground. Do you understand? In the station. You hear me!" She was absolutely hysterical. "He can't fly into battle. Not again! Never . . . Never!"

"Shh, Galene. It's all right." Fain pulled her against him and held her close. She was literally shaking like a child. "I'm not going to let your son be harmed. I swear."

And still she sobbed hysterically.

What the hell had happened to Talyn?

Her armband buzzed with the warning, summoning her to take command of the battle. Her breathing ragged, she stepped back to silence it. "I've got to go." When she met his gaze, he saw the terror that ran soul deep. "He's all I have in this universe, Fain. Please, don't let him fly into an attack again! Please! Keep him on the ground. Whatever it takes."

What did she want him to do? Shoot the kid? He had a feeling that was the only way to stop Talyn from doing what he wanted, and given the size and rage-factor of their son, that would probably only piss him off more. "You're his commander. Order him to stand down."

She snorted at that. "He's too much like his father." She glared hatefully at him.

Wiping at her eyes, she pulled herself together to rush to the command center for her post.

Torn between his duty to protect the station, and a need to make sure she was all right, he ran to the hangar bay where his fighter was docked.

Hoping to make it out before he got into trouble with his

child, he was halfway to his fighter when Talyn and ten of the Andarion guardsmen met up with him.

Shit. Fain closed his eyes and ground his teeth at the bad timing.

Of course, Talyn headed straight for him. Because, yeah, that was the kind of luck he had. "If you have ships, we can assist."

Effing awesome. Either he angered his son or the woman who held his heart in a merciless grip.

You're so screwed, Hauk.

Talyn sneered at his hesitation, misreading its cause. "We're not going for your throats, old man. We came to defend this station. We're allies who understand that a threat to one is a threat to all. We are Andarion. It's not in us to sit out during a fight. None of my soldiers will shoot down a Tavali fighter."

"That's not what I was thinking. I was merely considering the sheer number of body parts I'm going to have to fortify with blast armor should your mother catch *you* in a Tavali cockpit."

The slightest bit of amusement quirked Talyn's lips. "She won't hurt you for this. I'm the one she'll beat."

Yeah, right. Not after what he'd just witnessed. It was *his* balls she'd want on a titanium platter. "What about the doctor's orders?" That seemed like the safest excuse Talyn might buy.

"We're not lifting off from a planet. The G-force in a launch tube won't hurt me. It's nothing like escape velocity."

True, but . . .

Fain glanced around the Andarions with Talyn, who waited for orders. If he held Talyn back and let them go, it would impugn his authority with his soldiers. Make him look weak and ineffective. On Andaria, that was the worst sort of an insult to a commander.

She's going to geld me.

But he couldn't bring himself to harm Talyn or his reputation.

Knowing he was screwed, Fain jerked his chin toward his personal fighter that was faster and more maneuverable than most. "She's fueled and ready to launch. I'll assign ships to the others. What's your call sign?"

"Pit Viper."

Horrified, Fain went stock-still at the last name he'd expected to hear. The main reason being he'd thought Viper was long dead.

That familiar sick feeling returned to his gut. "Viper-Ichi?"

A snide smile toyed at the edges of Talyn's mouth before he answered. "Yeah . . . nice to finally meet you, *Blister.*"

Minsid hell. His son was the archenemy he'd once put a fierce bounty on with The Tavali. They'd faced off many, many times in battle.

Until about seven years ago when the Porturnum, at Fain's direction and under his direct command, had ambushed Viper and brought him down in one of the worst firefights Fain had ever been in.

Now, he understood why Galene had broken down the way she had. They'd blasted Talyn's ship apart with a weapon Darling had specifically designed for the trap they'd laid. How the hell Talyn had survived it, only the gods knew. Nothing but genetic fragments should have been left of him.

That alone said it all about his son's superior skills as a pilot.

Talyn leaned forward to whisper, "Don't worry, old man. I never told her who shot me down. I'm Andarion. I don't hold grudges in war. We're soldiers. We know when we don the uniform what we're risking." Talyn stepped back and turned toward the young major who'd approached him on the *Storm Dancer.* "Reaper, you're with me. No heroics."

Reaper. The other pilot Fain had been hell-bent to send to his maker.

And he was just a kid *now.* He must have been an infant in that firefight.

Pain racked him hard while he watched Talyn's uneven gait as his son headed for the fighter Fain had been flying when he'd brutally assaulted Talyn and no doubt given him that limp.

Worse? He'd meant to kill him that day.

In that moment, Fain wished Galene had shot him in the head on his arrival. Anything to save him from *this* pain and knowledge.

How could I have harmed my own child?

Disgusted with himself, he was headed toward Dancer's fighter when he heard someone let out a shrill catcall whistle.

"Own that walk, Sexy Baby T!"

Talyn stopped midstride.

For the first time, Fain saw the boy really smile, at the sound of Morrtalah Deathblade's voice. "Morra!"

As soon as she reached him, Talyn gave the extremely tiny female a fierce hug.

The green-skinned Phrixian was so small, she looked like a

toy doll in Talyn's massive arms. She buried her hand in his braids and kissed his cheek before she finally released him.

Frowning, Talyn glanced around the bay. "Where's Qory?"

"Still en route to base. He won't arrive for a few more days." She tugged at Talyn's Andarion flightsuit. "Don't worry, precious. I'll make sure and keep that cute bottom of yours intact for Lish and your mom."

Fain watched the easy way the Phrixian interacted with his son as they crossed the bay to their fighters. She even held on to Talyn's pinkie and swung his arm as they walked. He envied her that casual friendship. The ability to make Talyn's stern features soften ever so slightly as they bantered. It was obvious Talyn liked her a great deal.

Sighing with regret, he showed the other Andarions to ships before he climbed into Dancer's fighter that had been delivered a few days ago when his brother had agreed to stay here and help him get settled back in.

When Fain called for clearance, he realized Galene had taken control of the battle. The sound of her voice in the background did the strangest things to his breathing. Her voice was deeper than most females'. And she'd always liked to issue orders to everyone. It had driven her siblings crazy. Made his older brother furious to be around her. Keris couldn't stand it and had bitched anytime Galene visited.

Strangely, Fain had never minded. He'd always liked the fact that she was open and quite verbal with her needs and wants. There was no guessing with her. No games.

And as was evidenced by the hole in his chest, she didn't pull punches. With her, he'd always known exactly where he stood. *I have to be a sick bastard to find that charming.* Yet he did. It was one of the best things about her.

Not wanting to think about that, he launched with his squadron and did a quick search for Talyn's position. His heart raced as he realized his son was already in the thickest part of the fighting.

Sheez, no wonder Galene had been so insistent Talyn stay out of the battle. Had he intentionally gone for the worst of it? There was no other explanation for how much heat the boy was already taking.

Without thinking, Fain headed straight to Talyn's side to try and protect him as best he could. At this point, League fighters were everywhere. Of course, some of that was probably due to the assault Venik had made the day before on one of their outposts. The Tavali leader was using this war for his own profiteering. Until now, Fain hadn't minded. But as he saw his son narrowly escaping a blast that would have killed him had it made contact with his ship, he was resenting the hell out of it. Especially when it dawned on him that none of Ven's children were in this fight. Two of them were tucked in the command center with Galene, and Ven's daughters and their crew were safely across the galaxy. Not even Ven was out here for the battle.

That was bullshit. Fain had never put anyone into a fight he wasn't willing to participate in himself. That was the move of a politician, and War Hauks were anything but.

Something proven more than true as he watched Talyn's brazen skills. He was both proud and horrified by how fast his boy maneuvered in battle.

Just don't get hurt, kid. Galene would definitely cut his balls off this time.

Galene ground her teeth as she watched the massive war exploding on her battle screens. There were three hundred Sentella-Tavali fighters and eleven Andarions against five hundred League pilots. That would have been bad enough, but this was the first time Talyn was in a fight that she was directly commanding. And it was taking everything she had to keep herself together and focused. To not scream in terror every time someone came near him.

She could kill both him and Fain for this!

And this was exactly why she'd never once attended any Ring match her son had been in. She couldn't stand it. Not after watching the brutal brawls Fain had barely walked away from when he'd been a boy. Even now, she could hear his mother berating him for showing mercy by not killing every opponent he faced in the Ring.

"You shame your lineage, Fain. Keris wouldn't have allowed that coward to live after that pitiful display."

Glaring at her in complete defiance, Fain would spit out his bloody fang guard. His response to her condemnations had always been the same. *"And Keris isn't a Ring champion, Matarra. I am."*

Now, as Galene again watched Fain fight, she was consumed by sheer terror while he maneuvered to take a blast that was aimed for Talyn. A shot that landed dead on Fain's fighter.

I don't want to care. She didn't.

Yet . . .

She was every bit as choked up and nervous watching Fain as she was for Talyn.

Please be okay. She didn't want to watch him die. But the fighting was brutal. Mechanically and by rote, she called out orders and sequences while trying to keep herself from making this personal. Both Fain and Talyn were highly competent warriors, relying on her to stay calm and emotionless. To treat them any differently was an insult to both. And it could get them killed.

But as she saw a cluster of fighters descend on Fain, her entire body locked up with fright. Worse? Talyn flew straight into the thick of it to help his father.

Fain cursed as his controls short-circuited from the blasts he'd been taking. He rebooted the targeting system—not the brightest thing to do in a fight, but he had no choice. Nothing else was working. He was being hammered so much, his head and body were bouncing all over. While his dampners came and went, his shields were holding. However, they wouldn't be able to take much more without cracking and leaving him with his ass in his hands.

As his systems came back live, an alarm blared, letting him

know he was about to be fired on. He aimed for his attacker, then paused as he realized it was Talyn.

Payback's a bitch.

For a full minute, he couldn't breathe as he stared at his son and waited for him to fire and end his life.

An instant later, Talyn really did take the shot.

CHAPTER 6

The blast of Talyn's shot lit up the darkness. Fain braced for impact. But rather than striking his ship, it narrowly passed him by and went straight into the League fighter he hadn't even known was there.

Fain gasped as he realized Talyn had just saved his life. Unbeknownst to him, the League pilot had held him completely dead to rights.

He watched Talyn peel off after another fighter. "Thanks for the assist, Viper."

Talyn didn't say a word. Not until the fight was done and they were both back in the bay.

Fain went over to him to shake his hand and thank him for it personally.

With a furious glower, Talyn brushed past him. Then, he stopped and turned back.

He shoved his blast helmet into Fain's chest so hard, it would no doubt leave a bruise. "Just so you know, old man. If I'm going to kill you, I'll do it face-to-face. Warrior-to-warrior. I'm an Andarion, not a pussy coward who takes a cheap shot against someone who can't fight back when they're under fire and wounded." And with that, Talyn headed for the hallway to his quarters.

Hurt and embarrassed even though he knew he deserved Talyn's verbal assault, Fain sighed heavily. He should be used to his family rejecting him. With the exception of Dancer, it was all he'd ever known. And it was why he was so fiercely protective of his little brother. Why Dancer, alone, held his full trust.

Still, it cut soul deep that he'd disappointed his son.

Again.

All he'd ever wanted was what others took for granted. Friend or blood who wouldn't turn on him and make him feel like utter shit to be near them. Why was it so hard to be around others?

As he left the hangar, he met Galene in the hallway. Cursing silently in his head, he couldn't wait to hear what he'd done to piss her off, too. How much he'd disappointed her.

"Are you all right?"

The concern in her tone shocked him. "Um, yeah."

"Sure you don't want to see a medic? You took some harsh fire."

Terrified of the concern he heard in her voice, he drew up short. "What kind of shapeshifter are you? What have you done with Commander Batur?"

She scoffed at his question. "Fine, asshole. Not like I really care." With angry strides, she took off after Talyn.

"Well, you're just pissing off everyone today, aren't you?"

He grimaced at the Hyshian assassin as she came up behind him. "Don't start on me, Jayne. I'm not in the mood."

She held her hands up in surrender. "Sorry." She cocked her head to stare at him with an unsettling intensity. "So what went wrong with the two of you, anyway? Did you really love Omira that much?"

Fain pulled the small ring off his pinkie and handed it to Jayne. Everyone, including Dancer, assumed it was Omira's, and he'd never once corrected them. But the truth was when Omira had figured out who it originally belonged to, it'd driven her into the arms of a human. To this day, he could hear her cursing him for keeping it, even though he'd never once cheated on his wife.

At least not physically. And he'd done his best to keep his heart loyal to Omira, too. It wasn't his fault that it'd refused to leave Galene's hands.

When he'd left Omira after he'd caught her in bed with her ex, that tiny ring and the clothes on his back were the only possessions he'd taken with him.

He knew the moment Jayne deciphered the Andarion writing in the band. Her eyes widened and she let out a shocked gasp.

Shaking her head, she sighed. "Like father, like son." She returned the ring to him. "You need to show *that* to Lena."

He returned it to where it'd rested on his hand since he was eighteen. It was all he owned that he'd fight or die to keep, and many sentient beings had learned that lesson the hard way.

"Why? So she can finish ripping my heart out? No, thanks. I've done enough damage to both of them. Best thing I can do is just stay out of their way and let them live as if I don't."

Jayne caught his arm as he started past her. Scowling, she pulled her hand back to see it covered in blood. "You're hurt?"

"Not the first time. Won't be the last." But as he started past her, the floor slanted. Next thing he knew, that fetid bitch known as gravity rose up and slapped him hard across the face.

Fain heard the monitors a split second before he opened his eyes and saw them. That he expected. What he never thought to see was Galene holding his hand.

I have to be dead.

He grimaced at her as she reached to call for the doctor.

"Don't move, Fain. You have a massive head injury."

It must be bad. Even Talyn was standing in the doorway and had to move aside for the medics to come in and check him.

But honestly, to have them there, with him, he'd take the injury. For the tiniest moment, he allowed himself to pretend that he actually had a family that loved him.

He had a sort of brotherhood with The Tavali, but it wasn't the same as a real blood family and he knew it. End of the day, they wouldn't weep to see him gone. Wouldn't give his death much more than a passing *too bad* thought.

The last time he'd felt like he truly belonged to someone had been in Galene's arms when they were kids.

Never since.

Even now, he could still see her young, bashful face as she pressed her cheek to his and held his naked body close to hers. "I love you, Fain. I live only for the day of our unification when everyone will know exactly how much you mean to me. I shall scream it through the streets. Fain Hauk is my husband and I love him more than anything!"

Laughing, he'd rolled and pulled her body over his. "And I shall tattoo your Batur lineage all the way down my arm so that everyone will know that you mean more to me than even my own revered family heritage. A War Hauk I may be, but it is a Winged Batur who owns me. Mind, body, and soul. Forever."

Fain glanced down at his left arm to the hand Galene held. Heat stung his cheeks.

Galene ran her hand over the sprawling Batur tattoo that entwined around his Tavali markings before she stepped back to allow the doctor to treat him. She moved to speak in a whisper to Talyn, who nodded, then left.

Fain heard the Andarion doctor speaking, but paid her no attention. Not while he was watching the only female who had ever held his heart.

Galene pressed her lips together as she tried to sort through the conflicting emotions Fain stirred. Especially those that had ripped through her with serrated talons the moment she'd stepped into his hospital room and had seen her specific Batur lineage inked in bold blue and black hues down his entire left arm.

Shoulder to wrist.

Nothing had ever shocked her more. Not even the time

Talyn had repainted her walls with her favorite and extremely expensive lipstick when he'd been a toddler.

Fain hadn't borne that tattoo the last time she'd seen him naked.

No, it'd been done long after they'd parted ways. And she could tell by the way the tattoo had faded that he hadn't done it recently, either. He'd been carrying her lineage with him for years.

But why? Why would he have marked that on his flesh after abandoning her? None of this made sense.

How could he both abandon her *and* honor her lineage?

Talyn placed his hand on her shoulder. "You all right?"

"Not sure." She glanced back toward Fain. "Tell me, honestly. What do you think of your father?"

"You've physically or verbally spanked my ass every time I've ever answered that question. Believe it or not, I can be taught."

She snorted. "You hadn't met him *then*. Now . . ." She gestured toward the male she wanted to both kiss and kill.

Talyn let out a tired sigh. "What do you want me to say, Matarra? Like you, I'm still mad as hell at him for what he did to us. But I don't really know him well enough to comment on his motives or decency. He's a complete stranger to me."

But he wasn't a stranger to her. At least he hadn't been, and in the back of her mind, she saw the precious boy she'd once loved.

Cursed with an obnoxious, bullying older brother who'd been possessed of a severe drug and alcohol problem, Fain had spent the better part of his youth trying to cover for Keris. Or worse, doing his best to protect his younger brother from everyone who thought Dancer was worthless, and should have been left out to die as an infant. Only Fain had ever seen the good in his little brother, and any time Dancer had been threatened, Fain had thrown himself into the line of fire to protect him.

Just like he'd done today for Talyn.

Why do I have to love the very creature I hate most?

Emotions shouldn't be *this* complicated.

Talyn pulled his link out to check it.

"Felicia?"

He shook his head. "I'm a little worried. I haven't heard from her since I left a message asking her to call, and that's not like her. She's not even responding to my nudges. You don't think anything happened, do you?"

"I'm sure she's fine. Did you contact her brother?"

"He said he spoke to her and that she's fine. Just really busy with work and the upcoming holidays."

"Then don't worry so. She's ferocious."

That finally made him smile. "True enough." He returned his link to his pocket. "They need a battle report in the con. I'll go take care of it for you."

She pressed her cheek to his. "Thank you."

"Call if you need me."

Galene watched as Talyn walked toward the nearest lift bank. He really was the very image of his father. Something brought home a second later when the doctor and nurses scattered out of the room like insects fleeing an exterminator.

"No one took your damn ring!" the doctor snarled before

she and the others left him. "Up his dosage!" The doctor handed her pad to the nurse on her right. "And give him an enema while you're at it."

Suppressing a smile at something that was far too similar to Talyn's soured demeanor whenever he was confined to a hospital bed, she slid into the room with a chiding tsk and used a phrase that Felicia normally said to Talyn in similar situations. "You should be nicer to the ones who give you shots."

"I can't stand a thief," Fain snarled.

"Interesting words coming from the mouth of a Tavali pirate."

Fain sneered at her words. "Taking from a government drunk on its own power is one thing. Stealing from an individual—" His words stopped dead as she returned the ring to him.

"As I recall, it's my ring, is it not?"

A deep blush stained his caramel skin as she slid the ring back onto his pinkie to cover the lighter skin tone that said he never removed it from his hand.

"Why did you take it?" he groused.

"Again, it was mine."

His eyes brittle, he clenched his fist around her ring. "That you hurled in *my* face."

He was right. She'd wanted him to choke on it that day in the locker room. "I was a little distraught at the time." She lifted his left hand to twist the ring on his finger. "Intriguing engraving you added inside the band. Should I ask why you felt so compelled?"

Anguish swam in his eyes. "What do you want me to say,

Stormy? Please, for the love of the gods, give me the words that will make you forgive me for making the worst mistake of my life."

Grief and pain choked her as she let her touch linger on his rough callouses—callouses that told her just how hard and harsh a warrior's life he'd led over the years. "No words," she whispered as she brushed her fingers over the intricate Batur tattoo that ran the entire length of his arm. "What made you do this?"

"I told you I would."

"A promise a boy made to a young girl . . . long ago, in the heat of passion." She shook her head. "This makes no sense to me."

He reached for her hand and slid it over his heart to hold it there. "There was only ever you for me, Galene."

"Then why did you tell me you loved Omira?"

"I never did. You accused me of it. But I had never touched her until after you broke off our pledge. Never even really noticed her in our class while we were in school. It was a lie told that you believed."

"Then why not tell me the truth?"

Pain racked him as he grappled with a past that left a bitter lump in his throat and a burning hole inside his heart. "Because you would have cried and begged me to stay with you. And I would have killed my brother to have you as my wife. I thought that if I was gone and you hated me for it that you'd marry Merrell and have a good life. That was all I ever wanted for you."

A tear slid down her cheek. "I hate you, Fain Hauk."

"And I love you, Galene Batur. Instead of engraving 'Forever Galene's' inside your ring, I should have put 'Galene's bitch' there instead. That's what I really am."

A tear slid down her cheek. "You're such a bastard."

He lifted her hand to his lips and placed a kiss to her palm, just like he'd done when they were kids. "Worthless from my first breath to my last."

More tears followed as she saw the scars he bore. His body was a roadmap of the horrors he'd been through. Jayne was right. Nothing had ever been easy for Fain. "Why did you marry Omira if you loved me?"

"Given our last encounter in the locker room, I knew you were done with me. That you would never take me back. And you know my mother. Once our pledge was broken, my parents threw me out. I'd embarrassed them publicly. And after Chrisen and Merrell spread their lies, no Andarion female would have me. Not that I wanted one of them. But Merrell wanted you, bad enough to kill Dancer and Keris for it. That was what he told me he would do if I didn't leave you to him. I knew if I stayed on Andaria, I'd crawl back to you and bury my brothers, regardless of the guilt that would have killed me over it. While Omira wasn't my first choice, she was kind to me . . . at least, in the beginning. All I really was to her was an escape from the father she hated. Once the new wore off and she realized the nightmare of having an alien husband, she couldn't stand me either."

"Yet you stayed?"

"We were married. I'd made an oath to her. Better or worse.

I just didn't realize what all *worse* entailed. And a part of me believed I deserved every scar she carved on me for hurting you the way I did."

Galene brushed her hand through his dark and bleached braids, straightening them over his chest. "I want to claw out your eyes and stab you until you're dead at my feet."

He turned his head away.

She caught his chin and forced him to look at her. "I have always loved you, Fain Hauk. From the first moment I met you and you offered me a drink of your malt. You were the only thing in this life that I've ever wanted. Why did you never once come find me?"

He tightened his hand on hers. "Oh, Stormy, you have no idea how many times I wanted to. But by the time I was free again, so many years had gone by that I didn't dare. I figured you were married, with kids. And I knew the sight of you with someone else would destroy me. So I stayed as far away from you as I could. But you were always in my heart. Always."

She would deny it, but the ink on his arm bore out his words with a bold, tangible honesty.

And so did the tormented sincerity in his eyes.

Galene trailed her hand over his tattooed shoulder and watched as chills sprang up on his skin in the wake of her touch. Her Hauk had always been the most beautiful of all males. Even now, he was everything to her.

"Where do we go from here, Fain?"

"I don't know. The last thing I want to do is hurt you any more. Or, gods forbid, worse."

Before she could stop herself, she leaned down and placed a gentle kiss to his lips.

Fain closed his eyes as he savored the feel and taste of his precious Galene. Sucking his breath in sharply, he buried his hand in her braids and held her close. He lost himself to the taste of her, to the sweetness of her breath mixed with his. "Stay with me, Stormy. In all the darkness of my life, you are the only light I've ever known."

She broke off their kiss with a sob. "I don't know if I can. I want to forgive you. I do. But it's not that easy. You didn't just break my heart, Fain. You shattered it. I've never been able to trust any male near me after what you did. None . . . only Talyn."

Fain swallowed against the bitter lump that choked him. How he hated the pain he heard in her voice. Most of all, he hated himself for having caused it. "Will you give me one more chance? Please. I swear to you that I'll never abuse it. And you won't regret it."

Galene bit her lip as she heard the last words she'd ever expected him to utter. She wanted to slap him and walk away. To be as cold to him as he'd been to her that day she'd gone to tell him she was pregnant.

But what she saw was the wounded boy she'd loved more than her life. The one who used to swing her up in his arms and make her feel so warm and protected. So treasured. The one she'd thought to live the rest of her life with.

Now . . .

"You're the most aggravating male ever born."

"Completely unlovable."

She fought hard to suppress her smile at his adorable grin. "Yes, you are." She flicked her nails at him. "So why do I still care for you?"

"Told you. I'm irresistibly fluffy."

More charmed than she wanted to be, she rolled her eyes at him. "I think I must be the one with a head injury."

He quirked that adorable grin at her. "C'mon, Stormy. Let me court you. If I fuck up again, you can have Talyn kick my ass."

"You know he will. He did break *every* single record you ever set in the Ring."

He visibly cringed. "The joy in your voice as you say that stings me deep."

"Good."

Fain brushed her knuckles against his fangs. "One chance? Please?"

Against her better judgment, she nodded. "But be warned, War Hauk. If you break trust with me this time, I *will* end you. Painfully, and with relish." She jerked her chin toward the part of his body that was bulging under the thin blanket. "And *that* stays in your pants until such a time as *I* say so. You hear me?"

He whimpered at her cruelty. "You're a vicious *mia*. But fine. I accept your terms."

Yet as he made that bargain, Fain had no idea just what he'd opened himself up for. Something that became crystal clear over the next few days as Galene held him to his word.

And then some.

Once he was released from the hospital, she forced him to

endure the strictest Andarion courtship rituals—the very ones they'd spent their youth trying to get around. Right down to having Talyn, as her closest male relative, chaperone them. She refused to be alone with him.

Even now, Fain had to ask for his son's permission to dine with her. It was so effing galling.

More so because Talyn truly enjoyed making him squirm. Irritated to the brink of murder, Fain entered the command center where Talyn was currently on duty with his adjutant. The major laughed as soon as he saw Fain approaching them.

Gavarian cleared his throat. "Commander Hauk on deck, Commander."

Fain glared at the Andarion major for announcing him with such vicious glee.

Talyn's eyes gleamed as he turned to face him. "You need something, Hauk?"

It also irritated the hell out of him that his own son out-ranked him, and the two Andarion officers took a great deal of sadistic pleasure in reminding him of that fact every chance they had. "Can I have a word with you in private?"

Talyn handed his control band over to his adjutant before he followed Fain out of the room and into the hallway. Crossing his arms over his chest as the door closed behind them, he glowered at Fain.

Refusing to be intimidated, Fain growled low in his throat. His son wasn't about to have even a modicum of mercy on him. "You know what I want."

"Have you accomplished anything new? Added more honors to your lineage?"

"In the last nineteen hours?" Fain sneered at him. "You're not really playing this shit with me, are you?"

"You have to prove yourself worthy of her courtship. My mother's a Winged Batur and the prime commander of our armada, after all. An Andarion female of the highest honor and blood lineage. What do *you* bring to this relationship?"

"You're such an asshole."

There was the slightest quirk at the corner of his lips. "Just like my father, I'm told."

Before Fain could comment, the door opened to show Gavarian. "Commander? There's another transmission."

Fain didn't miss the rage in Talyn's eyes as he brushed past him to rush back into the room. He followed and watched as Talyn tried to run a quick trace and analysis.

"What's going on?"

Talyn glanced around the room, then spoke in an archaic version of Andarion that was taught only to those in the highest command positions. "We suspect a spy among your crew. Someone's bleeding information about secure Sentella movements to The League."

Fain started to laugh at the ludicrous suggestion. Then thought better of it. While Tavali were supposed to be loyal to each other beyond reproach, they weren't always. They were, after all, profiteering pirates. "You sure?"

Talyn gave a curt nod. "Unfortunately, we can't catch a long enough transmission to locate the source of it. Or identify the traitor."

"You're sure it's not an Andarion with your crew?"

"Not sure of anything." Talyn sighed heavily as he took the band back from Gavarian. He snapped it onto his wrist, then glanced askance at his adjutant. "Did you detect more details this time?"

"Too well encrypted, and they never transfer long enough to catch more than the very end of it. What I got, I sent over to Morra."

Fain frowned. "Then how do you know it's intel?"

Talyn gave him a droll stare. "How else would I know that your brother left Andaria yesterday with his wife and children and a royal Phrixian escort, and is heading toward a Sentella outpost before rendezvousing here? Or that Darling Cruel and Caillen de Orczy are meeting with Nykyrian eton Anatole at the Andarion palace?"

He was right. Fain hadn't spoken a word to anyone about that. Someone had to be monitoring his transmissions with Dancer. "I'm being bugged?"

"Unless there's a Trisani on this station we need to know about."

Fain cursed. "None that I know of. And you're sure it's going to The League?"

"Not completely. But it's being transmitted toward an area they control, so we're operating under the assumption that it is."

Fain looked around the room. Aside from the three of them,

there were only two others currently in the center. He was the only Tavali. "Can they understand us?"

Talyn shook his head. "Only Gavarian. They're not cleared for this. Besides, they're monitoring other transmissions and not even paying attention to us."

"You sure?"

Gavarian snorted. "Since I've been shagging the captain's sister and mother for the last year, pretty sure they're clueless."

Neither Andarion, both of whom were captains, looked up at something that should have been massive fighting words had they heard them.

"Satisfied?" Talyn asked.

"That they can't understand us? Yeah. Think so. That we have a spy? Not even a little. Does your mom know?"

"No. We just caught this earlier today. I was about to report to her when you showed up to annoy me."

Fain chose to ignore the barb. "Then I'll cover the con while you make your report."

Talyn inclined his head to Fain before he handed over the command wristband. "Thanks. I'll be back in a few."

As he stepped away, Fain stopped him. "By the way . . . you never answered my question about dinner with your mom."

An evil grin curved his lips. "I'll speak to the commander on your behalf and see what she says."

Fain clenched his teeth as Talyn headed out and left him in charge. He wasn't sure which one of them he wanted to strangle more.

Mother or son.

But as he turned back toward Gavarian, he realized something. Talyn doted on this kid. Even when they'd been in battle, he'd made sure to cover him and keep him safe. Like a mother hen with its only rooster.

Or Fain with his little brother.

"So . . . how long have you been Talyn's adjutant?"

Gavarian glanced up from the report he was typing. "That's classified."

Fain arched a brow. "Excuse me? You do know I'm his father, right?"

"Then you should ask the commander."

"Are you shitting me?"

Gavarian's expression turned to stone as he continued to read through his report. "The commander is an Andarion of high honor and exemplary moral character. It is my honor and duty to serve him with utmost devotion and discretion."

Aghast, Fain stared at the kid. "I just want to know more about my son."

His features softened. "I owe the commander a debt that can *never* be repaid. And I know how much he zealously guards his privacy. From everyone. The last thing I would ever do is hurt or upset him . . . not out of fear, but respect."

"You love him?"

Gavarian inclined his head to Fain. "He's family to me. And where I come from, that term means something."

Family . . . that word tugged at Fain's memory as he read the lineage name on Gavarian's formal dress uniform. While Andarion hard battlesuits and field uniforms had the names of high caste soldiers who could be used as political hostages by their enemies attached with patch strips that could be pulled off whenever they went into action, formal uniforms had their names stitched in. The assumption being that the formal uniforms were only worn in areas where their soldiers weren't as likely to be taken. "Ezul Terronova? Are you related to Lorens?"

"My father." Gavarian narrowed his eyes suspiciously. "You know him?"

"He was friends with my older brother, Keris. Long time ago. Good male. I trust he's well?"

That succeeded in melting some of the polar ice caps from the major. "He is, indeed."

"Still in the armada?"

Gavarian shook his head. "Retired seven years ago."

That news surprised Fain and filled him with dread. "Why so young? He wasn't injured, was he?"

"No, sir. My grandfather retired as one of the tadara's advisors, so my father stepped in to replace him."

That made sense. As he recalled, Lorens's father had been a bit older than most Andarion males when he'd finally scttlcd down and had his children. "Glad to hear it. Out of the males Keris ran with, Lorens was the only one I respected." He swept a gaze over Gavarian. "You must take after your mother."

Gavarian grinned sheepishly. "That's what they tell me."

Fain laughed as he realized how that had sounded. "Sorry. Wasn't trying to insult you. I meant in looks, only."

"It's fine. I'm used to being mocked and belittled. Had a steady diet of it from birth."

Shocked by those words from someone whose bloodline would rival the queen's, Fain stared at him. Unless Andaria had changed a lot since he left, no one should have dared insult someone with Gavarian's rank and caste.

Gavarian laughed at his confusion. "I have a younger brother. Three older sisters, and more male cousins than anyone should ever be cursed with. None of whom pull punches with me or respect my birth order."

"Ah. Got it. Siblings and cousins can be their own special kind of hell."

"You know it." Gavarian frowned and tapped his ear. "Major Terronova," he said, letting Fain know that he was answering a call.

Fain stepped back to give him privacy. While he waited, he went over the transmission and saw red. That was entirely too much private information for the wrong parties. He didn't like the thought of anyone knowing where his family was, at any time. Nothing good could come of it.

This was war and The League was after their lives. *All* of them. Especially anyone with ties to The Sentella's High Command, which was Dancer, Nykyrian, and Jayne.

His gaze went to Gavarian. Barely two years younger than Talyn, he was in the height of his youth. They were all too young to die. It was the one thing he'd always hated most about war. The young paid the steepest price for the pride of the old.

Too many years of saying good-bye to friends and family had soured him on the whole bloody business of it.

Gavarian returned to his side with a strange expression.

"Something wrong?"

"It was my brother. Apparently, he's been assigned to the unit that's escorting *your* brother and sister-in-law here."

Fain arched his brow, uncertain why that caused the ire in the major's voice. "Why does that upset you? Don't you like your brother?"

"Adore him. It's the other cargo he's been assigned to that I have to keep from the commander that concerns me."

"How so?"

Gavarian's gaze turned to steel. "You should be warned that the commander doesn't like surprises, at all. And if he can't get ahold of his female on a daily basis, he will panic. You should probably tell him that she's coming."

"That would spoil the surprise."

"Let me reiterate that the commander doesn't like surprises. And I doubt this one will endear you to him. You said you wanted to know your son better, Commander. . . . I can promise you this amount of stress isn't the best way to go about it. He won't appreciate it. You should tell him Felicia's en route. Save you both a lot of pain."

Before Fain could comment, the door opened to admit Talyn and Galene. She drew up short the moment she realized he was in the room.

For a full minute, Fain couldn't catch his breath as he saw her there in her tight workout clothes and glistening skin. Her braids were pulled back, exposing a wealth of sexy neck that had never failed to drive him crazy with lust as he ached to brush his lips down the entire length of her throat. Even as kids, he'd told her that on their unification day, he wanted her hair worn down, otherwise he wasn't sure he'd make it through the ceremony without embarrassing them both. And right now, he was rather sure he was drooling all over himself.

Galene froze as her gaze met Fain's. Honestly, she hated how hot and gorgeous he was in the dim light. How much his commanding presence affected her. It was getting harder and harder to remember why she didn't like him. Especially when he had that adorable bashful expression he only had around her. He was so arrogant and in charge with everyone else. Ruthless and powerful. Only she had the ability to take the cock out of his walk.

And that made him completely precious and irresistible.

Unable to meet her gaze, he handed the command band over to her. A tingle went up her arm as his fingers brushed against hers. Worse, it set her to trembling. In that moment, all she wanted was to taste those lips and have him hold her like he did all those years ago.

Stop it, Galene. You're not a child. You know better than to put your faith in hopeless sagas of heroes and fairy tales. And especially in the hands of a male who has already betrayed you.

Life was brutal. She knew that better than anyone.

And they had serious business to attend to. "Thank you, Fain." Dismissing her useless sentimentality, she snapped the band around her wrist and moved to review the transmissions Talyn and Gavarian had intercepted. While she did so, Gavarian had the two captains leave the room for their breaks and he jammed any unwanted signals or video that might be set to overhear their conversation.

Are you sure you trust the major? Fain signed to her out of his sight.

Galene smiled at his concern. "I consider Vari another son."

Gavarian took his suspicion in stride as he set the last of the jammers. "It's all right if Hauk doubts me, Commander. I'm a stranger to him. He knows nothing of our history together."

"Meaning what?" Fain asked.

Talyn passed a knowing smirk to Gavarian. "If you knew us, you'd understand the loyalty we have to each other. Out of the four of us, you're the one who's untested."

Fain went ramrod stiff at that.

"It's not a stab at you," Talyn said drily. "Merely a statement of fact. Now we have lethal matters to address. The League is after The Sentella and appears to be targeting your immediate families for murder."

Fain sighed heavily. "We knew that was coming."

"Yeah, but this . . ." Talyn handed him a chip. "Is detailed information on where they're located at present, and their upcoming schedules. Case in point, I didn't even know your brother was expecting a baby or that Caillen dc Orczy just had a son a few weeks ago. Never mind that his wife, Desideria, is currently residing at the Andarion Palace with Darling's wife and Maris Sulle's son and husband, along with all of Nykyrian's children and current wife, as well as Syn's son and wife. Or that their rooms were moved earlier today to a more secured part of the palace."

Honestly, Fain hadn't known all that either. "That is highly disturbing."

Gavarian nodded. "There are also schematics for the Caronese Winter Palace, the main Sentella base, and information on Syn's in-laws, and Cruel's brothers and sister. Even Jayne's grandmother and aunt are listed here, as well as her daughters' schools. It appears they're planning one massive blitz on everyone, all at once."

"So that if they don't get one of you, they'll take out enough of your families to gut you all. Period."

Fain winced at something that would definitely take down Sentella High Command. Even though the commanders weren't related by blood, they were united in a friendship tighter than any familial bond. "We have to let them know what's going on. I can fly out on my ship, which is secure to Sentella lines, and transmit. Tell The Tavali I'm doing a patrol. No one will suspect anything. Even if they pick up the secured transmission, they'll assume I'm talking to Dancer or Ryn. No one will question that."

"What if you can't reach them all?" Galene asked.

"I keep going out until I do. I'm not about to let them get blindsided by this."

Gavarian crossed his arms over his chest. "You'll need a wing with you. Otherwise, their traitor could turn you in for their crime. Use you to goat them. At this point, everyone needs to watch their ass and no one needs to do anything suspicious, without an alibi *and* a witness."

Fain shook his head. "I'll chance it. The only one I trust with my life is my brother, and he's not here. No offense, but I'm not revealing Sentella hailing codes to anyone."

"I'll go with you, then."

They all turned to stare at Galene.

"Ah, hell no," Talyn growled.

Smiling, she caressed her son's cheek. "It's fine, *keramon*. If he behaves inappropriately, I'll let you know."

Talyn curled his lip in distaste. "I still don't like it." He narrowed his gaze at Fain. "Don't you dare crack a smile about this."

"Wouldn't dream of it." But inside, Fain had to admit he was grinning ear to ear at the prospect of being alone with her. He just wished the circumstances were less dire. That was the only thing that allowed him to temper his joy.

A tic started in Talyn's jaw. "I need to get back to work."

Fain inclined his head to him. "We'll head out to hail my brother and as many of the others as we can."

Talyn glanced over to Gavarian. "Major, go with the commander and—"

"No," Galene said, cutting Talyn off. "Vari, stay with the commander and guard his back."

By the stony expression on Gavarian's face that somehow managed to convey his sudden onset of irritation, Fain could tell this wasn't the first time he'd been caught between them.

The major let them bicker for several minutes before he cleared his throat. "Can I grab a sandwich and bathroom break while you two *discuss* the rest of my shift?"

That succeeded in cracking the sternness from Galene's features. "You're both awful. Keep your major, Talyn. I don't want you alone on this station until we know who our enemies really are. I trust Fain with my safety. If you don't want to think of my sanity where you're concerned, think of Felicia's. Don't make me put a call in to her about *your* reckless behavior. You know I will." She wagged a warning finger at him.

Gavarian burst out laughing, then quickly covered it with a cough when Talyn glared at his adjutant. "Sorry, Commander."

"Fine . . ." Talyn ground his teeth as Gavarian took up his seat on the other side of Talyn and began monitoring the scanners.

Galene wiped at the sweat on her neck. "Can I grab a shower on your ship?"

Fain had to force himself not to react to the image of her naked in his room that question evoked in his mind. Yeah, she was a cruel Andarion. "Sure."

She passed the command band over to Talyn. "I'll grab a change of clothes and meet you in the hangar in a few minutes."

Before Fain could regain enough brain activity to do anything more than sputter, she was gone and he was facing his son's furious glower.

"Don't you dare make her cry."

That boy was never going to see anything but the worst in him. Sadly, he had a bad feeling there was nothing he could do about that. "I have no intention of it."

Talyn sighed in aggravation as he watched his father leave. Alone with Gavarian, he was torn between his military obligation and the need he had to make sure Hauk kept a respectful distance from his mother's heart. If Hauk said or did anything to her . . . he'd paint the walls with his father's blood.

"This is strange."

"What?" He turned back toward Gavarian.

He held the earpiece out for Talyn. "It's about Commander Hauk. Did you know he was renting space on the station for a female and her male dependent? Someone named Vega Jaswinder."

Talyn went cold at those words. "Excuse me?"

His features stern, Gavarian nodded. "It's in the latest transmission out to The League. According to this, Hauk has a long-term relationship with the woman, and makes regular visits to her living quarters for about an hour at a time, twice a week, whenever he's in residence." Gavarian screwed his face up. "I don't want to gossip about someone, T, but to me, that sounds an awful lot like Andarion rec time."

Yeah, it did. And as Talyn reviewed the transmission, he cursed under his breath. Gavarian was right.

If this was correct, Fain Hauk had a Tavali mistress. And Talyn was going to kick the male's ass all the way back to Andaria for it.

CHAPTER 7

Fain slowed as he neared his ship and saw two female Andarion pilots coming in from patrol. A group of six Tavali males were trailing after them, catcalling and harassing them as the females did their best to ignore the unwanted attention.

"What? You think you're too good for us?" The largest man cut the females off.

By the look on her face, she wasn't amused. Fain waited for her to tear the human male apart. But the Andarions were under strict orders not to start any incidents while here. And the one thing about the Andarion military . . .

They followed orders. Come hell, high water.

And even stupid humans.

Then the man did the worst thing he could—he took her arm. While humans might freely touch each other without invitation, that wasn't done in Andarion culture. It was considered a vile intrusion of personal space, and punishable with harsh sentences in their law courts.

If you lived long enough to be reported for it, that was. And as bad as it was to touch a male uninvited, no male *ever* touched a female he wasn't related to. Even doctors and medical staff had to ask permission before they treated patients of the opposite sex.

"Hey!" Fain snapped as he quickly closed the distance between them. "What is this?"

The Tavali turned on him with an angry snarl, then relaxed. "Hey, Hauk," he said, mistaking Fain's words as a greeting. But at least he let go of the female's arm. "Want to join us for some fun?"

Both females eyed Fain with stoic curiosity. Since he was fully clothed and his Outcast scars were covered, they had no way of knowing he'd been thrown out of his family or what specific blood lineage he was tied to, since Hauk was a fairly common surname on Andaria. They treated him as any Andarion would one of unknown origin—with cool deference. They would do so until the proper family and lineage pecking order was established.

Their names, rank, and caste were on their battle helmets, which gave Fain a distinct advantage over them. Had he not been disinherited, he would have outranked them both socially and militarily. But that being said, they were both aristocrats from high-lineaged families and most likely pledged or married to males who were even higher ranked than they were.

Not that it mattered. No one should be subjected to this kind of hazing. Male, female, or unspecified.

"You're not in a bar and they're not slags trolling for creds.

Show the *taras* respect or I'll show you a side of me you don't want to meet."

The tallest man stepped around the Andarion pilots to rudely invade Fain's personal space. A human move for intimidation. However, it was *his* eyes that widened as he realized he only reached Fain's shoulder and that Fain's height wasn't augmented by his footwear choice.

He was just that damn huge.

With a sneer, he glanced to Fain's sleeve, where Tavali wore their National flags of allegiance, personal Canting and rank.

As a Rogue, Fain's uniform bore the UTC flag, and his Tavali Canting of a fanged skull, sickle, and commander's ribbon rocker.

"You should remember that you don't have a Nation backing you, Rogue. Rather, you rely on the good will of us all to keep you flying."

Yeah, right. That was a vast oversimplification of his status in their world. And highly untrue. The Tavali had a lot of money invested in their Rogues that they didn't have in the others. While not bound to the UTC the same way as the others, they were still extremely valuable to *all* the higher-ups. And not as easily replaced as the rest of the Tavali pilots.

But these Baits were too stupid to know that.

Fain snorted. "I don't rely on Jack or Shit. Least of all a human piece of waste. You want to try and strip my Canting, go for it. I'd love to have you in a Calibrim." Calibrim was a test of arms in a Tavali law court, overseen by their officers, and fought to the death. Very similar to the Andarion Ring fights

Fain had literally cut his fangs on. Only difference was that the human pirates weren't nearly as fierce in battle.

They surrounded him.

"Why wait?" the shorter human goaded.

To Fain's shock, the two Andarion pilots took position at his back to let the humans know they would fight with Fain. Orders be damned.

"What's going on here?"

The sneer on the human's face turned salacious as he saw Galene in her workout clothes.

And that set off Fain's temper to a dangerous level. He grabbed the human by his jacket and slammed him hard against the ship nearest them. He struggled against Fain's iron grip only to learn just how strong an Andarion male really was.

"Let me educate you about Andarion culture," Fain growled at him in lethal warning. "Commander Batur is the blood mother of an Andarion prince, slag. That means you don't look at her. *Ever*. It's a death sentence to do so. On Andaria, females are venerated and you do not speak to a female until you have been deemed worthy and properly introduced to her by one of their males, or she speaks to you first. Furthermore, it is a male's place to ensure an Andarion female's safety, and we will rip the throat out of anyone who doesn't show our females their due respect. And while you might not like it, they are here under Venik's truce and at the behest of the UTC. *All* Nations. You will respect them and abide by their customs or so help me gods, I will force-feed your innards to every last one of you. Understood?"

Since he was turning blue from the grip Fain had on his throat, all he could do was nod weakly.

Satisfied he'd made his point, he released him and stepped back to see the others in similar choke holds from the females.

Fain grinned. "I should have added that our females are extremely capable warriors in their own right, and I intend to rescind their orders on no offensive contact with Tavali. If they're verbally or physically accosted again, they're allowed to defend themselves by whatever means they deem necessary."

They released the men.

Galene approached him slowly as the humans scampered away. "Commander Hauk, and Tiziran Fain of the Sovereign eton Anatole, may I present Colonels eton Xu and ezul Yetur."

"Thank you for your assistance, Commander," Colonel eton Xu said with a respectful bow to Fain. "We weren't quite sure how to handle it."

"No problem. Please pass along to the other females in your squad what I said. If anyone else causes you problems, do what you have to and I'll deal with the fallout from it. I promised Tahrs Nykyrian that I'd personally guarantee everyone's safety, and I stand by that."

Yetur saluted him. "Thank you, Highness."

As they walked off, he caught a strange adoring smile on Galene's face that made him uneasy. "What's that for?"

She reached up to brush one of the braids back from his cheek. "You just remind me of a noble boy I knew a long time ago."

And she reminded him of long-forgotten dreams. For a full

minute, he couldn't move as he stared into those pale eyes that held him captive in a way nothing else ever had.

Galene reached up to finger the place on his sleeve where the other Tavali wore tribal markings and allegiance. His biceps tingled from her gentle touch. "Why are you Rogue?"

Fain's throat tightened instantly as grief and pain over-whelmed him. Memories surged with a vengeance that left him dizzy. It was why he didn't want to think about the past. Why he did his best to have no one around him. Sentient beings asked too many questions. They wanted to know things like what he'd done and where he'd been.

Why he didn't run his own crew.

Stuff he didn't want to remember. Dust-covered memories that were best left undisturbed.

"We should head on out." He stepped around her and led the way to his ship.

Galene frowned at the curt way he'd ignored her question. At the deep anguish she'd seen in his eyes when she asked about it.

But then Fain had always been that way. He'd never spoken much about his family or his feelings. Even as a boy. It just hadn't been his nature.

Of course, when Keris had been alive, he'd viciously mocked and criticized every word out of Fain's mouth. To the point that Fain had literally responded with grunts in his brother's pres-ence. And his parents hadn't been much better. Demanding and impatient, they'd expected only the best from their sons.

Utter decorum. Perfect grades. Stellar athleticism.

As a girl, Galene had been terrified of Endine Hauk and her shrewish tongue. And Ferral Hauk had held a glower that could freeze the core of a sun. It'd taken her years before she'd felt even remotely comfortable around either of them.

To this day, she stung from Endine's cruelty the one and only time she'd made the mistake of asking her to adopt Talyn back into the Hauk bloodline after he'd been born.

"Why would I adopt the hideous bastard seed of a whore who publicly humiliated me after I slashed the bloodline of my own son I suckled at my breast? You made your bed, bitch, lie in it! Now take your disgusting bastard and crawl back to the gutter where you both belong."

Her only solace from that horror was that Talyn had been too young to understand the insults his own grandmother had given him.

If only *she'd* been so lucky.

But that was then, and thankfully Fain had been born with his grandmother's heart and not the black lump of soulless coal that functioned as his mother's.

As Fain led her onboard his ship, she paused. "Where are the showers?"

He took her to the crew deck and a small shower stall. "You won't have water until after I launch. It'll take about five minutes for it to flow." He jerked his chin to the small room across the hall. "You can wait in my quarters until then. There's a launch seat in the wall."

"Okay. Thanks."

He opened the door, then left her alone. As soon as he was gone, she felt strangely awkward to be in his intimate quarters without him. She didn't even know why, really. Other than this was his home whenever he wasn't docked on a planet or base.

With nothing else to do, she glanced around the small room that held a medium-sized bunk, monitor, fridge, sink, and small personal cooking unit. Very basic, serviceable, and clean. Sterile even.

It was so . . .

Cold.

Try as she might, she couldn't see Fain here. It would have to be cramped for an Andarion of his size.

What did he do here? Other than sleep or lose his mind from absolute boredom?

How could he not run a crew? It was rare for anyone to not have at least a copilot. For safety reasons, if nothing else. Space travel was a harsh and lonely mistress, fraught with unseen dangers that came up fast, furious, and unforgiving. Did his personal survival mean so little to him?

"Buckle in. We'll be launching in three."

Startled by his deep voice over the intercom, she folded the emergency anchor seat down from the wall and harnessed herself to it.

The monitor turned on to show Fain's face.

Galene quirked an amused smile. "Checking up on me?"

Color stained his cheeks. "Wanted to make sure the chair worked. It's never been used before. At least not since I've owned the lady-ship."

She pulled playfully against the straps. "I'm all secured, Paka. You can launch."

Snorting at her use of the Andarion word for dad, he obeyed. To his credit, the ship slid smoothly into space under his masterful skill. And when the screen went dark and he told her she was free to use the shower, she actually missed seeing his handsome face. She barely caught herself before an invitation for him to join her slipped out.

I am so messed up.

But she couldn't help it. She still loved him more than she ever wanted to admit to. And she hadn't been with anyone else. No other male had ever touched her. Not even for a kiss.

Only Fain.

While she could have easily registered for a sanctioned relationship with a male years ago, especially with her military rank, she'd refrained. She'd told herself that she hadn't wanted to hurt Talyn with it or risk how an Andarion male might treat her son, given Talyn's low caste. But the real truth was, she'd never wanted to risk anyone else hurting her the way Fain had. Never wanted to feel the pain of having her heart ripped out and callously fed to her.

Damn you, you bastard! She could still feel the raw anguish that day in the locker room when he'd stood there, staring at her, denying nothing about Omira. Still feel the deep betrayal of learning he'd married that bitch, and that they were living together in wedded bliss while she was struggling on the streets, alone and pregnant with his child. She hadn't even been eligible for her obligatory military service or their barracks housing because of the pregnancy. She'd been forced to wait until Talyn was six months old before they'd allow her into armada training, and her son into the military nursery program.

Even then, they'd refused to allow Talyn to be kept with the other children lest he taint them with his father's Outcast status. Her meager pay had been docked substantially for his segregation fees, and they'd been given the worst in base housing because of Fain's crime in defaming his prestigious bloodline. For years, she'd endured humiliation and shame. Had watched the way others scorned and mistreated her beautiful son.

Gah! It was so frustrating. This endless cycle of wanting to kiss Fain and beat him senseless for everything she needed to hate him over.

Trying not to think about it, she showered quickly. But it wasn't until she finished that she realized she couldn't open the door.

"You've got to be kidding me." Horrified, she tried every way she could think.

Nothing worked. Embarrassed and humiliated, she hit the intercom.

"May I help you?"

She froze at the unexpected, sexy Andarion female voice. "Who is this?"

"Storm. And you are?"

Pissed off, in short. "Galene."

"How may I help you, Galene?"

"You can start by telling me who you are."

"I already told you. I am Storm."

Was she intentionally trying to start a war? "And what's your position on Commander Hauk's ship?"

"I am Commander Hauk's ship."

I'm such an idiot. Storm. *Storm Dancer.* This was the AI autopilot. Duh . . . But in her defense, most ship systems didn't have a voice that could double as a porn actress. Nor were they usually so sentient sounding. This one appeared to have a sultry, sardonic personality, something that was highly advanced for a ship's system. "Oh. I'm trapped. Can you open the shower door for me?"

"Of course, Galene." The hydraulics hissed. Still the door remained closed.

"Is there a problem?"

"One moment, please. I am running diagnostics." Yeah, that was a bit snotty in tone.

Awkward and exposed, Galene tried to remain patient, but it wasn't easy. No one wanted to be trapped naked on a ship. In a small cube.

After a few extremely long minutes, Storm returned to the intercom. "Fain? Forgive me for disturbing you. But I fear we have a matter with the shower door that requires a manual override. Do you wish me to automate my body for it?"

Galene's jaw dropped at that stunning disclosure. "And what does this body look like?"

"I'm on my way," Fain said hurriedly. In fact, he made record time getting to her, which *really* made her wonder what he feared so much.

Crossing her arms over her bare chest, she listened irrita-

144

bly as he struggled with the controls in the hallway. "Having trouble?"

"Did you hit the release on your side?"

How stupid did he think she was? Struggling for patience, she clenched her teeth. "I did. It's not opening."

"The lever on the right?"

"The yellow one?"

"Yes."

"Not working." She glared as a bad feeling went through her. "Did you do this on purpose?"

"Hell no!" He dared sound exasperated with *her*? Really? "Why would I intentionally do something that I know would piss you off?"

He had a point. "You swear it?"

"I swear." When he finally opened the door, he had his gaze locked to hers. But she saw the battle inside him not to lower it. His breathing ragged, he held a towel out to her like a bashful teen.

"You okay?" she teased.

"Not really."

"Am I torturing you?"

"Yes."

"Good."

That brought a smile to his gorgeous lips as he swept a heated gaze over her body that she had yet to cover with the towel. "You are a cruel, cruel female, Galene Batur. You sure *you* didn't do this on purpose to lure me down here?"

His charm stole the anger and irritation from her. She

actually felt bad for accusing him of it. "I don't mean to be cruel, Fain. I just don't want to be hurt anymore."

"And that's why I'm standing here, harder than hell, not touching you when all I want to do is make love to you until neither of us can walk straight." With those words, he turned and started toward the flight deck.

Galene caught his arm. The moment his gaze returned to hers and she saw the raw hunger and need inside him, she froze in place. There was so much she wanted to say. But she didn't know where to start. Nothing made sense to her. None of her feelings felt right. The hatred and pain, the love and need. They tripped over each other and left her so confused.

His gaze softened as he dropped his hand to gently finger the old stretch marks left by her pregnancy. While Talyn had been born prematurely, the surgery from it had still left her scarred. In more ways than one. The physical marks had never bothered her. The close call with Talyn's life was never far from her thoughts. Three times since then she'd had a doctor tell her to pick out funeral clothes for her son and to prepare herself mentally for his loss. *That* had been the first time.

She prayed to the gods that her son continued to defy them all.

"I'm so sorry I wasn't there for you, Stormy. When was he born?"

"The first day of the year. A little after midnight."

"Did you have a hard labor?"

She shook her head. "He came nine weeks early. It was less

than ten minutes from when I entered the hospital ER to when they had him in an incubation bed."

His hand trembled against her waist. "Were your parents there?"

"Only your yaya Hauk. Corinne had me hidden in her guesthouse during the last few weeks of my pregnancy. She's the only reason Talyn survived at all. I don't know what I would have done without her kindness."

He frowned at that. "Why didn't she adopt him, then?"

"Your grasparan refused. Once he found out we were staying there, he demanded we leave immediately."

Fain cursed under his breath. "How old was Talyn?"

"Six months. But it was fine. By then, he was old enough for me to take my turn in the military. Since I was no longer under the official protection of my family, I lost my waiver. Corinne kept us going long enough to get me off the street until I could enter military housing."

He winced. "So that's why you didn't go to medical school."

"Actually, I did go. It took a while, but I finished. Third in my class."

"Then why didn't you leave the military?"

"By the time I was done, Talyn was beginning his service and I didn't want to abandon him to it. He never complained. Still, I knew how they treated lack-Vests. Had I left, he'd have had no one to do anything for him at all."

Fain pulled her into his arms and held her like he used to when they were kids. He cupped her head with his hand and wrapped his arm around her waist. It was a hold of utter protection. The kind she'd missed most. Even though she felt his erection against her hip, he kept his word and made no moves on her.

A perfectly behaved Andarion male. Just as he'd always been. An honor to his lineage and family.

Leaning her head back, she stared up at his searing eyes and the torment that melted away all the hatred she'd nursed for him through the years. "What about you?"

Fain brushed his hand through her wet braids as he refused to remember the bitter years he'd spent away from his Storm Dancer. They didn't matter and he didn't want to think about them right now. All he wanted was to savor this precious moment with her. He wouldn't let anything taint it. "I survived."

She arched a brow. "That's it?"

"What do you want me to say? That I went through hell? Yeah, I did. But the War Hauk family motto is . . . Indurari. Through blood pain we conquer and endure. Out of the bad, comes the good. By our challenges, we are strengthened. Ever strong. Forever onward." He quirked a lopsided grin. "Fuck you, fate."

She pulled at his braids and rolled her eyes. "You are so aggravating."

"So Dancer tells me." And yet she beguiled him in a way no one ever had. Before he could stop himself, he lowered his head slowly, giving her time to deny him. When she didn't, he gently kissed her.

Every part of his body erupted as he breathed her in and

tasted her lips. Growling, he deepened his kiss and pressed himself closer to her body, dreaming he was already inside her. Dizzy and breathless, he ran his hands over her velvety-soft skin, wishing he could turn back time and redo his entire life.

If only it were that simple.

But dreams were for fools. And wishes were for better males than him. Males who didn't owe their souls to someone else . . .

Pulling back, he smiled down at her and rubbed his nose against hers. "Will you have dinner with me?"

"Of course."

"Will you have sex with me?"

She snorted at him. "Now you're pushing it."

"You're the one standing naked in my arms."

"That's to punish you."

"It's working." He pressed her hand against his cock. "At this rate, I'm going to die of testosterone poisoning." Which could actually happen to Andarions. It was a real concern for the males of their species.

"Is that why you have a porn actress voicing the AI of your ship?"

That should probably embarrass him, but instead he was amused. "A male has to have some vices. She was the lesser evil. Besides, I modeled her voicetrack after *you*."

"I do *not* sound like that."

"Yeah, you do. You were ever the sexiest female born. None could touch you in that regard. The sultry strains of your voice saying my name alone were oft enough to tilt me right over the edge, love."

She opened her mouth to ask him if he was seriously trying to tell her that he'd walled himself up on this ship with her memory when the AI rudely interrupted them.

"Fain? I have Ambassador Dane queued for you. Do you wish to proceed with your communication? Or should I take a message for you?"

She saw the bitter regret that flashed across his features. "Hold the line. Tell him I'll be right there. That it's imperative I speak with him. Don't let him close the channel."

"Sure thing."

"Go." She nudged him toward the flight deck.

Inclining his head, he took off at a dead run. But as he reached the ladder, he paused to glance back at her. The raw, ragged heat in those precious Andarion eyes singed her and left her breathless.

Not sure what to feel about it all, Galene returned to his room and dressed.

By the time she rejoined him, he was speaking to Ryn Dane, the Tavali ambassador for the UTC. Like his younger brother, who was the Caronese emperor, Ryn had dark red hair and steel blue eyes that betrayed a razor-sharp intelligence. Even though he and Darling Cruel were only half siblings, related through their father, their features were strikingly similar.

"You're certain about this, Hauk?"

"Very."

"Well, that's utterly disappointing and highly disturbing. But the saddest part is, it's not unexpected or even surprising. Just pisses me off that a Tavali broke Code. Love to lay hands on

that bastard and personally strip their Canting and life blood."
Ryn paused as he saw Galene over Fain's shoulder. "Commander
Batur . . . it's an honor to formally meet you. I can see where
Talyn gets his fierceness."

"Excuse me?"

Fain stepped aside and flashed a grin at her. "Ryn's the one
who helped Talyn apprehend Eriadne years ago when Cairistiona
took the throne."

Heat stung her cheeks at the slight she'd inadvertently given
someone she owed the universe to. Ryn had saved Talyn's life
that day, along with their strike team they'd sent in to retrieve
the queen who'd fled Andarion justice. A strike team that had
comprised Morra and Qorach.

She owed this man everything.

"Forgive me, Lord Ambassador. I didn't realize that was
you." Strange, she hadn't remembered that before now. The
only thing she really recalled about that event was the danger
Talyn had faced, his injuries, and that when the dust had finally
settled, Cairistiona had been crowned tadara and Eriadne had
been effectively quelled.

Ryn smiled without malice and in good spirit. "It was an ex-
ceptionally long time ago. Think nothing of it. I'm just glad I was
there to help then and now. . . . Small universe, sometimes."

"Yes, it is. And I'd completely forgotten that The Tavali captain who helped them with their mission was related to the
Caronese emperor."

Ryn gave her a playful wink. "There are days I'm sure my
little brother would like to forget it, too."

She laughed. Handsome, refined, and suave, Ryn appeared to be an easy man to get along with. No wonder The Tavali had chosen him as their ambassador in dealing with the recognized nations and governments. Even though she knew Ryn came from a long line of Tavali outlaws and rogues, there was something innately trustworthy and honest about him. An air of jovial serenity that was quite contagious.

Ryn turned his attention back to Fain. "I do have shocking news for *you,* by the way. Guess who I have on board to join the confab at your Port StarStation . . ."

"No idea."

"Trajen Thaumarturgus *and* his vice admiral."

"You lie!"

"No, I swear on my father's immortal soul. I actually have him *and* his advisors heading in. Their ETA is seven days."

Gaping, Fain shook his head in total disbelief. "How?"

Ryn shrugged. "Sacrificed six goats and a virgin."

"That's all it took?"

Galene really wished she wasn't completely lost in this conversation. "Who's Trajen Ta . . . ?"

"Tuh-mar-dar-gus," they said slowly and in a strange synchronicity, as if they were used to doing it for others.

Luckily, Fain elaborated. "He's a ghost."

Galene arched a brow.

"No, really." Fain held his hand up in an Andarion sign of honor. "He's the leader of the True Black Flag Nation—the first of the Tavali clans. They come out for no one and nothing. Ever. Total phantoms who operate under their own law code. By the time you see them, you're dead. Tray's more myth than reality. I honestly don't know of anyone who's actually ever seen him."

"Wow . . ."

Like Fain, she was extremely impressed with Ryn's abilities to command such a person to their side. "How did you find him?"

"He came to me." Ryn grinned at Fain. "My grandfather's the one who fostered him into our Nation and he defected over to the Gorturnum a long time ago. I've known him all my life, but like you said, he's reclusive as hell. I haven't seen him away from his territories in decades. Apparently, his right-hand field admiral, Dagger, has a vested interest in this fight, and talked him into joining on."

"Damn, Dane. You *are* good."

"My mother is proud. Speaking of, I shall convey your news to the others. Have no fear, *drey*. They will know and none will be the wiser for it."

"Thanks."

Ryn struck his heart twice in rapid succession with a closed fist before opening it in a Tavali salute.

Fain duplicated the gesture then closed the channel.

"Feel better?"

He didn't answer her question directly. "You?"

"I'm not sure. You trust Dane?"

"More than most."

"Why?"

"I don't know much about him, and that says a lot in this community, given how high profile he is among The Tavali. He's kept his scandals down to none, and no one knows his business. What I do know, he's had several chances to move in on his brother's throne and never has. Same for his mother's Tavali chair and rank. He's a man of rare integrity who actually understands loyalty."

"You're right. That's a rare thing." Galene frowned as a strange expression passed over Fain's face. Even odder, a light seemed to flash behind his pupils, illuminating them and the iris of his eyes.

What the . . . ?

"Buckle down."

While the female in her would have balked at a civilian male barking an order like that at her, she recognized a military command when she heard one. She obeyed without question as Fain went to the con and strapped himself to the command chair.

"What's going on?"

Before he could answer, the hailing alarm sounded. His ship answered for him.

"This is *Storm Dancer*. STA1-LY-8-GENC-NCOB-ORFC-Y."

There was a brief pause. "Serial and captain?"

Fain took over. "You have my UCC. I don't see why you need that, especially since you have yet to identify yourself or your business."

"We are a League cruiser on patrol in search of rebels against our nations. Now identify yourself or be arrested. You have three seconds to respond."

"Captain Chryton Doone. STA1-8LY-5831930-GENCX."

"Crew?"

"One organic copilot. One mecha."

"We need visual confirmation."

Galene's stomach heaved at that. There was no way they wouldn't know her face. She'd been prime commander of the Andarion Empire for almost a decade. Had dealt with The League more times than she could count.

We're captured.

Fain passed an evil grin toward her. "Trust me?"

"Have I any choice?"

He snorted, then hit the release on his seat. It shot back, suspending him in the middle of the control room in a thick plasma bubble.

Galene gasped as she realized what she'd seen earlier in his eyes when The League cruiser had arrived. Fain *was* the ship. Holy gods of Andaria. This was a technology every nation had been trying for centuries to perfect.

And The Tavali had it.

Stunned, she watched as he took absolute control of every part of the craft and went against The League cruiser and the fighters it launched against them. While the bubble he was in kept him cushioned, the impact was harsh on her, but she remained quiet so that she didn't distract him.

Fain cringed as one of the blasts got past his shields and struck his side. The bad thing about being hardwired to the ship was that he felt every strike against the hull as a physical blow to his own body. And in the back of his mind was the knowledge that Galene was with him.

She was in danger.

He was violating his oath to show her this technology. No Rogue was supposed to expose their neurobinders to any non-Tavali under any circumstance. But he couldn't maneuver the ship like this without a crew, and he wasn't about to let The League take her.

Laws be damned.

Life be forfeit.

The Tavali could take his Canting and his head if they wanted it. He wasn't about to surrender her to her enemies for anything. And honestly, he preferred to battle this way. It was much more personal. Like being in the Andarion Ring. Fist-on-fist. When connected to the ship, he *was* in space. He could feel the pressure of the vacuum pressing against the metal. It smothered him. And at the same time, it freed a part of his soul.

He saw all and nothing. The darkness and the light. It gave him an understanding of the vastness of the universe and how small he was in it. How extremely insignificant.

It was why most pilots couldn't pass the tests for Rogue. Why they cracked within a few weeks, or months.

Less than one percent of one percent could master the physical and mental stresses it put on the body. Never mind the synchronization process of bonding to the ship. It took a full year for the neuromapping of the brain and ship circuitry to merge into a unified whole. Another year before a pilot could actually master the ship as part of the body.

Suicide rates were high among the Rogues, usually within nine months after that initial stabilization of pilot and ship—

although a lot of them ended up as fatal "accidents" that were believed to be disguised suicides and not the operator-errors officially filed on the log books.

Eventual insanity rates were even higher. Rarely did they make it a decade before their brains frayed beyond repair, and most ended up in unresponsive comas. Fain was one of the few who'd managed to hold it together for any length of time. It was the only reason Venik had ever allowed him to live.

He'd thrown Fain into this as a joke, fully expecting it to kill him. He'd thought it hysterical irony to merge Fain with the very ship he'd been enslaved on. A cruel way to get back at an Andarion.

Yeah . . .

It hadn't worked out quite the way Venik had planned. Never underestimate a Hauk's survival instinct, or the need to be the burr up the ass of anyone out to do him or her harm.

There was a reason Fain's family was legendary.

Fain turned and shot a blast at the League fighters as they closed rank around him. They had no idea what they were facing. They thought this was a divided crew.

Not a single living organism.

He skidded past them and headed back toward Tavali-controlled space. But it wasn't until he banked around the southern moon of Nebyla III that he realized something.

There were no Tavali reinforcements here. No patrols, and there should have been at least one.

He was flying dark.

Minsid hell. This had been a setup! Whoever had been

transmitting those facts about The Sentella had done this to get Galene out here to contact them. They knew she'd leave the station to make a solo report to the Command where there would be no risk of her being overheard.

And like a fool, he'd headed straight into this trap.

Something proven as more League forces dropped in around him. They shouldn't have been here without a massive Tavali counterstrike. This entire sector should have been secured and locked down by Venik's troops. Only someone high up in their Nation could have pulled Tavali patrols back and cleared it for The League.

"Surrender your ship, Hauk. There's no need in dying to-day." The fact they knew his name further confirmed his suspicions.

He laughed at the order. "Haven't you heard? War Hauks don't surrender, *giakon*. We take our enemies with us to the grave." He dove under the cruiser.

And straight into a huge swarm of fighters.

Fain skimmed two and rammed a third. One of his engines sparked, causing his nose to bleed and his leg to go numb from the impact. Ignoring it, he twisted and dodged as another group came up on the side and from behind.

He turned to fire on them, then stopped.

For a full second, he couldn't breathe as he saw Chayden, Morra, Qory, and Talyn leading in a rescue team.

Galene finally made a noise of protest as she heard Talyn calling orders over his comm. "Oh good God, is that my embryo?"

Fain laughed at her term for her gargantuan son. "Yes, it is."

"I'm going to kill him!"

Fain fell back and let the others take over. Normally, he'd have stayed in the thick of it, but he wasn't supposed to be engaged in solo battle with a *witherwin* onboard. He could get into all kinds of trouble for this.

Even lose his ship and Canting over it.

And since there were Tavali in the mix, the best thing was to back off and disengage himself from the ship before someone realized he was flying Rogue.

As if Chayden suspected what was going on, he flew in to provide temporary cover and give Fain time to pull out from the neural connection. "Psycho Bunny to Blister, why don't you take your precious cargo back to camp and let the big boys finish cleaning house for you?"

Galene arched a brow. "Psycho Bunny?"

Fain snorted. "I have no idea why they call him that. I'm told he killed the last human who asked."

The lights on his console sparked before the hailing alarm went off.

Galene looked about nervously. "What's that?"

"Your embryo requesting landing clearance on my ship." Fain set the sequence for Talyn and Gavarian to enter the *Storm Dancer*'s hangar bay, then freed himself from the psilinks so that he could manually control his ship.

The moment his seat righted and the connection severed, pain split his head in two. Agony sent him to the floor with a major nosebleed.

"Fain?" Galene rushed to his side to check on him.

He couldn't speak as he struggled to breathe. Damn, it hurt. That being said, he'd take the pain to feel her hands on his body as she rubbed his back to comfort him. To see the concern in her pale eyes as worry knitted her brow.

How sick was that?

"I'll be all right, Stormy."

She brushed her hand across his cheek. "You don't look all right. Are you sick?"

"I pulled out too fast. It happens whenever I sever the tie without the right sequence." He pushed himself to his feet. Honestly, he was shaky and weak. Sick to his stomach. Wiping at his brow, he was just getting his bearings when Talyn literally sprang through the flight deck door, threw his helm to the ground, and seized his mother in a fierce hug.

Talyn held her with her feet dangling well above the floor. "Are you okay?"

"You're crushing me."

"Are you okay?" Talyn repeated.

"I'm fine, but for the fact I can't breathe, *tana*."

Only then did Talyn loosen his hold. He took a step for Fain.

Galene grabbed him. "Don't."

"He endangered you. I think that requires a little limping on his part."

She shook her head. "I don't want to hear it from the likes of you, given how many years you've shaved off my life. Now behave."

The hostility in Talyn's eyes said that they'd be having words later.

Fain sighed heavily. Talyn was never going to accept him as his father.

Whatever. Familial scorn was what he'd been bred on. Nothing new there. He only wished it didn't hurt so much to see it on Talyn's face.

Ignoring it as best he could, Fain took manual control of the ship and headed them back to base while the others stayed behind to battle their enemies.

"Did you get a message through before you were attacked?" Gavarian asked as he moved to stand by Fain's side.

Fain nodded. "Barely. Why?"

"I don't know. Before we left, I heard something weird with The Tavali that I didn't understand."

"What?"

"Just another tail end of a transmission that said they needed to strip and bury Slag-wart's Canting. Any idea what they're talking about?"

"Yeah. It means to take my Tavali standing and remove me from citizenship."

Gavarian scowled. "Slag-wart is *you*?"

A tic started in his jaw as Fain gave a subtle nod. The term was one that instantly launched him to a level of violence he didn't often reach without Dancer or Darice being around and lipping off at him. If he knew who'd used it, he'd love to have their throat in his fist. " 'Slag' is The Tavali term for a conscripted or enslaved member of a bound crew."

Or a whore.

"Then how do you know they meant you?"

How he wished he didn't. Unfortunately, there wasn't anyone else it could be. "Slag-wart is Venik's pet name for me, i.e., I'm the blister on his ass."

Gavarian arched a brow at the bitterness Fain couldn't keep out of his tone. "Then why do you fly for him?"

Acerbic memories surged as he tried to keep them buried in a place where they wouldn't hurt so much. An impossible task, really, but Fain was nothing if not a glutton for foolish endeavors.

"I wasn't given a choice." He wiped at the blood that continued to run from his nose. "When I was taken, Venik embedded a kill switch in my brain. One push and my head explodes like a melon. Either I do what he says, or I die."

Which, in effect, made him Venik's whore.

Galene gasped as those words horrified her. "Are you serious?"

The dead earnestness in his pale eyes chilled her. "Last thing I'd ever joke about."

She couldn't believe his blasé tone. "Who knows about this?"

He cast his gaze around the three of them. "You three, Venik, the surgeon who set it, and Syn, who tried once to burn or dig it out."

"And he couldn't?"

Fain shook his head at her question. "Had he gotten to it within a few days of the implantation, he might have been able

162

to extract it. But it grew into my brain fast. Extracting it or burning it out now would kill me instantly."

So he was still enslaved to Venik, with no real freedom. That's what Jayne had hinted at when she'd said Fain's life hadn't been a picnic, either.

What else was he hiding?

"Why would Venik do that to you?" Talyn asked.

Fain let out an exasperated breath before he answered. "He thinks it's hilarious to own a member of the famed War Hauk lineage as his personal pet." He met Galene's gaze and the torment behind that blank expression made her stomach ache for him. "It seems Keris was right, after all. My only purpose in life is to serve as an attack dog."

Galene winced at his dry tone as those words took her back in time to when Fain had been accepted into the North Eris Medical Academy. He'd been so excited when their counselor had given him the news at school. Less than one percent of applicants were ever accepted into their prestigious program. It was the hardest medical school in the entire Nine Worlds to get into. And unlike her, Fain had done it without a prestigious medical family background to rely on.

He'd done it on his own, with no help from anyone. Just like Talyn's Felicia.

Ecstatic that his hard work and extra hours after school had paid off, Fain had run all the way home to tell his parents the incredible news.

When Galene had called him later, his happiness had

vanished completely. He'd worn that carefully guarded, jaw-locked expression he always held around his parents, grand-parents, and older brother.

"What's wrong?"

"Nothing."

His curtness had wounded her. "So what did your parents say about your acceptance letter? My father is thrilled to have—"

"I'm not going to med school with you, Galene."

"What? Why?"

"War Hauks aren't doctors. It was a stupid thought."

She'd scowled at him over the link. "I don't understand. You worked so hard to get in. You took all those advanced classes. . . . It's what you wanted to do. All you ever wanted to be."

Keris's bitter laughter had echoed in the background. "Don't be ridiculous. They only let him in so that they could brag about having a War Hauk on their attendance roll. Fain's an idiot. Only thing he's ever been good at is getting his ass kicked and being an attack dog. Last thing any Andarion wants is some-thing as dumb as him treating them when they need a real doctor."

Fain's eyes had been as dead then as they were now while he stared at her. "My father signed me up for my obligatory service this afternoon. I'll be entering the military this fall."

Galene saw that hurt boy now in the fierce male before her. Still defiant in the face of those out to own him and force him into a life he'd never had any say in.

Closing the distance between them, she rested her chin on

his shoulder and placed her hand at his hip. "You are not a dog, Fain."

Fain savored those words as much as he savored the way she held him.

Like she used to.

For a moment, he wasn't the cybernetic animal Venik and the others had turned him into. He felt Andarion again. Like he had control of his future.

Strange how out of all the beings in his life who'd sought to own and control him, the only one he'd ever wanted to give himself over to was her.

And she was the only one who'd refused to ever control him.

Not wanting to think about that, he flew them back to the station, where an entire squad of Hadean Corps soldiers waited for their arrival. Unfortunately, by the time he saw them, the comptrollers had possession of his ship and everything was locked down to drag him into the bay.

Bloody minsid hell . . .

Fain ground his teeth at what that meant for him.

Talyn unbuckled himself and moved to stand by his side to stare out at the armed enforcers. "What's that about?"

Shit to come.

"They're Hadean Corps. Tavali enforcement."

"Yeah?" Talyn prompted.

Fain didn't say anything more as he shut down his engines and opened the hatch. "Don't worry. It has nothing to do with you or your mother." His stomach cramped with anger, he headed down the ramp.

Sure enough, the captain of the Corps came forward.

"Commander Hauk, you're being remanded into custody, pending investigation and hearing."

Galene gasped. She rushed toward them. "What's the meaning of this?"

The captain cuffed Fain's hands behind his back. "It's Tavali business."

"Fain?"

He met her gaze and offered her a teasing grin. "Just answer their questions honestly, *keramia*."

Galene stood in stunned shock as they hauled Fain away and he didn't protest.

Kareem Venik came forward to greet her. "Commander? Would you mind answering a few questions?"

Talyn stepped between them. "She doesn't go anywhere without her escort."

Kareem nodded. "Fair enough. Please, follow me."

Galene trailed after Kareem, while Gavarian and Talyn provided a tight shadow to her. With every step they took toward the lockup center for the station, her fear for Fain tripled. "What's all this about? Why did they arrest Commander Hauk?"

"I'm not at liberty to discuss that with witherwins."

"Witherwins?"

"Non-Tavali." Kareem paused at an office and opened the door. He allowed them to enter first. By the expression on his face, she could tell he, too, was bothered by what was happening.

So she decided to try a more motherly approach. "Kareem?

I know you consider Fain family. Please . . . I don't want to see him hurt or in trouble. What can I do to help?"

He glanced nervously toward a corner. The furtive gaze made her wonder if they were being watched or recorded. "If you don't mind, Commander, I'll ask the questions." He gestured for her to have a seat.

She sat down as Talyn and Gavarian took positions behind her. She had to give Kareem credit that their stern glowers didn't send him fleeing. Lesser creatures would have lost their nerve. Or at the very least, control of their bladders. Especially given the scornful sneer on Talyn's face that promised a sound beating should the wrong word fall from the Tavali's lips.

With exception of clearing his throat, Kareem betrayed no sign of discomfort. "Commander? Um . . . can you lead me through your attack? I need to file a report on what exactly happened during the fight. I just need your debriefing on what led to the encounter and what actions Commander Hauk took during and after it. You're not in any kind of trouble. This is a routine report. Nothing more."

Yeah, right. She knew better. His careful tone and rigid manner belied those words. "Commander Hauk and I were flying out to try and signal his brother when we were attacked."

"Why were you out there? Why not contact his brother from the base?"

"That's Sentella business."

"Yes, but you didn't have to leave the station for that."

She arched her brow at his tone. "Are you accusing me of something?"

"No, Commander. Just curious why you left, is all. Seems strange."

"And as the Alliance commander, I don't answer to you. If your father has questions, he can take them up with me himself." She rose.

"Wait, Commander, please. I didn't mean to offend you. But there is one more thing I do have to ask you."

"That is?"

"Are you a trained and licensed pilot?"

Fain crossed his arms over his chest as he stared through the plasma bars at Venik. Completely calm and uncaring about his owner's fury, he blinked slowly and methodically. Then he cursed as his nose started bleeding again. From experience, he knew it'd be plaguing him like this for days to come.

As would the current headache that throbbed like a mother.

He'd never wanted the neural implants. Ven had forced this shit on him. Now he wanted to hang him with it.

Typical.

Fain wiped the blood away and dared Ven with his gaze to say anything about it.

Curling his lip, Venik started forward, then remembered the bars that would have seared him had he made the mistake of touching them. "Have you any idea the shitstorm you could bring down on both our asses for that stunt you pulled? You owe me, Hauk! Or have you forgotten how I found you?"

Fain laughed bitterly at the reminder Venik threw in his face every time they locked horns. "Yeah, I remember that day. How could I ever forget you dragging me out of my confinement cell by my hair, with my hands shackled behind my back, then shooting out both my knees before you held me down on the ground with your foot on my throat, and bragged to your crew about how easy it was to quell a mighty War Hauk kid who was already half dead from starvation and months of being brutally beaten by his slavers. Yeah, Ven, you were some big fucking awesome Tavali badass who defeated my worn-out piece-of-shit hide." He clapped sarcastically. "As always, I am in awe of your awesome fighting skills."

Venik pulled out the trigger for Fain's implant and held it up for him to see it. "I should have killed you."

"Probably." Fain gestured at the small trigger. "Still not too late. You wouldn't even have to get your hands dirty." He glanced at the drab gray walls. "Place could use a bright splash of color. Nothing better than brain matter on steel to put the fear of the gods in your enemies. Go for it."

For a full minute, he thought he might have finally pushed Venik too far.

But just as Venik started to press the release to kill him, he growled and returned it to his pocket. "I don't know why I tolerate you."

"I'm the only one who tells you the truth. Without fear."

A tic started in Venik's jaw while he stared at Fain as if trying to see into his soul.

After a long wait, he finally hit the release for the bars. "Yeah, you crave nothing. Never have. All the years I've known you,

you've never asked me for anything except time away from service to see to your brother's needs. Never anything for yourself. It's why I don't believe the lies someone's spewing against your honor. But trust doesn't come easy to me and you know that. You know why. As you said, you have plenty of reason to hate me. More than most. And I understand that, too. I did things to you that I regret in hindsight. Unfortunately, I can't change what I did to you because I hated others. We both have to live with my mistakes, and for that I am sorry. I met you at a bad place in my life. And you paid for a hatred that wasn't yours." Ven let out a heavy sigh. "But don't make me have to kill you, Hauk. End of the day, I will do it if I have to. You know I will."

Fain snorted. "Now you're just trying to turn me on. Don't make promises to me you're not going to keep. That's just wrong, Ven."

Venik rolled his eyes. "You're a sick bastard."

Without commenting on something they both knew was true, Fain took his gear from Venik and strapped his blasters to his hips as he headed back toward the hangar.

But as he left the retention area, he almost collided with Galene, who was waiting in the hallway.

He froze at the sight of her. And at the tender expression on her face.

"Was all that true?"

"What? That I'm an asshole? Yeah. It's what everyone keeps telling me. Talyn said he even took a survey and everyone agreed unanimously on that one core fact about my personality." He expected her to duplicate Venik's expression and sounds of irritation, but for once, she disappointed him.

Instead, she reached up to brush the braids back from his face and cup his cheek in a tender gesture of affection. She traced the line of his eyebrow with her thumb. "It amazes me how similar you and your son are to have had no contact with each other. My two little lorina twins."

Those words choked him. It was the first time she'd really called Talyn his, without it being meant to hurt him. "So we both chafe your ass, huh?"

She sighed with a light smile at that. "At times . . . Talyn, like you, verbally shoves everyone back to protect himself. If he goads them into rejecting him first, then he controls the rejection. That way, when they insult him for things he can't help, it doesn't bother him. He feels as if he earned it and he can accept their hostility and judgment without pain. Just like you always did as a boy."

Fain fell silent as he realized how right she was. As a War Hauk on Andaria, he'd been judged by everyone. Because of his family's fame and legacy, and Kcris's overachievements, so much had been expected of him that it'd been hard to function, especially as a kid. That was part of what had led to Keris's drug addiction. They were all walking freaks of nature. Everyone stared at them. Wanted to meet and touch them.

Wanted to put them down and show that he and his brothers weren't any better than anyone else. And they weren't. They'd never said they were.

Yes, they were the direct descendants of the celebrated

family that had held off foreign invaders, and paid for it with their lives, but in his mind, in the minds of their family, that was what Andarions did.

All Andarions.

It didn't make them special. It was just expected. They fought when confronted. No matter the size of the enemy. Unfortunately, the rest of the Androkyn didn't feel that way. They'd swung between hostile and rude, or worshipful and frightening.

Keris had found comfort from the pressure of that condemnation and expectation in drugs. Dancer had found solace in befriending their prince, who was an even bigger freak than they were. And so Dancer's fame had been deflected to Jullien, whose notoriety and life under a biting microscope outshone his.

Caught between them in age, Fain had been hung out to dry. The only place of comfort he'd ever known was in the arms of the female in front of him. Galene had never judged him by his family or lineage. She, alone, had seen him for who and what he really was. And after she'd left, he'd had no one at all.

Now the warmth of her hand seared his skin. And with it came a surge of raw misery that washed over him as he stepped back, out of her reach. "Don't, Galene."

She scowled at him. "Don't what?"

"Don't show me the light and then damn me back to the darkness." He couldn't mentally handle it again. It'd taken him too long to get to a place where he could function without her.

Too long to find peace in a universe that begrudged him a life he'd never asked for.

Bitter and pissed, he glanced past her shoulder to where
Venik stared curiously at them. Brax was just one of many
reasons why he couldn't let anyone close to him. "I don't know
what I was thinking. It was a stupid dream."

And he'd been an idiot to believe for one minute that he
could ever have a normal life again. She was the prime commander for the Andarion armada. Best friend to the Andarion
queen.

He was an Outcast.

Yes, Cairistiona had adopted him, but that wasn't real. She'd
only done it to strike at his mother—the bitch she hated who
had embarrassed Cairistiona when they were young.

I'm done being a pawn. It was time to remove himself from
the game before he brought any more shame to his family. And
hurt to himself.

His heart breaking with a reality he could never change, he
left and headed back toward his ship.

For a few heartbeats, he thought he was home free. Until
he heard Galene approaching him from behind.

She pulled him to a stop. Her hesitant touch and the long-
ing it brought wrung more pain from him than he would have
thought bearable. It took everything he had not to crush her
against him and run as far away from here with her as he could.

But Ven and the others would find him. They'd drag him
back. There was no escape. He'd never been free.

He could never be free.

Galene's breath caught as she saw the utter misery in Fain's
eyes. The unguarded pain on his face. "Chayden and Morra

pulled the logs on your ship and doctored them before The Tavali got to them. They told me what you risked for me. And I told Kareem that I assisted you in the battle and with the flight. I didn't know why he asked until the interview was over and Chayden met me outside to tell me that you weren't supposed to show me what you did. Why would you risk a death sentence?"

"You know why, Stormy."

"No, I don't." She scowled up at him. "You confuse me so much, and . . ." She cursed as her earpiece went off. Stepping back irritably, she tapped it. "Commander Batur."

Fain watched the emotions play across her beautiful face. Galene had never been able to hide her feelings well. It was one of the things he'd loved most about her. He never had to guess. She let everyone know exactly how she felt about everything.

"Is there a problem?"

"Another transmission." Biting her lip, she hesitated. "I want to finish this discussion."

He snorted bitterly. "I'm not going anywhere."

To his shock, she took his hand in hers and led it to her soft cheek. Closing her eyes, she nuzzled his fingers and placed a tender kiss to his palm that left him hard and aching. "What did Venik mean when he said he did things to you that he regretted?"

"He turned me into a cyborg."

She shook her head. "No. There was more to it than that."

Looking away, Fain dropped his hand as old memories surged. "I don't want to talk about it. It doesn't matter."

She cupped his cheek and forced him to meet her gaze. "Yes,

it does. You can try to bury it, but it always comes back to hurt you. No one knows that better than I do."

He winced at her words. "I *never* meant to hurt you. I thought you'd forget about me and have a better life. I swear to the gods, I did."

"I know that now. And it wasn't that bad. Not really. My fears for Talyn notwithstanding, we had a good life for the most part. The best memories of my life have been because of you, Fain, and the son you gave me. You would have been so proud of him. He has been an honor to us both."

"Spoken like a true Andarion mother."

She laughed. "Come with me. Learn about the son you haven't known. The two of you have been strangers long enough."

He swallowed hard at the sensation of her hand on his as he felt the old surge of protectiveness hit him. The ferocity of it was overwhelming. For a full minute, he couldn't breathe. It was a fire in his blood unlike anything else he'd ever experienced. And only Galene had ever made him feel it.

Damn. It was why he would always be stupid for her and her alone. She owned him more than Venik ever could.

And she didn't need a kill switch. One frown could gut him. One harsh word was like a knife to his heart.

Hating how much control she had over his life, he followed her back to the command center, where Talyn and Gavarian were again on duty. Only this time, they had Tavali with them, so they were much more guarded with their words.

Talyn passed a warning glance to the one Tavali to let them

know whom he was most suspicious of before he greeted his mother. "Commander." He handed his band over to her. "The League seems to be in retreat, for now."

"Thank you, Commander." She smiled at her son and his military decorum. "Why don't you and the major take your breaks?"

"Yes, ma'am." As he started for the door, it slid open to admit a small human male.

Galene was stunned at the boy's presence.

The nine-year-old was bashful and adorable. With brown hair and sad blue eyes, he quickly scanned the group and stepped back at the sight of Gavarian and Talyn, who were giants in comparison to his small size.

Talyn scowled at him, but gentled his tone when he spoke. "Civilians aren't allowed in here."

The Tavali closest to the boy laughed. "It's all right. I'm sure he just wants his dad."

Fain sucked his breath in sharply as Talyn arched a brow.

"His father?" Talyn asked.

The Tavali pointed to Fain. "Hauk."

If expressions were lethal, Fain's guts would be smeared all over the instrument panel behind him. He wasn't sure who hated him most in that moment, Galene, Talyn, or Gavarian.

The only one who didn't hate him was Warwyk as the human boy ran toward him and leaped into his arms for shelter.

Fain cuddled him to his side out of habit. Dreading their assumptions and anger, he faced the Andarions and cringed. "I can explain."

That familiar tic started in Talyn's jaw. "Forgive me, Commander. I was going to tell you about this later. It seems Hauk has a mistress on the station. I knew she had a boy who lived with her. I assumed the child had another father. Otherwise, I would have forewarned you."

Galene's gaze darkened as both Tavali began laughing.

"Shut up," Fain snapped at them. He let out a tired breath as he faced Galene, Talyn, and Gavarian. "You three, follow me."

Galene shook her head. "I'm not about to meet your mistress, you bastard!"

Sighing, Fain met War's wide-eyed stare. "War, tell the lady who you live with."

"M-m-my sister," he whispered. "Why are they so mad at you, Paka?"

Fain shifted the boy to his other hip. "It's a misunderstanding. Now what has you so upset?"

War's lips quivered as tears welled in his eyes. He fisted his hands in Fain's braids for comfort. "It's Vega . . . she done threw me out and locked the door. She said she don't want no man around her ever again and that so long as I have a penis, I can't come in anymore. I like my penis, Paka, but I love my sister. Do I really have to choose between them? I mean, I guess I'll choose my sister, but I'd really like to keep them both if I could."

Fain let out a long sound of frustration. "Oh dear gods."

War's hands tightened in Fain's hair. "Can I come live with you, Paka, if she don't let me back in?"

"Don't worry, *mi tana*. I'll get you back in with her." Fain rubbed the boy's back as he glared at the three Andarions who were still glowering at him.

Ignoring Talyn and Gavarian, he focused his attention on Galene. "Since I know nothing about being a pubescent girl, would you mind helping me find out what's going on with his sister?"

That took some of the ire out of her gaze.

"Excuse me?"

"His sister just turned fifteen. Apparently something must have happened at school today. And since I'm male, I don't think she wants to see me, either. Never mind tell me what has her so upset as it's probably something to do with being a female. So please, can you help us figure out what's going on with her and why she wants to turn her little brother into a sister?"

That took the anger out of all three of them as they exchanged curious frowns.

"Okay," Galene said slowly. "Let me see this Vega."

With a smug stare, Fain carried War and led the three of them down to The Tavali family quarters.

When they reached the children's deck, Galene slowed down. "Is this an orphanage?"

"Yeah."

Galene glanced at Talyn, who looked as sheepish as she felt. "Sorry, Hauk," he said sincerely. "When I saw the report that you were paying for their place to live . . . I leapt to a bad conclusion about you."

Fain set War back on his feet and took his hand. "It's fine,

178

but next time, ask." He knelt down in front of the boy. "War, this is Talyn and Gavarian. I'm going to take the commander and see what I can do to talk to Vega. Stay with them and we'll be back in a few minutes, okay?"

His eyes widened before he whispered loudly, "Are they going to eat me?"

Fain laughed. "No. You'll be safe. Promise." He held his pinkie out for the boy, who quickly locked and shook pinkies with him.

He led Galene toward the back of the gated orphanage, to the small condo Vega and War shared.

"Are they yours?"

Fain gave her a droll stare. "No, Galene. Talyn is the only child I have. He's the only one I'll ever be able to have. I was sterilized before I married Omira because she couldn't stand the thought of carrying my baby. Vega and War were cargo on a ship I took five years ago. Their parents had been slaughtered and they were headed to Ladorja to be sold as slaves. Since they had no other family left to take care of them, I brought them here."

"Why haven't you adopted them?"

"How? I have no papers. I'm an Outcast and a slave, too. While I technically fly under my own Canting, Venik still owns me. He never filed the paperwork to free me. If anyone runs my DNA, I'm owned. So legally, I can't adopt."

"What about Cairistiona?"

He snorted. "She hasn't made a public announcement. Even if she does, I'm still legally Venik's bitch on most planets outside of the Andarion Empire. Changes nothing." He stopped at a door and knocked.

"Go away, War!"

Galene arched a brow at the high-pitched, hysterical tone. "Vega?"

"Ah, gah! I'm going to kill that little tattle-butt! I mean it, Hauk! Go away! I don't want to talk to you or any man! Take your penis and go!"

"Vega! Open the door and talk to me."

"No! You suck! All men suck!"

"I'm not a man. I'm just male."

"You have a penis, too. You suck!"

He sighed heavily. "Okay, I can't argue that. Will you talk to my friend Galene? She's female. She thinks I suck, too."

Galene smiled at his words. "He's right, Vega. He is definitely a total male jerk."

There was a slight rustling on the other side. After a few seconds, the door opened to show the tear-streaked face of an adorable young teen. With black hair and blue eyes, she passed a sullen glare to Fain before she stepped back to let Galene enter.

When Fain started in, she slammed the door in his face.

"I'm just going to stay out here, then," he said loudly. When they didn't respond, he sighed heavily.

After a few minutes with no response, he turned and went to check on War. He found him and Talyn and Gavarian playing griball with several other boys.

Smiling, he watched his two sons. It was the first time he'd seen Talyn let his staunch military persona down. Other than that brief glimpse in the transport when he'd texted with Felicia.

Talyn smiled as he lifted War up to dunk the ball. War raised his arms in delighted triumph and sat back on Talyn's muscled shoulder. And when Gavarian picked the ball up and joined in, it reminded Fain of how he used to play with his brothers when they were kids.

Gods, how he missed those days before Keris had gotten mixed up with his wife and drugs. Yeah, his older brother had always been a bit of an arrogant dick, but he had been a good playmate at one time.

And Dancer . . .

Fain's first real memory was peering over the crib to see Dancer the day they'd brought him home. He'd been underweight and so tiny. Frail. Fain had held his hand out and Dancer had latched on with a powerful grip that hadn't seemed possible for such a delicate creature. They'd locked gazes and Dancer had squealed and kicked his legs as if to say, "Hey, *drey*! I've got you, and I'm never letting go." It was a silent pledge they'd made in that moment that the two of them had never broken. No matter what.

And that was what he wished most he'd been able to give to Talyn. A little brother like Dancer. It was what everyone deserved.

Talyn flipped War over his shoulder and caught him before he hit the ground. Laughing, War picked the ball up and tossed it to Gavarian before he wrapped his arms around Talyn's neck and hugged him.

The expression on Talyn's face said the gesture startled him, but wasn't unwelcomed. Closing his eyes, he squeezed War and rocked him like a proud parent.

Not wanting to disturb them, Fain started away. He'd only gone a step when War's voice stopped him.

"Paka! You didn't tell me you were Talyn's paka, too."

Shocked that Talyn had claimed him, he met his son's gaze. "Uh . . . yeah."

Talyn passed the ball to him. "You know how to play?"

"Little bit."

"Want to join us? Two on two?"

"Sure. Who's on my team?"

War slapped at Talyn's leg. "I'll take Talyn. Brothers gotta stick together."

Talyn laughed. "Hear that, Vari? You're out in the cold."

Gavarian made a sound of extreme aggravation as the other boys left the court. "Typical." He jerked his chin at Fain. "All right. Let's shame them, Hauk. Show them what we're made of."

Galene pinned the braid against Vega's head. "You are very beautiful."

The girl gave her a tenuous smile in the mirror. "You think Hauk's mad at me for what I said?"

"Nah. I've said much worse to him and he's forgiven me for it."

Vega laughed.

"C'mon, let's go find our males." Galene led the girl out of her condo. She had no idea where to search, but Vega stepped past her and led the way to a small rec area where several kids were playing. It wasn't until they reached the griball court that she saw the boys locked in what appeared to be a death match.

Vega paused to frown at them. "What are they doing?"

Galene sighed at the fierce way they played. Luckily, Talyn was large enough that he was able to keep War sheltered so that Fain and Gavarian couldn't trample the much smaller human. Though it appeared at times, they were trying. "I believe they're actually playing."

"They look like they're trying to kill each other."

She couldn't argue that. But as she watched them, it drove home exactly what fate had deprived them all of. It was the first time she'd seen Fain and Talyn interact as something other than adversaries.

Gone was any hostility. Other than that innate male competitive drive they all had. But it wasn't the same as what they normally had when they faced off. This was what it should have been.

Playful and good-natured.

It also showed her how much of his father's natural athleticism Talyn had inherited.

And even though it wasn't in Fain's personality to lose, she saw him pull back so that Talyn, with War in his arms, could cut around him and allow War to score the final goal.

"Wahoo!" War shouted. "We won!" He latched on to Talyn's neck and bounced in his arms.

Laughing, Gavarian wiped at the sweat on his face. "No fair. Next time, I call Talyn."

War's eyes widened as he saw his sister. He jumped from Talyn to run at her. "Vega! Did you see my goal!" Then he pulled up short and cupped himself. "Oh wait. I still have my penis." Biting his lip, he looked around nervously.

Vega groaned and covered her face in embarrassment. "It's fine, Warwyk. Shush!"

His excitement returned. "Did you see my goal?"

"I saw. You did awesome."

He ran back to get the ball while she approached Fain sheepishly.

"You feeling better?" he asked in a concerned tone.

She nodded. "I'm very sorry for how I acted."

Hugging her, he passed a nervous glance to Galene. "No problem." Then he introduced her to Talyn and Gavarian.

Her eyes bulged as they pulled their uniform jackets back on over their bared chests and fastened them. She murmured a pleasantry before she grabbed War's hand and all but dragged him toward their condo.

Fain scowled at her actions.

Galene laughed. "She's becoming a young woman."

"Yeah, I know. I worry about her here by herself. I try to come down a couple of times a week to visit them. Make sure everything's okay and that no one's bothering them."

"She told me. She also said that you've put the fear into a couple of boys she has a crush on."

Fain grinned proudly. "Do what I can."

Galene shook her head at him. "Well, that was what had her upset. One of them asked her to a dance and she didn't have a dress. She tried to earn the credit for it and it was stolen by an older boy."

The humor faded from his eyes. "Who?"

"It's fine. I'm taking care of it."

"Who took her credits?"

She placed her hand on Fain's arm. "I'm taking care of it, Fain. Just breathe." Kissing his cheek, she offered him a smile. "I need to get back to the command center. Try not to kill our son."

Talyn snorted at her humor.

As she started away, Fain stopped her. "You never answered me about dinner."

"Tomorrow night. My place. I'll see you at six."

Those words thrilled him, until he caught the glower on his son's face. "I take it you'll be there?"

"Wouldn't miss it for anything."

Fain silently groaned as Gavarian let out an evil laugh at Talyn's grim, promising smirk. Wonderful. "Looking forward to our quality time together."

That seemed to relax the sternness from Talyn's face. "Why don't you grab the kids and we can get something to eat now? You can take something to Mum, while Vari and I feed them."

"You trust me?"

"More than The Tavali in the command center."

"So I'm the lesser evil?"

"For the moment." Talyn offered him a drink of his water. "Get the kids. Dinner's on me for being such a jackass."

As Fain rounded up Vega and War, he realized that when they weren't on duty, Gavarian and Talyn were more akin to family than friends or coworkers. They actually argued like two brothers.

"Do I have to separate you two?" Fain asked as they almost came to blows over the last piece of cake in the cafeteria-style restaurant.

"Nah." Gavarian reached for a slice of pie. "Let fat ass have it. He has a female. If Felicia doesn't mind being crushed by his gargantuan weight, who am I to deprive him?"

"At least I have a female."

Screwing his face up, Gavarian silently mocked his words like an angry teen with his father.

"Why aren't you married?" Fain followed Gavarian toward a table. Given his social standing and rank, it was unusual for an Andarion of Gavarian's age to be single.

Sadness darkened his gaze. "My wife was killed in battle against The Tavali two years ago. My mother keeps nagging me to remarry. But I'm not ready."

"I'm sorry."

He shrugged as he found a vacant table for them and set his tray down. "You didn't know."

An awful feeling went through Fain as he glanced to Talyn's leg. "It wasn't . . ."

"No. Different fight. I was grounded by then. I tried to get her to ground out with me, but she didn't want a command position. She lived to fly."

"Now he spends his time with the cheapest females he can find. Which is why I give him a hard time over it." Talyn set his tray down by Gavarian before he went to help Vega and War with their food.

Gavarian nodded at Fain. "Yeah, I prefer no commitments. Those females don't want emotional ties any more than I do. We share an even exchange of goods . . . if you know what I mean."

As the kids returned with their trays, Talyn handed Fain a to-go box and drinks. "I'll make sure they both get back to their condo and are locked in."

"Thank you." Fain ruffled War's hair. "You two need anything before I go?"

"We're okay, Paka."

He glanced over to Vega and arched a brow.

She stood up to hug him. "Sorry about earlier."

"No problem." Fain leaned down to hug her. She kissed his cheek before she pulled away.

"Goodnight, Paka."

" 'Night. Be kind to Talyn and Gavarian. Don't make them crazy."

Fain left them, but paused at the exit to look back and watch as they joked and ate together. A strange warmth spread through him at the sight. Gods, how he hated the years he'd missed with Talyn and Galene as a family.

Sick to his stomach over it, he headed back to the command center where Galene was taking a status report from the Andarion prime commander for the day. She was impressive in her role of elite military ruler. Unlike his mother, Galene wasn't condescending or belittling with her leadership. She held an inner calm that allowed her to listen and take charge with a bold confidence that was contagious. She was absolutely inspiring. How he envied her that ability.

Personally, he was an asshole. He rubbed everyone the wrong way and reveled in that ability most of the time.

As she finished her call, she turned toward him with an arched brow. "Something wrong?"

He smiled. "Just in awe of your military skills. You remind me a lot of Hermione Dane."

"Ryn's mother?"

Nodding, Fain closed the distance between them. "And yes, it's a big compliment from me." He held the box out toward her. "I brought you some dinner."

"Oh!" She sucked her breath in and bit her lip in the sexiest move he'd ever seen. "Thank you! I'm actually starving."

So was he, and it wasn't for food. Damn, it annoyed him how she could reduce him back to the days of insecure teenage stupidity with nothing more than one simple coy look. It wasn't fair that she had so much power over him and he didn't appear to have any effect on her at all.

She took her food to eat at the small desk where she could monitor the station and communications.

"Mind if I join you?"

Returning to her seat, Galene scowled at his question as she unpacked her food. "I assumed you would."

He sat down beside her and fumbled in his own box.

A light, adorable smile played at the edges of her lips.

"What?" he asked, dreaded its meaning.

"Talyn must have picked this out."

"How do you know?"

"It's disgustingly healthy. He still eats like he's training for the Ring. Even Felicia complains that he's permanently damaged his taste buds from it."

Laughing, Fain held his food out toward her. "Want to trade?"

She peered at it suspiciously at first, then nodded eagerly. "I forgot what a gourmet you were. You still cook?"

"Not as much as I did. It's hard to come by and keep spices in space. And you can forget baking on a cargo carrier."

She shared a bite of her food with him. "I'm sorry."

"For what?"

"That you can't do something I know gives you pleasure." She twirled her fork in the noodles and took a bite.

Fain sat quietly as painful emotions choked him. No one had ever known him better than Galene.

Not even Dancer.

Because she had never judged or mocked his dreams, he'd shared things with her that he would have died before he told anyone else. And it made him remember the things she used to do when she was young. The way she lived so voraciously, as if trying to suck the very marrow from the bones of life.

189

"You still talk to your sisters?"

Sadness darkened her eyes. "No. My family cut all ties with me when I left home."

He winced.

She covered his hand with hers. "Don't. I made that choice. I could have given up Talyn and they would have moved forward with another contract."

"Why didn't you?"

Galene debated on how to answer his question. In the end, she spoke the honest truth. "He was your son. And mine. Yes, my life would have been easier. But no life is without hardship and tragedy. If I had to have such misery in mine, I'd have rather had it with my baby beside me than to have been left wondering where he was. How he was doing. If I'd ever see him again. And yes, he has *every* bad habit of yours. I swear to the gods. It's as if they cloned you when he was born."

"He must have made you crazy, then. All my mother ever did was bitch about what a burden I was to her and her sanity."

Galene fell silent as she caught the pain underlying his teasing words and she remembered some of his mother's harsher criticisms. "Actually, they're some of my favorite parts of your son. He's very thoughtful and kind. Sweet even." She inclined her head at his food. "Notice how well balanced your icky meal is."

He laughed. "It is, indeed."

She fed him another bite of her much tastier spicy noodle dish. Then she tsked as he made a mess of it and she was forced to wipe his chin with her napkin. But her smile faded as she caught sight of one of the scars in his hairline from the brain surgery where Venik had either implanted his kill switch or the neurobinders for his ship.

"You okay?"

Galene nodded. "Just admiring your handsomeness."

"Careful, I might begin to think you like me."

"Ah now, we can't have any of that," she teased.

Fain fell silent as memories rose up to choke him so fiercely that it was hard for him to swallow his food. Gods, how he'd missed this female. Being with her now made it so much worse. It just brought home with a stinging clarity how much of his life he'd screwed up.

She licked at her fingers while she ran over reports. "By the way, are you aware of how much Vega adores you?"

"Excuse me?"

Glancing up, she typed and did three other things, all the while carrying on a conversation with him. Damn, he'd forgotten how well she multitasked. "She told me about how you saved them. That you defied Venik's orders so that you could keep them here as your family, even when he threatened to kill you if you didn't get rid of them."

Without conscious thought, Fain reached up to touch the old scar that ran through his parietal lobe where they'd embedded the chip that could one day end his life.

Or render him a vegetable.

Venik had been hotter than the core of a sun when Fain had returned from that mission, hauling two human kids with the cargo he'd been sent after.

"What the hell are you thinking, Slag-wart?" Venik had

grabbed him by his neck and shoved him back into the wall. "We're not running a nursery. We've got enough orphans from good Tavali who've fallen. We don't take in strays."

Fain had ground his teeth to keep from speaking. In that mood, Ven wasn't about to hear anything, anyway. But being a slave himself, Fain had refused to be part of a system that ruined another set of lives. "I'll pay for their room and board."

"With what? I already own you."

"I can make extra runs."

A cruel smirk twisted his lips. "You really want to keep them? You can pull time in the arena." He slapped Fain's cheek twice. "How 'bout that? You still want them now?"

Fain would always give Venik credit. He knew how to hit the rawest nerve to wring the most pain from anyone. "Yeah. I still want to keep them."

Ven had pushed him back. "Fine. You can report for duty tonight. I'll make sure they add you to the menu."

Sick to his stomach, Fain had headed back to where the kids were waiting on board his ship. Only ten, Stellavega Jaswinder had barely come up to his knee. But that look of vulnerable courage as she held onto her brother's hand and comforted him had reminded him so much of Galene that he'd been lost to it. Smiling, he'd held his hand out to her. "It's all good. I'm going to take you to a place where there are other boys and girls, and a nice lady who watches over you. If you have any problems, you can always call me and I'll take care of it and you."

That was one of the few promises in his life he'd been able to keep. And he was grateful to the gods for it.

Sighing, he shrugged as he met Galene's curious stare. "They're good kids. And I knew Ven wasn't going to kill me. He might make me wish he had, but he's got too much vested in me as a pilot and Tavali to end me for anything other than personal betrayal."

"Are you sure about that?"

"Yeah . . . I've pushed him enough to know it conclusively."

Galene didn't speak again until The Tavali in the comm center left and they were alone. Then, she pinned him with a stare that made him instantly uncomfortable. "Did you really get a vasectomy?"

"What made you go there?"

"It's been on my mind since you mentioned it."

"Why?"

"Just wondering. It's not something an Andarion does lightly."

Since it was against every organized religion on their planet and their entire cultural teachings, yeah. Andarions were taught to protect and expand their bloodlines with as many children as possible. "I know."

"So why did you?"

He shrugged. "Omira didn't want a hybrid baby. She was afraid of what it might do to her to carry it. I didn't care enough to argue. Given how the humans and Andarions treat mixed heritage children, I figured it would be for the best, anyway. Kid would have a hard enough time without a mother who couldn't stand it, on top of everyone else."

"If you felt like that, why did you marry her?"

"I was alone, Stormy. Cast out of my race and family. She was in a bad situation at home, and she was desperate to get away from her abusive father. While I knew I didn't love her, I knew I'd never hurt her. In the beginning, she was nice to me so it was easy to pretend that it wasn't so bad."

"Then what happened?"

He held his hand up. "While I was at work, she found a photograph of you where I had it hidden and realized it was your ring she had. By the time I came home, she was all kinds of insane and gunning for my ass. Since it was inscribed in Andarion, she got it translated and came for my testicles. She confessed that she didn't love me either, that she'd only used me to get away from her father."

"Oh, Fain . . . I'm so sorry."

He sighed. "That wasn't the worst. She told me that she was pregnant and threw me out of the house. Sadly, I didn't believe it. I thought she was lying to hurt me. Three days later, I came home to get a few things and found her in bed with her old boyfriend . . . and I saw the test that confirmed her pregnancy. I knew then that she'd been cheating on me for a while."

Rising to her feet, she pulled his head against her stomach and held him close. "I hate that you went through that. You didn't deserve it."

"For leaving you, I did, especially the way I did it. I should never have allowed Merrell and Chrisen to threaten me and drive me from you."

"You were just a kid. Really. What could you have done?"

"I don't know. . . . But I think it's why I'm so suicidal with

Ven. Having given up my life to them, I don't give a shit what Ven does to me now."

She pulled back to stare down at him. "You should. I care." And with that she gave him a kiss so sweet that it left him reeling.

Closing his eyes, he breathed her in as she teased his tongue and tasted him fully. He cupped her face with his hands and savored every last chill her kiss gave him. In that moment, he forgot where they were. Forgot all the years they'd been apart.

All he remembered was that he needed her to live.

His blood rushed through his veins with so much intensity that it left his breathing ragged and his body so hard it physically hurt to not be inside her.

Suddenly, Galene pulled back with a gasp.

Since he had no blood left in his brain, it took him a second to catch up to her as she returned to the panel and began pressing the screen. "W-w-w-what is it?"

"Did you hear that?"

Honestly? The only sound he could hear was his heart pounding in his ears. But as he strained, he caught a masculine voice speaking in Andarion to someone.

A female.

There was something familiar about both voices. Yet he couldn't quite place them. "Wait . . . is that—"

"Eriadne," she finished for him. "They've released her from her confinement."

"Is that her speaking?"

She shook her head. "No. Believe me, I know that bitch's voice."

He scowled as they continued to speak. "Who's Nyran?"

"Merrell's youngest brother."

"I thought he was dead."

"So did I."

Fain's breath caught as the transmission cut off as if the sender realized they were listening. Sitting back, his head spun. At one time, Ven had been in bed with Eriadne—literally and figuratively—double-dealing against the Andarion race. Was it possible he might be doing it again?

"This is bad, Storm."

Resting her chin against her folded hands, she nodded. "You've no idea."

Her dread-filled tone made the hair on the back of his neck rise. "What?"

"Talyn killed Chrisen and Merrell. He tore them apart in Ring matches after they were tried and found guilty of attempted murder on Felicia, and plotting against Cairistiona. He's also the one who brought in Eriadne, single-handedly. I mean, Morra and Qory and Ryn helped him, but he was the sole Andarion on the raid. He's the one who personally arrested her and was here on this station when Nyran's mother, Parisa, was killed. Nyran vowed to see him in his grave over their deaths. And Eriadne . . . if she ever lays hands to him, she'll gut him."

Fain hesitated before he told her something he'd never breathed a word of. Not to anyone.

Ever.

"You know she's why my father lost his legs."

196

"Excuse me?" she breathed.

Fain swallowed and took a moment before he revealed the best-kept Hauk family secret of all time. Something not even Dancer knew. He'd only been told because of what had happened with him and Galene. It'd been his father's final blow to Fain's ego and was what had caused his father to hate him so incredibly much.

"For these worthless bastards you shit out, I gave up my legs? I should have let Eriadne kill them and kept my body intact!"

Fain winced as he forced that memory aside and explained it to Galene. "Because my father shamed Eriadne's family by sleeping with my mother while he was pledged to Cairistiona, Eriadne offered him a choice—he could give up the lives of any son he fathered with my mother or the legs he stood so proudly upon. Since he was a War Hauk, Eriadne couldn't legally demand his life or imprison him without a major shitstorm, but that was her offer to him. It's why he hates my mother so much. Why he's so bitter and mean to everyone around him."

"I thought he lost them in battle."

"That's the lie Eriadne forced us to tell. He had to sign a nondisclosure and agree to say they were lost in a battle with The Tavali. And it's why the Anatoles have had such a hard-on for my generation. Why they had Dariana marry Keris, and then kill him, and why they went after Dancer. It's partly why I didn't fight harder to stay with you. I kept thinking that if I stayed, one day they'd hold our child over my head, and I'd be like my paka, hating my sons for what they cost me."

"You could *never* be like your father."

197

Maybe, but there were times when he heard his father's words in his mouth, and thoughts in his head. Times when he felt that same level of bitterness toward the universe. It seemed the harder he tried to run from it, the quicker he came back to the gates where he started. "I just wanted the feud between my family and the eton Anatoles to stop."

He pressed her hand closer to his cheek and savored the warm comfort. "Gods, it's so unfair that we have to make the hardest decisions when we're so young. And then spend the rest of our years living with the consequences of them."

She let out a bitter half laugh. "You think you'd make better decisions when you're older? I don't know about you, but I still screw up routinely."

He laughed, then gave her a light kiss.

Until their reality returned. "They're going to be coming for us."

"I don't care about that," Fain assured her. "They can come for me. But you're right. Eriadne won't rest until she holds Talyn's head in her hands."

Jumping as if startled, Galene looked down at her link. A tiny smile lit her face before she held it up to him. It was a picture of Talyn, Gavarian, Vega, and War in the kids' bedroom in their condo. She pressed the message button.

"Night, Paka!" War and Vega said in unison. "Our brothers put us to bed and locked us in. See you tomorrow!"

Vega blew him a kiss, then rolled over to snuggle her little brother.

198

Talyn stood up and angled his link toward himself. "Just letting you know they're well fed, in bed, and safe, and we're heading to our rooms. Well, I'm heading to mine. Vari's probably going to troll slag—"

"Bite it, you smug, giant asshole," Gavarian snapped from off camera.

Talyn flashed a boyish grin that exposed his fangs. "Goodnight, Mum. 'Night, Hauk." The transmission ended with him threatening and teasing Gavarian as they left the kids' condo.

"Are they always like that?"

She nodded. "It's good, though. Vari's the first one Talyn's age who's ever treated him like a friend or brother. Until Vari started hanging out with him, he was always so serious and stern. Like you whenever you were without Dancer. It's good for him to be teased and to laugh like a normal young male."

Made sense. Most wingmen shared that close bond, since they were responsible for each other's lives in battle.

Sadly, Fain had never known that. As an Andarion soldier, his last name and lineage had kept him apart from his peers. No one wanted to be a team member with a Hauk.

They only wanted to show them up.

And speaking of . . .

"I want to check something with that transmission. I'll be back in a little bit."

"Be careful."

He treasured those words as he left the commcen and headed

toward the housing area. While he walked, old memories burned raw. He saw his parents fighting as he'd ducked and covered from their vicious hostility in Keris's room. Things had always gone nuclear around Keris's birthday.

But nothing compared to this fight.

"This is all your fault! You brought your lesser genes and tainted my blood with it and you see, you *see* what you've done!"

"Me? Don't you dare blame this on *my* family! Not when it was your worthless ancestor who just handed the throne of Andaria away! Who does that? A fool! Hauks have been idiots from the very beginning of our history and now you see what it's gotten you?"

"Yes, I do! A bitch for a wife and three pussies for sons!"

In their room, away from their fighting parents, Keris had turned on Fain then and seized him so fast, he hadn't even had time to defend himself before his brother had struck him so hard, it'd dazed him. "This is all your fault! They're going to hate me even more because you had to go and fuck a human whore! I hate you!" Furious, his brother had rained down blows faster than he could fight back.

Dancer had run to protect him, but Keris had lifted his brother from his feet and body-slammed him into the wall.

Then, he'd dragged Fain out of the room by his hair. Everything after that had happened in rapid succession. The screaming and shouting.

In the end, Fain only remembered Keris holding him down while his mother marked him as an Outcast, and then being shoved half-naked and bleeding out the door and told to never bother them again.

Dancer had snuck through the bedroom window with a backpack for the two of them. "I'm coming with you."

Stunned and aching, he'd stared at his brother who was still healing from his own surgeries that had been caused by Chrisen's treachery and now Keris's abuse, and choked on his tears. Dancer had looked more like a small child than a half-grown Andarion male. "You can't, Dancer. You have to stay."

"Not with *them*. They're all nuts. You're the only one I have I can rely on. You know that."

Sadly, he did.

Scared for his little brother, he'd pulled Dancer into his arms and hugged him, then kissed his head. "C'mon. I'll take you to Yaya Hauk's. But you can't come with me. I don't have any place to stay. And you still need medical care."

"I don't want to be here without you, Fain. I won't survive on my own."

"That's Keris's bullshit, D. You're a hell of a lot stronger than they know. I'd put you at my back a thousand times faster than I ever would Keris. Screw his military badges and honors. You're more War Hauk than anyone in our family. Never let them tell you otherwise. And don't worry. I'll never be far away from you. You need me, I'll always come."

How he wished he'd made that promise to Galene and Talyn. And how simple it'd seemed then.

The reality . . .

"Hey, Fain."

He paused as he almost collided with Morra. Damn, she was the tiniest thing he'd ever known. "Hey, sorry. I didn't see you there."

She flashed an adorable grin. "Yeah, I know. It's the frog thing. We adapted to blend in with our environments."

"I thought that was chameleons."

"Nah, I'm more original. And harder to see." She winked at him.

Laughing, he shook his head as Jayne joined them and handed something to Morra. "What are you two up to?" he asked them.

"On our way to see Galene." Jayne tilted her head as she frowned up at him. "Are you okay? You have that look Hauk gets whenever he's worried about something, but doesn't want anyone to know."

Jayne had lived with her Trisani husband for too long. She was beginning to pick up on Hadrian's same psychic abilities.

"I'm fine."

Morra passed a droll stare to Jayne. "He's not fine."

"Yeah." She met Fain's gaze. "Don't worry. We know what's going on. I was on my way to tell Lena that Hadrian and the kids are secured. I can't reach Nyk right now as he and a crew of my compatriots are in a sector where they dare not transmit. I tried to get through to the palace, but all I got was Cairie's staff. For an obvious reason, I didn't dare leave a message."

He cursed under his breath. "You have any idea where Jullien trotted off to?"

She shook her head. "He went underground years and years ago, after The League approved a death warrant on him, issuer unknown. To the point, some say he's dead and buried in a hole on some backwater outpost in an unmarked grave. And let's face it, he wasn't a warrior or survivalist, by any means. I don't think he ever tied his own shoes or buttoned his own pants. Cairie got a birthday card from him that first year, but nothing afterward. He hasn't touched his accounts or sent any kind of message in a decade. Basically, he's been little more than a ghost since he handed Kiara over to Nyk's enemies, and Nyk promised to paint the walls with his brain matter should he ever invade Nyk's personal space again."

"You think he took refuge with Eriadne?"

"Who knows with those two? Like her, Jullien was always a slimy little bastard. I've heard she blames him for his cousins' deaths. So much so that she's the one who contracted for his life with The League. Other reports claim that they've been seen together for years. Personally, I don't know what to believe. If he is alive, he has to be shacked up with family. The gods know no female would have him. Not without his titles and inheritance."

Fain gaped. "Wait . . . his parents couldn't pull The League kill warrant?"

"They tried to block it, but couldn't. When all was said and done, Jullien was the direct cause of the abduction and near murder of Kiara, who at that time was the Gourish princess, and is currently the future queen of Andaria and Triosa. Even though Cairie's the reigning Andarion monarch, The League stepped in and let the order for Jullien's execution stand. Since he's no longer heir to either empire, his parents couldn't say shit to stop it. They'd have to reinstate him, and that they won't do for fear of him going after Nyk again to get the throne. So if any bounty hunter or League assassin comes across Jullien, he's dead. And if Nyk ever lays eyes on him again . . . he won't even be a fond memory."

Fain grimaced. "What level warrant is it?"

"Thrill-kill."

His grimace turned to a wince. Thrill-kill meant the issuer wanted Jullien violently tortured before death——with proof of it before payment——and his remains desecrated. While he was no fan of Jullien's, a thrill-kill warrant against a prince who was incapable of protecting himself was harsh. And the fact that neither of his parents would reinstate him to protect him from it was even harsher.

All hail Andaria.

And that was why Fain had left their empire when he did. They were a cutthroat race, and the Anatoles were the worst of them. It was that very ruthlessness that had made him leave Galene in order to protect her from such atrocities.

Morra frowned at him. "Why are you so interested in Jullien, anyway?"

"Weird transmission came through. Just trying to make sense of things that don't quite fit together. And I'll breathe a lot better when Dancer's here and I can lay eyes on him."

Jayne nodded. "Yeah. I'm only now starting to breathe again after I heard from Hadrian. Nothing's more terrifying than to know you've got family in harm's way and to not be able to get to them."

Fain caught the strange expression on Morra's face. "Where's your family?"

"Qory's with Chayden. Nyk's headed in here. Talyn's in for the night, I'm here with Jayne and on my way to see Galene."

Now it was his turn to scowl. "Pardon?"

"My father was murdered when I was a girl. My mother died when I was a teen. All the family I have is Sentella."

Fain felt bad for the Phrixian. "Sorry."

She offered him a kind smile. "You didn't know, handsome. It's all good. Truth never offends me. I'll always take the bitterest truth over a sugared lie any day."

"Woman after my own heart. And speaking of, I won't keep you two from Galene. There's something I need to check on."

Jayne hesitated. "Don't worry, Fain. Sentella's got your back."

"Thanks. Appreciate it." He watched as they walked off. While he believed Jayne without a doubt, the problem was, he didn't know who had their backs in this fight.

The way it was looking, The Tavali were about to hang them all out to dry.

Even him. And there was nothing he could do to save the very ones he loved most.

CHAPTER 8

Fain was a lot more nervous than he should be for something so ridiculously simple. He shifted the flowers in his hand, wondering for the millionth time if they were too much.

Or too little?

If his hair was in place? His clothes were acceptable? Had he shaved close enough? He'd heard Galene bitch for days about Talyn's goatee, so he'd gotten rid of his this morning.

Had he used enough deodorant? Or too much? Maybe he should have bought some aftershave. . . .

Galene used to hate that on a male, but Talyn wore it. Perhaps her tastes had changed over the years.

Damn. He hadn't been on a date since before Talyn was born. He couldn't remember really how to do this.

It's just dinner, dumbass. Relax. You ate with her last night.

Yeah, but this was different.

They'd made plans for this. Set it up.

With his gut clenched tight, he knocked on the door of Galene's room, and waited.

No one answered.

Scowling, he checked the time. He was a couple of minutes early.

Okay, almost half an hour, but it wasn't *that* early. Her shift had ended hours ago. She should have been back by now and relaxing with her programs. Not that he was a stalker, per se. He just happened to know her schedule.

And routines.

A little better than his own.

Oh, shit, I am a stalker.

Trying not to think of that, he knocked again and listened.

This time he heard a muffled shout and something that sounded like it'd been dropped. Terror consumed him. Opening the door, he reached for his blaster and started to call out when he heard Talyn's angry voice in the bedroom, growling in Andarion.

"Dammit, you're hurting me! Stop ramming the hole! You're not in the right position! You have to be on your knees when you slide it in!"

To his further shock, Gavarian responded in an equally irritated tone. "Oh bite it and stop being such a damn crybaby. Just shift a little. It'll go in if you just relax and breathe, and quit clenching so tight you could make a diamond from the pressure. Breathe slow and easy, and it'll slide right in the hole. You'll see. We just need more lubricant. Now stop being so hostile and let me do this or I'll leave you to jack it by your-self."

Talyn hissed. "Let me shove it up *your* ass, and we'll see how relaxed and hostile *you* are!"

"Gah! You're such a dick. How does Felicia stand doing this with you?"

"For one thing, she's a lot more gentle and her hands are smaller."

"I don't see how *that* would help."

His mouth hanging open, Fain started to withdraw when he caught sight of Gavarian in the bedroom, on his knees in front of Talyn.

Well, they weren't having sex, but to be honest, he'd have rather they were than face the reality of what they *were* actu-ally doing in there.

For a full minute, he couldn't breathe as he stared at Talyn's lower right leg resting on the floor by Gavarian's side while the boy entered data on a small tablet in his hands.

He removed the link from the leg and began to reattach it to Talyn.

Talyn hissed in pain. "It's still not right. You're missing the hole. Pull it off!" He reached for his crutches, then froze as he caught sight of Fain in the doorway. "Don't you fucking knock, old man?"

Fain closed his gaping jaw. "I did. You must not have heard me." Sympathetic pain for his son wracked him fully. No wonder Talyn limped and favored that leg so. The memory of all the scars on his son's body went through his mind and he cursed himself for not being there for them when they'd needed him most.

But he was here for them now.

Setting the flowers down on a side table, he stepped forward, into the room. "If you want, I can do that. I used to help my father with his integrations when I lived at home."

Talyn wiped at the sweat on his forehead before he nodded. "Fine. Just get it on right, since Gavarian can't seem to manage it."

Gavarian growled at him. "Don't yell at me. I'm not the one who twisted it. I told you not to play ball last night. But did you listen? No! You never listen 'cause you always know better."

Talyn mocked him in the same manner he'd mocked him the night before.

Ignoring him, Gavarian rose and stepped back so that Fain could take over. He reviewed the data on the tablet and checked the diagnostics. Then he double-checked the couplings and swabbed them out with disinfectant before he added more gel to the connectors. The trick was to slide it in smooth and quick before either he or Talyn moved even a millimeter. Something he and his brothers had learned to do fast since their father was prone to knock the shit out of them if they hurt him in the process of reattaching his limbs.

Bracing the cyber foot against his own thigh, Fain gripped Talyn's real knee and the prosthetic calf muscle. "Ready?"

Talyn inclined his head to him and held on to the chair's arms.

Fain slid the leg into place.

For a full minute, Talyn didn't move or breathe as he no doubt waited for pain to kick in. "Is that it?"

"Should be. Can you move anything?"

Talyn wiggled his toes and finally let out a relieved breath as he slumped back in the chair. "Thank the gods," he said with a happy note underlying his raspy tone. He slowly moved his leg back and forth to make sure it wasn't malfunctioning.

Fain had to give the surgeons credit. When attached, it looked completely natural. Unless you were right up on it, there was no way to detect the faint line that marked where Talyn's natural leg stopped and the cybernetic replacement began. It even felt real to the touch.

"What happened to cause that?"

His features sullen, Gavarian picked up the pad and link. "You should know, Hauk. You were there."

"Vari," Talyn chided, "don't."

But it was too late. Over and over, Fain replayed that firefight against Viper and Reaper in his mind. It'd been a brutal fight. No wonder Galene had fallen apart at the prospect of putting Talyn back into a cockpit. Pain struck him hard in the pit of his stomach at what he'd unknowingly cost his son.

And Galene.

"I'm so sorry, Talyn. I would *never* have hurt you had I known."

Talyn shrugged with a nonchalance Fain would never fathom. "It's okay. Really." He glanced over to Gavarian. "My leg for Vari's life was a fair trade as far as I'm concerned. And it could have been worse. Could have been my head I lost, or something else not so easily reattached."

Gavarian snorted. "You weren't saying that ten minutes ago when you were threatening to kill me." He took the pad and cord out into the living area.

As Fain started away, Talyn stood and caught his arm. "Seriously, Hauk. Let it go."

"How can you stand to look at me?"

Talyn answered in an honest tone. "I fought in the Ring for over a decade. Open and Vested. With Warswords and without. Honestly? I never thought I'd live to this age. Every time I entered a match or flew down a launch tube for battle, I fully expected to lose my life or a limb in the fight. I made peace with both possibilities a long time ago. We're warriors and we're Andarions. It's what we do."

Still, Fain couldn't imagine how his son could stand to be in a room with him and not kill him for what he'd taken from him. It made no sense. "You have every right to hate me."

"I do hate you, old man. But not for *this*. We all make mistakes. The gods know, I'm not perfect. So I'm not going to hold what happened in battle against you when you had no idea who you were facing off against. We do what we have to, to survive war. And I don't fight for myself. I never have. I fight for what I love."

"Your mother."

Talyn nodded. "For your sake and hers, don't ever let her know you had anything to do with me losing my leg. Don't even let her know you were there that day. *She* won't forgive you."

"I still don't understand how *you* can. And if you don't hate me for the leg, what the hell else could you possibly hate me for?"

Talyn pulled out his link and turned it on. He showed Fain the lock screen photo of him with his arms around Felicia. They appeared to be on a camping trip and inside a bright yellow tent. When Talyn unlocked it, Felicia turned and said in the sweetest contralto, "Love my sexy baby!" Then she gave him a loud, audible kiss.

Swallowing hard, Talyn turned the screen dark and slid the link back into his pocket. "Every day I wake up and have her in my life, I have no real problems with anything or anyone. I'm just glad to be here. I don't know why my mother loves you like that, but she does. Whenever you come around, that sadness inside her vanishes and she lights up in a way she never has before. While I might not get it, I won't stand between you. So long as you treat her like she deserves, I'll do anything I can to help you. My personal feelings be damned."

In that moment, Fain felt even more like shit that he hadn't told Talyn Felicia was on her way here. He should. But he wanted to see Talyn's face when his son saw her unexpectedly.

"What I hold against you, Hauk, are all the years I watched my mother suffer because you weren't there for her. I hate you for every lonely tear she's ever shed in your name."

The front door opened. "Talyn?"

"In here, Mum."

The sound of her voice filled Fain with both panic and joy. Damn, that female had way too much power over him. It made a mockery of Ven's kill switch in his brain.

He followed Talyn out of the room to find Galene with Morra and Qory. They were each carrying two large covered trays of food. And Vega and War came in the rear of the group with small bags of chips in their hands.

After kissing Talyn on the cheek, Galene flashed a dazzling smile at Fain.

Suddenly, he felt out of place. "Did I misunderstand our plans?"

Galene laughed. "Not at all. You're a little early. But it's fight night and we always have dinner together while we watch."

Baffled, Fain looked from Talyn to Gavarian to Qory and Morra and back to Galene. "I thought you hated fighting."

She arched her brow. "I'm Andarion. I love the Ring. Not when my son or pledged are the ones bleeding in it, but for the rest . . ."

"She loves it." Talyn pulled back a lid and snuck a crunchy bit from one of the platters. "More than even I do." He snuck another piece and handed it off to War, who grinned before he ate it.

Morra sidled up to him. "Don't look so disappointed, Fain. This is a family tradition she's invited you to."

He locked gazes with Galene. "Really?"

Galene nodded. "Only Felicia's missing from it. Talyn and I have been doing this since he was in nappies. Even when I couldn't be with him, we'd watch together via links whenever we could."

And it was something she'd started doing with Fain and his brothers and father and uncles when they were kids. As physicians, her family had never cared much for the sport. But every weekend, his had come together for the big fight. His mother and aunts would prepare food and everyone would crash wherever they could find space at his paternal grandparents' massive house. Since the event was vastly chaperoned, Galene's father would drop her off for it, and they'd sit on the floor in front of the screen next to Dancer and their cousin Dimie.

How weird that Galene would carry on a Hauk family tradition without him when he'd basically abandoned it after his mother had disowned him.

Galene handed plates of food to the kids and helped them sit in front of the screen before she returned to make a plate for herself.

Morra passed an ale off to Qory and waters to Talyn and Gavarian. Since they were Andarion military, they weren't allowed to imbibe. She arched a brow at Fain. "Hearty or boring?"

"The good stuff with bite in it."

She popped the cap and handed him the bottle. Galene gave him a plate before she grabbed a water for herself and headed toward the living room with the others.

"Who's fighting?" Fain started to sit next to Qory, but Galene grabbed his belt and pulled him down beside her.

Too stunned to argue, he balanced his plate on his legs and set his drink on the table next to the couch.

Talyn licked the sauce from his fingers. "Torrid and Gallows."

"Who you banking on?"

Talyn shook his head. "Only gamble with my life, Hauk. Never my money."

Galene tossed a pillow at her son. "Not my favorite thing about him, either."

Sitting on the floor, next to the kids, Gavarian picked up his link to place his bet. "So who's going to win?" he asked Talyn.

"Gallows. Six rounds in."

"Thank you."

Fain frowned. "You sound like a prophet."

"He's never wrong," Galene, Gavarian, and Morra said simultaneously while Qory nodded in agreement.

"Then why don't you bet?"

Talyn rubbed at his leg. "Loyalty. I only put creds on a match when I know a portion's going to the fighters, or Erix's the trainer."

"Erix? He's still training fighters?"

Talyn grinned. "Yeah, I know, right? The way he complained about me sucking the life out of him, I'm stunned he didn't retire with me."

Fain laughed. "He did the same with me. All the time." He deepened his voice to mimic his old trainer. " 'I swear, Hauk, you're sucking the last few good years of life right out of me.' "

Talyn laughed. "You do that well."

Frowning, Morra looked back and forth between them. "Didn't he know you two were related? I mean . . . c'mon. You're dead ringers for each other, and no snide comments about how Andarions look alike to foreigners, 'cause I know better."

Talyn snorted. "He never really said anything. But yeah, I think he knew. I always suspected it was why he took me on as a lack-Vest."

"What do you mean?" Fain asked.

"Just that he wasn't known for taking pity on punk kids. And every now and again, I'd overhear him mumble something that sounded suspiciously similar to 'just like his useless paka.' I assume he had to mean you."

Fain laughed at his spot-on impression of Erix's gruff tone. "He never called me useless."

"True, but I like to embellish." Talyn ate another bite of his ribs.

Fain shook his head as he considered his son's words. "But you do bet, though."

Talyn shrugged. "Not a bet when it's a sure thing."

The more Fain learned about his son, the more he respected him and regretted how little he'd had in the making of such a great Andarion male. Then again, maybe that was a good thing. Had he been around, Talyn might not have grown into such an exceptional being.

The gods knew Talyn was definitely a better male than Fain had ever been.

Warwyk popped his head up. "Commander Galene? May I have some of the cake pieces?"

She narrowed her eyes at his plate. "How much did you eat?"

He held it up for her to see. "All."

"Wow! You inhaled that! By all means, sweetie. Go grab what you want."

With a happy shout, he ran to the kitchen to get another plate full of sweets and chips.

Laughing, she leaned against Fain's shoulder and made his heart quicken. "I forgot how much boys that age eat. I could barely keep Talyn in groceries."

"You can still barely keep me in groceries." He wiped his hands on his napkin. "Hey, War? Can you grab me another plate, too?"

"Sure, Big T!"

As the fight started, Talyn checked his link and frowned.

Qory signed at him to ask what was wrong.

Talyn let out a heavy sigh. "Still haven't heard from Felicia. I'm really getting worried about her. She knows what a psychotic asshole I am so she doesn't normally stress me."

Qory silently laughed.

From his seat on the floor, Gavarian passed a covert hate-filled scowl at Fain. Since they were traveling through League-controlled space, there was no way to safely contact them right now. Especially not with an unknown spy on the loose. "I'm sure she's fine. Just busy."

Galene brushed the hair back from Talyn's face. "Don't worry, baby. I'll have her brother check in on her. You know Aaron and the others would never let anything happen to your Felicia."

"Yeah. I just don't like being out of touch. I can't stand not talking to her. I have to know she's okay."

Galene gave him a hug and light kiss before she leaned back against Fain as if no time had ever passed. As if she'd forgiven him completely . . .

Shaken by the familiarity and emotions he couldn't even begin to define, Fain drank his ale while they bantered and chided each other the way he used to do with his family and friends back in the day. He watched silently as War and Vega teased and played with Gavarian and each other. It was so surreal and dream-like.

Then all of a sudden, for no reason whatsoever he felt like such an outsider.

I don't belong here. With them.

Worse, he was a danger to them. If Ven or someone else hit the button, he'd take out every person in this room. . . .

I'm a walking bomb. A bomb their enemies could exploit . . .

Panic set in with iron claws that shredded him. Everything was so painfully obvious now. While he'd known Morra and Qory for years, it'd always been at a distance. They were friends of his brother and Jayne.

Because of the years he'd spent as a slave and the fact that he was bonded to his ship and had a kill switch that could be detonated at any second and destroy anyone standing near him, he'd never bothered to make friends of his own. The only exception had been Bastien Cabarro, and even he had vanished one day without any explanation. Fain knew now that Bastien had been betrayed and imprisoned by The League in a situation as bad as his, but it'd only been recently he'd learned his friend's fate.

And they'd only become friends because Bastien wouldn't take no for an answer. Like Gondarion spiderweed, he'd latched on to Fain and wouldn't let go.

218

But Bastien was the rare exception who'd made it past Fain's carefully guarded defenses that kept everyone in the universe at a safe distance. Mostly because Fain hadn't wanted to go through the pain of being abandoned again. Not after everyone had shunned him over Merrell's lies, and Omira's faithless betrayal. Once in a lifetime was enough for him.

Now . . .

What am I doing?

He didn't belong in a family anymore. He didn't even know how to be in one. Too much time had passed. Life had gone on. He was a solo operator. A Rogue.

And as the fight ended just as Talyn had predicted it would, the walls seemed to close in on him as they became even more jovial and "normal."

Suddenly, Fain couldn't breathe. He felt stifled and over-whelmed. This wasn't right. It wasn't what he knew or was used to.

I have to get out of here.

Galene froze as she saw the panicked look in Fain's eyes. He reminded her of a trapped, feral animal. "Fain?" She reached for him.

He shot off the sofa and was across the room, faster than she could blink. "I need to go. I have something I have to take care of. Um . . ." Frowning, he glanced around at the others as he patted his pockets as if seeking something. "Thanks." He was gone so quickly, she barely realized he'd touched the door.

"That was so weird," Morra said as she picked up plates and threw them out. "Even for Hauk."

Galene gathered the kids' plates. "What do you mean?"

"You know, he's always reclusive. I've never seen him around anyone except his brother."

Qory gestured at them.

"Yeah," Morra translated for him. "He doesn't even have his own crew. He runs completely solo."

"Paka doesn't like people," Warwyk said as he threw away their cups. "He says they wear on his nerves. Except for us." He gestured at himself and his sister. " 'Cause we're little people and even though me and Vega outnumber him, we're still small enough he can toss us over his shoulder and tickle us into submission."

Vega rolled her eyes at his simple explanation. "That's not what he means, Warwyk. He loves us so we don't get on his nerves. But he doesn't trust anyone else at his back. Not even Tavali."

Galene hadn't really given it any thought before.

Now . . .

"Would you excuse me?" She left them to follow after Fain. Assuming he went back to his Tavali quarters, she tried there first.

She knocked on the door and waited.

No one answered. Since she was the CO of the facility, Fain had given her a master key for Andarion housing. She wasn't sure if her card would work on his room or not, but it was worth a try.

Galene slid her key in and pressed the lock. The door opened to a large, dark flat. "Fain? You home?"

Turning on the lights, she stepped inside and froze. The floor was covered with the flyers that were constantly being shoved under their doors. By the amount, it was obvious that Fain didn't spend much, if any, time here. While the entire place was furnished, there was nothing personal inside it. It was eerie and quiet. Like a museum or library. One that included a heavy layer of dust over the furniture and counters.

Yeah, he didn't live here.

Where else could he be staying?

Scowling, she ran over Vega's words. Now that she thought about it, she'd never seen him with anyone. He only spoke to Venik when he had to.

He ate alone. Worked out alone.

There was only one other place she could think to try. . . .

Galene hesitated as she pressed the controls for Fain's ship. It seemed like a stupid idea, but where else could he have gone?

Like his flat, the ship was dark, except for security lighting. She started to leave until she heard the faint sound of music playing.

Frowning, she followed it to the captain's quarters. The door was open, and there, on the small bed, sat Fain with his hands propped on his bent knees while he played his link.

Alone.

The jacket he'd worn earlier was hanging in his open closet with the rest of his clothes, letting her know that this really was where he made his home. Not in the station quarters he'd been assigned.

Yet it was almost as sterile here as it'd been there. The beauty of his parents and their strict, military rules he'd been raised with. His mother had never allowed Fain any kind of freedom at home. Endine Hauk had run her house like a barracks.

A place for everything and everything in its place. Keep only what you can carry. Males didn't need any kind of excess toys or items, except for weapons. He hadn't even been allowed to put posters up on his walls for decoration. Not even a picture frame.

Obviously, Fain still lived that way. There were next to no personal items here. Only the link in his hands, the blaster on his hip, and her ring on his finger. Just what he could carry.

"What are you doing?"

He jumped with a curse that would have been comical if her heart wasn't broken for him. "What are *you* doing here?"

"I came to find you."

"Why?"

"I was worried about you."

He frowned as if he couldn't conceive of that. "I'm fine."

But he wasn't. There was a deep, dark sadness in his eyes. One that made her ache for him. "Why did you leave so suddenly?"

"Fight was over." His tone was flat and emotionless. "I guess I should have helped clean up. Sorry."

But she wasn't buying it for even a second. Galene crossed the room to stand by the bed. "Fain. Look at me."

He hesitated before he complied.

"I want the truth. Why did you leave?"

"I felt . . ." He lowered his gaze to the floor. "Like an intruder."

Sitting down on the bed, she cupped his face in her hand and forced him to look at her. "That was not my intent. I wanted you to feel *included*."

He covered her hand with his and closed his eyes. "I don't know how, Stormy." He pulled her hand down to stare at her fingers as if they were foreign objects to him. "You asked me why I put your lineage on my arm. Because I wanted to remember what it was like to have someone beautiful to hold on to. But I realized tonight that it's gone and that nothing can bring it back. I failed all of you. In the worst ways imaginable. I was never there when you and Talyn needed me, and I don't know how to make it better. The last thing I want to do is cause you harm. So it's best if I just stay away."

Tears blinded her as her memories surged. Fain had no real understanding of family.

Only rigid obligation.

His parents had never been loving. They gave because it was what they "had" to do. She remembered when they were kids and Fain would get sick. His mother would criticize him for taking her away from work, and as soon as she got Fain home, she'd leave him for his older brother to tend. Something Keris had resented and he'd made sure that Fain knew just how much he hated caring for him. So Fain had learned to "not bother" his family whenever he was ill.

Not even for broken bones.

All his life, Fain had been charged with taking care of others. But not once had anyone ever taken care of him.

It was time for that to change.

"Come back with me, Fain."

His scowl deepened. "Why?"

"Because I want you there."

His eyebrows shot north. "For?"

She had to force herself not to roll her eyes. He was so much like Talyn it was criminal. Laughing at him, she took his hand and tugged at him. "Not for what you're thinking. You need someone to take care of you."

He snorted at that. "I'm more than capable of taking care of myself."

"This isn't about being capable or need. I *want* to take care of you. Now get on your feet, Pirate, and follow me."

Fain started to argue, but the tone of her voice told him it would be all kinds of stupid. Besides, he didn't want to fight with her anymore.

Deep down in a part of his heart he didn't want to admit existed, he wanted what he'd seen tonight. That kind of camaraderie. Kinship.

Family. Just once in his life, he wanted to belong to someone.

Sliding his link into his pocket, he got up and pulled his boots on, then he shrugged his jacket on and locked down his ship.

"Why aren't you using your Tavali quarters?"

He shrugged nonchalantly. "It's not home."

"Where is?"

"My ship."

This time, she did roll her eyes. "I'm serious, Fain."

"Yeah. So am I."

She paused to stare up at him. "You honestly live on your ship?"

He nodded. "Dancer lets me crash in his guesthouse sometimes, but I don't spend a lot of time on Andaria."

Because until recently, it would have meant his life if he'd been caught there. As an Outcast, he'd have been imprisoned by law should anyone have recognized him and reported him to their authorities. It said a lot that he'd risk that to visit his brother, especially given his mother's hatred of him.

"I'm surprised your mother never turned you in."

"She tried once. Nyk put the fear of the gods into her. And now that I've been returned to caste, thanks to Cairie, it's a little easier to visit, but I still don't spend a lot of time there. Too many bad memories."

"But you have addresses on different planets?" She'd seen them in his file.

"They were just mailboxes, over the years. I always lived in ports, unless I was under Tavali orders and doing illicit activities for Ven or Eriadne."

"You never put down any roots?"

He shook his head. "Never had a reason to. Dancer's the only family I have and he's always been mobile with The Sentella. I tended to stay within a few days' reach of whatever address he had."

In case his brother needed him. He didn't say it, but Galene knew the reason. Dancer had always come first with him. "You talk to him a lot?"

"Not really. Just kind of grunt at each other in passing."

Laughing, she opened the door to her flat and let him enter first. Everyone had already left, and Talyn was cleaning up the last of their dinner and snacks as they came in.

He scowled at Fain as he closed the fridge.

Fain drew up short at the sight of his son, who was wearing nothing but pajama bottoms. But the wardrobe choice wasn't what shocked him. It was Talyn's bloodred eyes that he'd kept covered with contacts up until now.

Stralen.

Shit.

Like father, like son. Whereas Talyn's must be permanent, Fain's had faded a few hours after Talyn's conception. Had he ever slept with Galene again, it might have become permanent. But there was no way of knowing now.

"You going to say something?" Talyn challenged him in that deep, angry voice.

"Are you?"

"Boys!" Galene warned. "Play nice."

Talyn jerked his chin at Fain. "Why's he back?"

"I asked him."

Grabbing his water, Talyn snorted and headed for his connecting room. "Thought I raised you better."

Galene shook her head and sighed. "I swear he's your clone."

"Not really."

"You think not?"

"No. I'd have kicked my ass."

Sighing heavily at him, she took his hand and led him to the couch. "Come on, Fain. Let me show you your son."

He had no idea what she meant until she connected her link to the monitor and spent the next few hours showing him countless photos and videos of Talyn from birth to adulthood.

And he didn't miss the fact that his son was every bit as solitary in nature as he was. Only where he'd chosen his path, Talyn hadn't.

Speaking of the beast, Talyn stuck his head through the door. "I'm heading to bed. Need anything before I go?"

Galene paused the photos. "Nah. I'm good. You're on first, right?"

"Yeah."

She got up and kissed his cheek. " 'Night, precious. Sleep well."

"You, too." He hugged her, then pulled back to pin Fain with a stern grimace. "Don't keep her up too late. I know all about how the two of you'd stay awake the entire night talking when you were kids. And she's got a long day tomorrow. Don't make me come back in here and separate you two. I mean it."

Fain snorted as Talyn returned to his room and shut the door. "Told him that, did you?"

"I told him lots of stories about his father."

"But never my name?"

"He knew. He just never asked." She smoothed the frown from his face as she returned to sit beside him. "Don't, Fain. I wasn't completely honest with you about the past. I was trying to hurt you."

"You succeeded."

"I know and I'm sorry." Her expression contrite, she sat back on her knees by his side and toyed with his hand.

Fain tried not to let it mean as much to him as it did. Just as he tried not to notice how warm and sweet she smelled. How inviting her skin was. "So why did you keep the Hauk Fight Night tradition?" he asked, trying to distract himself from the need he had to pick her up and carry her to the bedroom that was just a few feet away.

She bit her lip in the most adorable way. "I wanted Talyn to have something of yours. Something I knew you'd have shared with him had you known you had a son."

"Does he know?"

"He knows."

Galene traced the line of his eyebrows as she marveled at having him with her again. She brushed her hand through his braids that were laced with white strands where he'd bleached out sections. "What made you do this to your hair?"

He gave her a droll stare. "Got tired of being mistaken for Dancer."

She laughed, then sobered. "I've missed you so much."

Fain held his breath as she slowly leaned in to kiss him. His heart pounded at the sweet taste of her. At the scent of her perfume filling his head. He buried his hand in her braids and held her close as she slid fully into his lap.

He growled in satisfaction and cupped her shapely bottom.

Her hand was just about to hit gold when the lights came up and Talyn angrily cleared his throat.

Glowering, he stood over them like an irate parent. "Excuse me? No unification . . . *no* unification. You two need to back off and leave space for the imagination."

Galene burst out laughing at the old Andarion sayings that parents used with their teenaged children. "Go to bed before I spank you."

"All right. But you two need to keep it down or take it to your room. You're kind of grossing me out. Really don't want or need a ringside view of my conception. If you're going to get any louder, please let me know so I can bunk with Vari or something. Sheez! You do know that I'm right on the other side of that wall, right?"

Galene gave him a dry stare. "We're going to bed."

Talyn arched a brow.

"Your father will be sleeping on the couch."

Talyn wagged his finger between them. "Okay, I'm trusting you two to behave."

Laughing, Galene laid her head on Fain's chest. As soon as Talyn had shut his door, she nipped Fain's chin. "Brings back old memories, eh?"

"Not really. Talyn's a lot larger than any of your brothers or father. Scarier, too."

"That's because he takes after *his* father." Kissing his lips, she rolled off him. "I'll get you a blanket and pillow."

Fain pouted, but didn't say anything as he admired the view of her shapely rear while she walked away from him. He should probably protest, but honestly, he'd dreamed of this too many times to complain about the fact that she left him with the worst hard-on of his life.

While it wasn't perfect, it was better than he deserved.

Fain came awake to the smell of warm coffee and something sweet. It took him a full minute to remember where he was.

In Galene's quarters, on her couch.

He heard her speaking to Talyn in the softest of whispers. Just the sound of that light whisper sent a chill over his body.

"Don't forget to play nice with The Tavali."

Talyn snorted. "I'm not three, Mum." He picked up a bag of what must be his lunch Galene had made for him and glanced inside it. Then in a very childish voice that was meant to be an obvious mockery of the words he'd just uttered, he asked, "Did you remember to pack some of those sweet cakes I like so much?"

She laughed. "Of course I did, and I put extra in there for Gavarian, too, so that he won't pout with you again."

"Thank you." Talyn finished his coffee and set his cup in the sink. He glanced over to the sofa.

Fain made sure to feign sleep.

"Does it bother you that I let him stay the night?"

Talyn hesitated before he answered her quiet question. "Do you know what I remember most about being a kid?"

"My nagging you to stay clean?"

He laughed, then sobered. "How many times you said 'I wish your father were here to see you do that.' You never once let me say a word against him. Not for anything. If I ever tried to blame him for being gone, you made sure that I understood you were the sole reason he wasn't around . . . that you'd made the decision to stay silent and that had he known about me, he'd have never left. Aside from Felicia, who tolerates my sorry, surly ass, you are the strongest female I've ever known. I figure Hauk has to be an incredible male to win your loyalty and especially your heart. All I want is for you to be happy, Mum. So, no, it doesn't bother me to see him on the couch, if that's where you want him. Or anywhere else you want to put him. I'm a grown Andarion. You don't have to worry about my feelings, or tiptoe around them. You just worry about yours and know that if he hurts you, I will kill him for you and hurl his body into space."

She laughed and kissed his cheek. "I love you."

"Love you, too." He gave her a gentle hug and left.

Galene turned everything off and headed back into the living room.

Curious about her intentions, Fain continued to feign sleep.

She came over to him and brushed the hair away from his face before she placed a quick kiss to his cheek and pulled the blanket up to his chin. Then she returned to her room and went back to bed.

For several minutes, Fain didn't move as something warm and sweet swept through him. He hadn't felt like this since the day she'd conceived Talyn. Since they'd lain in the shelter of the cave where he'd once played with Dancer and listened to the rain pelting down outside.

Warm. Wanted.

Loved.

Don't be stupid. You're the father of her son. That's all you are to her.

But it felt like more. Worse? He wanted it to be more with a desperation that left him so vulnerable it terrified him.

Pain choked him as he looked down at the tattoo on his bare arm. For years, it'd been his sole comfort. Memories of Galene and the hope that he'd done right by leaving her had been the only thing that had gotten him through utter hell.

Now he knew the truth. He'd screwed her over badly.

As he started to get up and go to her, his link went off. He dropped it, then caught it before it hit the floor and alerted her that he was awake.

It had to be Dancer. His brother was the only one who ever called him, especially at this ungodly hour.

He unlocked the screen to see a very short encrypted message.

ETA 9 hours.

Yeah, it was his brother, and that made him smile. He couldn't wait to meet this mysterious Felicia and see his son finally smile.

Plus he'd feel a lot more relaxed once Dancer was safe and he had one person on this station he could trust with Galene and Talyn's lives.

With Vega and War.

'Cause deep in his gut, he knew something bad was brewing and it was about to hit. No matter how hard he tried, he couldn't shake the feeling. And while he'd been at war before, he'd never had this much to lose.

That was what made all this even more terrifying.

CHAPTER 9

F ain?"

Fain paused at the sound of Ven's voice. He turned and waited for the Tavali to catch up to him on the suspended walkway that connected their shopping area to the command and business sections of the station. "What'cha need?"

"We have a problem." Brax handed him a small chip. "That's a transmission we picked up. One of the Andarions is working with The League."

Fain put it in his ear and listened to it. It was the same transmission Talyn had intercepted earlier. "The Andarions claim it's a Tavalian."

"And you believe that?"

Why wouldn't he? "There are a lot more Tavali here than Andarions."

Ven shoved him back and grabbed him in one massive fist. "You need to remember what uniform you wear, Slag-wart."

How could he forget? "I know exactly where to put my loyalty."

Ven tightened his fist before he released him. "You better."

Fain didn't move as Ven and his entourage moved off.

Disgusted, he headed into the commcen to find Galene and warn her about his encounter. But she wasn't there. Just two Tavali, one Sentella he didn't know that well, and Talyn and Gavarian.

"Commander Hauk on deck," Gavarian announced.

Fain gave him a droll stare. "You don't have to do that, kid."

"Does it annoy you?"

"Yeah, it does."

Gavarian grinned. "Then I have to do it. Consider it my duty and pleasure."

Talyn snorted, but said nothing as he continued to review reports from their allies.

Fain closed the distance between them. "Where's Galene?"

"Commander Batur's in conference with Tadara Cairistiona and Emperor Cruel." Damn, whenever Talyn went into his official military mode it was truly impressive. The kid was unflappable.

With nothing else to do while he waited for Galene to finish up, Fain listened to the newsfeeds with Talyn. Things were heating up everywhere. The League was out for their blood in the worst sort of way.

They'd attacked another Andarion outpost and hijacked a

Caronese freighter that had been carrying medical supplies to aid those orphaned in the fighting. In better news, The Sentella had obliterated two of The League's primary weapons depots and freed a number of political prisoners who'd been wrongfully seized.

But things were going to get worse before they got better. Provided they all didn't get killed for treason.

Suddenly, the door behind him slid open to admit Dancer, Sumi, and a hooded female who was tiny for an Andarion adult, but that meant she was slightly taller than Sumi. And in keeping with noble Andarion fashion whenever the high-Caste traveled off-world, no part of her body showed at all.

For once, Gavarian didn't say a word to announce their presence. But the relief on his face was tangible. In fact, he looked like a pregnant woman who'd just given birth after a three-day labor.

Ever the stern military commander, Talyn straightened from the control panel to scowl fiercely at them. "Civilians aren't allowed in here," he barked at Dancer. "You need to leave."

Dancer didn't betray a single emotion as he stood his ground. "Fine, Commander. Give us the key card to your room and we'll go."

Talyn's snarl deepened. "Excuse me?"

Two graceful hands, brightly painted in keeping with the Andarion holiday season, emerged from the folds of the dark blue cloak to lower the hood and expose a mass of waist-length, curly brown hair. Fain had never seen such an abundance of curls in his life. They sprang out to frame the breathtaking face of a joyous imp. Bashful and sweet, she stared up at Talyn with love gleaming in her silvery-white eyes.

"Licia!" Talyn breathed before he raced across the room to scoop her up in his arms and kiss her as if his life depended on it. Cradling her head with his hand, he pressed his cheek to hers and held her with her feet suspended well above the floor. "What are you doing here?"

With bright musical laughter that betrayed her happiness, she kept her arms wrapped around his shoulders as she savored his touch and played in his braids. "Your aunt and uncle showed up at the condo and said that your father sent them to ask if I wanted to come stay with you while you were stationed here. I hope it's okay?"

"Of course it is!" Biting his lip, Talyn finally set her back on her feet. Breathless, he cupped her cheek and swept his gaze over her as if he still couldn't believe she was real. "Where are your things?"

She turned to show him her small backpack beneath her cloak. "You know me. Travel light. Besides, I didn't want to waste a single second getting to you." Wrinkling her nose and giggling in the most adorable way, she danced around to face him again. And Talyn was just as giddy. He couldn't stop smiling at her while he brushed the hair back from her face.

Their obvious love and adoration for each other tightened Fain's throat. It reminded him of how Galene used to look at him when they were kids.

How she still lit up his heart every time she came near him.

And he was grateful beyond repayment to his brother for doing him this favor.

Fain cleared his throat to get Talyn's attention off his female, but it was hard and took several seconds before his son dragged his gaze away. "Go on and see Felicia settled. I'll cover the remainder of your shift."

Talyn hesitated. "You sure?"

Nodding, Fain pulled his key card out. "And swap keys with me. I had them exchange our quarters earlier. After last night, I figured you'd want more room and privacy while Felicia was here. Mine should be freshly cleaned and stocked for you. If not, let me know and I'll get maintenance right on it."

Like a little kid who'd just been handed the gift he never thought to have, Talyn slung Felicia's pack over his shoulder and complied. His hand hesitated on Fain's. "Thank you, Hauk. Really."

Fain clapped him on the shoulder. "My pleasure, kid."

Talyn returned to Felicia's side and took her hand to lead her out.

Felicia bit her lip in the most precious way as she glanced over her shoulder at Fain. "Um, Talyn? When did you get a father?"

Talyn paused to look back at him, too. It was the first time Fain saw something more than contempt or hatred in his son's eyes as he regarded him. "The minute you walked through the door." He kissed her hand and left the room.

Fain should probably take offense to the fact that Talyn hadn't introduced them, but given his son's eagerness to be alone with his female, he'd let it slide. He'd have been the same way at that age.

Introductions and manners always took a backseat to stralen hormones and emotions.

Dancer and Sumi closed the distance between them.

"Hi, Sumi." Fain kissed her cheek.

She gave him a light hug. "That was really sweet. Good job."

Embarrassed, he shrugged her praise off. "Where are the kids?"

"Kalea saw a candy store out in the mall area so Darice was kind enough to take her for some, while we brought Felicia here." Sumi stepped back and caressed her slightly distended stomach. "I'm going to go check on them and make sure Kalea hasn't driven him to murder her with her billion and two questions about everything."

Dancer snorted at that. "Yeah, right. Get me some of whatever you get for yourself."

She wrinkled her nose playfully at him. "Will do."

As soon as she was gone, Dancer arched a brow at Fain.

"What?" he asked irritably.

"Nothing." Dancer pulled out a large envelope. "I picked up those papers you requested. Everything's in order."

"Thanks. I owe you."

"Nah. Just sorry it took so long. League has most of this sector locked down tight. We had to do some creative navigating to get here without battle or confrontation, and I wasn't taking any chances, given my cargo."

That he well understood and was grateful for. "Glad you made it."

"Yeah. Me, too."

Fain set the papers aside. "So what do you think of Felicia?"

"Not what I expected."

"Meaning?"

"She's sweet, Fain. Quiet and bashful. Very, very reserved. For some reason, I'd assumed the Iron Hammer's female would be much more brazen and tough. In your face."

"Like Sumi?"

"Yeah. But I think a strong breeze could knock Felicia over and scare her. I've never met anyone more timid, especially not an Andarion female."

Dancer was right about that. Most Andarion females were tougher than the majority of human males. And he noticed Gavarian was choking as they spoke as if he knew something they didn't.

Ignoring him, he continued to speak to his brother. "What did you find out about her?"

"Her father's Saren ezul Terronova and her mother was born Marna eton Nykyrian."

Fain's eyes bugged at *that* noble lineage. Those were two of the original royal bloodlines that were only trumped by that of the current queen of Andaria. In fact, Cairistiona was an ezul Nykyrian—through her father, who was descended from the daughter of the first Nykyrian who'd been granted a royal title. An eton Nykyrian meant that Felicia's mother was descended from the original prince . . . damn. Felicia's mother was more noble than the current tadara's father had been.

As for the Terronova lineage . . .

It was only trumped by the eton Nykyrian and eton Anatole lineages.

"Are you shitting me?" He glared at Gavarian, who grinned at him.

"Oh? Did I fail to mention that Felicia is my aunt?"

It took everything he had not to shoot the kid where he so smugly sat. "Yeah. You left that bit out."

"Oh . . . By the way, Hauk, Felicia's my aunt."

No wonder Gavarian was so close to Talyn, and that they trusted him so completely. The little shit *was* family. It was all starting to fall into place now.

Dancer scowled at him. "Your father's Lorens ezul Terronova?"

Gavarian nodded. "All my life . . . since birth."

He looked back at Fain. "Lorens is her older brother, who adores her."

Fain let out a low whistle. "I give Talyn credit for choosing so well." But why a female with a lineage *that* impressive would be a paid companion boggled his mind. Even being bastard-born, Felicia could have negotiated marriage with any male she wanted.

Hell, she could have probably commanded a prince.

"She really loves him. I wish you could have seen her face when we went to pick her up. At first, I thought she was going to call security on us. But once I proved to her that I really was his uncle, she packed so fast, she left a vapor trail."

Fain laughed at that.

Until the door opened and showed Galene entering the room. She stalked toward him like a feral lorina out for blood.

Had he not been standing with a wall at his back, he'd have fled from the steeled look on her face. *What the hell did I do now?*

A little scared, he was frozen to the spot. Until she stopped in front of him, reached up, and pulled his lips down to hers. Fain relaxed as she kissed him with a passion he hadn't tasted since they were kids. It left him breathless and hot, and with a hard-on that should be declared illegal. And no doubt was obvious to all.

Pulling back, she smiled up at him. "Thank you."

"For what?"

"Making Talyn so happy." She hugged him like she used to do. Her breath teased his ear, sending chills all over his body. "I passed him in the hallway, with Felicia. He was practically dancing."

Fain savored the sensation of her body pressed against his. The only way to make this better would be to have her naked in his arms. "Anything to make you smile at me."

She rolled her eyes at him until she noticed Dancer. "And thank *you*. Felicia said you were a sweetheart to her the whole time, and that you and your wife and kids treated her like family."

"You don't have to thank me. I don't see how anyone could be unkind to her. It'd be like kicking a toothless kitten."

Galene let out a low laugh at that. "Yeah, you keep thinking that."

"Meaning?"

"Felicia's not as meek as she seems. Threaten Talyn and you'll find that out *real* fast. Even Qory's afraid of getting her riled."

Dancer scoffed. "I'd have to see it to believe it."

The door opened.

Galene turned to look past Dancer. The moment her gaze focused on the newcomers, her entire world shattered in a blinding wave of pain.

It was her worst nightmare.

Fain's ex-wife.

Worse? The pregnant human bitch stood there with a dark-haired girl in her arms, and an Andarion boy by her side who was almost identical in looks to Fain.

Vasectomy, my ass!

CHAPTER 10

For a full minute, Galene couldn't breathe as she stood face-to-face with the last person she'd ever expected to see again. Omira Hauk. Fain's human *wife*.

"Stormy," Fain said in a low tone. "It's not what you're thinking."

She raked a hostile glare over him as her fury erupted. "You faithless bastard!" Unable to deal with it, she stalked from the room with his lies ringing in her ears.

Fain followed her out into the hallway. "Galene, please!"

"Go back to your human! Or else I *will* kill you!"

"She's Dancer's wife!"

Galene stumbled at the last thing she'd ever expected to hear. Dancer's wife? What the hell?

How sick were they?

Catching herself against the wall, she turned back toward Fain, stunned beyond imagination. "What?"

"That's not Omira. I swear! It's her sister Sumi, and she's Dancer's wife. Not mine."

Galene scowled as she tried to digest his explanation. Could it be true?

Dancer and the tall, lithe blond woman who was still holding the little girl in her arms approached them slowly. The boy stayed back as if he was afraid she might harm him.

"I'm not Omira," the woman said slowly. "I know I look a lot like my sister, but I'm quite a few years younger."

She was also taller, now that Galene saw her with less fury in her heart. And much prettier.

Completely dumbfounded, she turned back toward Fain for more explanation.

The little girl frowned at Dancer. "Paka? Why's the pretty lady so mad at everybody? What did we do to her?"

He took her from her mother. "No one's mad, Lee-lee. Just a little misunderstanding."

Galene shook her head as she finally accepted a harsh truth. "This must be awkward at family reunions."

Sadness darkened the woman's eyes. "Not really. My sister died a long time ago. The only family I have now is standing in front of you." She gestured at the boy with them. "This is our son, Darice."

Galene felt an instant kinship with the woman who had no other family. "Sorry . . ." She hesitated, trying to recall the woman's name.

"Sumi."

"Sumi, I know what it's like to be alone. I didn't mean to overreact."

Fain let out a reserved sigh. "I should have warned you, Galene. But honestly, I don't even think about them being sisters. It just doesn't come to my mind at all."

That more than anything told her that he was being truthful about his feelings toward Omira. If he'd really loved her, he wouldn't be able to stand being around Sumi. Seeing her pregnant with his brother's children. The pain of it would be unbearable.

Instead, he really didn't care.

She smiled at Sumi's stomach. "When are you due?"

"Next year."

"Congratulations."

Rubbing her belly, she smiled warmly. "Thank you."

Fain took the little girl from his brother and brought her over. "Kalea, meet your aunt, Galene."

With her finger in her mouth, Kalea frowned at her. "Are you a girl aunt or a boy aunt?"

"Beg pardon?"

Sumi, Dancer, Darice, and Fain laughed.

Sobering, Fain explained it for her. "She knows Maris Sulle as Aunt Mari."

"Oh." Galene joined their laughter. Maris was the Andarion ambassador for Caron. He was also flamboyantly gay. "I would be a girl aunt."

Kalea launched herself from Fain's arms into Galene's. "Nice to meet you, Aunt Galene."

Closing her eyes, Galene savored the sensation of holding a small child again. She hadn't held one this age since Talyn had been a toddler. And Kalea weighed a lot less than he had at her age. She was so incredibly tiny and delicate. "It's a pleasure to meet you, too, Kalea."

She dug a handful of hard candy out of her pocket and held it up to Galene's face. "Would you like some? My brother kept most of it 'cause he said I'd eat too much and get a stomachache, but I think he's going to eat it 'cause he always does. Darry's mean that way."

Laughing again, Galene shook her head. "No, thank you. You can keep it."

"Okay." Kalea kicked her legs to signal she was ready to be set down.

Galene put her on her feet and watched as she ran to Dancer.

"Paka? Lee-lee needs a bathroom. Quick!"

He passed an irritated smirk to Sumi. "Why does she always come to me with this?"

With an evil laugh, Sumi held her hand out to Kalea. "Come, sweetie. Mommy needs one, too."

Dancer sighed. "Now that I'm not afraid for Fain's life, I'll see them settled. You two . . . play nice." He chucked Darice on the shoulder and led him in the direction Sumi and Kalea had taken.

"Am I forgiven?" Fain asked as soon as they were alone again.

"Does it really not bother you that she favors Omira so much?"

He shook his head. "Like you, it shocked me the first time we met. But as soon as I realized it was Sumi grown up, I had no problem with it at all. She's a perfect match for Dancer . . . and she's now my real sister since Cairistiona adopted us both."

Galene gaped. "*That's* Tizirah Sumi?"

"You didn't know?"

"I assumed she was Andarion. Not human."

He let out a light, sarcastic laugh. "The tadara is an interesting and highly unconventional individual."

"Tell me about it. I spent years as her main protector."

"Really?"

Galene nodded. Then she narrowed a glare on him. "Any more surprises I need to prepare for?"

"That's probably it. I hope. Like I said, I didn't even think about it. Or I'd have said something."

She fell silent as she grappled with everything she'd learned about him. And speculated on what else he might have forgotten to mention. "You don't have any other children I need to worry about meeting unexpectedly, do you?"

Pain darkened his eyes. "No. As I said, I had a vasectomy right after I left you, and you've met the sole two kids I take care of. You're the only one who gave me one hell of a son. Be nice if he could stand being in a room with me, but it's better than nothing, I guess."

"Like his father, he's not as hard-assed as he seems. Talyn's extremely tenderhearted."

Fain burst out laughing. "Sure he is. Have you met your kid?"

Galene suppressed a smile as she pulled out her link and put Gavarian in charge of Fain's shift. She glanced past Fain, toward the commcen. "Can I have you for a minute?"

248

He arched a brow at her word choice.

She rolled her eyes. "Put it in your pants, Pirate. I want you for something else."

Pouting, he stuck his head back in the center to tell them he was taking a break before he grabbed the paperwork Dancer had brought and rejoined her. "Is it too much to hope that you were fibbing and we're going to have a little fun adult time, after all?"

"Yes. It is, but . . ." She took his hand and led him toward the mall area of the station.

When she neared a small bistro, she stopped to peek around the corner of a wall. "Look over there."

Fain did and his breath caught.

He'd been wrong. Talyn hadn't taken Felicia straight to bed. Rather, he'd taken her straight to food. And his giant son sat next to Felicia, who fed him bits of her sandwich as they laughed and playfully cut up like two teenagers. Gone was any hint of the mighty Iron Hammer, or the staunch military commander who fiercely glared at everyone around him. Only the uniform remained the same.

For the first time, Talyn acted like a normal Andarion youth. He was even more relaxed with her than he'd been during fight night or while he'd played ball with Gavarian and the kids.

Stunned, Fain stepped back to face Galene, who gave him a satisfied smirk.

"Be nice to Felicia and there's nothing Talyn won't do for you. She is his heart and soul. He's never been that way with anyone else."

Fain cocked his head as he stared down at his own heart. "I understand, completely." He brushed the backs of his fingers along the line of her jaw. "I miss laughing with you like that."

Galene licked her lips as she felt her will weakening. But this wasn't the same bashful boy who'd once held her, and she knew it. Fain was a fierce pirate now. Comfortable in his skin and his role in an extremely violent world. She saw that more and more as he dealt with his Tavali brethren.

Still, she wanted him. And when he dipped his head to kiss her, she buried her hands in his braids and held him close. His scent filled her head and made it spin. His tongue swept against her fangs and raised chills all over her. No male had touched her since the day she'd conceived Talyn. None had ever really appealed to her.

Only Fain.

He owned her heart. He always had.

And when he pulled back, it took everything she had not to drag him to her room and strip him naked.

He nipped her chin playfully before he left her and headed toward Talyn and Felicia.

Talyn sobered at his approach, but he wasn't quite as hostile toward him as he'd been in the past. He wiped his lips and hands before he inclined his head to Fain. "Felicia, meet my father. Fain Hauk."

She arched a curious brow. "Which Hauk lineage?"

"My brother who brought you here is Dancer of the Warring Blood Clan of Hauk. Our biological mother is descended of the Sovereign Anoles."

"Wait . . ." She passed a narrowed glare toward Talyn, who appeared suddenly sheepish. "As in the second cousin of the tadara?"

Fain nodded. "Our grandfather was. Our mother is a third or fourth cousin. I never could keep it straight, much to her chagrin and constant shrill degradations for my failings over it."

Her jaw still slack, she glowered at Talyn. "You're descended from the royal house *and* your father is of the original thirteen War Hauks, and you *never* told me?" She cuffed his shoulder. "You beast! How could you not tell me something like that after all the times I've asked you?"

"I'm an asshole. But I'm *your* asshole," he teased her with a devilish, lopsided grin.

She laughed at him as he cupped her hand and kissed her knuckles. "I can't believe you!"

Fain set the sealed folder in his hand down on the table near Talyn and pushed it toward him. "I also had Dancer pick that up for you on Andaria."

Scowling, Talyn opened it. Then he gasped as he pulled the paperwork out. "Is this for real?"

Fain nodded. "Everything's been changed. All your military and personal records now show you as a fully Vested tiziran, with both your mother's and my lineages."

His breathing ragged, Talyn placed Felicia's palm against his cheek. He slid from his chair and went down on one knee by her side. The joy in his eyes brought tears to Fain's. "Will you honor my lineage with yours, Felicia?"

"Of course I will!" Tears flowed down her cheeks as she

nodded without hesitation. She threw herself into his arms and held him close. Sobbing, she reached out toward Fain. "Thank you!"

His throat too tight to speak, Fain took her hand into his as Galene wrapped her arms around his waist and leaned against his back.

"Thank you, Fain."

He savored Galene's touch much more than her gratitude as he released Felicia's hand. "It was the least I could do. I just wish I could have done it sooner."

She squeezed him tight before she stepped away to look at Talyn's new IDs and papers. "I'll call Marna as soon as it's morning in Eris. We can start planning the unification ceremony for next year."

Felicia wiped at her eyes as she kissed Talyn and returned to her chair. "I'd rather we do it as soon as we can."

Galene frowned. "Why? You've waited this long. . . ."

"I'd rather no one question our baby's lineage."

Fain wasn't sure who was more shocked by Felicia's words. Him. Galene.

Or Talyn, who stared bug-eyed at her.

His hand shaking, Talyn placed it against her stomach. "You're pregnant?"

She nodded. "I was going to tell you later tonight."

His features pale, Talyn's breathing turned ragged. "How long have you known?"

Felicia cringed. "A little over a month. I was planning to stay with Jayne and Hadrian once I started showing so that no one would know."

Because Talyn, as a lack-Vest bastard, would have been imprisoned for impregnating her. Especially given her noble lineage. The Andarion high court would have most likely castrated him over it.

"You told Jayne before me?" Talyn asked in wounded disbelief.

She cupped his face in her hands and offered him a sad, teasing smile. "I was terrified when I ran the test, Talyn. I didn't know who else to confide in. Had I told your mother, she would have told you immediately. My brother and father would have strangled us both. My mother would have screamed at me for being careless and endangering you, and you would have insisted I get medical care without waiting, and they would have arrested you as soon as they confirmed the pregnancy. I couldn't let them do that to you." She fingered the prison brand on his neck. "Not after the last time. I wasn't about to take a chance with your life or your career. Not when I know exactly how pig-headed you are."

Covering her hand with his, Talyn shook his head. "It's okay, Licia. You saved me from my own stupidity. Not like you haven't done that a few times before." He kissed her lips. "I don't want anything to taint this for you, baby. You know how much I love you, and I couldn't be happier. Jail or no jail. And I actually prefer the no-jail option." He looked up at his mother. "You're going to be a yaya, after all."

Galene walked into his arms and held him close. "Congratulations, Talyn. I can't wait!" she said breathlessly. "I know the baby will be an honor to us all."

Feeling like an outsider again, Fain started to leave, but Galene reached out and took his hand.

"Where are you going?"

"I figured you'd want to be with your family to make plans."

Talyn stood up slowly. His expression stern, he held his hand out to Fain. "You *are* family, Hauk."

Stunned, Fain took his hand and allowed Talyn to pull him into a hug. He clung to his son, unable to believe that this moment was real. "I'm so sorry I wasn't there for you, Talyn. But I swear to every god of Andaria that so long as I have breath in my body, I will be here for you from now on."

Nodding, Talyn released him and returned to Felicia's side. "So what are you planning to tell your parents?"

She swallowed her bite of Talyn's ice cream. "That I was abducted by aliens and surgically implanted."

Talyn laughed. "Now that I think about it, I might ought to store my sperm before you tell them. Lorens is likely to kill or geld me."

"Don't worry, baby. I'll protect you."

"Good. 'Cause he's scared of his little sister. I don't intimidate him at all."

Felicia scoffed. "That's just what he wants you to think. Trust me. The last thing Lory ever wants is to walk into a Ring and face *you*."

Galene gathered the papers and badges, and sealed them back in the envelope. "Don't lose this."

"If he does, it's all on official record now. Only you or the courts or tadara can ever take his Vested status from him. He is and will always be a legal eton Anatole." Fain met Talyn's grateful stare. "And both my brother and Sumi have agreed to adopt you if you want to be entered as a War Hauk. After all, it should have been your birthright, and they've promised to honor it, if you want. You now have three highly prestigious lineages to choose from, aside from Felicia's."

"Gah, I don't know what to say to that. Thank you, Hauk. Seriously." Talyn passed a bashful grin to his mother. "But if it's okay, I think I'll stick with Batur for myself. It's been good to me. And I'll leave it up to Felicia and Matarra as to which one is best for the baby to use."

Galene stroked his cheek. "Ever *mi courani*." Then she tugged playfully at his goatee. "Felicia? Would you please make this mess on his beautiful face go away? I positively *hate* it. He looks like a farm animal."

Felicia laughed. "But I kind of . . ." Her voice faded out as Galene cocked a brow at her. "Am thinking it should be shaved."

Talyn snorted. "I look like an infant without it."

Galene ruffled his braids. "You'll always look like an infant to me. Just wait until your baby's here. Then you'll finally understand why I still want to cut up your steaks."

"If it's a boy. If it's a girl, I'm locking her in her room until I'm dead and gone." He passed a smug look to Felicia. "Or pledging her to priesthood."

"You will have no control over her pledging. That's up to me and our mothers."

"Yeah, but I have full control over whether or not the male you pledge her to is anatomically correct on their unification day."

Fain burst out laughing. "How do you manage to deliver lines like that in such a dry, serious tone?"

"It's his sexy surliness. I would say it's what I fell in love with, but it was his sexy shyness that won me over."

"I always thought it was my large . . . condo you coveted."

Felicia let out a sound of supreme annoyance. "Oh my God, Talyn! Your mother's standing right there! Watch what you say in front of her!"

But there was no apology in his expression at all, as he took a bite of Felicia's food.

"And on that note, we shall leave the two of you alone. Good night, kids." Galene kissed Talyn's cheek, then Felicia's.

Inclining his head to them, Fain stepped back to make room for her.

Talyn rubbed his bearded chin against Felicia's fingers. "Goodnight, Hauk."

" 'Night, son. Felicia."

" 'Night, Mum. 'Night, Paka," she said sweetly before she fed Talyn more of his dessert.

To Fain's shock and delight, Galene took his hand in hers and led him toward his post.

"What time is your shift over?"

He checked his chronometer. "Another hour."

"Mine ended before I took my call with Cairie, so I'll leave the door to my side of the condo open . . . if you feel up to it, why don't you come in for some tea?"

"What? With no Talyn there to scowl at me like an angry father?"

She gave him a smile that hit him like a fist in his gut. "No scowling Talyn. You finally found a way to get rid of him, it seems. And that was a clever device for moving your room closer to mine."

"Ah, you caught that ulterior motive for switching rooms with him, did you? And here I thought I was being really slick."

She sobered before she placed a kiss to his cheek. "I'll see you later . . . maybe."

The sensation of her lips on his skin lingered like a tingling caress as he watched her walk away with that sassy, sexy swagger that was unique to her. Every part of him wanted to run after her, but he couldn't abandon his post. Not when he was covering for Talyn. The last thing he wanted to do was get his son in trouble. And he was still pissed at what he'd seen written in his son's military file.

Actions taken against Talyn because of Fain's youthful stupidity. Honestly, he was stunned Talyn could bear to be in the same room with him. It said a lot about both Galene's and Talyn's character that they could tolerate him at all.

Trying not to think about it, he went back to the commcen, where Gavarian returned the command bracelet to him and introduced Felicia's escort, the Andarion captain who definitely looked like Lorens. The boy was practically a clone of Keris's onetime friend.

"This is my brother Brach. Brach, meet Fain Hauk."

Fain inclined his head to him. "So, you're warning me this time who your family is?"

Gavarian grinned. "I told you, I don't give up the commander's private details. Not without clearing it through him first."

Brach snorted. "He doesn't care who takes a shot at me. My ass isn't sacred to him."

Gavarian nodded in cantankerous agreement. "And there is that."

"Commander?"

Fain glanced to the Tavali on his right who had spoken. "Yeah?"

"There's something weird coming through. But I don't know this language." She handed her earpiece over to him.

Fain pressed it against his ear and listened. "You recording it?"

She nodded. "Do you know what that is?"

"I think it's Phrixian. Call Morra and get her up here."

"Yes, sir."

Fain caught random words from the years he'd spent listening to Darling and Maris switch in and out of languages and dialects when they were drunk, or angry and fighting with each other, but he couldn't really understand what was being said.

Morra came in, pulling on a jacket. "Yeah, boss?"

He handed the earpiece to her. "Phrixian?"

She inserted it and nodded. "Naglfari bastards . . . Hope all their dicks rot off."

Fain and half his on-duty staff choked at that unexpected comment.

"It sounds like a report for Kyr. Some kind of bargain . . . no, pact is more precise. Blood brothers?" She handed the ear-piece back to him. "It just went dead as if they realized they were being heard. Did anyone get a trace?"

The comm officer shook her head. "Somewhere on this sta-tion. Nothing more precise than that."

Crossing her arms over her chest, Morra scowled. "There aren't any Naglfari here, are there?"

"Not that we know of. You're the only one I knew who could even identify the language."

Morra cursed. "They definitely have to be Naglfari for you not to know their race. Let's face it. Schvardan stick out. Hard to hide in a crowd when you're lime green and glow in dim light."

Definitely had a point. Fain brought up the file. "Here's the whole thing."

She replaced the earpiece to listen. By her darkening expres-sion, Fain knew it had to be bad.

"What is it?"

"Not real sure. They're speaking in code and using terms that don't make sense."

"Such as?"

"The pickle is in the jar, and the lid is open." She deepened her frown. "And if I'm the one they're calling the pickle, I'm going to have their pickles for lunch."

He ignored her venomous threat. "What is that supposed to mean?"

"I told you, it's mostly random phrases like that. The prize is at the top of the closet. Don't forget to turn out the lights and brush your teeth. What the hell? I think they're on drugs."

Fain growled in frustration. "Did the voice recovery work?"

His comm officer shook her head. "I can't break the encryption."

Fain pulled his link out and called Dancer. "Hey, I have a file up here I need you to work magic on. We need to ID the real voice on it."

"On my way."

Fain hung up and sighed as he tried to figure this out.

What are you up to, Kyr. . . . He did his best to understand the mind-set of The League's prime commander. There was only one person he knew who *might* be able to guess it.

He glanced back to the comm officer. "Get me a copy of the file to send."

As they worked on it, he stepped out of the room for privacy and called Maris Sulle, Kyr's younger brother and Darling Cruel's best friend. He was also a member of The Sentella and one of The League's most wanted criminals. He motioned for Morra to follow him to Galene's office.

By the time Fain reached her desk and took a seat, Maris answered the call with a groggy yawn.

Fain cringed as he realized it must be the middle of the night wherever Maris was. "Sorry, Mari. I didn't check the time or your location."

"Mmmm, it's okay, sexy. Is something up? Besides me and you at this unholy hour." He yawned again audibly. "Then again, it may not be unholy wherever you are, but I hope it is. I believe whole-heartedly in sharing my misery."

Fain tried not to be amused at that comment. "I just had an interesting call we intercepted from Kyr. But it's codespeak and in Phrixian. You're the only one I know who might be able to translate it."

"Or Saf." Maris yawned again. "He'd know better than I, especially if it's League code. Can you please send him a copy and wake him up? Besides, he can handle the sleep dep better than I. I'm the one with a husband and infant, and he's the one gallivanting about with cheap women and no responsibilities these days as we're all still spoiling him terribly."

"Yeah, sorry I woke you."

"No problem." A baby started crying in the background.

"I've got him," Ture said near the link.

"Thanks," Maris responded before he returned to the call. "File's here. I'll get right on this with Saf and see if we can figure it out." He yawned yet again, making Fain feel terrible for waking them.

"I owe you."

"Anytime, sweet cheeks. I'll call as soon as I have something."

As Fain hung up, he noticed Morra was texting someone. "What are you doing?"

"Notifying Ryn since Nykyrian's en route with Syn. He's letting me know that their families are being prepped and locked down." She showed him the text. "I'm personally responsible for Sumi and the kids until they arrive, and am senior Sentella officer under Hauk and Jayne." She put the link in her pocket. "I'm not to let Hauk's family out of my sight for three seconds."

"What was that?" Dancer scowled as he walked in on that last bit.

Fain laughed at the thought of Morra babysitting Sumi and Dancer in their bedroom. "It sounds like a plan."

Morra chucked Dancer on the arm. "Always around to ruin your fun, eh, big guy?"

Dancer shook his head. "Just knock first before you enter. If Sumi comes awake to a stranger in the room, she'll open fire on you."

"I've heard that about your lady. And that Kyr is still nursing his rib cage from his last encounter with her."

"That he is. My Ger Tarra is fierce."

"In that case, I shall awaken the hulk that is Q and send him in first." She winked and clicked her tongue at him. "Later, fellow air-breathers."

Dancer laughed as he turned toward Fain. "She really hates the Nagls, doesn't she?"

"With a burning passion. And now that you're here, I'm handing the helm over and going to update Galene on this. Call if you break the encryption or need me."

"Will do."

• • •

Galene smiled as she saw the paperwork she'd filed go through. "Is there anything else I need to do?" she asked the female Tavali.

"No, Commander. It's pretty much standard from here. Everything checks out. While this isn't quite the normal procedure, I can't see a reason why this shouldn't post immediately. Our goal is to place as fast as possible, so we're happy to facilitate all inquiries."

"When will I have an answer?"

"We should have official paperwork cleared within a few hours. Once you have notice, you can take possession immediately."

Joy rushed through her at that. She couldn't wait to surprise Fain with the news. "Thank you. I can't wait."

"No, thank you. We appreciate your interest and hope to have this finalized no later than the morning."

"Wonderful!" Galene hung up. Yes, this was a big commitment and change, but it was one she wanted.

For Fain.

No, for all of them. Watching Felicia with Talyn had reminded her so much of her youth, when she had made those plans with Fain. They had been robbed of sharing Talyn's childhood together. But she would make it up to Fain.

Starting now.

Her link went off. She picked it up, and bit her lip as she saw the message from Venik. This was the most important of all. *Please, please be a yes. . . .*

With a deep breath, she opened his text with breathless anticipation.

Commander,

You insult me with such a request. The Tavali does not let our Rogue pilots go. Hauk owes tithe to me and I'm not about to give up such a valuable asset. Do not waste my time again with any more ridiculous inquiries where he's concerned.

H.A. B.V., Lord Porturnum

Tears blinded her as she read the cold, callous words and felt her hopes and dreams crash and burn with each one. So much for freeing Fain from Venik's service.

He was right. Brax would never let him go.

Leaving the center, Fain walked the metal corridors with a deep feeling of severe trepidation. Everyone he passed, he wondered if they were the traitor. Who would be so stupid? The Tavali weren't like other Nations. They were a highly trained, fierce warrior culture that was supposed to hold honor sacred above all. While they didn't hesitate to screw over non-Tavali, you were never, ever supposed to do harm to those who flew under Tavalian Code and Canting.

It was an automatic death sentence. The only reason Ven had gotten away with what he'd done to Fain was because he'd done it before Fain had earned his own flag. And it was why Ven hadn't blown his head off since. Why he might threaten to, but always backed down from actually pulling the trigger.

At this point, there would be an inquest and Ven would have to answer for Fain's death. He'd have to justify it to the UTC or lose his own Canting and standing.

And Fain knew what Ven did.

He wasn't worth it. So, for now, he was relatively safe from Ven's threats. Provided he didn't push his owner too far. There was a point where Ven wouldn't care, and would react without reason. Luckily, Fain hadn't found that point-of-no-return yet.

"Hey, Hauk."

He inclined his head to Kareem's older brother, Stanis, who looked more like his Qill mother than his half-Andarion father. He was one of the few Tavalian who was almost equal to Fain's massive height and build. "Hey, Stain. Didn't realize you'd made it back to the station."

"Yeah, just docked. Was headed in to say hi to my dad. What about you?"

"Coming off shift and headed for RNR."

Stain nodded. "You look like you could use some."

"Yeah, haven't slept much. There's been some weirdness going on."

"That's what Kareem said. Heard you had a run-in with The League in the middle of our territory."

"I did, indeed. It was a bold move on their part."

Stain laughed. "Definitely. Glad you made it out."

"Not half as glad as I am."

"Hear, hear, brother." Stain shifted the package in his hand to the other arm. "Well, I'm off to pay respects. See you around."

He inclined his head as he watched the shorter male walk away. While Fain had never envied Ven his position or money, he had always envied him his family. Four sons and four daughters, all brilliant fighters and pilots.

And Malys Venik was no slacker herself. An incredible Qillaq warrior, she was hopelessly devoted to her husband and children. But she wasn't the most affectionate of women. Because she came from a warrior culture even more severe than the Andarions, it left her a bit cold and even less maternal than his own mother. Fain had often suspected that was what led Ven to occasionally find comfort with others when his wife was away for long periods of time.

Either that, or a death wish on Ven's part. If Malys ever learned of his dalliances, there was no telling what she'd do to her husband. For one thing was a given about all Qillaq females.

Their males only cheated once.

Why Ven would risk it, Fain couldn't imagine. He'd have given anything to be so lucky. And with that thought on his mind, he entered his side of the condo first so as not to startle his new roommate.

The door that joined his quarters to Galene's was ajar.

An awful feeling went through him. That wasn't like her. While she'd said that she would leave it open, that just meant she wouldn't lock and bar it. Not that she would actually open it like *that*. Galene didn't like open doors. She never had.

This can't be good.

Please, please be okay.

Drawing his weapon, he crouched low and pushed the door open with his foot.

His heart hammering, he froze at what he found there.

CHAPTER 11

Galene looked up with a gasp to find Fain pointing his blaster at her. She held her hands up, afraid of his intent. Faster than she could react, he dropped his weapon straight to the floor and rushed to scoop her into his arms.

"You're all right," he breathed raggedly in her ear as he held her with trembling arms. He laid his head against her shoulder and held her so tightly that she could barely breathe.

"Fain, you're hurting me."

He loosened his hold, but still didn't release her. "I thought you'd been attacked . . . I-I didn't know what I'd find."

Melting at his obvious fear, she pressed her cheek to his head and buried her hand in his braids. "No, *keramon*. I'm fine. Just waiting for you."

Fain pulled back at that to see the dimly lit room where she'd set out a full service for them, along with snacks and warming towels. And a low, slow song from their youth. It was only then he realized she was dressed in a long maroon gown—Hauk maroon—and a robe that left very little of her lush body to his imagination. Instantly hard, he smiled at her. "You're seducing me?"

"Am I?" she teased.

Closing his eyes, he kissed her and let the taste of her lips soothe his ragged nerves. The warm, rose scent of her body lotion filled his head. He began to relax as he finally heard the words of the song. It was the same one that had been playing the night of their dance when Galene had last told him she loved him.

Unable to believe this was real, he pulled back to stare down at her. "Is this a new torture where you're about to kick me out and send me to my room?"

Cupping his cheek in her warm palm, she rubbed her nose against his. "I know better than to tease an Andarion male. I wouldn't do that to you."

He frowned at her. "I don't understand."

She laughed bitterly. "Neither do I. I still want to claw out your eyes and leave you bleeding on the floor."

"Mmm, I love when you sweet-talk me like that."

Laughing, she nipped his chin, then opened his shirt and slowly peeled it from his body. Her fingers lingered over the scar on his shoulder that Keris had given him during his Endurance when his brother had kicked him with his spiked boots on their ascension while Fain had been drilling anchors to the side of the mountain they were scaling. That "fun" action had almost sent Fain plummeting to the ground. Galene had been so angry when she found out about it, Fain had actually been forced to disarm her and keep her from Keris for weeks.

After his unwillingness to allow her to physically harm his older brother, she'd finally "poisoned" Keris in retaliation with a concoction that had left his brother sick and cursing her for a solid week. But she'd been completely unrepentant. *"You ever hurt or endanger Fain again, and next time, it'll be coming out both ends, and your nose!"*

No one had ever taken up for him the way Galene had. Gods, how he loved this female.

She kissed the faded scar. "Do you ever think about Keris fondly?"

"Sometimes. Then I remember what a bitter, jealous asshole he was and how often he used Dancer for target practice."

"I know he was hard on you, but he loved you."

"I would emphatically disagree."

She fingered his scar with a frown. "And I sat with him in the stands during your fights. Every time you hit the deck, he'd rise to his feet and clutch his prayer beads, whispering a prayer under his breath until you were back up again. Then he'd take my hand and pretend to be tough. But I could feel him trembling in fear for you."

"Really?"

She nodded. "I know he never told you, but he was so proud of you. Every time you won, he'd jump up and scream as loud as I did."

"And then criticize my skills as soon as he got near me."

"Only because he wanted to please your mother."

Fain ran the backs of his fingers along her jawline. "You were the only one who ever made me feel strong and capable. Wanted.

I weep for every second of my life that I've lived without you by my side."

A beautiful smile lingered on her lips as she undid his pants. He held his breath, praying she didn't stop. If she did, he might very well die on the spot. Her gaze held his as she slowly slid her hand down to cup him.

Fain moaned out loud at the sensation of her stroking his cock. Tears choked him as tenderness and guilt overwhelmed him. Of all the beings in the universe, this was the one he should never have caused harm to. Yet he'd done more harm to her than even his worst enemy. For that alone, he wanted to kick his own ass.

Galene bit her lip as she saw the tender emotions playing across his face. She leaned in to kiss the scars that marked almost every inch of his chest. Some were from claws, knives, or blasts, and others were from wounds she could only guess at.

So much pain and suffering.

And always alone. Her poor Fain had never had anyone to love him and see him through his tragedies.

As she glanced up, she saw his eyes turn vibrant red. At first, she thought it might be from his neurolink with the ship. But as she studied them closer . . .

"Fain?"

He fingered her cheek. "I was always stralen for your touch, Stormy. Like Talyn, I hid it as a boy out of fear. It was why I left so suddenly after we made love that rainy afternoon. I was terrified that if your parents found out we'd been together before our unification, they'd punish you for it."

271

She buried her hand in his braids and tugged at them. "You've lied to me so many times. Kept so many secrets."

"I know, and I'm sorry. But I was so scared they'd hurt you and I didn't know what to do or where to turn. I had no one I could rely on, other than myself, and we both know what a piss-poor Andarion I am. Keris treated me like shit and never listened to anything I had to say. My parents were always disappointed in me, and told me to figure everything out for myself. And Dancer had no one else to protect him. Since Chrisen and Merrell couldn't touch Keris until Dariana got her claws stuck in his heart, they came for me from the moment I started school until our graduation. I had no quarter from any of them and their scheming hatred."

He squeezed his eyes shut. "Then when Chrisen crashed and trapped Dancer inside their pod to prove to me how easily they could kill him and get away with it, unless I agreed to break up with you . . . I felt so helpless and lost. I didn't know what to do. Chrisen said if I told anyone, Jullien would have me jailed and Dancer would be killed instantly. I knew they meant it and that they'd carry out those threats without reservation or hesitation."

Galene pressed her cheek to his as old memories surged. Fain had cut school the day of the accident to be with her. They had snuck into her parents' pool house to be alone and had spent the entire morning planning their unification ceremony and where they'd live while she went to school and he did his military service. They'd practiced their vows and dreamt of a future that would never be theirs.

Fain had just left the bathroom when his link had gone off.

Even from across the room, she'd been able to hear his mother shrieking at him. Hanging up, he'd grabbed his backpack frantically.

"What is it?"

"Dancer." It was all he could choke out.

Galene had gone with him to the hospital. His parents had looked at him as if he was the most repugnant creature alive. But it'd been Keris who'd grabbed him by his throat and shoved him against the wall.

"Where were you?"

Fain had slammed his hand down and broken Keris's grip. "What happened?"

His mother had raked him with a sneer. "Dancer was burned and will be deformed for the rest of his life. Which, if the gods have any mercy, won't be much longer."

Horrified by her callousness, Fain had scowled at them. "How was he burned?"

"He crashed the pod he was flying," his father snarled. "Almost killed Tahrs Jullien and Tiziran Chrisen Anatole. We'll be lucky if the tadara doesn't demand my life and Dancer's for it! You were supposed to be in the pod, you worthless bastard! Where were you?"

Keris had punched him so hard, Fain had staggered back. "Hope you're happy, *brother*. Your little adventure today cost Dancer his life and entire future. Good job, you selfish asshole."

Unable to listen to any more, Galene had stepped forward and pulled Fain back. "It wasn't Fain's fault. He was with me because I needed him."

Only then did they back off.

Endine had shaken her head. "I hope for your brother's sake, for all our dignities, he doesn't survive surgery." She'd stalked off.

His father had limped toward Fain. "That hybrid bastard is the one who dragged him out of the wreckage and ruined his future. If you're the warrior you should be, you'll kill that rank bastard tomorrow and save what little family honor we still have." Then his father had stormed off after his mother.

Keris had spat at Fain before he followed his parents and left Fain alone in the waiting room with his guilt and pain.

Aghast at their actions and aching for him, she'd rubbed his back, trying to offer a solace she knew she couldn't. "I'm so sorry, Fain."

The raw agony in his eyes had been excruciating. "It's all my fault. I did this to Dancer."

"You didn't do this. Had you been there, you'd have crashed, too, and been scarred."

He'd looked at her as if she was repugnant to him. That expression was what she would spend the rest of her life believing had sent him into Omira's arms. "I should have been there. I should be the one in a coma, not Dancer!"

Galene had stepped forward to hold him.

Hissing at her, he'd run down the hallway, into the bathroom. She'd followed after him and paused, knowing she couldn't go inside.

Through the door, she'd heard his rage and temper as he trashed the facilities. An act of desolate agony that had caused them to call for security. Her parents, who'd been doctors at the hospital, had responded to the call instantly, and her mother had forced her to go home while her father had gone into the bathroom to talk to Fain.

Over the next week, Fain had stayed by his brother's side, only leaving long enough to take his finals and attend obligatory graduation functions. Abandoned by his parents and Keris, who'd forsaken Dancer, Fain had refused to speak to anyone.

Even her.

She'd felt completely helpless in the aftermath. Yet on their graduation day, Chrisen had told her that Fain had wanted to see her. That he had something important he wanted to tell her about their future.

Knowing she was already pregnant, and eager to share her own news, she'd rushed to the locker room where Fain had shushed her and brushed her aside so that he could shower and dress for the ceremony, "without any more stress on my back." That was what he'd coldly said to her.

Since Dancer's crash, he'd been avoiding his home by staying at the hospital, and had decided to dress at school instead of his mother's house where he'd have been subjected to her constant insults and tirades. If not actual physical abuse.

Wounded by his callous words, Galene had left him. But as she stepped outside the locker room, she'd found Merrell lurking by the door. As she tried to brush past him, he'd grabbed her arm.

"Fain doesn't want you, Galene. Dear gods, how blind are you?"

"What do you mean?"

"He's been screwing Omira Antaxas for weeks now. Ever since the accident, she's been with him at the hospital and everything."

Snatching her arm out of his grasp, she'd sneered at the smug prince and that utter stupidity. Fain would never do anything like that. "You're lying!"

"I saw them together. So did Jullien. Just ask him, if you don't believe me. All the Hauks are twisted. Didn't you know? Their entire lineage is chromosomally damaged. Keris is a drug addict. Dancer's deformed, and Fain's a human-lover. Before your unification, you might want to check his DNA. I've heard his own father knows that Fain isn't his. It's why his skintone is so much lighter than his brothers'. And they doubt Dancer's paternity, too."

Galene had wanted to deny it, but she'd heard those rumors. And she'd seen Keris high on several occasions, even though it was strictly forbidden, and could mean his life if he were caught.

Shoving Chrisen away, she'd gone to Fain, only to have him break her heart by denying nothing. . . .

"Galene?"

She blinked as Fain's deep, melodic voice pulled her back from the past, into the present.

He cupped her face gently. "Where did you go?"

"Back to a boy who gave up everything he had to save his brother's life." Tears gathered in her throat as she placed her finger over his lips to keep him from speaking. "Shh, Fain. I know the dirty politics Chrisen and Merrell practiced. The lies they told and crimes they committed. I can't imagine having to make the choice you did. Especially alone, at that age."

"I should have killed them."

"No. If you'd done that, Talyn would have been the bastard son of a felon. A traitor who murdered royal sons. It would have been even worse for him. But had you told me then, I would have run with you, and never looked back."

"And they would have killed Dancer . . . just as they killed Keris. The only thing that saved Dancer's life was my leaving. It forced my parents to keep him, even though he was scarred."

Because it would have been the highest mark of dishonor for them to disown two sons. One child was an acceptable loss. That meant something had been wrong with that child. Disinheriting two meant that the parents had failed in their roles. And since Keris was dead, it would have ended the Hauk dynasty on Andaria. Something his proud father would have never allowed to happen.

For Dancer, Fain had given up everything he cherished.

Her hand trembling, she brushed the braids back from his face. "My noble warrior."

Fain shook his head. "There's nothing noble about me. I'm just an Androkyn."

"No, you were never so simple a creature, Fain Hauk."

Smiling, he picked her up to whisper against her lips. "My precious Storm Dancer." He slid her down his body so that her gown caught on his pants and exposed her to his questing hands.

She sucked her breath in sharply as he boldly explored her and left her breathless. "No male has ever touched me, save you."

"Good. I'd kill anyone who dared lay a hand to you, Stormy. I've never been one to share what I love with anyone." He pulled her gown over her head and dropped it to the floor.

Galene shivered as the cool air raised chills on her skin. Only the heat of his body warmed her now. She nibbled at the whiskers on his jaw, delighting in the way they teased her tongue and lips.

Fain closed his eyes and savored the sensation of her breath on his skin, of her hands sweeping over his back and pulling his pants lower. He kissed his way down her body until he was kneeling between her legs. Looking up at her, he nudged her knees apart so that he could finger her and then taste the part of her body that he'd been craving since the moment he saw her waiting in the Andarion landing bay.

He knew his eyes were glowing vibrant red in the dim light. He could feel that surging rush of possessive emotion. The need to protect and cherish.

All for her.

As a boy, he'd been torn apart by those unfamiliar stralen urges. As an adult, he fully understood what they meant. "Stormy? If we do this . . ."

She brushed her hand over his lips to cut his words off. "I know. It's time for you to come home, Fain. Let's forget the past and start the future we should have had."

Those gentle words wrung a growl from him as he rose up to capture her lips. Unable to stop the flood of adrenaline and possessiveness she awoke inside him, he entered her.

Galene cried out at the unfamiliar sensation of a male filling her body.

Holding her weight, he froze. "Are you all right?"

She buried her face against his braids and nodded. "I forgot how large you are."

More gentle than she could fathom, he cupped her breast as he swirled his tongue around her ear. "I won't move until you're ready."

Smiling at him, she slowly began to thrust her hips against his.

Fain growled again as the stralen inside him rushed forward. It'd been so long since he felt it that he'd forgotten the intensity of the hormones and adrenaline. The feral need to protect everything he loved.

"I love you, Galene," he breathed. It was a stupid confession, but it wasn't like she didn't know it. Not like she couldn't look into his red eyes and see the truth.

There was no way to hide it now. Not that he wanted to.

She'd been right. He'd hidden too much from her. Never again would he be so stupid.

Closing his eyes, he bit his lip and savored the warmth of being held by her. Of finally feeling like he was where the gods had meant for him to be.

This really was home.

"*Kimi asyado.*"

I love you tremendously.

Galene couldn't breathe as she heard the words she'd lain

awake at night missing. As she felt Fain's strong arms around her again while he slowly thrust against her hips. She pressed her cheek to his—the deepest expression of Andarion affection. "I love you, Fain Hauk. You worthless bastard."

He laughed at that. "But I'm *your* worthless bastard."

She joined his laughter until he took control of their lovemaking. Her laughter died under a fierce groan at how good he felt inside her.

Screaming out, she came in a blinding wave of pleasure.

Fain savored the sound of her literally purring in his ear while she clutched at him and arched her back against the wall. Closing his eyes, he surrendered to his own release. Weak and panting, he leaned his forehead against the wall and held her against him as he shook all over.

Galene nuzzled his neck, raising chills the entire length of his body.

When he pulled back, he saw the same regret inside her eyes that he felt for all the years together they'd missed. "I should *never* have let you go."

"You had no choice."

"That's the lie I've always told myself."

"It's not a lie, Fain. It just wasn't meant to be for us."

The way she said that made his breath catch. "What are you saying?"

"That the gods themselves conspired against us. Maybe there was a reason for it."

"Yeah, Merrell was an asshole." He scooped her up in his arms and carried her to the bedroom.

"What are you doing?"

He quirked a grin at her. "Making up for lost time."

Hours later, Galene swallowed hard as she slowly traced the myriad of scars that marred Fain's bare back while he napped by her side. Honestly, she wasn't sure which ones angered her most. The deep, vicious marks from a whip that had to be from his days as a slave, or the surgery scars from when Venik had fused Fain's spinal cord with his ship.

Tears blurred her vision as she tried to imagine the horror he'd suffered. How much rehabilitation must have gone into merging him with his ship's systems. She knew from Talyn's injuries just how long and arduous such recoveries were. Not just physically, but mentally grueling.

And Fain had done it without anyone there to help him through it. No one to wake up to.

That broke her heart.

She knew from her brief conversations with Dancer that he had no idea what Fain had been through. He stupidly thought his brother had joined The Tavali by choice. Dancer had no knowledge that Fain was still enslaved to Venik or that he'd been bound to a cruel human master for a time. One who had used him as nothing more than a cockfighter in the worst sort of blood sport. One that made the Andarion Open Ring fights look like kids' play. Fain had been stripped of his name, his heritage.

Everything.

When Venik had taken custody of Fain, he'd been nothing

more than a piece of feral property. Marked and tagged, and issued a value like other pieces of stolen cargo.

How she wished she'd never gone snooping into Fain's Tavali service files.

But she'd known that Fain would never tell her anything about his past. Her male was too good at keeping his secrets.

With the sound of his soft snore warming her, she pressed her lips to his shoulder and traced the lines of his tattoo. Just as she started to brush her fingers against the small hairs around his navel, he woke up with a beautiful fanged smile.

He shifted slightly to give her more access to his body. "Surely you're not still hungry for me?"

Laughing, she nipped at his shoulder while she gently cupped and caressed him. "Maybe."

He kissed her as he rolled so that she could straddle his hips. But before she could do much more, her link went off with Talyn's ring.

Worried that something might have happened, she grabbed it and answered. "Hey, baby. Is everything okay?"

"Yeah. Sorry, I didn't mean to worry you. Lish and I have something we're doing and we kind of need you here. You got a few?"

"For you? Always. But I'll need a couple of minutes before I head over."

"No problem. And do you know how to reach Hauk? I tried, but he's not picking up his link."

She traced the line of Fain's nose. "Um, yeah, I might know where your father is. Why?"

"Could you bring him with you?"

Now that was a strange request. "Sure. You need me to bring anything else?"

"No. That's all we need."

"All right. I'll be there shortly." She hung up.

"Is something wrong?"

Galene hesitated. "Not quite sure. Talyn didn't sound right."

"Because he asked for me?"

She rolled her eyes at him. "No, silly. His tone of voice was odd." Scooting off him, she pouted. "Sorry."

"Don't apologize. I could die happy right now."

Strangely weak and yet thrilled by his words, she traced the arch of his brow. "Come take a quick shower with me."

Fain obeyed, and followed after her. But when Galene moved to soap his body, he found a whole new level of heaven and hell. "How can you possibly make me this hard again? *Krikkin ey,* it's like being a teen again. Aggravating as hell."

She pulled her hand away. "You want me to stop?"

Catching her wrist lightly, he pressed her open palm against his sac and gently rubbed himself against her smooth skin. "No. But unfortunately, I don't want to piss off Talyn. He already hates me enough." With a heavy sigh, he finished his shower and dressed, while trying not to focus on how incredible her body looked both in and out of her uniform.

As he fastened his shirt, she stopped him. "What are we going to do about your eyes?"

Fain winced as he realized they were still vibrant red. "I have a bad feeling it's permanent this time."

"Do you have any contacts?"

He shook his head. "I never bothered with them, as you were the only female who ever awoke it in me. And since I never thought you'd ever touch me again . . ."

She bit her lip. "What are we going to do?"

He shrugged nonchalantly. "Fuck them all. They need to know if they touch you or Talyn, they have me to deal with. It'll do them good to fear me." He took her hand and pressed it to his cheek. "No more hiding."

"They better not hurt you. Trust me, the only thing worse than a stralen War Hauk is a pissed-off Winged Batur on the rampage. We can go places Hauks only dream of."

Laughing, he kissed her hand and allowed her to lead him to Talyn's new apartment.

He wasn't sure what to expect.

And when they walked in, they both drew up short at what they found.

Dressed in Batur blue, Felicia wore an old-fashioned Andarion wedding gown. The kind that was at least a hundred years old and very delicate and beautiful.

No longer sporting his moustache or goatee, Talyn was in his military dress uniform, and they were surrounded by Gavarian, Brach, Jayne, Morra, Dancer, Sumi, Darice, Kalea, Qorach, Vega, War, and Chayden.

Even more shocking, Felicia's parents were on a split-screen monitor, along with her brother Lorens.

Talyn arched an inquisitive brow at the sight of Fain's eyes, but didn't say anything about it.

"Paka! Paka! Paka!" War shouted as he launched himself into Fain's arms and hugged him tight.

"What's going on?" Galene asked hesitantly as she moved closer to the monitor.

Felicia's mother, who looked a great deal like her daughter, let out a fierce growl. "They don't listen and are being impossible. I told them that they can do this, but that it won't exempt them from a formal unification when they return home. She is my only daughter and he's your only son, by the gods. They are not robbing me of a glorified, humongous ceremony where I can shove my daughter's union down the throat of every snotty family member I have. Especially to a prince *and* a War Hauk!" She paused in her tirade to frown at Fain. "I'm Marna eton Nykyrian, by the way. You must be Fain eton Anatole. It's an honor to meet you, Tiziran."

He inclined his head to her respectfully. "And you, Tarra eton Nykyrian."

Galene smiled warmly. "And I believe Fain is well acquainted with Saren and Lorens?"

"We are," they said in unison.

Felicia cleared her throat. "Now, if my mother can refrain from yelling at me for the next few minutes . . . as you can see, Talyn and I have decided to have a simple Andarion wedding."

"A *common* wedding," Marna mumbled.

"It's legal," Felicia said in a gentle, patient tone. "It's even how the tahrs himself married Tizirah Kiara."

"And they had a formal ceremony later, did they not?"

Rolling her eyes at her mother, Felicia let out an exasperated breath. "Yes, Mum. And don't worry. Talyn and I are more than willing to take our vows a hundred thousand times, once we're home. You will get your grand unification ceremony with all its glory and pomp. We promise. We will take nothing from you."

Talyn laced his fingers with Felicia's. "Please don't be angry at Felicia, *mu tara*. This was all my idea. Having been raised as a bastard and with us at war, I didn't want to risk anything going wrong. I want to make sure both she and the baby are taken care of. Now that I can legally give her a lineage to be proud of, I didn't want to wait another minute. She and the baby need the protection of my lineage with hers. It's not worth the chance of waiting to get home to do a formal ceremony."

That finally succeeded in calming Marna down. "Galene, I've said it before and I'll say it again. Thank you for raising such a wonderful son. He is an honor to you, and this is why I love him as if he were my own."

"Hear, hear," Saren agreed. "And I should mention that I released Felicia's vestal accounts as soon as she told me the news. I put her, Marna, and you, Galene, on them. Spend to your heart's content. There's enough in there to throw her the unification ceremony of the century. One so large, even the tadara will be envious. . . . And since she waited so long to marry, the interest has really accumulated. It should adequately cover everything and make quite a nest egg for her and Talyn. Not that Talyn needs it. I still stipulate he's worth more than I am."

Lorens laughed. "Given the size of his condo and toys, I think he's worth more than both of us put together."

Ignoring them, Talyn turned toward Felicia and lifted the sheer blue veil away from her face. His red eyes glowing, he stared down at her with a tenderness that choked Fain. He knew exactly how his son felt.

With a tender smile, Talyn took her hands into his. "Doctor Felicia Orfanos, born of the houses of ezul Terronova and eton Nykyrian . . . my only heart, my one true soul, and my guiding star, here before these witnesses, I proudly proclaim you as my Ger Tarra Batur, now and forevermore." He kissed her knuckles.

Her lips trembling, Felicia smiled up at him. "Lieutenant Commander Talyn eton Anatole, tiziran of Andaria, the famed and mighty Iron Hammer who has made grown Andarions weep in terror, born of the Warring Blood Clan of Hauk and the Winged Blood Clan of Batur, you are my fierce, shining strength and ever heart. As such, I proudly claim you now and forevermore as *mi Ger Tana, mi courani*." She kissed his hands, then lifted her lips to kiss him.

With tears in her eyes, Galene took Fain's hand and gave him a tenuous, proud and loving smile. He pulled her against him and held her close as they watched their son accept his new wife.

War and Vega threw glitter over them and shouted in happiness.

Marna sniffed back her own tears as she and Saren congratulated them. Lorens chimed in, too. Felicia thanked them and blew them a kiss before she turned their monitors off while Morra, Chayden, and Qory all congratulated Talyn.

Jayne sniffed as she approached Galene and Fain. "Isn't she beautiful in my grandmother's dress? I can't believe it fits so perfectly! Right down to being Batur blue for them."

Galene frowned. "How did you get it here?"

Grinning, Jayne winked at them. "Trisani husband. He told me to pack it before I left home. Said I might need it." She glanced back at Felicia, who was laughing and hugging Gavarian. "I learned a long time ago not to argue or question Hadrian's weird dictates." She reached up and playfully tugged at Fain's braids. "Nice eyes, Hauk."

"Yes, they are," Dancer agreed as he came up behind her. "I hope this means I have to buy two unification presents?"

Fain glanced over to Galene. "We haven't discussed it. There's still a lot to consider. Let's face it. We all know what an asshole I am."

Dancer snorted as Sumi came over to hug Galene. "Congrats on the grandbaby." She cut a meaningful look to Fain. "And on other things."

Galene felt her cheeks heat up as they became the focus of everyone's attention. "This is Talyn's and Felicia's moment. Let's not take anything away from them." And with that, she moved to hug Felicia and kiss her cheek. "I've loved you since the moment I first saw you in the hospital and you told me you were Talyn's female. I can't tell you how much this means to me to officially have you as my daughter."

Felicia blushed. "Thank you, Commander."

"Matarra," she reminded her.

Smiling, Felicia bit her lip. "Yaya, you mean."

Galene hugged her again. "I love you so much, *mia*."

"I love you, too."

She turned to her son. "And you . . ." She squeezed his finally clean-shaven chin. "You're much more handsome like this."

He screwed his face up. "I still hate it. But Felicia made it worth my while."

"Talyn!" Felicia gasped.

"What?" He blinked innocently as he looked over to her. "What'd I say?"

Felicia groaned out loud as Jayne placed her arm around her shoulders and grinned. "Don't be so horrified, Lish. Face it. If it has an engine or testicles, it's bound to give you trouble."

Fain let out a nervous breath as he approached his son. "I'm thinking we should make a quick exit. They're starting to turn on us. This can't be good."

Talyn nodded. "For once, we're on the same side." Then, he indicated Fain's eyes with a jerk of his chin. "Sorry I interrupted the two of you. Now I know why you weren't answering your link when I called."

Fain cringed at Talyn's words. "It's not what you think."

"Yeah, it is. But it's all right. At least I finally know."

Fain scowled. "Know what?"

Talyn turned so that his back was to the rest of the room before he dropped his voice to a faint whisper only Fain could hear. "Why you left her. You didn't do it because you were the dick I thought you were. You did it to protect her."

"How do you know?"

He pointed to his own eyes. "Curse of being stralen. It makes us do incredibly stupidly wrong shit for all the right reasons to protect what we love."

Fain snorted a short laugh at that. "Ain't it the truth?"

Nodding, Talyn held his hand out to him. "Clean slate, Hauk?"

"Clean slate." He took Talyn's hand and pulled him in for a warm hug that he savored.

Galene paused as she caught sight of Fain and Talyn embracing. But what brought tears to her eyes was the expression on Fain's face. The love and pride he had for Talyn. She'd waited a lifetime for this moment and it was far sweeter than she'd ever imagined.

Warmth rushed through her body that the two of them were finally making an effort to put the past behind them and start fresh. A warmth that strangely thickened as Darice and Dancer joined them, and she saw two generations of War Hauks standing together for the first time in decades. Then, she looked over to Felicia, who was holding Kalea and tickling her belly while she laughed with Vega, Morra, and Gavarian. Qory, Brach, and Chayden were joking silently in Qillaq sign language.

It was an odd family, to be sure. But it was all hers and she loved every one of them.

"You okay?"

She glanced over her shoulder at Jayne. "Fine. Just thinking."

Jayne wrapped her arms around her neck and held her like she used to do when Talyn was little and Galene had felt so alone and lost. "I've never seen Fain look so relaxed and happy . . . or you, for that matter."

Closing her eyes, Galene allowed her cousin to rock her. "And that's what scares me, Jaynie. I've never had so much to lose before. Nor so many trying to take it from me."

Hours later, Galene came awake to the sweet, precious warmth of Fain's naked body pressed against hers. His thigh was wedged between hers with his tattooed arm draped over her hip while he had his face buried deep in her braids. He held on to her as if he were afraid of letting go, even to rest. How he could manage to sleep, never mind actually breathe like that, she couldn't imagine. But it didn't appear to bother him at all.

After the small reception in Talyn's apartment, they'd taken Vega and War home, then returned to her condo where they'd spent the rest of the night making up for all the years they'd been apart. She'd made love to him thoroughly and had tasted every vast inch of his lush, muscled body until he'd begged her for mercy.

And a nap.

She never wanted to leave this bed or his arms again. A smile curved her lips as a wave of complete serenity engulfed her.

Until she heard a noise in Fain's room. It was a light scraping, but enough that her heightened Andarion hearing picked it up clearly. It was moving through the living room, coming closer to her bedroom.

"Fain?" she whispered, shaking him slightly.

He woke much slower.

She rolled to her blaster on the nightstand an instant before her bedroom door blew apart.

Cursing, she opened fire on her attackers.

Fain slid from the bed to search for his reserve blaster in the tangled mess of his clothing. She heard him cursing himself for his carelessness.

Meanwhile, their silent attackers spoke to each other in a language she didn't know.

All of a sudden, her blaster jammed. Her heart stopped as she realized they had her dead to rights. She grabbed the lamp to bash them, but before she could blink, Fain launched himself with a growl at the one aiming for her. He slammed the assassin against the wall and literally ripped his throat out before snatching the blaster from the assassin's hand and shooting the closest one. He kicked the falling assassin into a third, then launched himself over their bodies to catch the fourth one and break his neck before he spun around and shot the third one.

Turning, he went to make sure there was no one else in the living room.

A second later, he was back in front of her as an alarm blared from the hallway. "Are you all right?"

Stunned and a little afraid of him, she nodded. Honestly, she'd forgotten just how brutal War Hauks were in battle—how ruthless—and never more so than when protecting family. Since she'd never seen Talyn in a Ring match, it was a side of her son she didn't know. Mostly because she'd never wanted to know what all her son was capable of doing to another sentient being.

It was why everyone on Andaria lived in fear of the War Hauk bloodline. Why their names and family were so celebrated.

Fain placed his cheek to hers. "Call Talyn and warn him in case there are more," he whispered. He stepped away to pull on his pants, then took off to check on their son—still barefoot and without a shirt.

Galene didn't hesitate to obey. Like Fain, she wanted to make sure her son was secured.

Talyn answered a moment later in a groggy tone.

"I've been attacked, baby. Fain said to warn you. They might be headed for you and Felicia."

That cleared his fogginess instantly. "I'm on it. You okay?"

"Yeah." She heard the sound of blaster fire outside Talyn's room.

An instant later, Dancer's voice was in the background, checking on Felicia and Talyn.

"I'm on my way to you." She hung up and pulled her clothes on before she swapped her charge cartridge for a fresh one, and tucked in a few extra. Just in case.

In the hallway, she saw the bloody trail Fain had left. Her throat constricted at the sight of the carnage. *Please don't let that blood be his.*

It was awful and it left her sick to her stomach.

But in all honesty, she was impressed. There were bodies

everywhere. Fain had torn them apart as he headed to secure Talyn and Felicia. She only prayed that he'd made it.

By the time she reached Talyn and Felicia's room, her fears had almost paralyzed her. Yet the moment she saw Felicia with Morra, Jayne, Qorach, Sumi, Kalea, and Darice, she calmed. They had Felicia surrounded like a treasured crown jewel.

"Where's Talyn and Fain?" Galene asked.

Jayne hugged her. "They went out with Dancer, Vari, and Brach to chase after the bad guys. You okay?"

"Rattled. They hit Talyn's old room first." Tears made her vision swim as she glanced to Felicia. "Had his father not changed rooms with him, they would have probably killed him in his sleep."

Felicia rose to her feet with a growl. She grabbed the blaster from Morra's hip and headed for the door in a feral, determined stride.

Qorach caught her and shook his head.

"Q, out of my way! No one goes after Talyn's back. No one! By every god of Andaria, I'm going to find them and skin them alive while they scream!"

The only thing that kept Felicia from attacking the mountainous Qill in an effort to get past him was that her link went off with Talyn's ring. She pulled it from her robe pocket.

"Baby?" she breathed.

"Hey, Lish. We're good. They were League assassins. We cornered them and they killed themselves before we could capture them. You all right?"

"Fine. Where are you?"

The door to her room opened to show Talyn and Fain, with Dancer, Vari, and Brach pulling up the rear. Talyn slid the link into his pocket before he disarmed Felicia and gathered her into his arms.

Fain hesitated in front of Galene.

Relieved that he was still breathing, she quickly examined the blood on his body to make sure it wasn't his. "Were you hurt?"

"No, thanks only to your quick reflexes. I didn't even know they were there. They'd have had my ass, had you not shot them while I fumbled for my blaster." Fain kissed her before he turned his attention to Talyn. "They went for you first. Thank the gods you weren't in your room." He scowled as he glanced about. "Did they go after anyone else?"

"No." Morra jerked her chin toward Galene. "They only went after Galene and Talyn."

Raw, unmitigated fury tore through him over that. He'd just started for the door when it opened to admit Venik, who wore a similarly enraged expression.

The Tavali leader's gaze swept the room as he took inventory of the occupants and their varying stages of dishabille. His gaze narrowed on Fain as he raked him from head to bare feet. "You all right, Hauk?"

Fain wiped at the blood on his face. "More pissed than I've ever been in my entire life. I want the throat of the Porturnum bastard who sold us out to The League."

A strange darkness descended over Venik's features. "No one attacks my base." His scowl deepened as he noted Fain's eyes. "Stralen? Really?"

Fain gave him a snide smile. "Told you it was complicated."

"Everything with you always is. I should have finished killing you when I dragged you off that ship. Teach me to show mercy." He sighed heavily. "We're searching for more League assassins. Everyone's being scanned for IDs, prints, and DNA. All of you have to submit, too. I want anyone who has any ties, past or present, with those bastards. I intend to feast on their entrails."

"I'll come back positive for League ties." Sumi stepped forward. "But I can assure you, I have no love for them, and I didn't do this. I went rogue from my post, and have a staggering price on my head as a result. You can check the reports. Last time I was with Kyr, I almost succeeded in ending this war. If I'm ever near him again, I plan to finish him."

"So you're the woman who almost gutted him. Good job. Shame the slimy bastard escaped."

"Yes, it is."

Fain got his brother's attention. "Did you get anywhere with that recording I sent over?"

"No. The bitch got erased."

He glared at his brother. "Erased?"

Dancer nodded glumly. "I was going to tell you later." He passed a meaningful stare toward Galene. "Didn't want to ruin your night."

Fain ground his teeth. "Well, whoever that little bitch is, he's about to learn what three stralen War Hauks are capable of. I will find him . . . or her, if I have to tear this entire station down, rivet by rivet."

Venik opened his mouth to speak, but the lethal expression on Fain's face backed him down instantly.

Fain moved away from Galene to check the charge levels of his weapons. "We need to split our families up to keep them from becoming a bigger target."

Dancer nodded in agreement. "Nyk has reinforcements headed in."

Galene's and Talyn's links started buzzing with an alert tone.

Fain scowled as they checked the message. "What is it?"

Gasping, Galene went pale. "The League and her allies just bombed the Andarion palace. The heaviest strike was made against the royal family wing."

"Where's Nyk's family?"

Dancer appeared to be one step away from hurling. "They came in for our wedding and have been staying at the palace with Cairistiona ever since . . . even Nyk's father."

With tears in her eyes, Galene handed Fain the link.

Fain cursed before he passed the link to Dancer so that he could see the photo that had been sent to Galene. "They didn't just strike the palace, *drey*. They leveled it. No survivors."

CHAPTER 12

While Galene had held Fain's utmost respect before, he truly saw the depth of her mettle as she kept herself together in the wake of this news. Her spine went straight and her chin lifted defiantly. She met Talyn's gaze. "Tough times never last."

"But tough Andarions do," Talyn finished for her as if it was something she'd said so many times that he knew it by heart.

She inclined her head to him. "We secure our family here. And we move forward with a retaliatory strike. Kyr has to have something he cares about. I want that weakness found and destroyed." She met Dancer's gaze. "Has the tahrs been informed of this?"

"No. They're flying dark so that they can reach us without The League picking them up."

"Then let me know when he lands so that I can inform him."

Dancer indicated him and Jayne. "That's our job. We're

his family and he'll need us. I owe it to him to tell him personally."

Galene choked on a sob. "And Cairie and Tylie were my family."

Talyn started for her, then paused as Fain gathered her in his arms.

Galene patted him on the back before she stepped away and took his hand and Talyn's. "I'm fine. Until bodies are found, we will hold hope sacred in our hearts and pray that they made it to shelter. It's possible they had warning and evacuated."

A slim possibility. But it was one that allowed her to move forward and function.

She narrowed her gaze at Fain. "How many Tavali can you muster?"

"How many you need?"

"A hundred thousand."

His eyes widened at the number. "I can do it. But it'll take some time. Maybe as much as a week to get them mobilized to one place."

"Rendezvous them at Qaris and let me know as soon as they're all there. A group that large will draw notice, so they need to arrive within an hour of each other. Once amassed, I want a strike force with them from the north and us from the south. Every Leaguer in this galaxy is about to get a taste of Alliance vengeance."

Venik let out an evil laugh. "I like your female, Hauk." He saluted Galene. "I'd like to put dibs on the salvage of whatever remains from this."

"If there's anything left of their ships, it's yours to raid." She stepped back. "Now, if you'll excuse me, I have research I need to do, and a battle to plan."

Fain started after her only to find Talyn in his way. The expression on his face said that he was one breath away from ruining the rest of Fain's life.

Or ending it.

"Is there a problem?"

"Don't leave her alone, Hauk. She's not as strong as she pretends to be. She had a very close and strong kinship with the tadara. When no one else was kind to her, Cairie was. They've been best friends for thirty years. Please help, Mum. She has to be dying inside over this."

Cupping Talyn's head, Fain pulled his cheek to his son's. "I love you both," he whispered in Talyn's ear. "And I won't leave her alone."

"Thank you. And for the record, I'm glad you weren't in my bed tonight when they attacked. It's my honor to fight by your side."

Fain tightened his hand in Talyn's braids as those words brought tears to his eyes. Unable to speak past the fierce wave of love that surged inside him, he released his son and went after Galene.

He found her in her office outside the command center. True to Talyn's words, her hands were shaking as she made notes and researched data.

"Stormy?"

Tears glistened in her eyes as she looked up at him. "I was only three the first time I met her. Did you know that?"

He closed the door and crossed the room to stand beside her. "No."

She sniffed back her tears. "It's the first real clear memory of my life. I was in the palace with my paka, who'd gone to give her a physical to make sure she was still fit for military duty while pregnant. I was sitting on the floor, playing outside her suite, when I heard the clicking of sharp boot heels against the marble floor. I looked up and saw the most beautiful female I'd ever seen in my life. Tall. Strong. Proud. Her head high, she wore her red battlesuit like the mythic goddess Kadora. She stopped by my side and smiled down at me."

Galene wiped at her eyes. "I dropped my gaze to her blaster. I'd never been that close to one. 'Are you afraid of me, little one?' she asked. I shook my head no. And she smiled so beautifully and asked if I wanted to touch her weapon. When I said yes, she took it out, ejected the charge cartridge, and handed it over. I was beguiled. My father horrified. He started fussing at me for wasting the tizirah's time. But Cairie quickly shushed him and told me that she wanted me in her armada when I grew up. That she respected my courage and fire."

Covering her face with her hands, she wept as if her heart was broken.

Fain knelt on the floor by her side to gather her into his arms.

"I loved her so much, Fain. You just don't know."

"I'm so sorry, Storm. But you said it yourself. It's possible she wasn't there."

Galene held on to him and to those words. She let his strength melt into her and was grateful to have him here. It was the first time since childhood that she'd had someone she could lean on. While Talyn had done his best to fill that role, she'd always been extremely aware of the fact that she was the parent and that she was supposed to be strong for him. Something that had been so incredibly hard at times.

But with Fain . . .

She could be weak and needy. She didn't have to pretend that this didn't hurt her to the core of her soul. And as that thought went through her mind, she remembered that Fain had also been close enough to the tadara that she'd adopted him. That he was a lifelong friend of others who'd perished.

They *were* his family.

"How are you doing?" she breathed.

He looked away, but not before she saw the heartbreak he was holding inside. "I just keep thinking about the kids. Cairie's lived a long, full and good life, and I'm Andarion enough to appreciate that and be at peace with it. But the kids . . . Zarina's only a few months old, and Thia's just entering the prime of her womanhood. She looks older, but she's just a baby. So full of life and wonder . . . like her brothers. The twins are a wrecking crew of disaster. Jayce and Adron would make Saint Sarn a cursing atheist, and yet I love spending time with all their annoying questions. And Kiara . . . she's the gentlest soul I've ever known." He shook his head. "I refuse to believe they're gone." He spoke between clenched teeth. "I won't accept that."

Galene bit her lip as she sniffed daintily. "Thia's the same age you were when Keris died."

That succeeded in wringing a single tear from him. Angry, he wiped it away. "Did you know Keris's last words to me were '*titana tu, giakon*'?"

She cringed at words that were basically *go fuck yourself, you castrated coward*. "Why would he say that to you?"

His red eyes glistened with grief-stricken agony. "I'd just found Omira in bed with a man and I'd tried to go home. My parents slammed the door in my face and threatened to call the enforcers on me if I didn't leave, so I went to Keris's. I just wanted five minutes of shelter. Instead, he sucker-punched me, insulted me, and left me in the rain on his doorstep."

"I'm so sorry, Fain. Did you never try to speak to him again?"

Shaking his head, he sighed wearily. "I took what little money I had that night and bribed a ride from a Tavali to Rook, hoping I could find work on someone's crew. Since I was Outcast, I had no papers. No Andarion could hire me, and no one else would touch me without legal documents and a birth registration. So I was left scraping for whatever illegal crew was willing to pay me under the table and not ask questions about my background. A week later, I went into a bar for a job prospect, and ended up getting drugged and enslaved. Ven liberated me right before Keris took Dancer on his Endurance. I was planning to talk to Keris to make amends once he was back from it . . . never had the chance. Never was able to say that I was sorry, for everything."

He blinked back his tears. "I was the only one there when they cremated him. All I kept thinking was that I should have been there for Dancer when he fell during his climb, and for the years after that when everyone blamed him for Keris's death. That he was alone in that house with our parents' hatred, and with no brother there to help him through it."

"You were always there for him."

"No. I was only there to help piece things back together after everything fell apart. But I was never there when he really needed me. Anymore than I was there for you or Talyn."

She placed her finger over his lips. "Let it go, Fain. Life is hard. For everyone. We are all warriors fighting our way through it. As I've always said to Talyn, tough times never last. But tough Andarions do. I learned that from watching you as a boy. Your parents, grandparents, and Keris treated you like shit and yet you never once spoke against them. You'd just lift your chin and carry on. 'Barking dogs don't bother me,' you used to say. 'Sooner or later, they reach the end of their yard and hit a fence. I'll keep going past it, and won't hear them any-more.'"

"I was young and stupid."

"Young, yes. Stupid? Never."

He placed her hand on his cheek and savored the warmth of her touch on his skin. "I weep for every nanosecond of my life that I lived away from you."

Overwhelmed by his sincerity, Galene kissed him. Like

Fain, she grieved for all the time they'd lost. All the years that had been stolen from them.

"Commander?"

Irritated by the intrusion, she pulled back from Fain to see the highest-ranking Andarion officer after Talyn and Gavarian, who'd been left on duty. "Yes, Gheris?"

"Sorry to intrude, ma'am, but you really need to see this." He moved to the monitor on her office wall while Fain rose to his feet. He turned it to the Andarion newsfeed.

Galene gasped as she saw Cairistiona's mother, Eriadne, on the screen. Ever regal and harsh, and with a frigid beauty, she was dressed in full royal Andarion battlegear as she addressed the media.

"It is with great sorrow in my heart that I stand before my fellow Androkyns once again. As you all know, my daughter forced me into exile against my will. Over the years, I've tried desperately to reconcile. And she would have none of it. When she began this war against the very League that was founded by our own proud War Hauks to protect us from invasion, I begged her to rethink her foolishness. Ever rebellious like her father before her, Cairistiona refused."

The queen mother gestured to the photos of the leveled Andarion palace. "I have just received word that there are no survivors of the palace attack. Rescuers are working diligently to extract bodies for state burial, but as you can see, there is very little that remains, and we will be lucky if we find any remains at all."

Eriadne sniffed back tears. "I, like all of you, am devastated by such a tragic loss of lives taken far too soon. But as the War Hauk motto says, *indurari*. Through blood pain, we conquer and endure. Andaria will continue on as she always has. And to ensure that no other Andarion family has to stand over the graves of their children for such a needless cause, I have again reclaimed the throne that was so violently taken from me, and entered talks with the prime commander of The League. Commander Zemin is more than willing to forgive our transgressions so long as we deliver the traitor Nykyrian Quiakides over to him for execution. With a heavy heart, I have agreed to his terms to sacrifice my grandson for the good of our empire. For the good of the families I don't want to see lose another loved one in a futile war that can only end in our inevitable deaths, and the end of our beloved empire and proud families."

Lifting her chin, she drew a ragged breath. "I am recalling all Andarion soldiers from their off-world posts and severing our ties with the Alliance, effective immediately. Failure to return home, and any who stand with this so-called Alliance against The League, will result in their being declared traitors to the empire. This includes Prime Commander Batur, who is currently overseeing Alliance forces on an enemy base. If she contacts me immediately, and returns, she and her staff will be forgiven for their actions against our race and their treason against The League. But they must go before The League and do contrition, purification, and reeducation for their actions. Once repatriated, we will welcome them home."

Galene ground her teeth at those words. Contrition, her left foot. She'd assassinate that bitch first.

"From this broadcast forward, Andaria is again part of The United Systems and falls under the protection of The League and agrees to abide by the laws of The Overseer." She inclined her head to her soldiers, who began burning the tattered Alliance flag they'd taken from the attack, and hoisting a United Systems flag over the remains of the palace.

Eriadne saluted the media. "All hail Andaria. We are forever united in purpose and we will strike with a precise hand." The queen bitch finished with the national Andarion motto. "Forever forward. Never back." And with that, she left the podium.

The media shouted questions as Gheris turned the monitor off. His gaze went from her to Fain and back again. "I will stand with whatever decision you make, Commander. But know that my sister was taken and raped under the former tadara's regime, by one of her nephews. She did nothing to punish those responsible, even though we knew who they were and could prove it. Instead, my sister was imprisoned and executed for treason for daring to impugn royal reputations. Tadara Cairistiona and Tahrs Nykyrian restored honor and law to our empire. Regardless of what you decide, I will not be part of handing Tahrs Nykyrian over to The League for his execution."

"Put your heart at ease, Colonel. My loyalties are with the tahrs. He is the true heir to the throne, not the former tadara. I have my own issues and grudges with that bitch. But I will not force any of you to follow my path. Tell the others that they can stay or go with no fear of retaliation from me. In this, I won't be their conscience. I understand that all of you have families at home. Go in peace or stay and fight." She offered him a gentle smile. "If they wish to go, escort them out immediately, and notify our home troops to expect them."

He saluted her. "I shall tell them, but I know their hearts are loyal to you. It's why Commander Batur selected us for this assignment. We all have issues with the former tadara and The League." He turned on his heel and left them.

Galene rose to her feet to face Fain. "That whore killed them."

Fain let out a heavy sigh. "As much as I'd like to say that no mother could do such a thing, I agree. She slaughtered most of her family to take the throne the first time. It only stands to reason that she'd kill the rest to regain it."

Galene reviewed the footage of Eriadne's speech without the sound. "Where's Tiziran Jullien?"

Fain moved to stand by her side. "She didn't mention him, did she?"

"No." She paused to show an old enemy in the background. "Nyran is there." She pointed him out. "But there's no sign of Jullien, anywhere."

"You think he was in the palace when it went up?"

She shook her head. "He was exiled when his grandmother was thrown out. To my knowledge, he hasn't been near Eris since. But why wouldn't she have mentioned him as stepping forward with her? It's weird. With the others gone, would he not be her sole heir?"

Her link rang with Talyn's tone.

She clicked it on. "Yes, baby?"

"Hey, have you seen the Andarion news?"

"That Eriadne has proclaimed herself tadara again. Yes."

"I know this is rhetorical, but are we staying or leaving?"

"I don't trust that bitch as far as I can spit . . . and I don't spit. The ninth sun will freeze solid before I return to an Andaria ruled by her. What about you?"

"You know *exactly* how I feel about her. And I know from experience how much faith you can put in her lies. But regardless of my personal revulsion, I will stand with my mother in all wars. That being said, Felicia's brother called to let us know that her father has been seized and is in custody, awaiting trial for treason. They're planning to execute him, and all of Cairie's loyal advisors. WAR is attempting to reestablish itself, but it's been awhile since we've had any contact with each other. After Cairie took the throne, we disbanded harmoniously, assuming Andarions no longer had to fear Anatole tyranny."

"Is Lorens safe?"

"Yeah. He's on the run with his family and Felicia's mother. He wanted us to make sure Vari and Brach don't return home until this is settled. I promised him that I'd sit on both of them like a mother hen."

"How's Felicia doing?"

He cleared his throat and waited a few seconds as if putting distance between him and her before he spoke in a whispered tone. "She's acting brave. But you know how much she loved Kiara and the kids. She was taking it hard before Lorens called. Now . . . if she could fly, she'd be on her way home to slaughter Eriadne herself. Thank the gods I was never able to teach her how to pilot a fighter."

Galene snorted. "We still have a traitor here. I'm assuming the new tadara wants us all dead. So stay with Felicia and keep her safe."

"What about you?"

"I have your mother," Fain said before she could answer. "I won't let anything happen to her. I swear it on my life."

Galene angled the link so that Talyn could see Fain. "My two fierce protectors."

Talyn saluted Fain. "Let me know if either of you need anything."

She hung up an instant before Fain's link went off.

Galene stepped closer to him to see who it was. She recognized the ambassador's seal. "Ryn?"

"Yeah." He answered it.

"Is your brother with you, Fain?" Ryn asked without preamble.

"Not at the moment, but he's here on the station. Why?"

Silent tears began streaming down Ryn's face. "Darling was in the Andarion palace when it was hit . . . with Zarya and Cezar." He barely choked the words out.

Fain struggled to breathe as those words struck him in the gut. Zarya was Darling's wife, and Cezar their infant son. In one blow, Eriadne had wiped out the Caronese emperor and his heir. "Oh God, Ryn. I'm so sorry. I thought he was with Nyk."

His hand shaking, Ryn raked it through his red hair. "We

haven't told Annalise yet. We can't. . . . She was way too close to her brother . . . she thinks Darling is headed for you. . . ." He paused to swallow and rub his hand over his face. It was obvious he wasn't handling it well, either. Like his half sister Annalise, Ryn worshiped his half brother Darling.

"Even though he's underage, Drake has assumed the Caronese throne with the CDS backing him. Maris had just headed out to you from the Andarion palace. Less than two hours before it was struck. He doesn't know about the hit, either, but his son and husband were also there. So was Desideria, Vashe, Lil. Shahara, Kasen, and Devyn." Ryn broke off into tears. "They took our families, Fain. *All of them*."

"I thought Ture was on Caron."

"No. They were planning to go, but they hadn't left yet. They wanted to make sure their husbands were safe first. And be together so that they could muster a rescue party if something happened." Fury burned deep in Ryn's eyes. "Tell Commander Batur that I'm mobilizing every fucking member of the Wasturnum for her to command and we are already en route for battle. As are the Caronese and Exeterians. We're going to ram our vengeance down the throat of any and every soldier dumb enough to don a League uniform." He hung up without preamble.

His own hand trembling, Fain slid his link into his pocket as he struggled to wrap his mind around the tragedy of the day. It was so overwhelming, it left him in a strange state of numbness. As if the pain had gone so deep into his soul that it cut through all the nerves.

Sadly, though, he knew it wouldn't last. Sooner or later, that numbness would pass and with it would come the true agony and reality of the fact that in one day he'd lost the majority of everyone who mattered to him. Everyone he called family.

Horrified, he stared at Galene. "How did they get past their forces?"

Galene shook her head. "We were betrayed. Someone had to give them our codes. There's no other way they could have infiltrated the net. Most likely Ilkin or someone else with the highest clearance . . . I-I should have stayed on Andaria."

"No. They'd have had you, too. The entire block where your condo was, as well as the Andarion armada command center, is leveled. Had you or Talyn stayed, you'd be dead with the others."

Galene wiped at her tears with the heel of her hand as she struggled for sanity in the midst of this utter lunacy, and the blinding need she had inside her to tear Eriadne apart. "This wasn't about the war. This was Eriadne using it as an excuse to punish us all for our part in dethroning her. She told us that if she had to wait a hundred years, she'd stand over our graves, crown on her head, and laugh at her vengeance against us."

Fain wanted to deny that, but given what he knew of the tadara and her bloodthirsty vindictiveness, he couldn't. "You were part of it?"

Galene nodded. "Talyn and I both."

"How so?"

"Chrisen started the fight by coming after me and Felicia, and threatening us. Talyn finished it in the Ring. He took Chrisen's life, and Eriadne took out contracts on his. Back then, WAR was in its prime."

"WAR?"

"Warriors Against Royalty. A radical group set on over-throwing Eriadne. We wanted no part of WAR originally. Not until Talyn was imprisoned by Chrisen and Merrell, for no other reason than being born your child." More tears glistened in her eyes. "When we got him back, he was broken, Fain. I'd never seen him like that, and I pray to the gods that I never do again. He was so angry and bitter by what they'd done."

"What happened?"

She drew a ragged breath. "Nykyrian had returned by a chance encounter with his mother and aunt. I helped to sober Cairistiona, and we went after that bitch for every wrong she'd ever done us. After it was over, I told Cairie to kill her. That so long as Eriadne lived, she'd be plotting all our deaths. But she's Cairie's mother, so Cairie refused. Just like she couldn't bring herself to hurt Jullien. So, she exiled them. Now . . ." She gestured toward the photos of the smoldering palace. "What kind of Andarion slaughters her entire family for power? That's a human move."

He pulled her against his chest. "I know."

The alarm to warn that aircraft were approaching sounded in the hallway.

Galene clutched at him. "That'll be the tahrs."

Fain's gut clenched with dread. This was the last thing he ever wanted to do. But he wasn't about to leave Dancer to do it alone.

Hand in hand, they went to tell Nykyrian and the others that their families were dead. Killed at the hands of his own ruthless grandmother.

CHAPTER 13

His stomach cramped with grief, dread, and barely restrained rage over the injustice of it all, Fain stood with Jayne, Dancer, Chayden, Sumi, and Galene as he waited for Nyk and his group to disembark. He really, really didn't want to do this. But he knew the others didn't relish the task any more than he did. No one wanted to tell Nyk, Syn, Maris, or Caillen that their families were gone.

Damn it to hell. . . .

Galene reached out and took his hand into hers. Fain didn't look at her, but the comfort of that single touch was almost enough to send him to his knees. Closing his eyes, he selfishly savored the fact that she was with him for this. That *his* immediate family was safe.

He just wished that he'd been able to spare his friends their pain.

Completely unaware of what had happened, Maris, Caillen, and Syn joined Nykyrian before they headed toward them as a single group. They were bantering among each other as they always did. Something that made this all the more difficult and painful to do.

The rest of the troops they'd brought with them were still disembarking and being rounded up by Tavali and Sentella officers, who were briefing them on what had happened.

Nykyrian scowled as soon as he saw them and realized they were a much more somber group than normal. He stopped dead in his tracks as if he had a bad premonition. "What's happened?" His accented tone turned brittle and thick.

Fain and Galene exchanged grief-stricken looks before Dancer stepped forward to clear his throat.

Sumi put her hand on Dancer's shoulder to steady and comfort him. He covered her hand with his and locked gazes with Nykyrian to answer the question. "The League . . . they got through Andarion defenses and leveled the palace and every-thing around it."

Fain watched Nyk receive those words with an icy stoicism that only a veteran assassin could manage. He didn't even blink. Caillen, however, staggered back until Syn caught his brother-in-law and steadied him so that he didn't fall.

Maris choked and sputtered. All the color faded from his face, leaving his dark beard a stark contrast to his skin. "Survi-vors?" he breathed, his voice cracking.

Dancer shook his head as tears filled his eyes.

Out of nowhere, Safir, Maris's younger, dark-haired brother, appeared to pull Maris against him and hold him tight to his chest as Maris screamed out in agony. The sound echoed through the bay, causing everyone to wince in sympathy.

Nyk still didn't move. He'd had six children in that palace, ranging in ages from four months to his oldest who was just entering adulthood. His wife had been there. His mother and father. Aunt and her partner. Not to mention his friends who were as close to him as any sibling could be, and their children and spouses.

It was so unfair.

And still Maris's soul-wrenching sobs echoed through the bay as Safir held him.

Caillen turned and started for a ship, but Syn caught him again. "What are you doing?"

"I'm going to fucking kill them all!"

"Who, Cai? Other than yourself?"

Tears fell fast and furiously down his cheeks. "Kasen was with them! My son and daughter! Shay and Dev were there! Damn you, Syn, you heartless piece of shit! How can you be so calm? Don't you care?"

His dark eyes filled with rage, Syn went for his throat.

Fain caught the blow that would have left Caillen on the floor, searching for his teeth, had it made contact with him. "Hey!" He put space in between them as Chayden moved in to take control of Caillen. "You need to calm down and remember that everyone grieves differently. Doesn't mean they don't care. You don't judge people in pain, and you damn sure don't lash out at them when they've lost what Syn has! There's not a one of us here who hasn't been gutted today. Now get ahold of yourself, Caillen, and breathe. This is not the time for us to turn on each other. We have to stand together now more than ever."

Caillen wiped at his eyes as Chayden pulled him into his arms to comfort him. Honestly, Fain was amazed at how well Chayden was holding together given how much he worshiped his sister and niece and nephew who'd been lost. "Don't worry, brother," he whispered against Caillen's head. "We're going to tear them to pieces. For Vashe and Lil and Des." He finally broke on a sob as he said his sister's name.

Fain turned toward Syn, who was as stoic as Nykyrian. But then they had no choice. Death had always been a brutal part of their lives, and especially for Syn. "You all right?"

Syn gave a slow, subtle shake of his dark head. "I just had my heart ripped out and fed to me. Of course I'm not okay." He passed a look to Nykyrian that if Fain didn't know better, he'd swear they were two Trisani speaking with telepathy.

Then again, they'd been friends for so long, the two of them *could* read each other's minds. And in this, they were united in malice.

Justice was all about making two bodies where only one had been. Kill them all and let the gods sort it out.

With a cold-blooded snarl, Nykyrian met Galene's gaze. "Jullien in charge of the attack?"

"No. Nothing's been mentioned about him. Your grand-mother has resumed the throne and is returning Andarion allegiance to The League. Ambassador Dane notified us that

Emperor Cruel's brother Drakari has been voted in by the CDS, and he's preparing a retaliatory strike as soon as he can muster one."

Jayne rubbed Nykyrian's arm to comfort him as Morra and Qory joined their group. "Eriadne and Kyr are demanding you surrender to them immediately for a public execution."

Nykyrian actually let out a chilling laugh. "Eriadne should know by now how hard I am to kill. The bitch doesn't have an army *that* large." Without a word, he walked back toward the hangar. "Fuel my ship," he called to one of the workers. "I want to launch immediately."

Dancer ran after him. "Nykyrian? What are you planning?"

He turned on him with a snarl. "Nykyrian's dead. This is about Nemesis rising to strike down the bastard who dared to take what I love. And I'm going to shove it down his throat right before I put him out of all our miseries."

"Wait!" Safir shouted as he let go of Maris to follow after Nykyrian. "Kyr didn't do this."

Nykyrian turned toward him with an arched brow. "Explain."

"Don't get me wrong. My brother's guilty of a lot of malice and cruelty." He gestured toward his bruised and battered face that was still healing from the round of torture he'd suffered at Kyr's own hands. His brother had even sheared off Saf's long black hair—an act of disgrace for an assassin, and done for no other purpose than to shame Safir, who'd been one of the League's best assassins. And all because Saf had refused to kill Maris, and had helped his brother escape Kyr's troops by

allowing Maris to use him as a human shield rather than murder Maris in cold blood. "But I know he's not responsible for
attacking the palace."

"Yeah, right." Syn narrowed his gaze. "What makes you so
sure about that?"

"The children." Safir glanced to Maris, who was finally starting to calm down. "You've always wanted to know what made
him change that summer when he was seventeen. . . . His wife
and daughter were brutally slaughtered."

Maris wiped at his eyes. "He was never married."

"Yes, he was. You can ask Zander if you don't believe me.
He's the one who told me the story a few months ago. It's why
Kyr assaulted you so vehemently at your wedding to Tams. In
his mind, you were callously throwing away what he'd been
denied."

Maris scowled. "I don't understand."

"She wasn't of noble birth or Naglfari. A common foreigner
Kyr met and fell in love with. He worshiped her, but because
Kyr was heir, Father refused to allow him to marry her and
betrothed Kyr to another female. One of our own. Kyr balked
and joined The League to get away from Phrixus and Father's
dictates. Father was furious, and to punish him, he had Kyr
moved from the League armada that he'd joined to assassin
training as punishment so that Kyr wouldn't be able to marry
anyone at all. What Father didn't know was that Kyr had already married the woman, and that she was pregnant with his
child. About a year later, Huwin Quiakides found out about the
marriage and ordered his wife and child killed, per League

dictates. Kyr was on a link with her, trying to get to her to save her, when she died. He heard everything. And it destroyed him."

Nykyrian cursed under his breath. "That's why he turned psychotic when I took the warrant on my father and killed him."

Saf nodded. "He wanted the kill himself. It's also why he has never once, as prime commander, ordered the death of any child. Think about it." He looked to Maris. "It's why Terek wasn't killed when his mother was. Why the League assassins left your son in his crib, safe and unharmed. Kyr made it clear that if any of us touched a child, he would slaughter us where we stood." He turned back to Nykyrian. "He trained you. You know how he thinks. What his policies are. Better than anyone."

Sumi let out a nervous laugh. "It's why he never harmed Kalea. He threatened it, but I had the best of care until I delivered her. My training didn't begin until after Kyr had been assured I was fully healed and physically able to endure it."

Nykyrian glanced away as a tic started in his jaw. "Yeah, I would call bullshit, but that actually explains some of the stranger things I saw him do when I was in The League with him. Still, it changes nothing." Closing his eyes, he visibly struggled with his anger and guilt.

Jayne tried to hug him.

He gently moved away from her side. "I don't want comfort, Jayne. There's nothing inside me right now, except the need to make that bitch who birthed my mother, and anyone who had a hand in this, bleed out of every orifice."

Caillen wiped at his tears with the back of his hand. "Are

we sure there are no survivors? Desi's tough. Shahara even more so. They had VIK with them. They could have—"

"Eriadne wouldn't have left a survivor. She callously served poison to her own brother and his kids, and watched them eat it and die in front of her. She kept my mother in a drugged stupor for almost half her life and handed me over to humans to torture and kill when I was just a child. That bitch has no semblance of a soul. . . . Dammit, I should have never left." Throwing his head back, Nyk bellowed with rage.

With tears in his eyes, Syn growled low in his throat. "I give them credit. They found a way to make sure none of us have a clear head for battle."

Nykyrian scoffed. "What she underestimated was our combined determination. We won't be burning the queen in effigy. She's the one we'll set fire to on the lawn of the palace grounds." His features even grimmer than normal, he started for the command center.

"Tahrs?"

They all hesitated at the unfamiliar sultry feminine voice.

Fain scowled as he saw the last thing he expected. A Gorturnum contingency.

And not just any group.

He knew by the female's Canting that this was Trajen's right hand. Vice Admiral Ushara Altaan. A female whose personal motto was to never go to bed angry, but rather stay up and plot revenge. While no one had any idea what she really looked like beneath her Tavali mask and heavy war-paint makeup, they all knew what happened to those who crossed her.

A closed-casket funeral, provided your loved ones were lucky enough to find some bone fragments or skin cells to run through a DNA scanner to identify your remains.

Dressed in typical Tavali gear, she wore a black-on-black tight leather battlesuit that hugged an extremely pregnant body. One that appeared four, maybe five months past her due date— which was doubly shocking since her last known husband had been brutally slaughtered years ago, and no male had been brave enough to go near her since.

Her face was painted stark white with thick, bold stripes beginning below her eyes and nose in sharp geometrical angles— gold, electric blue, metallic purple, and then three thin red lines in a distinct pattern of some ancient Andarion lineage Fain didn't recognize. That, along with her silvery-white eyes, height, and the hint of fangs when she spoke betrayed her Andarion heritage, but like Nykyrian and in total contradiction of their species, she had snow-white hair.

Nykyrian drew a ragged breath. "Admiral, this is a really bad time."

"I know, Highness, but really, you and your friends want to speak with me. Immediately and in private. I'm afraid I have to insist."

When Nykyrian started for the commcen, she recklessly stopped him.

"Again, Tahrs, I insist, and I'd rather we speak aboard my ship where I know we can't be overheard by a spy."

They exchanged puzzled frowns before Nykyrian finally agreed. Curious, they followed her toward her vessel.

323

Fain glanced around as more Gorturnum landed in the station. Venik was getting a full house. Something that would make him really cranky. Even though he'd agreed to it, he never played well with others. And he really hated when the other Nations ventured into his territory.

He also noted how nervous Galene was with Ushara's arrival.

"You said you didn't really know her?" she whispered to him.

"Yeah. No idea what this is about."

She bit her lip. "You think it's a trap?"

"It's not a trap, Commander," Ushara said with a smile as she rubbed her distended belly. "Let's face it, I'm not exactly at top fighting speed at the moment. I'm pretty sure you could take me in this condition. Not that I would risk my son in a fight."

Galene laughed. "Sorry, Admiral. I didn't mean to insult you."

"No insult. I don't blame you for being suspicious. These are troubling times."

Once they were all on board, Ushara closed the ramp and led them toward a conference room. Since they didn't know what to think, no one spoke. They merely waited and stayed alert for any sort of trick.

After they took their seats, Ushara turned on her monitor.

Galene and Nykyrian gasped as a recording of Jullien eton Anatole appeared. Only he looked a *lot* different than the last time any of them had seen him. No longer the corpulent, haughty prince they all despised, he was dressed in rugged

Tavali Gorturnum gear and had shed about two hundred pounds. Or more to the point, he'd turned that weight into lean, solid muscle.

With a raw masculinity he'd never had before, he pulled the skull-decorated blast helmet from his head to expose his thick black hair and whiskered face before he spoke from what appeared to be an underground shelter of some sort. "Greetings, brother. I know I'm the last creature you want to see right now, but I had to let you know that everyone's safe, and that I'm sorry I couldn't forewarn you about The League attack on the palace. By the time I found out what Nyran and Eriadne had planned, there wasn't enough time to call you or Matarra, and I wasn't sure either of you'd even believe me. I didn't know who else to trust. So I did the only thing I knew to do. I came myself to secure them."

Jullien turned the camera and panned it around to show them their families. Cairistiona and Aros stood together, beside Tylie and her partner Kelsei. They were a bit disheveled in their pajamas and coats, but that didn't matter.

They were blissfully alive and not being held prisoner.

Cairie smiled at the camera. "*Mi tana,* breathe easy. Jullien literally pulled us out minutes before everything went up in flames. We owe him our lives. I love you. Have no fear for us."

Aros inclined his head. "She's right. We're all fine." He stepped back to show the children, who were complaining about the toys that had been left behind, and Thia who grumbled about a broken nail and not having a hairbrush.

Shahara and Zarya were both napping on the floor, with

their children nestled beside them while Ture was changing Terek as the baby gnawed on his fist.

He smiled and waved. "I'm all right, Mare-bear. T, too. We just want you to be safe." He held Terek up to wave. "We love you."

Darling, who was working on rewiring Syn's mecha body-guard VIK for Syn's son, was the next one to speak. "Yeah, Nyk, I don't trust your brother, either. He's a bloody, traitorous bastard. We know it. But . . . He has given us one hell of a tactical advantage. The League thinks we're dead and that you're rattled and reactionary. So long as they think we're dead, they're not coming after us, and you can focus on kicking their asses with a clear head and single-minded focus. Use this to the best advantage possible and don't let either of my brothers do *any*-thing stupid while I'm gone. I know I'm asking a lot, but I'd like to still have an empire when I get out of here." Then Darling slid his gaze over to Jullien. "And if *your* brother gets frisky, don't worry. I will end him. Shahara will help. She already took two shots at him."

Jullien wore an irritated grimace as he turned the camera back on himself. "Anyway, Nykyrian, I know you have absolutely no reason to trust me. And I know you're fighting with one hand tied behind your back so long as you're worried about whether or not I'm going to betray you when you least expect it. So as an act of good faith, to let you know that I understand that I hold in my hands everything in this universe you treasure, I've placed in your hands my very heart and soul. The very means by which to destroy me. And with you being a former League assassin, I know you won't hesitate to do so if I fuck this up. . . . I have your wife and family in my custody. So I have sent to you *my* wife, daughters, and sons. Please, protect them. . . . I can't live without them, brother. They are all I have in this world. All that means anything to me. You are the only one I would ever trust them with."

Tears filled Jullien's hazel green eyes as he swallowed hard. "Shara, I love you, *munatara a la frah.* I'll be home as soon as I can. Don't you dare have Vidarri without me. And don't let Vasili fight without my brother winging him. I swear I'll loosen the noose on him soon, but he's not as skilled a fighter as he thinks he is, and I don't want to bury our son. He's just not ready to fight in this war. Kiss the girls for me, and tell Mira to be brave for her paka." The screen went black.

Nykyrian didn't move for a full minute.

Honestly, none of them did. They were too stunned by the male they'd just seen. That was *not* the soulless piece-of-shit prince who'd once made their lives hell. Not only had he seemed caring, he'd even appeared humble. Kind.

What the hell?

Fain could barely wrap his head around the stunning transformation.

No one had a change of heart that dramatic without some serious life-altering trauma behind it.

Who had taken the stick out of Jullien's ass and beaten him with it?

"Mama?" An adorable dark-headed little girl pushed open the door to peer in at them. "Are you in here?"

327

"Dammit! Viv! Leave Mom alone! What did I tell you!"

Ushara made record time for her condition rushing to the door. "Vasili! What have I told you about your language? And in front of your sisters, no less!"

"Sorry, Matarra. She got off the chain while I was trying to keep Mira from climbing the walls. Literally. I swear to the gods there has to be a spider in someone's DNA. And I am never having kids if it's yours."

As if to prove her older brother's point, the little girl shot between her mother's legs and ran full speed toward Nykyrian. She skidded to a halt by his side and stared up at him, bug-eyed and slack-jawed. Then she looked at Fain, Dancer, Galene, and Talyn in turn.

"Are you going to kill me?" she breathed at Galene.

"No," Galene gasped as she knelt in front of the child. "Why would you ask that?"

" 'Cause . . .'cause that's what all Andarions do to Fyrebloods. You kill us 'cause you don't like us and what we can do, and . . . and Paka says we gots to be extra careful 'cause bad Andarions hate him even more than they hate us. Are you bad Andarions who are going to kill my paka?"

With an indulgent smile, Ushara returned to brush her hand through her daughter's dark hair. "No, Viv. They're good Andarions. This is Prime Commander Batur." She took her daughter's hand and led her to Nykyrian. "And this one is your uncle that your paka has spoken of so many times."

Viv scowled at him. "But you don't look like my paka's twin. You look more like a Fyreblood. Are you one of us?"

Nykyrian scowled, then caught himself, as he must have realized how terrifying that expression would be to a small child. "No, I'm not a Fyreblood." They, like the winged flying clans Galene was descended from, were a very rare, pale-skinned, blond breed of Andarion that could actually breathe fire. At one time they had been revered as gods on Andaria. And as such, Eriadne had viewed them as a threat to her power and had ordered all members of their race hunted down and executed— just as she'd done the winged clans. It had been a brutal time in Andarion history known as the Purging Years. Another reason no one wanted Eriadne back on the throne.

After kneeling down, Nykyrian held his hand out for his niece to shake in greeting. "I'm your paka's fraternal twin. Not identical." He met Ushara's gaze. "You really married my brother? Willingly?"

Laughing at his dry tone, she nodded as she gently took her daughter from the room and handed her off to her brother.

Vasili looked much more like his mother. Tall and blond, with white eyes and fangs. But he was older than Nykyrian expected. Probably around eighteen.

He scooped Viv up in his arms and left them.

Closing the door, Ushara faced Nykyrian. "Jullien's not the same boy you knew. And I'm very sorry for what he did to you and your wife. Believe me when I say that Jullien is scarred by it, too. More than you'll ever know."

"It's not just what he did to Kiara," Dancer said bitterly as he crossed his arms over his chest and glared at her.

Galene nodded. "I'm in agreement with that. I'm not too

sure I won't shoot him in the head should our paths ever cross again."

Ushara sighed sadly. "I know. There are no secrets between us. My husband has much to atone for. But I would remind you all that there is no one here without a sordid past, and enemies aplenty who would level horrid tales about you as well." She turned to Nykyrian. "Especially you, Tahrs. You were a trained League assassin. The best who has ever lived. How many innocent souls stain your hands?"

"What I did, I did to survive."

"Yeah," Dancer chimed in. "And that goes for the rest of us. We didn't grow up in palaces, surrounded by guards who were willing to lay down their lives for our protection. With our every whim catered to."

She laughed bitterly. "No? What of Darling Cruel? Is he not a prince?" Then she glanced at Saf and Maris. "As well as the ambassador and his brother?"

They exchanged shamed looks at that. All of them knew the horrors that had come with Darling's noble lineage. As bad as their pasts were, they paled in comparison to the hell he'd been through.

And Maris's had been no better.

Ushara approached Nykyrian slowly. "Your grandmother told Jullien that she had you killed, and that if he didn't fall in line with her will, he would follow you to the grave, and that no one would mourn his passing. *No one.* He was only six at the time. When your mother learned of your death, and Jullien went to comfort her, do you know what she said to him? 'My precious Nykyrian is dead—he was my entire hope for this empire. Why couldn't it have been you who died?' "

Nykyrian winced.

Ushara ground her teeth as she swept a look over them all. "From the moment your mother crawled inside her grief over losing you, Jullien was an abandoned orphan left to find his own way, with no one there for him. Your father was so busy trying to save your mother from the drugs your grandmother was feeding her that for years he ignored Jullien completely. So Jullien was left alone to deal with a brutal grandmother who had coldly murdered her entire family, including her husband, children, siblings, and their children, as well as anyone else she viewed as a threat to her power. And while Tylie always adored you and your mother, she bitterly despised and belittled Jullien. Why? Because he happens to physically favor her brother who tried to murder her . . . as if he could help that. From the moment of his birth, everyone around him plotted his assassination. By the time he was twelve, nine attempts had been made on his life. Three of them by his cousin Merrell. But no one would ever believe him, and he couldn't prove it. When Jullien was ten and tired of being threatened and living in a constant state of fear that his own family was going to kill him, he begged your father to let him live on Triosa with him, and do you know what your father said?"

Nykyrian paled. "I can't imagine."

" 'I don't have time to fight with your grandmother for your custody. It's not worth the battle or upset. Besides, you won't be any more welcomed on Triosa than you are on Andaria.

As you know, my parents don't want you here and it would be awkward for you to live with us full time. You're much better off on Andaria where you kind of blend in with the population.'" Ushara let out a bitter laugh. "You probably don't remember your paternal grandparents since they died before you returned to Triosa. Count yourself lucky in that regard. How I wish Jullien had been spared their bitter cruelty."

Her eyes flared with rage as she swept her gaze around the room. "All of you mocked him for his obesity, but the only comfort he ever had was from an old Andarion cook he'd sneak off to see, and while she wasn't kind to him, she wasn't hostile either. His words . . . she tolerated me with a semblance of compassion. And when your grandmother found out about it, she had her executed for making Jullien weak and unattractive."

Dancer growled low in his throat. "That still doesn't excuse what he did to us in school."

She turned on him. "Jullien didn't crash your pod, Dancer. Chrisen did. When Jullien started back inside to save you, Chrisen grabbed and held him so hard that he still bears the scars from it. It's what they argued over. And while that accident damaged you, it saved your life. Merrell and Chrisen had planned to kill you when you joined the armada, just as they'd done your brother Keris. It was why Jullien hacked your League files and disqualified you for military service. It wasn't just because of your sister-in-law. And he picked on you around them because had he ever truly befriended you, *War Hauk*, they would have murdered you instantly . . . as they did every friend he tried to make, and both the females he'd been pledged to. Dear gods, by the time he was exiled from Andaria, he was afraid to even sleep with a female for fear of what they might do to her. And don't think for one minute, they spared him from their cruelty. Like your mother, he was drugged most of the time he lived at the palace. You all assumed he chose that lifestyle, but he didn't."

She turned toward Nykyrian. "As for the stolen ring incident when you were in school together, he was trying to save *both* your lives. Had your grandmother discovered you were alive then, she'd have executed you both. Merrell *and* Chrisen were already plotting how to murder you and him before anyone recognized you. He thought jail would get you out of their sights and keep you from their reach. It might have been misguided, but he was a child and every move he made was highly monitored and always reported. And let me reiterate that they kept him drugged out of his mind most of the time."

Nykyrian folded his arms over his chest as he glared at her. "And handing my wife over to my enemies?"

"Your adoptive brother, you mean? The man who was the stepfather of your daughter and an old friend of Jullien's? Aksel went to him and promised Jullien that he wouldn't harm Kiara. He'd sworn that he was only going to use her to get you out of the way and that she would be released unharmed. Jullien never meant for her to be hurt. And yes, Jullien did want you dead— just as you wanted him dead. He's not proud of that, but when you returned and your mother and father threw him aside for you, he felt like he'd lost what little he had. Need I remind you, it was *your* picture, alone, your mother wore over her heart. Not Jullien's. Your mother, your aunt, and your father turned on him when you came back, as if he was the one who'd sent you away. And your grandmother made it quite clear to him that if he didn't get rid of you, she'd kill you both."

"And assaulting Talyn?"

Fain arched a brow at Galene as instantaneous rage tore through him. "What was that?"

Galene nodded slowly as she gestured toward the mark on their son's neck. "When Talyn was assigned to his personal guard, Jullien had him branded a traitor, scarred as an Outcast, and thrown into prison. They broke both his legs and left him for dead on Onoria." Angry tears glistened in her eyes. "My baby was barely twenty years old and had *never* done anything to Jullien."

Ushara swallowed hard. "I know, Commander. I know. Merrell and Chrisen played on Jullien's insecurities and jealousy where his mother was concerned. She doted on you and Talyn, to the exclusion of her own son. And it cut Jullien to the root of his heart. Sadly, the whole horrible event started as a stupid prank Jullien was put up to by Merrell, that got way out of hand and quickly escalated to an extremely regrettable level. Merrell was the one who scarred and branded Talyn, not Jullien. And yes, I know it doesn't excuse it. Jullien knows it can't be forgiven. It's why he's intentionally stayed away from all of you for years now. He understands that his presence is nothing more than a bitter reminder of a past all of you are better off not remembering. And that you deserve to live without him around to steal even the smallest bit of happiness from your lives. He doesn't expect you to forgive him or even tolerate him. We accept the fact that we will never be a part of your family, that by his own actions, he lost that right long ago. But for now, you need him to keep them safe so that you can do what you have to, to ensure all your futures. All he wants is for you to understand that you can trust him. That he will die before he allows any harm to come to your families. We wouldn't have entrusted our children to you, nor would we have talked Trajen into joining the Alliance in this war if we weren't behind you and your cause one hundred and ten percent."

Suddenly, there was pounding on the door, followed by a shrill scream. "No! Let me go! They could be hurting her! Mama! Mama! Ma-ma!"

Ushara rushed to the door to open it and stop the hysterical screaming. An identical copy of Viv fell into her arms. "I'm okay, bobkin. No one's hurting me."

The little girl clung to her mother as she passed a belligerent glare at the rest of them. "Don't you hurt my mommy! I mean it!"

Nykyrian closed the distance between them and held his hand out to the girl. "No one here would ever harm you or your family."

"Not true for your paka," Caillen said under his breath. "*His* throat, we'd cut."

Chayden slapped him in the stomach hard enough that it made Caillen grunt in response.

Nykyrian passed a glare at him before he turned back to the girl. "I'm your uncle, Nykyrian. You're what? Five?"

"Almost."

He pulled out his link and turned it on, then scrolled through it and held it toward her. "I have twin sons who are your age. Would you like to see your cousins?"

Forgetting her fear, she left her mother's arms to look at his pictures. "They look like us."

"They do," he said gently. "They're named Tiernan and Taryn."

She smiled. "My favorite doll is Taryn! My name's Mira and . . . and my sister's Vivi. And . . . and . . . I have a mean brother named Visi."

With the grimace that was Nykyrian's version of a smile, he pulled the girl into his arms and gave her a hug. "Nice to meet you, Mira."

Ushara took her hand. "Now will you go and play while I take care of some things?"

"Okay. Sorry, Mama."

"It's fine, my heart. But Mama has some important things to do." She kissed Mira's cheek before she gently guided her out of the room.

Nykyrian rose to his feet, then turned toward Galene. "All right, Commander. We put you in charge for a reason. My brother has given us a rare opportunity."

She nodded. "We will take full tactical advantage of it."

As they left Ushara's ship, *Scythian Nights,* they met Ryn and his mother, who were leading a small, regal group of Wasturnum toward them.

Fain couldn't help smiling as he noted how markedly differ-ent Ryn's group was from Venik's Porturnum, and even the Gorturnum group they'd just left. But then each Nation of the Tavali tended to draw a certain caliber of individual to it. And everything from their style of ship to their Canting, names, markings, flightsuits, and battlesuits tended to reflect those various personalities.

The Septurnum, like Chayden, were their in-your-face, annoying gutter rats—an almost psychotic lot who sought the more questionable jobs that others passed on. If there was danger to be had, they were the suicide jockeys who wanted to embrace it with both arms, and cock out. They were the Tavali troublemakers who lacked all semblance of self-preservation. And if a Tavali was running afoul of someone's laws, and in particular The League's, you could lay odds they owed tithe to Gadgehe Hinto.

Venik's Porturnum were much more cautious, as a rule, and very paranoid because of the enemies they gleefully toyed with. They tended to be double-dealers, con artists, and fast-talkers. Always plotting something and out to make a quick cred. You had to watch your back with them, and were never quite sure where you stood. If you gambled with the Porturnum, you'd best count all your fingers when you left the table, 'cause you'd probably be missing one.

Maybe two.

Next were the Gorturnum—the original Nation that all the Tavali had evolved from. And as such, they were held with a certain reverence by the other pirate Nations. But that being said, their members were mysterious and extremely antisocial. So much so that their motto claimed they played hard to get along with. Like mythical phantoms, they moved swiftly and silently through the galaxies. In and out, quicker than anyone could blink. If you needed something done fast and with no witnesses left alive, you contracted with them. While others sought fame, the Gorturnum kept to themselves to an almost psychotic level.

Out of all the Tavali, they were the most loyal and secretive to their order.

And then there were the regal blue-bloods . . . the Wasturnum. Dignified. Honorable. They lived by Tavalian Code and Council, and brooked no slackers. Their members bled decorum and refinement, and yet there was also a barbarian undertone that said they could and would cut your throat while smiling in your face. That dichotomy was actually extremely unsettling. Like sitting down to have dinner with a lion, and you were never quite certain if you were going to eat with him or become part of his dinner should you say the wrong thing.

Or use the wrong piece of cutlery.

Even so, Fain had a lot of respect for the Wasturnum. As a rule, they operated aboveboard and you didn't have to constantly stand with your back against the wall for fear of a cheap shot.

And they were led by the infamous Hermione Dane. The ruler of their United Tavali Nations.

It'd been a long time since Fain had last seen her, yet eerily, she never seemed to age a single day. She was still youthful and seductive. Lethally graceful and elegant. As the supreme admiral of the Universal Tavali Council, she was their version of a queen. But it wasn't a position she'd inherited. All of the ruling Tavali positions were earned by deed, combat, service, and honor, and they were held by maintaining those, and could be taken away at any time.

By one mistake or challenge.

Citizenship, names, and Canting were honors that all members of their Nations held in sacred trust. You didn't violate Tavali Code. Not if you wanted to live.

Fain struck his Tavali salute and bowed his head respectfully to one of the few political leaders he truly revered. "My Lady Grand Empress and Supreme Admiral."

Her golden eyes were bloodshot from the tears she visibly struggled to hold back. To pay further tribute to the passing of Darling Cruel and his family, the white stripes of their black leather Wasturnum battlesuits had been electronically dulled to a dim gray—a Wasturnum custom of mourning, along with the red ribbon that was tied around their sleeve Canting.

For her and Ryn, the ribbons held a memento of Darling's that was special to them. Hermione's was a lock of red hair she must have kept from Darling's first haircut—another Wasturnum tradition. Ryn's ribbon held the ring from an explosive device marked with Darling's Sentella insignia. Darling's signature FU that he'd always left for the League prime commander to make Kyr lose his mind.

Fain was amused by Ryn's choice, and he recognized it for what it was. Not just a memento of Ryn's beloved brother, but a promise of vengeance against Kyr for daring to take Darling's life. While Ryn and Darling hadn't always gotten along, and though they were only united in blood by their father's lineage, they were forever brothers.

And they would kill or die for one another, without question.

Likewise, Hermione couldn't have been more upset had she been Darling's birth mother. Ever elegant and regal, with her cape slung casually over one shoulder, she was fiercely defiant and a creature of absolute power. Her long, dark red hair was braided down her back and she kept one hand casually draped over the blaster on her left hip.

"Commander Hauk." She bowed her head in greeting. "It's a pleasure to see you again." She placed a kiss to Fain's cheek. Then she grabbed Nykyrian into a motherly hug and choked on a sob. "I'm so sorry for your loss and ours. I can't believe Darling's gone."

Ryn stepped forward in case she needed him.

Nyk held her and whispered in her ear.

While Nyk did that, Fain pulled Ryn back from them.

When he started to protest, Fain cupped Ryn's jaw and leaned down so that he could whisper intimately to the Tavali ambassador without anyone else overhearing him. "What Nyk's telling your mother is something you cannot react to. Brace yourself and stow your expressions to show no emotions whatsoever. . . . Darling is alive and well. As are his wife and son. Everyone was pulled out before The League bombed the palace. Now act upset." Fain stepped back.

Like an award-winning actor, Ryn choked on a sob and

patted Fain on the arm. "Thank you, brother. I appreciate your sympathy in my darkest hour of need. I won't forget it."

Fain inclined his head, but he saw the relief in Ryn's eyes as well as the fire that had returned to Hermione's. Now *that* was The Tavali queen he knew and loved.

Hermione clutched at Nykyrian's hand. "From the moment he drew his first breath in this life, Darling has always been a son to me. For his father alone, I would have given up my Canting and name, and renounced Tavali citizenship." She cast a furious glower around the bay. "May the gods have mercy on the soul of whatever Tavali dared bring harm to Darling and his house, for I will not. Rather, as my esteemed ancestor Hestia Waring-Dane once did, I will rain down Hell's wrath upon them and take not just their Canting and name, I will have their throat. Tell Brax he better deliver their heads to me or else I will have his on my wall, and his balls as my earrings."

Ryn smirked at Fain. "That's my mom. Now you know why I'm still single."

Hermione passed an irritated glare at her son.

He gave her a charming wink. "Just like you, Mom. Independently owned and operated."

Chayden laughed. "Hey, it's better than me. I can't tell if I'm still single 'cause nobody likes me, or because I like nobody."

Caillen snorted at that. "That's easy. Definitely the former more than the latter."

Chayden passed a threatening look at him, which Caillen must have caught, along with a sudden memory of the fact that before Caillen had married Chayden's sister, he'd slept with Chayden's fiancée, and that was the sole reason they'd split up.

And why Chayden remained unmarried to this day.

Caillen quickly put Fain between them for protection.

Ignoring them, Hermione released Nykyrian and met Galene's gaze. "I stand at your ready, Commander. Let us know when and where to attack. My forces are at your disposal."

While Hermione headed up the ramp to greet Ushara, Ryn stayed behind.

"You're sure about Darling?" he asked Fain in a barely audible tone.

"Absolutely. He wanted us to make sure you didn't do anything stupid—his words—while he was in hiding, and cost him his empire."

Ryn cracked a half smile. "That's my little brother, Dumbass. And not like I could screw it up any worse than he did. I'm not the idiot who declared war on The League by telling their prime commander that I was going to raid and pillage the village and burn that—and I quote—motherfucker to the ground and there ain't nothing you bitches can do about it—end quote."

Dancer laughed. "Yeah, not one of his better days. But definitely one of his more entertaining speeches."

Ryn snorted. "Yeah, right. Let's hear it for the Cruel family's standard of diplomacy."

"Brother, I hear you. There's no problem so large that it can't be solved by an adequate supply of explosives," Chayden finished for him. "That's always been one of my favorite things about Darling."

Fain shook his head. "Yeah, *you* would like that, Psycho Bunny."

"And you . . ." Ryn swung around toward Talyn, who met him with an arched brow. "I hear that we have a new son to welcome to our family group. It's an honor to see you again, boy."

Talyn extended his arm. "It's good to see you, too, Ambassador."

Taking his hand, Ryn pulled him in for a hug. One that Talyn accepted without complaint. "Family don't shake hands. We maul like the gods intended . . . and I'm so glad I kept Ven from shooting you all those years ago."

Talyn clapped him on the back. "Me, too. It would have seriously screwed up my future plans."

Laughing, Ryn stepped back, then remembered he was supposed to be in mourning. He cleared his throat and sobered instantly. "Congrats on the unification."

"Thank you."

As Fain turned toward Galene, a sudden explosion rumbled and then rocked through the station. Alarms blared and lights dimmed. Their comms went off with warnings and summonses.

Fain paled as he read his link and his entire world tilted out of control.

No . . .

"It's the orphan decks . . . where War and Vega are housed." Without waiting on anyone, Fain took off at a dead run. His heart pounded in terror as he tried to call them.

No one answered.

Over and over he told himself they were all right as he kept trying to get through to them. That the lines were down or overloaded by others trying to contact loved ones.

Yet when he reached the section where they lived and saw the cordoned-off area that had been blown out and sealed so that the rescue teams could help the few survivors, he knew better.

No one in their building was left alive.

No one.

CHAPTER 14

F ain fell to his knees as pain racked him harder than any blow
he'd ever felt since that day in the locker room when
Galene had shattered his heart and left him barren and alone.
He couldn't breathe for it. All he could see were the faces of the
kids when he'd first found them, starving and terrified.

It's okay. I've got you. No one's going to hurt you again. I promise.

How could he have let them down, too?

"Fain?"

He blinked at Galene's voice, but couldn't speak past the agony that choked him.

She brushed her hand through his braids as aid workers and
Hadean Corps soldiers rushed around them to put out the fires
and help survivors. "Come with me."

"I've got to search for them. Maybe they're trapped. Maybe—"

"Come with me," she repeated in a tone that brooked no
argument or resistance.

He glanced past her to see Talyn watching them with a

peculiar expression he couldn't read. "You want to listen to her, Hauk. Trust me."

Numb, he nodded and allowed them to lead him back toward Talyn's condo.

By the time they reached it, silent tears blinded him as guilt flayed him for having left the kids by themselves. Damn Venik and their laws. He should have kept the kids with him and screwed Tavalian law and custom. This was all his fault. And he would never forgive himself. Never get over the loss of two lives that were solely on him. Two lives he'd sworn to protect and take care of. He was all they'd had.

And he'd failed them. He would never forgive himself.

Talyn opened the door to his condo.

"Paka! Paka! Paka!" War came running to almost tackle Fain with an unexpected hug.

Fain's breath left him with a loud whoosh as War's small body collided with his and filled his arms with squirming spindly limbs.

"See! I told you he wasn't caught in it." Vega frowned as she approached and saw Fain's tears. "Are you okay, Paka? Was someone hurt?"

Unable to speak, Fain grabbed both of them into his arms and burst into tears as he sank to his knees and held them in a crushing embrace. Relief and love exploded through him while he rocked them, knowing they were safe and alive. That by some unexpected miracle they'd been spared the horror of the day, and consequences of his stupidity.

Thank you, gods, thank you! He would never miss temple again after this. He owed Ornul and Eri prayer lights for the rest of his life that They, in Their divine mercy, had spared his kids.

It wasn't until he'd thought they were dead that he realized just how much he loved them. How much of his heart he'd allowed the two of them to claim. Since the day he'd lost Galene, and his parents had callously thrown him away, he'd done his damnedest to live the rest of his life without any kind of emotional entanglement. To keep everyone, even Omira, at arm's length.

Only Dancer and the memory of Galene had stayed with him.

Until the day War and Vega had wiggled their adorable little ways through his shields.

"Paka . . . I. Can't. Breathe," War choked out as if he were in absolute misery.

Snorting an irritated laugh, Fain let go of them finally.

"I think Paka went crazy," War whispered loudly to his sister.

Bug-eyed, she nodded.

Galene laughed at them before she stroked Fain's cheek with a gentle, understanding hand. "No. Paka had a bad scare. He thought you both had been killed in the explosion. I know from all the years of having your brother Talyn in similar situations that the only way to breathe again after such a horrible shock is to have the babies in your arms and feel with tangible proof that they're safe and whole."

Only then did Fain let go and take Galene's hand. "Thank you. But how did they get here?"

347

She jerked her chin toward Gavarian, who was watching him as if he was as crazy as War had proclaimed him. "Talyn sent Vari and his brother to secure them after the attack on us."

Fain finally saw that Felicia had been sitting at the table, doing schoolwork with them, on his arrival. "Thank you, Vari. And thank you, Felicia, for watching over them."

Before they could respond, Vega touched the tears on his cheek.

Fain met her haunted gaze. Her small hand trembled as she wiped at his tears.

"I'm sorry we scared you, Paka." Then Vega did something she hadn't done since she'd hit puberty—she sank down in his lap and laid her head on his chest to cuddle against him like a small child.

Closing his eyes, Fain held her and brushed his hand through her dark hair. "I'm just glad you're all right. And if you want to date, I promise I won't gut the little . . . male."

She laughed at that. "I can wait until you're ready. I don't want you in jail for it."

Fain smiled. "Very well. I'm told ninety is a prime dating age for a human female."

"Paka!" she snorted.

Gavarian moved to stand in front of them. "Well, since you're here . . . if you'll give me the new key card to your half of the condo, I'll get the kids moved in for you."

Fain scowled as he finally realized that all of Vega's and War's personal items were packed in bags and lined up against the wall. He glanced over to Galene in confusion.

Her features softened into the kind of smile he'd never thought to receive from her again. She pulled out her link and scrolled through it for a minute before she handed it over to him. "It went through earlier. I was going to tell you about it but then all hell broke loose."

Stunned, he felt his jaw go slack. "You legally adopted them?"

She nodded. "And named you as their paternal guardian. I found the loophole that allows you to legally be their father, and there's nothing anyone can do to stop it. It was the least I could do for you, after what you did for Talyn and Felicia."

Another tear slid from his control as he saw his own name listed as their father. He couldn't believe it.

A family of his own . . . The only thing he'd ever wanted in his entire life. A dream he'd been forced to give up so long ago that he'd refused to think about it. The pain had always been too raw and biting.

Now . . .

Rising to his feet, he pulled Galene into his arms and kissed her. "Thank you, Stormy."

She smiled up at him. "Don't thank me so soon, War Hauk. Parenthood is an equal share of awe and ah, crap."

"Thanks, Mum," Talyn said drily. "Way to nurture that healthy ego in your son."

She laughed at him. "Oh please! As if you need any help in that regard. Your ego is granite. I've seen the way you dress when you're not in uniform."

Talyn staggered back and covered his heart as if she'd shot him. "Ah, now that's just painfully mean." He turned toward

Felicia. "And you're the one who should really be offended since you buy most of my clothes."

Felicia let out the most feminine and strangely sweet snort Fain had ever heard. "True, but you seldom wear the ones I buy for you. Rather you live in those old things you've had since the day I moved in. Every time I try to throw them out, you find them again and return them to the closet."

Gavarian and Brach burst into laughter.

Until Talyn glared at them. That sobered them instantly. "Don't you hyenas have luggage to move?"

Gavarian passed an irritated smirk to his brother. "Yes, sir." But no sooner had he neared the luggage than a demanding knock sounded on the door, at the same time Fain's link went off with Venik's alert tone.

"What fresh irritant is this," Talyn said under his breath.

Assuming it was about the attack, Fain started to answer his link while Galene opened the door. The moment she did, a full Hadean Corps squad burst in, with their arms held at the ready.

Gasping, Felicia shot to her feet. Vega and War screamed and ran to take cover behind Fain. They gripped at his legs as Talyn moved to cover Felicia.

"What is this?" Galene demanded.

Fain tried to calm the children. Something much easier said than done, since War was trying to scale him like a ladder. The boy had hands that could double for suction cups. And Vega's death grip on his thigh wasn't much better. He was starting to lose circulation in it.

The captain moved toward Gavarian and angled his blaster

at him. "Major Terronova, you're under arrest. On your knees. Hands behind your head. Ankles crossed. Now!"

His jaw dropping, Gavarian held his hands out so that no one would mistake his intent and shoot him for it. "Whoa . . . What? Are you serious?"

When the captain went to grab the boy, Fain handed the kids off to Galene and shoved the captain back.

"Stand down, Hauk," he warned.

Fain refused. "This is bullshit!"

Venik walked through the squad to join the fray.

Before Fain realized what Venik intended, he felt something cold snap around his neck. An instant later, a fierce shock went through his nervous system. Had he been human, it would have rendered him unconscious or flat on his back.

As an Andarion, it just seriously pissed him off. Wanting blood, Fain growled at the pirate bastard who'd cuffed him.

"It's time you remembered your place, Slug-wart. I just lost three hundred people, and half of them were children. *You* brought the Andarions here. Fuck with me and I'll hang you with them. We have footage of that little prick walking in the area where the bomb was planted less than an hour before it detonated. And he had no business whatsoever on those decks. He's the only one who was out of place there."

Fain glared at Venik. "He was getting my kids to safety, after someone tried to murder my son in his sleep."

Venik shoved him back against the wall. "Get it through your thick, stupid Andarion skull, you don't have a son. You don't have kids. I. Own. You." He grabbed Fain by the throat.

The next instant, Venik went flying sideways.

"Get your hands off him!" Talyn planted himself between them. "My father's a War Hauk, you son of a bitch. You don't talk to him like that! And you don't ever lay hands to him!"

The expression on Ven's face made Fain's blood run cold, especially as every guard there aimed blasters at his child. Galene started forward, into the fray, but Fain waved her back and Felicia held her in place.

While it meant everything in the universe to him that Talyn had defended him, if he didn't diffuse this fast, it was about to go into total nuclear devastation. No one threatened Venik in his station.

No one.

"Stand down, Talyn. High Admiral Venik's correct. I'm not a War Hauk. I haven't been one since the day my mother slashed my lineage."

Ven straightened his clothes with an arrogant tug. "And who owns you?"

Fain had always hated it whenever Ven played this power shit with him. It took everything he had not to put the bastard through the wall. But so long as he had a kill switch in his brain, he had to cow to him or have his brains become part of the landscape. And while that might not have been all that important to him in the past, he now had a room full of reasons to swallow his pride and let Ven feel like he had control of him, when really, they both knew the truth.

If Fain wanted his freedom, Ven would be forced to kill him. 'Cause that would be the only way for Ven to keep him leashed.

No one hemmed a War Hauk down without their express permission and cooperation.

"You do, my lord."

"Who do you tithe to for your Canting?"

Fain felt the familiar ticcing start in his cheek. "You . . . my lord."

Venik nodded. "That's right. *I* am the one you answer to, for everything. And this little fantasy bullshit you've been living ends today. Get your things and report to slag quarters. Now!"

Galene wanted to weep as she saw the bitter resignation in Fain's stralen eyes. This was killing him and there was nothing she could do. Damn Venik for it.

It was just like watching Fain with his family, all over again. Every time he'd ever tried to have pride in something or to feel good about himself, either Keris, his father, or mother would rush to publicly humiliate him.

And you did it to him on his graduation day.

Galene choked as she realized that. All these years, she'd been focused on her own pain. She'd never once considered what she'd taken from him in return.

His last chance at one untainted memory. How could she have been so selfish?

While her parents had been kind and giving until that moment in time, his hadn't. Fain had never had anything in his life he hadn't bled for. Not one.

What do I do?

Venik faced the captain of the Hadean Corps. "What are you waiting for? An accommodation, or applause? How about I just kick you in the ass? Now arrest the major before I give in to that latter urge."

Fain scoffed indignantly. "No! I just told you what he was doing there. You've no reason to arrest him."

"And it still doesn't clear him of the matter. If anything, it makes it look worse, *and* implicates *you*."

He gaped in disbelief. "You don't really believe that?"

"Honestly? I don't know what to think anymore. Maybe I should arrest you both until I sort this out."

Was he serious? Stunned by his irrational logic, Galene shook her head. "I can't stay quiet any longer. This is insane and you know it. Fain would never do anything against you."

Venik turned on her. "No offense, Commander, this doesn't concern you. Blister is Tavali property. And until you can find me someone else who set those charges, I'm holding the major responsible. Now stand aside, or I'll haul all of you in for interfering with Tavali justice. *That* is my prerogative."

"You can't do that, Ven," Fain said from between clenched teeth. "C'mon. He's just a kid. You know what they'll do to him in lockup."

"He's older than you were."

She saw the involuntary flinch those words wrought and it made her wonder what had happened to Fain when they'd first taken him. It had to be beyond her worst horrific imaginings to make a mighty War Hauk of his caliber react like that all these years later.

And that made her sick to her stomach.

Fain glanced to Gavarian, then Talyn, before he returned

his furious gaze to Venik. "It don't make it right. I'll take the hazard. Just leave him alone."

Ven's gaze went past Fain to Gavarian as he debated the offer. "He has motive. His pregnant wife was killed in a dogfight with us. Did you know that?"

"He told me."

"And you still think him innocent?"

"I believe that he's not the kind of male to seek vengeance, yes."

"Then you're a fool, and he's going to lockup. Hell, I might even ship him back to Eriadne, with my compliments."

Fain cringed as bitter nightmares ripped through him. A part of him was tempted to keep his mouth shut. Gavarian was a grown male. A trained officer, with battle experience. Not the callow innocent he'd been back in the day.

But as he met the boy's steeled gaze that said Gavarian was more than ready to take them all on, he knew the truth.

For all that fire, Gavarian was too young to be in Tavali lockup alone with the types of animals who would be waiting for him. Criminals who wouldn't hesitate to take out every bit of their anger at what they perceived as social injustice on the son of an alien aristocrat. That kind of fury unleashed . . .

No one deserved it.

And he wasn't going to stand by and see it rained down on an innocent kid.

"I know he didn't do it. If he wanted revenge, he'd have taken it against me personally."

"Hauk," Talyn barked in warning. "Don't!"

Fain swallowed hard as he glanced to Galene and braced himself for what was to come.

Venik scowled. "Explain."

"Hauk," Talyn stressed one more time.

Fain ignored him and did the right thing, in spite of the consequences he knew would bite him hard on his ass. "The major and Talyn both saved my life. Twice. And they both know that I led the Tavali assault against them that got them both grounded out of the Andarion armada."

Galene sucked her breath in sharply as Talyn cursed Fain for his stupidity.

"And the major knows that I was the lead on the same raid his wife was flying in when she died. If he wanted revenge, he'd have killed me, or allowed me to die. He wouldn't have gone after civilians. He damn sure wouldn't have protected War and Vega for me."

Venik narrowed his gaze on Talyn and then Gavarian. "Is this true? Did you know that?"

Talyn sighed heavily. "Of course we did. Not exactly something you forget."

His gaze haunted, Gavarian gave a subtle nod. "Code name Blister tends to stick out."

"Very well . . ." Venik closed the distance between him and Fain. "You have thirty minutes to report to your new quarters. I want you there any time you're not on duty. You are not allowed any free time I don't give you. Understood?"

Fain glared at him.

"Do you understand?"

He understood. He just didn't want to verbally commit to something he had no intention of following.

Venik growled low in his throat. "Don't make me kill you, Hauk. I will if I have to."

"Do whatever allows you to sleep at night."

Venik's nostrils flared. "Captain. Stay here and make sure Hauk reports to quarters. If he fails to, I want him arrested. Shot if he resists."

"Yes, sir."

And with that, Venik and all but four of the Corps soldiers left.

Fain turned toward Galene. The sudden chill in the room told him it was time to go. He was no longer welcome here. Talyn had been right. She would never forgive him for what he'd done. And he didn't blame her at all.

"Why didn't you tell me?" Her voice was scarcely more than an anguished whisper.

"I told him not to."

She turned on Talyn with an angry glare. "You knew all this time?"

Talyn nodded. "From the moment I saw his ship and its serial."

"And yet you said nothing?"

"I didn't want you hurt."

Fain took a step toward her. "Stormy—"

"Don't!" she snapped, stepping out of his reach. Her eyes flared with hysteria. "You . . . you weren't there. You didn't see what you did to my baby." Her breathing ragged, she struggled to speak as tears welled in her eyes. "What was left of him after you blew his ship into twisted fragments. They told me to pick out clothes to bury him in! That he'd never again wake, or then walk. You weren't there while we watched him struggle every day, in anguished pain, so that he could relearn to speak, talk, and walk. To do the most basic tasks for himself . . . because of *you!*"

Those words struck him twice as hard given what he'd felt when he heard the explosion earlier. While he loved Vega and War, he hadn't carried them in his body. He could only imagine what she must have felt when they brought Talyn in from battle and she got that call.

Fain swallowed hard. "I would never have hurt him. Or you."

"But you did. Dear gods, how you hurt him! And me. So many times." Wiping angrily at her tears, she gestured toward Gavarian. "And Vari . . . he barely survived Lettice's death. You stole a part of his young soul when you sent her to her grave."

"I know. I'm sorry."

"And there are some things that sorry will *never* fix." She glared at him with the same ball-shriveling hatred she'd given him that day in the gym. "Just go."

Fain passed a glance to War and Vega, who stood silently beside Felicia. He expected to see condemnation on her face, too, but only sadness showed in her pale eyes.

And sympathy.

Without another word, he led the Hadean Corps out of their

condo and headed for his new quarters. There was no need to gather his things. He didn't have any.

Talyn moved to comfort his mother, but she shrugged his embrace away.

"I'm so mad at you right now, I could beat you myself."

He blinked in stunned shock. "Me?"

"You! You let him back into our lives, knowing how I would feel if I ever found out he's the one who took your leg from you. How could you? For that matter, how can you stand to even look at him, knowing what he stole from you? What he's cost you!"

Talyn gaped. "Really, Mum? You know, it was my leg *I* lost. Not you. But you know what? Look around this room." He gestured at Brach and Gavarian. "For almost a decade now, I've had two of the greatest brothers any male was ever lucky enough to claim. Yeah, they're a pain in my ass at times, but when I need them, they come, bitching every step of the way. Because of Hauk, I have the most devoted mother any child could have asked for. Yeah, there have been many times in my life I've seriously doubted your sanity, but never once have I ever doubted your love for me." He moved to brush his hand over Vega's and War's heads. "Now, I have an adorable new brother and sister to love. A brother and sister I'd have never met had Hauk not come back into our lives."

Then he pulled Felicia against him and pressed his cheek to hers. Closing his eyes, he gently wrapped his arms around her waist and held her. "And thanks to what Hauk did for me, I'm now fully Vested, and have the most amazing and beautiful wife by my side, with my own baby on the way. I'm the second highest ranked officer in the Andarion armada, and the most celebrated Ring fighter of my generation. If all I had to pay for that was half of one leg, then damn, Mum, I got off easy. And it was so worth it in my book. Hell, I'd have given them the whole leg, *and* an arm. Besides, it wasn't like he took a testicle from me. *That*, I might not have forgiven."

"Talyn!" Felicia gasped. "The children!"

Vega's eyes were as round as saucers while War ran to hide behind Gavarian, laughing.

Ignoring them, Talyn continued. "So to answer your question, I have no problem looking at my father. I'm too damn grateful to still be here with all of you to worry about something as trivial as a leg. Had he not shot me down, Lorens wouldn't have retired early, and I wouldn't have been able to move into your adjutant position. From where I stand, I owe him everything."

Galene hated whenever Talyn took the noble ground. It really made her yearn for the days when he was small enough for her to put into a corner.

Unwilling to cede this point, she turned to Gavarian. "How do you feel about it?"

Gavarian let out a tired sigh. "It would be really easy to hate Hauk for what happened. Honestly, there are times when I want to. Unfortunately, he's a decent bastard who makes hating him really hard. Besides, the truth is what I have trouble living with, not his part in my past. As much as I loved and adored Lettice, she didn't love me. Not like that. She was fond of me, but she preferred the life of a fighter pilot over that of a nobleman's or officer's Ger Tarra. Nothing made her happier than battling for glory, and she always said that she wanted to go out in the middle of a dogfight, in a burst of flames, during her prime. That she didn't want to grow old and wither in old age. She got what she wanted. So, like Talyn, I can't lay that at Hauk's feet. We are warriors. When we go to battle, we know what we risk. Blaming another soldier for fighting for his life is pointless. And now that we're on the same side, Hauk's shown himself worthy of his lineage. He is his son's father. I'm honored to fight with him."

Spoken like a true Andarion.

How she hated that little bastard for that.

But Gavarian made valid points that only made her hate him more.

Felicia stepped away from Talyn to approach her. With a kind smile, she rubbed Galene's arm in comfort. "If it makes you feel better, Commander, I want to claw out his eyes for hurting Talyn, too. Like you, I haven't forgotten what Talyn went through to get back on his feet. Between the two of us, we might be able to make Fain limp."

Galene laughed and drew her into a hug. "I love you, Felicia."

"Love you, too." She squeezed her, then let go. "And because of that, I want to remind you of something you once said to me. You've only loved two males in all your life. Talyn and the one who gave him to you. You said that if I ever met his father, I would know it instantly as they were so similar as to be virtually

361

indistinguishable from one another." She wiped the tears from Galene's face. "You're right. They're both extremely aggravating males. Gorgeous beyond belief. Proud and strong. Andarion, through and through. And as my mother said to me when I first told her I was in love with Talyn, 'There are times when you will look at him and want to eat him up. And the rest of the time, you will wish you had. But remember on those times when you're contemplating his murder that the aggravation will pass and you again want to gobble him up and wear him like a blanket. So don't kill him without giving me fair warning to save up for bail money.'"

Galene laughed again. "Thank you." She glanced around at all of them. "Thank you all for keeping me focused. And you're right. Staying angry at the past will only cost me my future. It's time I finally forgive him and let it go. There's no use in looking back and holding it against him. We can't change it. And I'm done making us all pay for it. In spite of it all, I do love him. Even when I want to kill him. I've lived my life without him and honestly, I like having him in it more."

Yet even as she said the words, she knew it wasn't that easy. There was still an enemy out to frame and kill them. And Fain didn't have the freedom they did.

He was Tavali property. Not that she understood exactly what that meant.

Determined to find out, she left them and went to search for Ryn Dane, or Ryn Cruel, as he was known whenever he wasn't among his Tavali brethren.

It took some time, but she finally located Ryn in the infirmary, lending aid to those who'd been injured in the bombing. As she tried to help, she quickly learned that "her kind" wasn't welcome there.

"We're not sure your group didn't set this bomb. Now stand aside, Commander."

Stunned, she gaped at the rude doctor, who brushed past her to tend another patient.

Ryn stopped by her side and offered her a bottled water. "Sorry about that. Everyone's on edge after the attack. They all want to blame someone who isn't in a Tavali uniform. It's easier that way. The thought that one of our own could do this . . . yeah."

"You don't think we had anything to do with this, do you?"

"No. But I'm not an idiot. I don't judge others by their culture or uniform. I judge them by their own deeds and words. One thing I learned early in life, from both my parents, was that rotten seeps into all barrels, and that injustice never discriminates. It hits everyone equally and without reservation or hesitancy." He took a deep drink of his water. "So what brings you here, Commander?"

"Tavali law."

He choked on his water. "Okay. What about it?"

"How can someone buy out a Tavali slave?"

He wiped his mouth with the back of his hand. "Make an offer to their owner. Just like anywhere else."

She'd already tried that offer and Venik had turned her down coldly by telling her it was against their Code. "Even if they're a Rogue pilot?"

He frowned at her. "Rogues aren't slags."

"Slag?"

He shook his head. "Sorry, term we use for conscripted, enslaved, or Canting-busted members."

Now she was really confused. Fain was both, and she knew it. Venik had told her such and refused to sell his contract to her. "But Venik owns Fain."

Ryn's scowl deepened. "He can't. Fain wears a Rogue's Canting . . . doesn't he?" He stepped back to call out to a passing Tavali. "Hey, Pettrew? Hauk's the current RA, right? I'm not crazy, am I?"

"Yeah, Dane, you crazy as hell, but Hauk is RA. I think he has at least another year before we vote again. Why?"

"Just checking the cerebrum. You know, I take a lot of hits to the head. Wanted to make sure nothing's been knocked loose. Thanks." He took another drink. "Yeah, he's a Rogue. Ven can't own him. Part of being a Rogue is that you fly independent of Nation and owe allegiance to none."

"That's not true in his case."

"You know this for a fact?"

"I do."

He capped his water. "Where's Fain?"

"Venik made him report to some quarters . . . I think he might have called them slag quarters?"

Ryn narrowed his gaze at that. "With a commander's rank?"

"Yes."

"That's bullshit." Ryn stepped over to hail Dancer from triage to join them before he led them away from the infirmary.

"What's going on?" Dancer asked.

"I'm not sure, but I want some non-Tavali backup in case I have to do something radically stupid to help your brother."

"Ah . . . Well, if you want that, we should call in Caillen. Radically stupid's his specialty."

As they crossed to the housing district, Talyn and Gavarian joined them. By the expression on Talyn's face, she knew something else had happened.

"What is it?"

"Morra picked up another transmission. She, Saf, and Maris are trying to break it. But I wanted to let you know and I didn't want to transmit it. We have Brach and Qory watching Licia and the kids. I have a bad feeling there are more fun surprises planted for us."

Galene's stomach knotted even more. "You think it's another attack?"

"That's my guess." Talyn jerked his chin at Dancer. "Where's your family?"

"On lockdown with Jayne until Nero can get here. Sumi's an extremely capable assassin, but she's a pregnant one at the moment. I don't want to take any chances with her or the baby."

"Believe me, I understand."

Galene slowed as she saw the cramped barracks area Ryn had led them to. While it was clean, it reminded her of a prison holding area. The walls were completely clear so that guards could see into the large room where rows of bunk beds were lined end to end.

Probably a hundred males occupied the space and lounged

around, either on the beds or the floor. They looked positively bored. And why shouldn't they? It didn't appear as if they were allowed any form of entertainment or privacy. Or even personal items in that holding cell. All they had were the clothes on their backs, and the same silver collars around their necks that Venik had placed on Fain.

And here she thought her original accomodations had been wretched.

"What is this place?" she asked Ryn.

"Part prison," he sighed, "all kinds of hell. It's designed to be uncomfortable to punish the Tavali whose ranks were busted, and they've been put here until they can earn their citizenship back. Or to motivate the others to earn rank to get out. No one who holds rank or Canting is ever supposed to be housed here."

Ryn stopped at the desk to speak to a guard. "Where's Commander Hauk?"

The guard didn't bother looking up from his monitor. "No one sees him without orders from Admiral Venik."

Ryn jerked the cable out of the wall.

Hissing, the guard rose to his feet to attack, then paled as he realized who was there. "Ambassador Dane . . . my apologies, sir. I-I-I didn't realize that was you."

"Obviously. Now where's Hauk?"

Before he could answer, a body slammed so hard against the wall, it cracked it. Chaos erupted inside the holding cell as humans and others shouted, screamed, and ran for cover. A blood-chilling Andarion war cry rang out.

It was the shout of a War Hauk in full-on battle-mode rage.

The kind that had made them feared by all otherworlders. And given rise to the terrifying legends of her race.

Three more bodies followed the first.

Dancer and Talyn headed for the fray with Galene pulling flank. But as they entered the room and saw Fain, they all three drew up short.

Holy gods . . .

While she'd seen Fain pull some stellar moves as a boy in his Ring matches, it was nothing compared to the power and grace of the full-blown War Hauk doing life-and-death battle before her now. He wrapped his legs around the waist of the Tavali in front of him, twisted, and went down on the ground, pounding and slamming him so hard, Fain had his opponent neutralized before the Tavali had a chance to react. Flipping without using his hands, Fain came up to take on his next opponent.

A guard moved in and Fain turned to catch his hand and disarm him.

More guards were rushing into the room.

Remembering Venik's orders for them to shoot him if he resisted them, Galene panicked. Before she could stop herself or rethink it, she ran forward.

"Fain?"

He swung around with a punch for her throat. She moved to block it. But less than a millimeter from contact, he froze as he realized she wasn't his enemy.

His breathing ragged, he stared down at her. Time froze as the absolute power and beauty of him hit her as hard as that blow would have had he not stopped it.

And it was almost as debilitating.

He blinked twice before he drew her in for the hottest kiss she'd ever tasted. His arms trembling, he lifted her from her feet and held her against his chest.

Then he carried her to Talyn and set her down. "Watch your mother. Keep her by your side."

She scowled as he lowered his head like a fierce predator and stalked the first Tavali he'd slammed into the wall. He grabbed the male by his shirt and hauled him to his feet.

"Where is it?" Fain demanded in a fierce, deadly growl.

The male wheezed and coughed.

"Answer me or so help me gods, I'm pulling your entrails out through your nostrils and choking you with them."

With a calmness that was astounding, Ryn walked up to Fain. "Um, Commander? I hate to intrude on this private beat-down you're having with your friend here, but before the Hadean Corps shoots you dead for it, might I inquire as to the source of this violent rage session you're having?"

"Sure," Fain said in the same mocking therapist tone as he held the man against the wall with one bloody fist. "I found the bastard rat who set the charge. And there are two more rigged to go off that he planted."

The color drained from Ryn's face. "Where? When?"

"What I'm trying to find out. Wanna help me beat the shit out of him now?"

Ryn drew his blaster and held it under the Tavali's throat. "Fuck yeah, I do. Where is it?"

"Up your ass." Laughing, he bit down hard.

Ryn cursed and dropped his blaster, then pried his jaw apart and tried to swipe something out of his mouth. "Suicide cap!"

The Tavali began convulsing.

Galene stepped forward with Talyn. "I need water. Fast. Step aside."

Ryn frowned at her.

"She's a doctor," Fain explained.

Ryn slung the Tavali at her and called out orders for them to assist her.

Fain stood back and watched as Galene calmly pulled out the medpack from the cell's wall unit, and went to work on the human with Talyn's assistance. Since Andarions and humans had a long-standing history of war between them, part of Andarion medical training was human anatomy. How to heal them.

How to kill them.

Neither he nor Ryn spoke while they watched Galene and Talyn do their best to purge enough poison from the human to keep him alive.

A Tavali med unit showed up a few minutes later.

Fain stopped them from replacing Galene and Talyn.

Ryn scowled at him. "What are you doing?"

"We don't know who's working with him. I'm not about to put him in the hands of a Tavali coconspirator who could kill him off before we get what we need out of him. Are you?"

Ryn turned toward the med team. "Get them out of here. Leave the gurney and gear."

"Are you serious?" The medtech gaped at them.

"Go! They need you in the infirmary to help with the wounded there. We're good here."

Grumbling under their breaths, they obeyed.

Fain took their gear over to Galene.

After a few minutes, Galene sat back on her heels and sighed. "I've got him stabilized, but I doubt he'll last long. It was keratol he ingested."

Fain cursed again at the fast-acting poison that shut down organs and quickly brought on death. "Will we be able to interrogate him?"

"No. But if we can keep him on life support until Nero gets here, he might be able to use his powers to get what we need. It's the best we can hope for."

Ryn pulled his blaster out and aimed it for the Tavali's head.

"Whoa!" Fain caught his hand before he pulled the trigger. "What are you doing?"

"Making myself feel better. Not productive, I know. But a little bloody violence goes a long way in consoling my soul."

"You know, I don't think it's your mother keeping you single, buddy. But *this,*" Fain took the blaster from his hand and held it up to his gaze, "might be the actual reason."

The color faded from his face. "My mother . . ."

"What?"

"That's where one of the bombs is. I know it!"

"What?" Fain repeated.

Ryn looked down at Talyn, who was still on the ground next to the Tavali. "We killed Parisa . . . me and Talyn. Nyran wants revenge on us. He wants to kill my brother and *mother.*"

"He's right. That would make total sense. She's the Lady Tavali. The symbol of your Nations and the head of them all. It would be like taking down the entire War Hauk family on Andaria. It would divide the Tavali clans into war against each other, and personally devastate Ryn."

Pulling out his link, Ryn called his mother.

She didn't answer.

Ryn bit his lip. "She *never* rolls my calls. . . . Something's happened to her. Something bad." His breathing ragged, he took off at a dead run.

CHAPTER 15

Fain was barely one step behind Ryn as he traced his mother's location through her link to where she was in the station. According to their intel, she should be in her apartment.

By the time they reached her quarters, they were both sweating. Ryn opened the door and froze so fast that Fain almost slammed into him.

Galene actually did collide with Fain's back. Then gasped as she saw what had brought them to such an abrupt stop.

Hermione Dane stood on the opposite side of the room, stock-still. Brax Venik sat in a nearby chair and was just as uncomfortably posed as she was.

"Don't move," Hermione breathed slowly and without moving her jaw. "There's a bomb." She cut her eyes toward the device that was wired beneath the table between them. "We tripped it and we're not sure what detonates it. But it hasn't gone off yet."

Fain nudged Galene back. "Call Syn and get him here stat. Tell Talyn to stay with our traitor. I don't want him near this."

"Agreed." She moved slowly and carefully back into the hall-way to make the calls.

Fain placed his hands on Ryn's shoulders to keep him from doing something stupid to save his mother. "Can you call Kere?" Fain used Darling's Sentella code name in case someone was listening in, hoping that if they were, they wouldn't know Kere and Darling Cruel were the same person. Since Ryn's little brother Darling was the most skilled explosives engineer in the Nine Worlds, he was their best bet on saving Hermione's life.

"Already coded. Waiting for him . . . Hey, Kere. I have a situation here." Ryn slowly pressed his ear to conference the call to Fain's link, too. "Fain and I are standing in front of an IED that is about to blow my mom to the gods. We need your help."

Darling cursed in their ears. "I need eyes on it."

"Yeah, we're not sure . . . hang on. Mom, what the hell are you doing!"

Hermione had sunk to her knees and was slowly and very carefully making her way toward the device with her own link. "He'll need visuals. I'm getting them for you. Conference my link in with his call."

"Oh my God, Mom! Stop moving! We don't know what we're dealing with yet. If you get killed, I'm going to strangle you!"

"And if you don't get behind a blast shield and into a hard-suit, I'm going to bust your Canting down to slag."

"All right, everyone! Let's calm down and regroup." Fain took a deep breath as he struggled with his own panic over the escalating situation. "How about we all discuss anything else we want to do *before* we do it? Huh? This is the time to work together, not have a free-for-all that could get everyone killed."

Hermione nodded in agreement. "Fine. My link's on. Conference and I'll pull back to wait. I won't do anything else. Promise."

Ryn concurred.

Darling took a second to look the device over. "All right. There's bad news, and some serious suck-the-joy-out-of-your-life news. Where's Hauk?"

"I'm right here."

"Not you, Fain. *My* wingman."

"He's in the hallway. You know how he is about explosives."

"Yeah, I do, which is why I asked. Send him on a bullshit and long errand across the station. We don't want Grandma freaking out on us. Now where's Mari?"

"With Nyk, I think. Or with Saf. I'm not exactly sure, but he's not here."

"Well, that sucks." Darling let out a tired sigh. "All right, Fain. Do you share Dancer's aversion to explosives?"

"Only if they blow up in my face."

"That's what we're trying to avoid." Darling paused a few seconds before he spoke again. "I need you in a hardsuit, with a blast box. Tell Syn to set the onsite dampners for that room to the sequence I'm sending to his link right now. You need a diffuser kit from him and he will have to be in the command center working in tandem with you to disarm it. If you two cannot work as a single unit and in the right order, we're all going to have a bad day."

"What can I do?" Ryn asked.

"Stay out of this. And don't argue. I know you're the best in a fight, but not when it comes to your mother. I need a clear head and not an idiot in the way. You want her out of there. Stay in the back and let us do our job."

"I'm taking advice on this from *you*?"

"Exactly. I'm speaking from experience, as I was the moron who got all of us into war because I went in to save my wife and I couldn't keep my mouth shut. Had I let all of you do your jobs and stayed home, you wouldn't be plotting my death right now. So, please, Ryn. I love Mama Dane, too. She's the only real mother I ever knew. So let me save her. I'm as upset by this as you are, and hanging on by a thread. We can only afford for one of us to be hysterical right now and I'm claiming it."

Tears glistened in Ryn's eyes as he looked at his mother, who gave him a sad smile.

"Danes don't flinch, baby. We stand and fight. They're not going to get me. Not today. Don't you worry."

He nodded. "Love you, Mama."

"Love you, too, Trey-vey."

Syn joined them and handed Fain a hardsuit. "Hey, I got the note from Kere that said you were in need of this." He glanced past him to see Hermione and Venik inside. "How you doing in there, Lady Tavali?"

"Pissed off and wanting to taste the blood of my enemies who dared to attack me here in my own space."

"Working on delivering that to you. Venik, what about you?"

"Get me out of here so that I can give her the head and throat of whoever did this."

"From what I heard, Fain beat you to that. It's why he's here." Syn set the blast box at Fain's feet, along with the diffuser kit. "You know how to use any of this?"

"Not as good at it as you or Kere, but I've had a few training courses."

"You pass any?"

"A couple."

Syn turned positively green. "Oh, goodie. Ryn, you might stand back . . . a lot. We're about to have Explosives Amateur Hour. My favorite form of entertainment . . . when I'm watching from far, far away."

After making an obscene gesture at the Ritadarion, Fain turned to give Syn his back so that he could fasten the couplings for the blast armor.

Fain glared at his brother while Syn suited him up. "Dancer, listen to me. I want you and Galene to round up your wife and kids, Talyn and Felicia, and Vega and War. And grab Gavarian and Brach, too. Get everyone to my ship and secure them there until this is over. I'm not playing this shit anymore. You'll all be secure there and no one will be able to touch you."

"That's against Tavali Code," Venik snarled.

"Kiss my hairy ass, Ven." Fain kept his gaze locked on Dancer's. "You already have access and clearance to board. Tell Storm to follow Level Two protocols. She'll lead you through how to scan everyone in for clearance. There's plenty of crew quarters for everyone. And supplies."

"I'm not leaving you to face this alone."

"You're less than useless with explosives, and you know it."

"You have the same trauma I do . . . for the same reasons."

Fain winced as he tried not to think about either of their childhoods. "Yeah, but I'm not the one who fell off the side of a mountain after a charge detonated in my face." He jerked his chin toward the end of the hallway. "Go on, Dance. You've already watched one brother die in front of you. I don't want to be your next nightmare. You have a baby on the way. Children to protect. I need you to keep *them* and my family safe. For me, little brother."

Instead of leaving, Dancer moved forward and jerked him into a tight hug. "You die on me and I'm following you into hell to beat your ass. You hear me?"

"I hear you."

Dancer yanked his hair before he let go and stepped back. "I mean it, Fain. Don't make me have to commit a mortal sin to damn myself to come after you."

"Go on." Fain playfully pushed him away. "You're annoying me. Get to the others."

Dancer took three steps before he turned to look back. Tears glistened in his eyes.

I love you, too, brother. Neither of them had to say it out loud.

Syn clapped him on the arm. "All right. You're in." He handed Fain the helmet. "Mic check."

Fain put it on and sealed himself in, then checked to make sure the audio and visuals were transmitting. "Check?"

"You there, Kere?"

"I'm here. We're ready as soon as you're in the commcen."

Syn inclined his head to Fain. "Good luck. I'm dragging Ryn with me so that he can have his nervous breakdown in a less distracting area."

As Fain reached for the box and kit, he realized that Galene had vanished while he'd been suiting up. That she hadn't even bothered to say good-bye to him.

Or good luck.

It stung a lot deeper than it should have that she'd abandoned him so quickly. For all he knew, he could be dead in the next few minutes. It was actually a good bet. And she hadn't even cared enough to wish him luck.

Don't think about it.

That was easier said than done.

"Fain? You with me?"

"Yeah, sorry. I was distracted."

"Um, okay, buddy. A bit of advice? Let's not get distracted while handling something designed to explode. Wanna stay focused. Trust me, your odds of survival go up exponentially that way."

"Titana tu, giakon."

"Yeah, keep it in your pants, Andarion. You're not pretty enough for my tastes. Now make your way to the device and try not to bump it or the table. I want you to slide up under it, slow and easy, with as little motion as possible."

Fain was barely under the table when Syn's voice returned to his ear.

"I'm tapped into the system, Kere. I've given you full access."

"Beautiful. Fain, freeze."

He heard Darling tapping frantically.

"Syn, power up their cross shields with their interior routers for me."

"Done."

"Lights will dim on my mark. No one panic, but Fain, tell Mama Dane and Venik to run for the door when they do."

"Lady Tavali. Ven. The lights are about to go dim. When they do, you need to rush from the room." Then, he counted down with Darling. "Three. Two. One. Go!"

The lights dimmed.

Both ran past him, into the hallway.

"Are they clear?" Darling asked.

"Think so."

"All right, you ready for this?"

"Yeah, lead me through it."

Darling brought the lights back up. "Gently pull the cover off and expose the belly of the beast."

Fain did as he said and grimaced at the mass of gnarled wires that were wrapped around explosive mineral clay. Though the clay was no bigger than his fist, it was enough to take out this entire wing of the station. "Hey, Syn? You need to tell Venik to evacuate the entire southern quadrant."

"On it."

Darling calmly continued talking Fain through the disarming sequence. "All right, Fain. What I need you to do now is count the third brighter orange wire from the left and isolate it."

Fain hesitated. "Brighter?"

"Yeah. See it?"

He blinked as he stared at all the wires in his hand. Orange . . .

"It's this one, *keramon*."

Fain went cold at the sound of the sweetest voice in the Nine Worlds as a warm body slid up next to him. "What are you doing here?"

"I had a feeling you didn't tell them that the reason you never passed those diffusing classes was because you were partially color-blind."

Darling cursed in his ear. "Is she serious? Are you serious? You can't see a full color spectrum and you're handling a minsid wired explosive? Hauk? Are you out of your Andarion mind?"

"Yes. When he was a boy, he got into a fight with Keris and his brother injured his retina and did a significant amount of damage that left Fain with dichromatism." She covered his hand with hers and moved it to one of the wires. "This is the third brighter orange one."

Grateful for her help, Fain cut it while he ignored Darling's insults for him and his parentage that continued without interruption through his link. "You need to go to my ship with Dancer where it's safe."

"I'm right where I belong. You need someone here with smaller hands, who is used to handling delicate instruments. I'm a trained surgeon, with a full range of color vision. I've got this."

"Stormy—"

"Strong alone. Stronger together." She took his hand in hers and removed his glove. Her gaze paralyzed him as she took the ring from his finger. Then she pulled off her glove and placed the ring where it had once rested on her hand. "I have loved you since the moment I met you as a child. You are my life, Fain Batur. If you die here today, then you're taking me with you. I don't want to live another moment of this life without you in it."

Love for her choked him as Darling finally shut up. By naming him like that, Galene was claiming him as her husband, before witnesses. According to Andarion law, that would legally bind them as effectively as a unification ceremony.

He touched his bare hand to hers. "And you are the air I breathe, Galene Hauk. I shall never allow harm to come to you."

Darling let out an irritated sigh. "Aw, that's all sweet and moving, but could we please focus on the bomb that's about to detonate in your faces?"

"Yeah, waiting on you to tell us what to do, Kere. What's taking you so long?"

He broke off into a round of Caronese Fain was glad he couldn't understand, otherwise he might have ended the emperor's lineage. "Galene, shine the light and follow this sequence. Dark blue, light blue, green, yellow, light orange, red, red, purple."

She quickly snipped them in the designated order while Fain held the light for her. "Done."

"Did anything happen?"

Fain arched a brow at Darling's anxious question. "Was any-thing *supposed* to happen?"

"No. Not necessarily, but . . ."

"But what?"

"You might want to jerk the device off that table and seal it in the box real fast. . . . Just in case the designer planted a fail-safe in it."

Fain obeyed, and locked the seals tight. "Yeah, okay. Now what?"

"That should be it. We should—"

The bomb detonated at their feet. Fain grabbed Galene and covered her with his body. He held her against the wall so tightly that she couldn't breathe. "Precious? I think we're safe. Is that not the purpose of the blast box?"

"She's right, big guy. You're crushing her for no reason."

But instead of letting go, Fain pulled his helmet off and let it fall to the ground. Then he did the same with hers.

Galene was completely unprepared for the ferocity of his kiss. It was demanding and hot, and left her breathless.

"All righty, Andarions. I'm going to . . . uh . . ." Darling cleared his throat. "Give you the room and leave you to that. Little uncomfortable for the rest of us."

Fain pulled back with an adorable, unabashed grin. "You ever risk your life like that again and so help me . . ."

"All you have to do is not risk yours." She pointed to the rank patch on her hardsuit. "Remember, I outrank you, soldier."

Smiling, he nuzzled his face against her braids. "Why did you come back?"

"Because I love you. I've always loved you."

Those words made his heart sing. Did he dare hope that she meant what he thought she did? "Am I finally forgiven?"

Cupping his head to her shoulder, she wanted to both beat and hold him for eternity. Why couldn't he make loving him easy?

But then that was part of his charm. "Yes. You're forgiven."

Fain closed his eyes as he savored the words he'd waited a lifetime to hear. If he died right then, he'd be content.

And all he wanted was to carry her back to his ship and make love to her for the rest of the month.

If only he could.

Sighing heavily, he hated responsibility. Damn adulthood. He wanted to send it back for a full refund. "We still have one more device to locate."

She nodded. "I know."

Fain tapped his link to unmute it. "Hey, Kere. Any luck on finding the third charge?"

"Working on it."

Fain picked up the box and carried it while Galene led the way to the hall. Hermione and Ven waited at the end of it. As he neared them, Fain handed the box and exploded device off to a Hadean Corps officer.

Hermione stood up on her tiptoes to kiss Fain on the cheek. "I owe you. Thank you for what you did."

"No problem. I'm just glad I overheard the slag bragging about setting it, and got here before it went off. What happened, anyway? How'd you find it?"

Hermione sighed. "We were talking. I got up to get a drink and I heard the release spring. Since we didn't know what tripped it, we didn't dare move for fear of setting it off."

Hermione had barely finished speaking before Ryn showed up and grabbed her into a fierce hug.

"I'm all right, Ryn."

"I know. I'm just not ready to be an orphan yet."

Fain scoffed. "Aren't you a little old to be an orphan?"

He glared at Fain over his mother's shoulder before he set her back on her feet. "Considering the fact that my mother bottle-fed me until I was thirty? No."

Fain laughed at something that was practically true. Hermione did tend to dote on and overprotect her only child like he was the most sacred creature in the known universe.

Hermione rolled her eyes at Galene. "The lies our children tell about us."

"Don't I know. My son horrifies me daily."

Ryn sobered as he faced Venik. "We lucked out with Fain discovering this one. But we're not going to get that lucky with the next one. You've got to figure they're either going after defense or family. Where are your kids located?"

"Most of them are on their own ships. Only Kareem is currently in port. Even my wife is out on my daughters' ship."

"That's not true," Fain said. "I saw Stain come in earlier."

Venik scowled at him. "No. He's out with his crew."

"No, he came in. Check the logs. He told me he was on his way to see you and Kareem when I met him."

Ven pulled out his link to look.

While he did that, Galene fingered Fain's eye. "Does that hurt?"

"What?"

She sighed heavily. "You've got a nasty black eye."

He touched it, then hissed as he realized it *was* tender. "Ow, damn. I didn't feel it until now. Guess the prick got a shot in, after all. Must have been when he broke the chair over me."

"Oh my God, Fain! He hit you with a chair?"

"Yeah. A few other things, too. He even lobbed one of the smaller humans at me."

Galene covered her face and groaned. "I wish I thought you were joking and making that up. Unfortunately, I know better. Gods, you are your son's father. What did I do to deserve *two* of you?" Shaking her head, she met Hermione's gaze. "Is it easier with human sons or males?"

"Not really. I never know what horrifies me more—the stories Ryn tells me, or the ones I know he withholds out of respect for my maternal sensibilities, or fear of what I'll do to him should I ever learn the true nature of his innate recklessness and brazen stupidity."

"For the record, it's definitely the latter." Ryn stepped back to tap his ear. "Yeah, this is Dane. Go."

About a minute later, while Galene and Hermione were still comparing war stories about raising stubborn sons as single mothers, Fain frowned as he watched Ryn stumble and go down to one knee. Unsure of what had happened, he moved to kneel by Ryn's side to see if he could help.

"Were there any survivors?" Ryn's voice was barely a whisper. His breathing turned ragged and pain-filled.

Scowling, Hermione joined them. She rubbed at her son's back.

Ryn held his hand to the link as he nodded. "Keep me posted." He hung up.

Hermione's frown mimicked Fain's and Galene's. "Baby? What is it?"

Ryn stared straight ahead as if he were in a trance. "The League hit Hinto's west fleet while they were en route to rendezvous with us."

Hermione cursed under her breath. "How many did they lose?"

"They're still trying to determine the numbers." His lips trembled. "The *Merry Crimson* went down in the fighting."

She winced. "How awful . . . Did Commander Hinto get out?"

A tear slid down his cheek. "I told her not to come. I told her to stay at her father's base." He balled his fists together and pressed them against his forehead as he broke off into a sob. "Dammit, Mack! Dammit! Why couldn't you listen to me for once in your life!"

Hermione's scowl deepened. "Ryn?"

He wiped angrily at his tears. "I married Mack Hinto, Mom. Five years ago in a quiet ceremony on Paraf Run. We didn't tell anyone 'cause we knew what it'd do to the UTC, and how you and her father would react to it." He pulled his link out and pressed a message on it.

Fain winced as soon as he heard the familiar lilting accent of High Admiral Hinto's only daughter. Much like with Ryn, there weren't many Tavali who didn't know Mack Hinto's fierce reputation. But where Ryn was known for his levelheaded decorum and smooth charisma, Mack was a spitfire hellion more likely to bomb her way out of a situation than to ever try to diffuse it. While few wanted to deal with her, even fewer wanted to take her on in battle.

That never ended well for her adversaries.

But the one thing everyone agreed on—she was the best pilot and strategist the Tavali had ever trained.

"Hey, me precious, Wassy baby boy, I'm sorry I missed you. And I don't want you upset when you hear this. I know you told me to stay safe and out of the fray, but you know that's not our way. Especially not after what them bastards done to your brother and his family. And Chayden's. You're a Dane. I'm a Hinto. You've got to respect that we will not let this go unanswered. Besides, you need me, love. I know how much Darling means to you. I'm not about to leave you alone while you're grieving for him. I know how strong you are, but even the strongest sword needs a steady hand in battle. I swore to stand by your side, through all life's challenges, and I meant it. I don't care what me father, or anyone else, thinks. I will always be there for you when you need me. I love you, Trevelyan.

For everything you're worth and even what you're not. See you soon, me love. I'm counting the seconds till I lay me eyes and hands upon you again." She finished the message with a kissing sound.

Ryn curled his link to his chest and sobbed.

Hermione wrapped her arms around him and rocked him while he cried. Fain ached at the pain he saw in her eyes. At the agony of Ryn's loss. He knew that misery personally and it sucked on a level unimaginable.

There was no way to console it.

Venik motioned him away from the Danes. Rising to his feet, Fain stepped over to him.

"You were right. Stain came in. He's been trying to find the traitor himself."

"That what he said?"

Venik arched an angry brow. "You doubt my son?"

Fain glanced over to Ryn. Honestly? At this point, he doubted everyone, except a tiny handful. But he wasn't stupid enough to say that to the boy's father. "What else did he say?"

"They found the third explosive device. It was planted in my quarters. Stanis and Kareem have a team there now, deactivating it."

"Good." Fain hesitated as he finally saw a crack in Ven's iron façade. "What is it?"

"Reality hitting me. You know how I feel about Hinto."

"You hate him with the burning fire of a million stars."

"Yeah, but no one deserves to lose a child. Not like that. It could have been my Circe or Berra or Maryl or Lyss." His breathing turned ragged. "My girls fly as a united crew, Hauk. One battle, I could lose them all. And Payne. He flies with them."

"Call them home."

"I already did. And my boys." His gaze burned into Fain. "Can I really trust you, Hauk?"

"Only you can answer that. I've never betrayed your trust. Even when I should have. There's nothing else I can do to prove it."

"Yeah, and it's why I don't trust you. I don't understand you, boy. I never have. Everyone wants *something*. But not you. You took whatever I did to you and you just kept going. No complaint. No slander. You just endured. And I don't know why."

Fain laughed bitterly as he glanced to where Galene sat with Ryn and Hermione, offering them her comfort. "I had nowhere else to go, Ven. No one wanted me. I had no papers. No country or allegiance. My only family was my brother. All I'm trained to do is make war and battle. To fight in a Ring and take as many lives as I can. Keris said it best years ago—I'm nothing but a trained guard dog. Taking care of others is all I've ever known to do. End of the day, dogs don't want nothing but a bed and a meal."

Sadness darkened Ven's eyes. "And that's how I've treated you all these years. I'm sorry for that, Hauk." He jerked his chin toward the bruise on Fain's cheek. "And I'm sorry about sending you down to slag. I was angry and lashing out. I wanted someone to blame and you were an easy target and in range."

"It's all right. I found the traitor there."

"And saved my ass yet again." Venik let out a tired sigh. "What are we fighting for, Hauk? Really?"

"You always battle for profit."

Ven laughed at that. "True, but what good is it if you bury your children?"

"It's not. Our children and their futures are the only thing worth warring for. That is the Andarion way. We don't look to the past, nor at ourselves. It is not our way of life that we preserve. It's *their* future, their rights, their freedom that we secure with our blood. We battle and lay down our lives so that they won't have to."

"Yet they are the ones who fight our wars and die in them." Ven swallowed hard. "We have to end this with The League. Sooner rather than later."

"That's what we're trying to do. But we can't negotiate with tyrants who don't respect us, or value the lives they are charged with securing."

"One life lights a thousand."

Fain nodded at the old Andarion saying that meant one being, no matter how insignificant he or she might appear, touched thousands of others, and that all of them were united together as an undivided whole. Take no one for granted.

Hermione and Galene helped Ryn to his feet.

When Galene started toward them, Venik waved her back. He faced Fain so that no one else could see or overhear him. "You have been a friend to me when I didn't deserve it. Loyal when you should have struck out. I want to know why."

"What do you want me to say, Ven? You're an asshole. We both know it. I'm no joy either. But . . . you saved me from Tyrth when you didn't have to. And, you didn't kill me when you could have."

"I shot out both your knees."

"You didn't kill me," Fain repeated. "You're certainly not the first to shoot me. Hell, my older brother did that twice, growing up. Dancer plugged me once in the side."

"By accident."

"Still, a shot's a shot." Fain smirked as he glanced over to Galene. "And my wife got me a few days ago, quite intentionally. At point-blank range. When I bitched about it to Command, Nyk was the first to point out that everyone wants to shoot me at some point. You and Storm just got the fun of it."

Ven snorted. "That may be, but you still haven't answered my question."

Fain fell silent as he sorted through his complicated emotions where Venik was concerned. There was a part of him that hated the bastard for things he'd done. But beneath that hatred and resentment was the truth he couldn't deny. It was what always brought him back and what stayed his hand from lashing out at the Tavali no matter how much he might want to. "When I was nothing and had been left abandoned and forgotten by friend and blood alike, you gave me a chance to regain my dignity. Yes, you made me earn it, in blood and sweat, but in the end, you allowed me to have a ship of my own and to fly unfettered."

Ven lowered his voice to a barely audible whisper. "I brutally wired you to that ship without your consent. To the very hell where they abused you every minute they kept you caged there like an animal."

"Are you trying to make me hit you?"

"No. I want to understand why you have saved my life, especially after what I did to you earlier. I humiliated you in front of your family."

Fain shrugged. "I've had worse. Trust me. Your little hissy fit doesn't even register on my scale of degradations. Like I said, I owe you more good than bad."

"You still feel that way, even after I made you trade your freedom for the Jaswinders'?"

Fain snorted bitterly at the reminder. "Yeah, okay. That one sticks in the craw a bit. Especially over the last few days of you peacocking around here and lording it over me. I have to say the urge to slam your head into something hard has crossed my mind . . . a few thousand times an hour."

Ven laughed. "Ever brutally honest. It's what I value most about you." He pulled out his link and scrolled through it. "I think I owe it to you to show you this."

Fain frowned at the encrypted message that had Galene's command badging on it. He wasn't sure what to expect, but he didn't care for the idea of his female conversing with another male.

Until he read it.

My Lord Porturnum,

I know this is a bit forward of me, and for that I beg your extreme indulgence. I've been doing some research into Tavalian customs and contracts while I've been here, and there is one matter that I should like to inquire about. While a lot of information isn't readily available, it is my under-standing that each high admiral holds a tithe or contract with the pilots who fly under them that binds that pilot to their Nation. The tithe is usually for the value of the ship, and in the case of a slave, for the value of the individual as well, and any special training or other undue expense they've incurred. I know that Commander Fain Hauk owes a tithe to you and I should like to pay it off on his behalf and buy his freedom or tithe from you. Would this be possible?

Thank you for your time. I look forward to your prompt response on this matter.

Galene of the Winged Blood Clan of Batur
LT Commander, Alliance Command

Fain stared in stunned awe of those words. Galene had tried to buy his freedom? He couldn't believe it.

Venik took the link from his hand. "I was a bit rude to your Ger Tarra in response to her request, and I apologize to you both. You're right. I'm an asshole. I'm selfish. Reaction-ary. I do what I have to, to get the job done. As a rule, I don't care who or what I have to step on to get my way. But, you have been a good friend to me. A loyal servant even when I didn't deserve it."

Fain wasn't quite sure where Brax intended to go with this line of conversation.

"I know I'm going to regret this. . . ." Ven motioned for Galene to join them. "Enough families have been destroyed today. It's time we start building them. As a unification present for the two of you, I'm releasing Fain's tithe. Blessed union to you both. May the gods shine on you always." He kissed Galene's cheek, then Fain's. "Now I'm off to secure my family and sanity as best I can."

Galene gaped as Ven left them. "Was that for real? Did he honestly just set you free? *For* free?"

His head reeling, Fain sputtered. "Ven's always been capricious and bipolar. . . . You really asked him about buying my tithe?"

The most beautiful blush stained her cheeks. "He told you that?"

"He showed it to me."

She visibly cringed. "Are you mad that I did that without asking you?"

"Mad?" Fain cupped her face in both of his hands. "How could I be angry over the kindest thing anyone has ever done for me?" Then he kissed her until she was breathless and he was so hard that he could barely think straight. All he wanted was to be inside her. To hold her and never again let anything or anyone come between them.

Stepping back, he rubbed his cheek against hers and took a deep breath in her hair so that the precious scent of her skin set his blood on fire even more. "C'mon, I'm taking you back and making love to you until we're both limping."

She snorted. "Gee, Fain. That's just the kind of romantic offer that makes a female's heart race with anticipation."

He cracked what he hoped was a charming grin. "Yeah, well, I was never fully housebroken. You knew that when you unified with me."

Galene would have protested more, but then he took her hand and kissed her ring with a gesture so tender that it made her forget how unrefined a beast he could be. Especially since he led her toward Hermione's chambers to check on Ryn—a thoughtful gesture that was very much a part of his character and why she'd always loved him. No matter how unruly or rough he could be, he was ever considerate of others.

"How's he doing?" he asked Hermione as she answered the door.

Hermione stepped back to show Ryn on the couch with his arms propped on his knees and his head resting in his hands. Misery was etched on his face and he appeared lost and bewildered. Completely bereft and devastated. "I've never seen him like this. How could he have loved her so much and me be so clueless about it?"

Fain shook his head. "None of us knew. I've even been on missions with them and had no idea. They hid it well. I actually thought they hated each other, the way they went at it whenever they were together."

"He told me . . . it was a ruse to keep anyone from growing

suspicious." Hermione choked on her tears. "I can't stand seeing my baby in so much pain."

Galene took her hand and squeezed it in sympathy. "I know," she breathed. "It's so much easier to take it ourselves than watch them suffer. I am so sorry."

"Thank you. The remainder of the fleet is limping toward us and should be here in a few hours, with Jupiter Hinto leading them. They have to make extensive repairs from the battle. Gadghe's headed back for their main base. My understanding is that his son has taken command from his father, since he's too upset to handle things right now."

Fain lowered his voice so that Ryn wouldn't hear him. "Was Mack's body recovered?"

"No one knows. They sent over that last transmission to say her ship went down, and nothing since."

"Then I'll find out discreetly when Jupiter lands and make sure to relay it to you."

Hermione rubbed his arm. "Again, thank you. Now go and secure your family. Then we'll plot our vengeance."

Galene glanced to Ryn before she spoke. "I already have a plan. I just need a few minutes with Tahrs Nykyrian before I move troops."

"I want to know the minute Jupiter calls for clearance."

All three froze at the sound of Ryn's deep, deadpan voice.

Her face pale, Hermione turned to face him. "Ryn—"

"I'm not an infant, Mom. Jory won't be in any better shape than I am. He's the only one who was at our wedding, and he worshiped the ground his big sister walked on. It's not fair to put all this on him and leave him standing alone." He joined them at the door. "Let me know when you're ready to attack, Commander. I'll be there. All I can say is that bitch Kyr had better buckle up. I'm going for his throat with everything I have."

Fain held his hand toward Ryn. When Ryn took it, he pulled him in for a hug. "United in purpose."

"United by bond." Ryn clapped him on the back. "Forever Tavali."

"Forever Tavali." And with that, Fain put his arm around Galene and led her away from them. "Hell of a day, huh?"

"Indeed. Makes me terrified of tomorrow."

As they headed for Fain's ship, his link went off with Nyk's ring. He clicked it on. "Yeah?"

"Conference me with Galene."

Fain tapped her link so that she could hear the call, too. "You're on. Go."

"You asked for Kyr's weakness?"

Galene met Fain's gaze as they paused to listen. "Yes, Highness?"

"There isn't one."

Galene gaped at Fain. "What?"

Nykyrian sighed in their ears. "We've gone over *every*thing. And I mean every last detail we could sift."

"He's right," Saf said through the speaker on Nykyrian's end. "I've talked to every member of my family. After the death of his wife, Kyr closed himself off completely. Mentally and emotionally, he shut down. From what everyone says, I was the only one he cared about. And you saw what that got me. He practically killed me, and he now thinks I'm his enemy. I know from being in The League with him that he has no one there he trusts. At all."

"We've got no eyes on him," Maris joined in. "Not one Sentella spy or agent has been near him. After Sumi's attack, he has sealed himself away."

Fain sighed heavily. "How do we stop him?"

"We have to kill him."

Galene flinched at Nykyrian's cold words. "Safir?"

He hesitated before he confirmed Nykyrian's statement. "I know he's my brother. But the brother I knew died a long time ago. My father has accepted it as a necessary action for the good of the Ichidian Universe and the United Systems, and is willing to sanction it. The Phrixians won't retaliate. They condone whatever action is necessary to secure Kyr's abdication from League power."

That was good, but she knew it couldn't be an easy decision for a father, even a Phrixian one, to make against his own son. "And once we've removed him, who would we trust in his position? We can't just dismantle The League entirely. While it has become corrupted, it did stand for centuries as a noble endeavor that protected all the systems from tyrants such as Eriadne and Justinian Cruel. Whether we like it or not, the Nine Worlds have grown to depend upon it as a necessary part of our governments."

"I agree. What I propose is a restructuring of how it's run, and who controls its power. Rather than one prime commander whose authority is absolute, we will need to reinstate the Overseer's Consulate to take command of League forces, so that one individual will never again be the sole authority. Rather, The League's prime commander will now answer to and take orders from the Consulate in the same manner as any military leader answers to the governing body of his or her world. And as far as Kyr's replacement, I plan to propose Lorens ezul Terronova for the position."

"You've heard from him?" Galene couldn't suppress the hopeful note in her voice.

Nykyrian nodded. "He's with an enclave of WAR. They've rescued his father, and several members of my mother's council. Lorens is requesting reactivation for his rank in the armada, and he wants Ilkin to step down so that he can take over. They plan to make an attack against Eriadne at first light . . . but only with your express approval."

"I trust him implicitly. And I gladly cede full control of Andarion troops to him. They're his to command. Please, reinstate his rank and oath, and I promote him to the acting prime commander of our armada in my absence. If he has a shot at Eriadne and Nyran, he is to take it on my authority with extreme prejudice and I will bear out all consequences for his actions. . . . Are the Caronese there yet to back him?"

"Almost."

"Good. I shall let Acting Governor Drakari know then to coordinate with Commander Terronova for his strikes. And, Highness?"

"Yes?"

"Can we requisition something else from Lord Drakari?"

"What would you like?"

"Two dozen of the best-trained Kimmerian Corps he can muster."

Nykyrian choked on her request. "And may I ask why you want us to hire assassins from a rival organization I can barely stand?"

She laughed at his offended tone. "The Sentella is the best of the best. No doubt. Unfortunately, The League knows your uniforms too well. As well as all your tricks and tactics."

"But not those of the Kimmerians," Nyk said speculatively. "You're right. I like it. They've *never* crossed The League before. It's definitely something Kyr won't see coming."

"You think the Kimmerians will join on?"

"We can try, and I can raise you one better for the cause."

"How so?"

"A former Gyron Force officer aching for payback on The League. My cousin is salivating for a way to get to Kyr. Whatever you're planning for the Kimmerians, I say we put Bas in charge of them."

Fain let out an evil laugh. "Yeah. I trained with Cabarro. He is all kinds of crazy. I swear that Kirovarian has Andarion in him somewhere. Strongest human I ever met. Fast. And unpredictable as hell in a fight. You never know what he's going to pull."

Galene liked what she heard. That was exactly what they needed. The best advantage when dealing with any enemy was unpredictability. "Then let's do it."

"I'll get started." Nyk hung up.

As they entered the bay where his ship was docked, Fain

pulled Galene to a stop so that he could marvel at the miracle of her being with him.

"Something wrong?"

"You are the most beautiful female I've ever known." He cupped her face and placed a tender kiss to her lips.

Galene wasn't sure about Fain's mood. There was a strange solemnity to him. One that honestly scared her. "What are you thinking?"

He pulled back with a scowl. "I don't know . . . something keeps tugging at the back of my mind. A detail I missed."

"What do you mean?"

Fain hesitated before he answered. "I'm not exactly sure. Just . . . I guess I'm being stupid." But as they boarded his ship, he turned around slowly to scan the bay. He couldn't suppress the sudden chill in his body.

And it wasn't because there were others on board. This wasn't his nervous system reacting to the additional heat signatures on his ship.

This was another matter entirely.

A premonition of a thing out of place. His subconscious picking up on a detail that didn't belong. If only it would clue his consciousness in on it.

Not that it mattered. He planned on being on high alert anyway. Because the one thing that had forever remained true in his life was that whenever things went right . . .

Everything backslid into hell.

Yeah, a shitstorm was coming for him. The deluge always did. He just hoped this time, he was the only one it took under and drowned. Because the last time he'd felt like this, his older brother had been murdered, Dancer had almost followed Keris into the grave, and Fain had lost everything in his life that mattered to him.

CHAPTER 16

N ykyrian stared down at the small child nestled in his arms, in absolute wonder of it. Her dark hair tousled, her cheeks were stained bright pink while she slept in blissful ignorance of the war that kept the rest of them from finding any peace at all. To her, the world was still fresh and new, a place of safety and love. She knew nothing of the real horrors he and his friends had survived. The absolute cruelty her beloved father was capable of.

Or him, for that matter.

And he prayed to the gods that she never did.

Innocent and sweet, she'd crawled into the lap of a heartless bastard who'd been trained to ruthlessly and methodically take lives and feel nothing for them as they died by his cold, steady hands. All at the command of an organization that had sold his services to the highest bidder.

Every life has a price. That was the League motto that had been drilled into him until it had replaced every last shred of his soul, and drowned out his conscience and humanity. As an assassin, his life had meant nothing to them or anyone else. Not even him. Either kill or be killed. Failure was not an option.

And in the darkest hours of a night very similar to this one, in the blink of an eye, a single innocent child and her mother had changed all that. When he'd lived in a place of numbness so deep he thought nothing could ever reach him again, the unexpected pleas of a mother for her innocent child's life had.

"Kill me. But, please . . . please, don't harm my daughter. She's an innocent. Too young to die for no reason. I don't care what you do to me, just don't hurt her. I beg you!"

It'd been the first time in his life that he'd seen a mother's love for her child. As foreign a concept to him then as war was to this toddler in his arms now. And that sole, unexpected plea, while the child's father's blood had dripped from his fingertips, had changed his life forever. There in that darkened room, on that fateful night, he had turned his back on The League.

One seemingly insignificant job. A typical, meaningless assignment.

Then in a single, unexpected heartbeat, everything had changed. That mother hadn't just saved her child. She'd given him back his soul and opened his eyes to what The League really was. To what he'd become.

A brutal tool.

A mindless animal.

Vowing to never again let anyone else have that kind of control over him, to wear no one else's leash, he'd walked away and founded The Sentella to save as many innocent lives from

The League as he could. And that little girl whose life he'd saved that night had grown into a fierce warrior herself—one who now wore a Sentella uniform, and fought for his cause with the same fervent passion her mother had given him. Nykyrian still watched over her and made sure that no harm came to her.

He always would.

Thankfully, she had no memory of his part in her past. Nykyrian prayed she never did.

But as much as he cared for her, it'd been another lady who had returned his heart to beating. Another innocent victim of The League who had given his hollow existence true meaning and purpose. Who had shown him love and made him understand it for the first time in his worthless life.

Without Kiara, he was nothing.

Mira mumbled and smiled in her sleep before she nuzzled against his chest and clutched at his shirt, just as his own children often did whenever he comforted them from whatever night tremors they had.

Distracted from his meandering thoughts, Nykyrian cupped her tiny head in his gloved hand. How could something so precious come from his traitorous snake of a brother? While he certainly wasn't without his own sins, Jullien was another beast entirely. Never would he have imagined his brother finding a conscience of any kind.

Not with both hands, a star chart, and an expert guide leading the way.

He just couldn't wrap his mind around the concept of Jullien loving *anything*.

Except his own repugnant reflection.

But then as he'd sat here, he'd begun to remember things he hadn't thought about in a long, long time. Memories of being in the palace with Jullien before Nyk had been sent away to die.

Of Jullien reaching out and being pushed away. By everyone. Ignored until Jullien acted out and was punished for it.

In school, it'd been the same way. Their teachers had taken a great deal of pleasure in pointing out Jullien's shortcomings and making him come to the front of the room more than anyone else. And because he'd been so overweight, and Andarion, the other students had been merciless to him. He was constantly getting into trouble for something.

At the time, Nykyrian had thought it justified and reveled in seeing Jullien punished and ridiculed. With some perspective and distance, he was no longer sure of that.

Yes, Jullien had been an ass. No question about that. But he'd also been isolated by his peers. For all his lineage and political standing, Jullien had been shunned and rebuffed by women.

Still, none of this made sense to him. How had his arrogant brother ended up as a Tavali pirate?

Nykyrian heard a light, aggravated gasp as Ushara came into the room and saw her daughter asleep in his lap. "How in the Nine Worlds did she get here? I've looked all over for her!"

The corner of his lips twitched in amusement as he saw the shadow of her standing there, hands on hips. "She snuck in a little while ago. She said she couldn't sleep. That her father always told her a bedtime story and that she needed to hear his voice so as not to have nightmares. Since he wasn't here, she thought my voice might work to keep them away, as we have the same accent."

Growling, Ushara rolled her eyes. "I swear Jules has ruined her. She's such a paka's girl. I can't do anything with her when he's not around." She moved to take her daughter from him. "I'm sorry she bothered you."

Nykyrian frowned as he realized Ushara had removed all her makeup. She looked nothing like he'd imagined. While most Andarions had dark complexions, hers was absolute porcelain— like a fragile, perfect doll. Especially given the whiteness of her hair and paleness of her eyes. It was a stark contrast to her black eyelashes and red lips. No wonder the Andarion clans had once believed the Fyrebloods to be godlike. She appeared ethereal and divine. Exotic and otherworldly.

Blinking as he realized he was staring rudely at her, he cleared his throat. "She was no bother at all. I actually appreciated the distraction. It soothed us both for a bit."

"You miss your children?"

Like a vital organ that has been savagely ripped from my body.

But assassins never admitted to such things out loud. Nykyrian clenched his teeth against the pain her innocent question wrought. "As with your Mira, at least one of them demands I rock them to sleep at bedtime. Kiara calls it stalling, but I don't mind. Rather, I dread the day when they grow too big for such things."

Ushara brushed her hand over Mira's dark hair. "I've never really been away from mine. Not until Vasili began his training for Canting. Even then it was rare until a year ago when Jullien apprenticed him full time as part of his crew."

"You didn't apprentice him yourself?"

"I couldn't. My rank's too high to run a single crew, and Trajen relies on me, as I'm one of the only few he trusts at his side. Had Jullien not taken a rank reduction so that he could sponsor him for me, I don't know what I would have done . . . other than gone mad from ragged nerves and stress." She smiled, exposing a bit of her fangs. "It's one of many reasons I love your brother. He knows how I worry. Still, I hate when they go out together. I know I have to let Vas grow up, but it's so hard when I still have the urge to burp him after he eats."

Nykyrian snorted. "I know exactly what you mean. I feel the same with my eldest and she resents me for it. She thinks I'm the most overprotective beast ever born. But I've seen too many shattered by cruelty to risk her, and I know what I'm capable of should any harm ever come to her. I would not hesitate to do my worst to any who make her cry a single tear."

She started to lift Mira from his lap.

Nykyrian stopped her. "You shouldn't be carrying her in your condition. I'm quite aware from my own wife that when females are near their due dates, their backs are stressed and aching. Show me where she sleeps and I'll carry her for you."

"Thank you." Ushara gave him a grateful smile.

With Mira in his arms, Nykyrian followed her from the council room of her ship down the narrow corridor to the crew quarters that were decorated to show where her children slept.

He paused in amusement at the door that bore the ghostly Gorturnum screaming-skull logo against a solid black background with the words *Vasili the Brave and Terrible* circling it. Yet it was obvious from the script and design that the picture was a holdover from her son's younger days, and done by his mother to amuse him. Just as his sisters' door had a more feminine version of the Gorturnum flag with their names so stylized in pink.

Nykyrian inclined his head toward Vasili's door. While the girls were obviously of an age to be Jullien's, and both had their father's dark hair, darker complexion, and greenish eyes, Ushara's son was another matter. He was as blond as his mother. "Vasili . . . I take it you were married before Jullien?"

"I was. Not that it matters to Jules or Vas. They've been completely devoted to each other from the very beginning. Yet even so, Jullien has always taken care to not try and replace his father in his affections." She swallowed hard. "Chaz was a good male. Strong and proud. Just like his son."

Sadness darkened her eyes as she opened the door to the girls' room. "Unfortunately, Chaz died long before he could see what a wonderful son he gave me." She touched the heart-shaped, winged necklace, marking it as significant to her, before she spoke again. "I never thought to find another male who would win my loyalty or heart." Releasing the medallion, she passed an amused grin at Nykyrian. "And *never* one of *your* ilk."

"Meaning?"

She led him to a bunk where Viveka was sleeping and pulled back the blanket for him.

Nykyrian carefully placed Mira in bed and tucked her in.

She immediately burrowed toward her sister, who unconsciously turned over and wrapped her arms around her as if she knew it was her twin, and, even in sleep, sought to protect her from any harm.

"An eton Anatole." Ushara spat the name as if it were poison on her tongue. "Your bitch of a grandmother brutally slaughtered my entire family and the rest of us Fyrebloods to the brink of extinction. Chased us to the very ends of the universe and has left us all haunted and scarred. Terrified of being found again. Honestly, there's a part of me that still feels as if I've betrayed their memories by being with your brother."

"Then why are you?"

She lifted her chin. "Why are you married to your wife?"

Nykyrian hesitated before he spoke the honest truth. There was no need to withhold something everyone already knew about him. "I can't live without her."

"Nor I without my Jullien. As I said, he is not the same boy you exiled, and he paid a steep price for all that was done in his past. It was only by losing everything he had that he gained his soul."

Nykyrian glanced down at the children and nodded. "Sadly, that seems to be the case more times than not. For us all."

As he left the room, he paused to stare at Ushara, who appeared both innocent and yet world-weary. "And you were right earlier. No matter how much we lie to ourselves about what a good person we are inside, sooner or later, we are all someone else's nightmare. Let us hope, for all our sakes, that history judges us with far kinder labels than what we've used to judge each other."

Fain couldn't sleep. Not while he had Galene's naked body nestled in his arms. He was too afraid to close his eyes and wake up to find this all a cruel dream. Even now, in the quiet hours, he couldn't believe that just a few feet away, contained in these metal walls that had once been his bitterest hell, in crew quarters that were normally empty, slept a family that belonged to him. A family that actually claimed him as a member.

Even better, a family that had been waiting for them on their return, to celebrate their unification.

Closing his eyes, he savored the memory of their impromptu surprise party. Talyn had been the first to pull him in for a hug. "Darling called and told us about your interesting union in the middle of disarming an IED. Don't think you're off the hook for a real ceremony. Either of you. If I have to suffer one, Hauk, you do, too." He'd released Fain to kiss his mother. "I'm a firm believer in spreading the misery."

"Talyn!" Felicia had chided. "You're so awful! What he means to say is share our joy."

"Yeah." Sarcasm had dripped from Talyn's tone. "That's *exactly* what I meant. So much so that I'm even willing to pay for the entire event. Whatever my mother wants, she gets."

Galene had kissed Talyn's cheek. "Thank you, but your father has already promised the same. He even told me he'd paint himself pink and wear feathers just so long as I actually showed up this time. Right, *keramon?*"

"Yeah, well, what the hell. You already left me standing naked in an auditorium full of strangers. What little dignity I have left is all yours to abuse."

Laughing, Talyn had passed him a bottle of ale and then toasted them while Vega and War had dusted Galene with "good luck" glitter that still clung to her skin and the sheets.

Fain continued smiling as he remembered the first family dinner he'd had since his parents had thrown him out. It'd been incredible.

And it terrified him. He had too much to lose now, and that reality tightened his gut. Anxiety made worse by the fact that Talyn, Gavarian, and Brach had gone out afterward with Chayden and Qory to help comfort their friends' loss over the deaths of their Septurnum brethren. Even though Chayden was a Rogue, both he and Qory had been fostered under the Septurnum Nation and had been adopted by Gadgehe as young teens—raised in the Tavali pirate lord's own household, as part of his immediate family.

And unlike Ven with Fain, Gadgehe had treated them like his very own blood-sons. Jory and Mack thought of them as siblings, and Chayden and Qory felt the loss of Mack as if she'd been their real sister.

War, misery, and death spared no soul, and took pity on no family. Today they had come for Ryn.

Tomorrow . . .

"Fain?"

He kissed Galene's shoulder. "I'm right here, Storm."

"Can't you sleep?"

"Not really."

Rolling over, she cradled him with her body. "I could have sworn I wore you out."

He smiled at the reminder of how thoroughly she'd made love to him. No inch of his body had been left unexplored or unpleasured. But even so, the mere scent of her skin, or sound of her voice was enough to make him hard all over again.

Kissing her, he took her hand in his and led it to his cock. "Obviously, I'm broken. 'Cause it won't go down for more than a few minutes at a time."

With a sweet laugh, she nipped his chin. "Apparently. My goodness, *akama* . . . However did you survive without me?"

"Never well. Always in abysmal misery."

"Mmmm." Dipping her head down, she kissed the skin below his slave's collar. "Is Venik ever going to remove this thing from you?"

"I'll have him remove it tomorrow. I'm hoping it slipped his mind, and that he hasn't reconsidered."

She froze. "He wouldn't dare. Would he?"

Brushing his hand through her braids, he swallowed as doubt stabbed him. "It wouldn't be the first time he's changed his mind about something he promised to do. Especially where I'm concerned."

"I'll kill him!"

Fain smoothed her furrowed brow with his thumb. "At least make him sign my manumission papers first. Trust me, we don't

413

want to deal with his wife. She's even more unreasonable and unhinged than he is. There's no telling what Malys might do. She's forever spinning out of control. And in extremely unpredictable ways."

Fire sparked inside Galene's eyes as she stared up at him in the dim light. "No one will hurt you again, Fain. On my honor. I will kill for you. Anyone. Anywhere. Any time."

Savoring every syllable, he kissed her and slid himself deep inside her body. This was where he belonged. Only here did he feel sheltered and welcome. She was his fortress of strength. His sole haven. And when she rolled him over so that she straddled his hips, he really did want to die before something came and robbed him of this, and left him alone again. He wouldn't be able to stand another day of living without her.

With hooded eyes, he watched her ride him and let the warmth of her body wash away his bitter memories and replace them with the promise of a better future. It'd been so long since he had something to look forward to that he wasn't even sure how to cope with it.

He was treading new, unfamiliar ground now and it terrified him.

Galene watched the emotions play across Fain's face as he gently cupped her breasts and arched his back to drive himself deeper inside her. Even scarred, he was still the most delectable male she'd ever seen. There was nothing better than wrapping herself around his hard, muscled body and feeling it flex against hers, and under her hands. No male had ever been made more perfect.

He awakened a hunger in her she hadn't even known she possessed. If she didn't know better, she'd think herself as stralen for him as he was for her. Impishly, she reached down to trace the line of his lips that held some of the glitter the kids had thrown over her earlier. He would probably die to know how much of it was on his skin and in *his* hair, too. But it looked good on him.

Fain nipped her fingertip with his fangs. Then he caught her hand and held it to his lips so that he could tease her palm with his tongue. Chills ran up her arm at the sensation of his breath on her skin. His eyes turned eerily bright red in the darkness before he rose up to kiss her.

With a deep, guttural laugh, he flipped and trapped her beneath him. He had that intense, predatorial stare now that she recognized. It meant playtime was over.

Rising up, he slid back inside her. This time, his strokes were deep and long. Desperate. He held her as if terrified of letting go.

"I'm not going anywhere, Fain."

He laced his fingers with hers and laid his cheek to hers. "If you do, swear that you'll shoot me between the eyes before you leave."

She sucked her breath in sharply. "What?"

He lifted himself up on one muscled arm to stare down with a sincerity that was chilling. Then he placed her hand against his wildly beating heart. "I mean it, Galene. You have always been with me, but now that I have you back . . . I would rather you put your dog out of its misery than leave it caged in the hell it's called home all these years."

"You are not a dog, Fain!"

With a cocky grin, he kissed her. "Of course I am. But I'm more than happy to be your bitch. You're the only one I will gladly let command me, and whose hand I would *never* bite."

She groaned at his humor. "Gah, you are so terrible. I hate the way you view yourself. I wish you could see yourself as I do. Just once."

Cupping her chin, he kissed her then and quickened his strokes until she was breathless from it. Then, in one blinding wave, she cried out as she came.

His eyes flared even brighter an instant before he joined her. He buried himself deep inside her and held her close as he nibbled and teased her ear. His whiskers teased her flesh.

It felt so good to have him in her bed. To have him with her. Period.

Galene held him tight in her arms. "Felicia was right. I just want to wear you like a blanket." She tugged his muscled arm over her breasts.

He arched a brow at her. "Should I ask why you were discussing that with our daughter?"

She laughed. "We weren't talking about *this*. Rather how aggravating males are in general."

"Not sure that's a better answer. Either way, I seem to come out a loser."

"Are you trying to pick a fight?"

He kissed her shoulder. "I would *never* pick a fight with you while you're naked. If I say something stupid, you have to remember that you've drained all the blood out of my brain hours ago, and left me with no ability to think clearly."

"Oh, you clever charmer. You've become far more debonair over the years." Her gaze fell to the collar on his neck and she felt a wave of sadness again at what he'd been through.

Alone.

And all because she hadn't stayed and fought for him . . . the one person she should have fought hardest to keep.

But never again. That was one promise she wouldn't break. Not ever. She would never again allow anyone to ever divide them.

Fain's breath caught as he saw the haunted expression on her face. Every time she glanced at the symbol of his slavery, it stole her joy. He couldn't stand it.

She deserved nothing but the best. And all happiness.

Kissing her lightly, he rolled from the bed.

"Where are you going?"

He reached for his pants. "To get this minsid collar off. I will not be the cause of your sadness anymore. I've given you enough tears. You will never shed another over something I've done. I promise you."

Galene choked on a sob as he entered the bathroom to wash. Not from sadness, but over the sheer joy she felt. Yet as she listened to the sounds of his dressing, a horrible dread consumed her. She'd meant what she said.

The gods had conspired against them from the beginning, and stolen too many years that should have been theirs. And though she didn't want to believe it, a part of her couldn't help wondering if they weren't cursed. If they weren't meant to be divided.

Her link buzzed.

Frowning, she pulled it over to see that it was the notification she'd set for Jory Hinto's arrival.

She flinched involuntarily before she returned it to the table and went to join Fain in the small bathroom. He was just leaving the shower as she entered.

"Something wrong?" He lowered the towel with a worried frown.

How she treasured that note of concern in his voice. The knowledge that she finally had someone to lean on. While she was strong and could stand on her own, it was nice to have someone at her back. To know that Fain would catch her should she ever stumble.

"Jory just requested clearance codes."

Fain cursed. "Is he coming in this bay?"

"It's what I told them to do. We have a few minutes before they arrive." She stepped past him.

Fain caught her hand. "Have I told you how proud I am of the commander you are? 'Course, you were always bossy. . . ."

She laughed at him. "And you, Fain Hauk, do honor to your forefather and namesake. In your eyes and form, I see that brave soldier who stood so valiantly and fought with his family to hold back an invading army to save our race. He had *nothing* on you."

Fain couldn't breathe as she spoke those words. It was the kindest thing anyone had ever said to him. "I love you, Stormy."

"And I, you. Forever and a day."

He heard a knock on his door.

"Fain?"

Reluctantly, he pulled on his pants and left her to open it, and greet his brother who was in the hallway outside Fain's quarters. "What do you need?"

"The Septurnum are arriving. I thought you'd want to join me in the bay."

"I'm just waiting on Galene."

She stepped out of the head, fastening the cuff of her formal suit.

Fain pulled his jacket out of his closet and shrugged it on, then followed Galene, Sumi, and Dancer off his ship and into the bay. Hermione and Ryn were already there, waiting with Nykyrian, Jayne, Syn, Maris, Saf, and Caillen, as well as Venik, Ushara, and a small welcoming party of somber Tavali. Ryn's eyes were red and swollen, but they were the only thing that gave away his broken heart. The rest of his composure was that weird mixture of rigid aristocrat and lethal warrior that was uniquely his.

Except for his left hand, where he finally wore a black wedding band that he idly stroked with his thumb.

Fain paused beside Ven and Ushara. Ven grimaced as he saw the collar on Fain's neck. He passed a covert glance to Hermione and Ryn before he quickly put himself between them to block their view and removed it. Had they seen it, Ven would have had some interesting questions to answer from the UTC, since the contract he'd made with Fain for the kids was technically illegal and in total contradiction to Tavali law. He was lucky Fain wasn't the type to rat him out. But having made the pact with full knowledge of what he was in for, he was Andarion enough to abide by the terms, no matter how appalling they were.

"Thanks." Fain rubbed at his neck where the skin had been chafed and bruised from it.

Without responding, Ven quickly slid the collar into his pocket before the Danes saw it. *Yeah, you should have thought about* that *before you locked it on my throat, huh, genius?* That was the bad thing about Ven, he didn't always think things through completely. He had a bad tendency to react first and then live to regret his impulsiveness.

Dancer moved to Ryn. "How you doing, buddy?"

"Gutted." His tone was emotionless and hollow. His eyes, however, betrayed an anguish that ran soul deep.

Fain hated to see anyone in that kind of pain.

Dancer placed his hand on Ryn's shoulder. While Fain had known Ryn for years now, it was nothing compared to how long and how well Dancer, Jayne, Syn, and Nykyrian had known him. Since Dancer was one of Darling's closest friends and his wingman, they shared a special bond. And given that the four of them had been protecting and training Ryn's little brother Darling since he was a teen, Ryn felt indebted to them and considered them an extension of his family.

And family stood together. Always. Blood with blood. Especially during times of grief and need.

As Jory's ship pulled in and docked, Ryn closed his eyes.

Jayne took his hand and rubbed his arm to comfort him. True to his princely bearing and tough Dane heritage, Ryn didn't show any emotion as he waited in somber silence. The only clue to his pain was his rapid breathing and the tight fists that he kept clenched at his side.

Hating that Ryn had to go through this, Fain took Galene's hand into his as the ramp lowered and a small party started down it. He immediately recognized the tall, blond, muscular Tavali dressed in the red and black colors of the Septurnum Tavali Nation at the rear of the group.

Vice Admiral Jory Woods Hinto, or Jupiter as he was better known. The code name, which literally translated to "godfather," had been given to him because when it came to making the impossible happen, Jory was almost Trisani with abilities. Had his father been anyone other than Gadgehe Hinto, Jory would have most likely been Gorturnum instead of operating under the True Red Flag Nation.

Yeah, he was *that* good.

As with the Gorturnum's nefarious pilots, Jory flew like a phantom beast through the most treacherous zones, undetected and never caught. In and out with a speed that left everyone wondering what kind of engine powered his ship. It was inhuman the things he could do, and his skills were legendary. Many speculated that his mother had to be Trisani or some other similar psionic species. No one could just develop the talent he had by sheer skill or experience.

But right now his movements were slow and methodical as he came off his ship, cradling his sister's limp body to his chest.

Fain winced at the same time Ryn's façade slipped and he stumbled back, then caught himself and straightened.

Jupiter cursed out loud. "How do you weigh so friggin' much when you're so krikken tiny? What do you eat? Lead pellets? I swear to God, Mack, I've carried titanium plating that weighed less than your fat ass."

Mack lifted the ice pack from her bright red hair and opened her eyes to glare at him. "Stop bitching, you little brat, and put me down. I told you not to carry me. But noooo, you wanted to show off your massive man-muscles to whatever woman might be present. Now you feel like a wimp and I feel like a blimp. Thanks. Like I don't feel bad enough. Mess with me and I'll puke all over you, and that'll learn you quick enough, won't it now?"

"Mack!" Ryn shot across the distance that separated them and swept her up in his arms before Jory had a chance to set her down. Laughing and trembling, he held her cradled like a baby in his arms as he spun circles with her. "I can't believe it! You're alive! You're here!"

With her eyes closed, she wrapped her arms around his neck and held him tight. "I'm so sorry we couldn't tell you, love. Dumbass burned out his subspace transmitters and by the time they were repaired, we were in League territory and didn't dare transmit."

"Hey now! Dumbass saved your life. You could show a little appreciation, you know."

"I am. It's why I'm not calling you a moron." She winked playfully at Jory, who laughed it off as he took her insults in stride. It was something the two of them had always done good-naturedly. As snarky siblings, they lived to trade insults. They didn't mean them and they both knew they would die before they'd ever allow the other to be hurt or allow anyone else to insult them.

Jory shook his head. "I would be offended, but I'm so glad she's still alive after that attack . . . she can call me anything at this point and I wouldn't care. Mack's got a free pass at me for at least a good decade or better."

Coming to a sudden stop, Ryn held Mack with one arm and pulled Jory to his chest with his other and kissed his cheek. "Thank you, little brother. I owe you more than I can ever repay."

"Actually, we owe you and Darling. Had y'all not made those mods to her ship . . . they had her tight-to-cross, Ryn. And they hit her with everything they had. It was one of the worst firefights I've ever been in." Jory sank his hand in Mack's bright red hair as tears welled in his eyes. "Anything you or Darling *ever* need. Ever. My life. My ship. It's yours."

He clapped Ryn on his arm, then wiped at his nose and sniffed. "Anyway, Da is really sorry he had to turn back. The League hit our north fleet and did some major damage to the Pharester station. As his vice admiral, he's authorized me to act in his stead for this mission. Whatever you need us to do . . . name it. I'm your number one bitch with a blaster."

Ryn rubbed his nose against Mack's as he smiled and kissed her. "I don't know how I'm going to fight now, since I have no plans of letting you go ever again."

She laid her head on his shoulder and then smirked at her brother. "Notice Trevelyan has absolutely no problem carrying me weight."

"Yeah, he's a freak. We all know it."

Ven rolled his eyes at their antics as he faced Fain. "Well, since I'm not needed and there's no family tragedy, I'm wandering off. Let me know if something comes up and needs my attention."

Fain's gaze went past Ven's shoulder to see the real reason Ven was drifting off—High Admiral and Presidium Trajen Dane Thaumarturgus was landing with his group of Gorturnum, and if Ven stayed around, he'd have to greet him as well. There was some kind of bad blood between the two of them, but no one knew what it was.

And Fain knew better than to ask after such questions.

He inclined his head to Ven. "I will."

And with that, Ven and his small contingency headed out.

Oblivious to them, Hermione cleared her throat and arched her brow at her son, who still held his wife cradled in his arms. "Have you forgotten something?"

"Um . . . yeah. Mack, meet my mother. Mom, meet Mac-Adough Hinto Dane, high commander of the *Merry Crimson*."

"Well . . . *was*. I'm rather in the market for a new ship at present, since me old one now lies in pieces, scattered about the galaxy. Know anyone interested in striking a bargain?"

Ryn screwed up his face thoughtfully. "Now that you mention it, the crew of the *Cruel Victory* could use a co-captain. I've been told Ambassador Dane's a bit of a prick to work with and can be extremely unreasonable and demanding, but something tells me you might be able to wrap him around your little finger and bend him to your whims any time you want. His crew would probably appreciate your presence on those days when he's particularly irritable and nasty."

Laughing, Mack kissed his cheek, then turned in his arms toward Hermione. "It's a pleasure to formally meet you, Lady Tavali. I'm extremely sorry that we kept our marriage from you, but I didn't want to compromise Trevelyan's standing either in the Tavali Nations or with the Caronese. I'm well aware of what everyone thinks of us Septurnum and of the longstanding feud between our clans. And how me father would feel about it all. The last thing I would ever do is harm your son in any way." She sank her hand in Ryn's red hair and toyed with it where it fell along his collar. "Trevelyan is everything to me."

Hermione kissed her cheek. "Call me Mom. And the honor is mine. What happened between the Septurnum and Wasturnum was centuries ago. It's time we heal our Nation and bring our people back together." She hugged them both. "Now go and rest, both of you. Ryn hasn't eaten or slept since he heard of the attack. My son loves you dearly and that makes you dear to me."

As they left, Hermione approached Jory and led him toward Galene to introduce them. "I know you're well acquainted with Fain. His wife, Galene, Commander . . ."

"Hauk," Galene said, to Fain's surprise. "I'm the one leading the Alliance."

Jory saluted her. "Pleased to meet you, Commander. I have some hacks to make to my ship to return her to speed, but we'll be back in service in a few hours."

"Take your time. We'll be making several waves against The League. If you don't make it out on the next run, we can place you in one of the subsequent ones."

Jory inclined his head. "I look forward to fighting with you, Commander Hauk."

As he walked away, Hermione glanced back to where Ryn had vanished with Mack. "He lets her call him Trevelyan. I can't get over that. He hasn't allowed anyone to use his given name since he was six years old, and he walked out of the shower, butt naked, and told me I was never to call him that again, under *any* circumstances."

"Yeah . . . okay," Fain said with a laugh. "Didn't even know that was his name."

Hermione nodded. "Oh, thank the gods this day ended much better than I was expecting. A few more victories like this and I might be able to sleep again."

"Speaking of . . ." Fain pulled out his link to call Chayden. "I'll let the others know that Mack is alive. It'll be a full load off their minds." He stepped away while they continued to talk war strategies.

Unfortunately, no one in their group answered his call.

He returned to Galene and Hermione. "It must be too loud for them to hear it. I'll go tell them in person."

"I'll go with," Jayne volunteered.

Galene pulled her to a stop. "Before you go, I meant to

426

tell you that Nero and Hadrian are due for arrival within the hour."

The color faded from Jayne's cheeks. "Hadrian? Why?"

"They're coming to find our spy for us."

Fain was glad to hear that. Two Trisani trackers would do it. No one could hide from that for long.

But Jayne didn't appear as happy about it as he was.

"I'll kill him!" Jayne growled. "I told him to stay out of this!"

Galene exchanged a frown with Fain. "Why are you so angry?"

Jayne lowered her tone to a furious whisper. "You don't understand the bounty on his head. If anyone *ever* learns he's alive . . ." She broke off into sputters. "He's not supposed to leave home. Ever!" She growled again, low in her throat. "I swear, he's not going to be happy until I kill him for his stupidity. Or someone else does it for me!" And with that, she stormed off.

Dancer hesitated as he watched her leave. "You want me to come with you or stay with Galene?"

"Stay with Stormy. I don't want her left alone. And in the mood Jayne's in, she might clip something off you're attached to, just on principle. While I think I'm safe, you . . . she might use for a scapegoat."

Dancer laughed. "You got it."

Nykyrian and Syn wandered over to him while Galene, Sumi, and Dancer headed back toward Fain's ship.

"You know Thaumarturgus?" Nykyrian jerked his chin in the direction Ushara had vanished.

Fain turned to see her walking down the ramp of the *Stygian*

Nightmare beside the most mysterious Tavalian ever bred. Dressed black-on-black, there wasn't an inch of Trajen's body left bare. Broad-shouldered, tall, and with an aura as lethal as any assassin to ever don a League uniform, Trajen carried himself with a predator's lope.

He wore no blaster, but the hilts of enough blades were visible to say he didn't need one to slay his enemies. And in a way, that was an even better testament to his sinister skills and willingness to take a life with his bare, bloodied hands. Not to mention, he had a crested Andarion Warsword strapped across his back. The only way for him to have such a weapon would be to have taken it in battle from the hands of a slain Andarion warrior.

No Andarion would have given *that* up without a brutal bloodbath. Andarions considered a family Warsword as part of a sacred heritage, and they were treated with extreme reverence. You didn't just go into a store and buy one of those. They were passed down through families, or taken as war trophies.

Case in point, the one Fain owned had come from the first Andarion he'd killed in battle. Dancer's was the very sword that had once belonged to the founder of their lineage from centuries ago that their grandmother had bestowed on Sumi right before their unification. Talyn's had been earned in the Vested Ring.

While a handful *could* be commissioned from swordsmiths, those numbers were strictly limited and had to be approved by the tadara herself, and no off-worlder was allowed to order one, under *any* circumstance.

Fain had to give credit where it was due. Trajen seemed to be everything he'd heard, and then some.

He glanced over to Nyk. "Know him strictly by reputation. Ryn and Ushara are the only two I've ever heard of who know him personally. And of course Ven and Hermione . . . but only because of the UTC. Even then, I don't think they've met face-to-face more than a handful of times."

Nyk turned toward Syn, who shook his head.

"He's a ghost. No record of any kind, anywhere. I got nothing when I did a trace. I'm thinking he was either erased or he's something we don't know about."

Nyk rubbed at his jaw. "If he was erased, Syn, he'd have a record."

"Not if he was good enough." Syn sighed. "At any rate, he's OU."

Fain scowled. "OU?"

"Origin Unknown," they said in unison.

"And we don't like that," Syn said. He winked at Fain. "It's scary."

Nyk shoved at him. "Go get some sleep."

"I'd rather get a drink, but I don't want my wife to gut me for it. Later." Syn headed for his quarters.

"You going to sleep?" Fain asked Nykyrian.

"No. I think I shall try to learn a few things about our new arrival." Nykyrian hesitated. "Doesn't 'Thaumarturgus' mean 'warlock'?"

Fain shrugged. "Not in any language I know. But I'm not as

fluent in as many as you are. That being said, Warlock *is* his call sign."

"Interesting," he mumbled, following after Ushara and Trajen.

As Fain headed out, he noticed that a lot more ships were landing. Both here and in other areas of the station. And when he saw that one of the ultra-lights that was being serviced and stored belonged to Ven's daughters, he sent a quick text to Ven to warn him that his wife was home, just in case Ven had wandered off somewhere he shouldn't be.

After all, they'd had enough excitement for one day. He was ready for a little boring.

Yet as he headed for the entertainment decks, he had a feeling that things were about to get lively again. Especially if Chayden was down in his cups with Caillen nearby.

"Hey, Sexy Baby T," Chayden whispered in a shout as he leaned across Qory to talk to Talyn. "The Tondarion Fire I drank wants to tell you a secret."

Talyn laughed at his friend. "You're drunk, Chayden."

"No, I'm not." He slammed his hand down on the table. "You still only have one head. So I'm still sober . . . ish." He belched, then ordered more drinks.

Qory signed at them, but Talyn couldn't make it out since Qory wasn't sober either and so his signs were slurred.

Chayden began chewing on a straw. "He says you should have a drink. See, I'm not so drunk I can't understand Qory."

Talyn scratched at his cheek. "We can't drink."

"Oh yeah, you're Andarions in uniform. Sucks to be you!" Chayden pulled a drink off the tray of a passing waiter—an alien who started to say something, then took one look at the massive size of Qory, Gavarian, and Talyn, then changed his mind about it.

"Yeah," Chayden said in a surly tone. "That's right. I got an Andarion set of Ring fighters and a Qill, and I'm a Qill-born Tavali and you're not! Ha!" Then he realized Brach was with them. "Oh hey, I got another Andarion, too!" He scowled at Talyn. "How many Andarions is that? Oh yeah . . . three. Three Andarions and two Qills and one bottle of Tondarion Fire. Yum. See, I can . . . do math. Not drunk."

Gavarian scowled at Talyn. "Qillaqs are interesting when they drink, aren't they?"

"They *are* something."

"You're something. And I'm a belligerent ass. Hole." Chayden guzzled the drink. "Hey!" He leaned against Brach. "You know what my greatest accomplishment was today?"

Talyn took a drink of his water. "Can't imagine."

"I kept . . . my mouth shut."

Talyn passed an amused frown to Brach.

"What's that mean?" Chayden asked.

"Nothing."

"Sure it does, but I'm telling you, for me . . . that's a major accomplishment. And I deserve another drink for it."

Laughing, Talyn reached for the snacks, then paused as he caught Gavarian's and Brach's eyes bugging wide. Curious, he followed their line of sight to see three extremely scantily clad, highly attractive females gliding through the crowd.

Yeah, okay. That was definitely noteworthy. Especially since one of them had on an outfit that really didn't leave a lot to the imagination. She might as well be naked in the room.

"Hey, hey, hey!" Chayden snapped, pushing Talyn's chin away from the small group as they sat down across from them. "Put those eyes on the floor and get the blood out of the protruding parts of your body. Fast. That there is the crew of the *Black Widow* . . . and tell me, Chay," he said to himself in a falsetto, "why is their ship named the *Black Widow*?"

Talyn gave him a dry stare. "Why is it called the *Black Widow*?"

" 'Cause their father is Braxen Venik . . . you know, head of the Porturnum Tavali, and one of the most ruthless, bloodthirsty pirates who's ever lived. Any male who looks at one of *them* and decides he wants to take a ride, gets a visit from Daddy and leaves the room in little bloody chunks." He jerked his chin at the two large, muscled males who came in behind the females and evicted the people from the table closest to them. Unlike their sisters, they held more Andarion traits than human. "And those, my Andarion pretty, are Braxen's sons. Payne and Stain, which is exactly what you will quickly be in and become should they catch you looking at their sisters."

Talyn laughed. "As you said, I'm Andarion. Some deaths, my friend, are definitely worth it. But as beautiful as they are, they pale in comparison to my most precious Felicia. There's nothing there that appeals to me, in any way."

Gavarian snorted. "Yeah, but I see all kinds of happiness awaiting *me*." He got up. "What about you, *drey*?" he asked Brach.

"Ah, hell to the yes. If I have to go out, I want it to be with a big bang."

"No!" Chayden grabbed them each by the arm. "Don't do it. Save yourselves."

"What in the Nine Worlds is going on here?" Jayne asked as she joined them.

Talyn sighed as he pulled Chayden away from Gavarian. "Our little Qillaq has imbibed a lot of Tondarion Fire. Honestly, I didn't know humans could have this much and not die from it. I think he passed internally pickled an hour ago."

Chayden ignored him. "Jaynie! Tell Vari not to diddle the Widows. Quick, while he's still a male."

"Um . . . yeah. Drunk as he is, kid, he's right. You don't want a piece of Ven's daughters. And it's not Ven you have to fear. They're half Qillaq. You have to earn martial rights to their beds, and they take two lovers at a time."

Gavarian flashed a devilish grin. "I'm really good with that."

"Two males."

His smile faded instantly. "Oh . . . not so good with *that*. I don't share well."

She laughed. "Didn't think so. But I do have some good news."

Talyn arched his brow. "Yeah?"

Before she could speak, Payne Venik approached their table and raked a sneer over Gavarian, Brach, and then Talyn. His gaze narrowed on Talyn's name and rank patches. At first, Talyn assumed it was from his Ring fame. Most knew him from the years he'd fought as the Iron Hammer. Even though he'd been retired for almost a decade, he still held more titles and records than any other fighter in Andarion Ring history.

But that wasn't the cause of his notoriety with the Tavali.

"Batur . . ." Payne shoved him. Hard. A bully-looking-for-a-fight move. "You don't have the right to look at my sisters."

Talyn barely caught his temper before he laid the idiot in his cold grave. Not only did Talyn stand a full head taller, he also outweighed the Tavali by a good seventy pounds. Or more. He knew from his years of fighting that he could kill the hybrid being with one blow.

Tempting. *Very* tempting.

And this was why they were forbidden to drink. Especially while they wore the uniforms that represented their nation and race.

"I wasn't looking at your sisters." Talyn tried to step away.

Stain cut his path off. "What? You think you're too good to look at them? You think 'cause they're hybrid, they're *beneath* you?"

They were trying to draw him into a fight. As the bastard son of an Outcast, Talyn was well acquainted with shit like this, since every ass-wipe Andarion had felt honor-bound to bait and taunt him for it since the hour he'd taken his first breath. It was what had made him such a vicious Ring fighter.

He cocked a brow at the Venik brothers. "Wait . . . I thought your whole problem with me was your fear that I *was* thinking so much of them that I was imagining they were beneath me already. No offense, but you really need to work on your communication skills. You're sending all kinds of mixed signals here."

Payne started forward, but Chayden caught him. "Hey, now . . . what's with all this . . . negative hostility, huh? We're all friends. Let's not be so *nasty*."

Stain curled his lip. "Stay out of this, moglidyte."

Talyn had no idea what that word meant, but by the amount of rage it awoke in both the normally easygoing Qory and Chayden, it had to be the Tavalian equivalent to *giakon*.

Or worse.

With a feral growl, Chayden launched himself over the table to go for Stain's throat.

Talyn caught him midair and spun about to ground him before he made contact and started another war between the Tavali clans. "Easy, Chay."

Chayden wasn't having it. In a mixture of Qillaq, Universal, and Tavalian, he spewed hatred and obscenities at them all as he did his best to move past Talyn.

Damn, he was like a tiny spider monkey. Or a fast-moving toddler.

Talyn literally lifted him up and set him down on a stool. "Sit your ass down! Stay there! Suck your thumb if you have to. But if you jump off that one more time, I will make you limp. I mean it!"

Chayden started to stand.

Talyn growled and widened his eyes. And exposed his fangs.

Retreating back to his seat before Talyn made good on that threat, Chayden glared at him, but wisely stayed put.

"Commander! Help!"

He turned to see Brach and Vari struggling to keep Qory trapped with the table, and away from the Veniks. As large and strong as they were, they were barely able to hold back the mountainous Qill.

And while Qory was gesturing furiously at them, no one needed Talyn or Chayden to translate the physical gestures for the words Chayden continued to spew at them verbally.

Jayne took over babysitting Chayden while Talyn forced Qory into retreat. Even though Talyn wasn't quite as large as the Qill, he was still one of the tiny handful of beings Qory shirked from putting headfirst through a wall, so it gave him a degree of leverage when dealing with the irate mountain that others, such as Vari and Brach, didn't have.

After Talyn got him seated and away from Felicia's brave nephews, he stepped back.

Payne was in his face again.

Releasing a tired sigh, Talyn stared down at the Tavali male as Vari and Brach took up positions to back him in what was obviously going to be a fight. "Really? Do I have to kick your ass? Is that honestly how you want this night to end? Don't you have a woman to curl up with? Boyfriend? Pet? Hell, anything would be better than nursing the busted ribs and broken jaw I will give you. And I would much rather be spooning my female in blissful peace than cleaning your blood out from under my claws, while she bitches at me for not holding my temper."

Payne curled his lip. "You're not the badass you think you are, Batur."

Brach let out a hysterical laugh. "Are you shitting me? Oh my God, it must hurt to be *that* stupid. You do know who you're taunting, right?"

Talyn slid his gaze past Payne to the boy. "Stay out of this, Brach."

Jayne stepped forward. "Payne, why are you doing this?"

He passed a cold, steely look to Jayne. "Because if I don't finish this, *she* will." He snapped his fingers. "Hadean Corps? Arrest Lieutenant Commander Batur for treason, and anyone else who interferes."

CHAPTER 17

"Commander Hauk?"

Fain paused at the sound of Morra's call. He waited for her to catch up to him and bit back a smile at how hard she had to work for it, given the size of her much shorter legs. It was so strange to him how so a tiny being could have such a large presence. She was so lively and animated that it was easy to forget the fact that he could just about carry her around in his pocket.

"Something wrong?"

"We finally broke the code." Wheezing a bit from her frenetic run, she held a link out to him. "I don't recognize the voice, but you might. And I have a better translation for it. It's still nonsense. Maybe it'll make some sense to you." She took several deep breaths as he turned the link on to read the transcription.

Fain scowled at the riddle.

Yeah, well, if I catch that pickle in another jar, I'm not going to shrivel it. I'm going to lop it off at the hilt, along with the berries and whatever else it's attached to. Mama don't play and she don't share her meals. Fire burns, but I consume, and I won't rest until I see it all in smoldering embers. There will be no shelter from the tide that rises. Let the rain drown it down. Show me the cow and I'll bring in the grinder. The rooster will be a hen and rue the day it left the pen to play.

A chill went down his spine as he recognized that syntax and cadence. Even without a voice to confirm his suspicions, he knew who spoke like that.

And why.

Something that was confirmed a second later when he thumbed the link on and it played out in the clear, husky voice of one pissed-off and betrayed female Qill warrior.

A female Qill he knew for a fact spoke flawless Phrixian because she'd thought it a quaint language to learn. . . .

Shit.

"Malys."

"Yeah. I should say so. They have to bear us a lot of malice to—"

"No, Morra. Not malice, Malys Venik. That voice belongs to Ven's wife."

Straightening up, she turned a darker shade of green. "What?"

Fain's head reeled as he debated what to do. How best to handle a very deadly situation. One didn't walk up and confront

Lady Porturnum. While Ven might dip his pickle in other jars, he always returned to the one who held his heart. And that was Malys. For all her faults and his, Ven would gut anyone who challenged her.

And explode Fain's skull all over the nearest wall if he breathed a word of this to Nyk or The Sentella and endangered her.

Morra reached for her link.

"What are you doing?"

"I'm reporting this."

He pulled the link out of her hand. "No. Bad idea."

"Fain!"

"I'm serious, Morra. You can't report this. Not yet. Let me deal with it first." The expression on her face said she'd definitely rather not. Honestly, he'd rather not, either. "You've no idea how explosive she is. You can't just march a group in there to confront her. She'll take out half the station before she goes down."

Morra finally relented. "I suppose there's a reason her name isn't Temperance."

"Exactly."

"Fine, gorgeous. I'll give you an hour. But I have to let the others know."

"All right. One hour." Fain handed her the link back. He started to tell the others about Mack, then decided against it. That could wait.

Malys couldn't. She needed to be neutralized immediately, before she did something they couldn't easily undo. Closing his eyes, he checked in with his ship to make sure everything and everyone was fine there.

Then he used his ship's system to tap into the station's line so that he could trace Malys and pinpoint her location. It wasn't something he did often. Mostly because he didn't care to track others.

Strange, though, Malys was in the command center. Not where she spent most of her time. Especially when Ven wasn't there. Running Tavali logistics and command just wasn't where her interests lay.

Yeah, this couldn't be good.

Curious, and honestly a little scared, he headed for her as quickly as he could while trying to remain nonchalant and not alert anyone else to the fact he was growing more terrified by the heartbeat of what Malys might be up to.

When he arrived at the main commcen, he found her with Kareem, her bodyguards, and two other Tavali. Kareem appeared a bit stressed and upset. Not the happy son to see his mother returned to him after a long absence.

Yes, Mom was home.

And she was pissed.

Ah, dear gods, what fresh hellacious fun is this?

"Something up?" Fain asked, trying not to betray his concerns too soon.

Tall, stacked, and lethal, Malys was dressed in skintight red leather, trimmed with white—the colors of the Porturnum Nation. Colors that heightened the caramel tones of her skin and accentuated her dark hair and well-painted eyes. The lady was striking and could easily pass herself off as the age of her daughters.

But she paled in comparison to Galene. Not just in looks. Rather, in every way imaginable.

Still, she was the lady of his Nation and he was supposed to respect her as such.

Malys turned on him with a shriveling glare. "This doesn't concern you, slag. I suggest you leave."

Well, so much for respect. She could kiss his ass with that tone. Fain stiffened at the insult. He really wasn't in the mood for it. Pointing to his sleeve Canting, he cleared his throat. "Rogue. Commander. Sir, if nothing else. And since the Alliance is currently in charge here and I'm the OOD, this is where I'm supposed to be." A slight lie, since he wasn't currently the officer on duty, but for some reason, the OOD wasn't in here. Which made him wonder where the Tavali coward had wandered off to.

Hell of a time for a break.

Kareem's eyes widened to the point it was amazing they didn't fall out of his skull. With an audible gulp over Fain's audacity, he stepped back so that he wouldn't be between them.

Yeah, no one back-talked the queen of the Porturnum Nation. It was all kinds of stupid. And on that point, Fain rivaled Caillen Dagan. But it wasn't in his genes to back down from anyone.

Ever.

Her eyes flashed with heated venom as she swept her gaze from him to Morra as Morra came in behind Fain, and then narrowed it in anger on her son. "Was it you or the slag who warned your father I was home? Is that why neither he nor his whore were in their quarters when I went after them?"

Fain crossed his arms over his chest. "My Lady Porturnum, you have much bigger problems right now than rounding up a roaming husband. I'm afraid I'm here to take you into custody."

"Excuse me?"

Fain let out a tired breath. "I would rather you come peacefully, but if I have to, I will drag you through the station, in cuffs."

She snorted disdainfully. "You're not male, or skilled, enough for that."

"Believe me when I say you don't want to test that theory."

She moved to stand in his face. An act of bold intimidation that didn't work at all, since she barely reached the middle of his chest. But he gave her credit as she stood on her tiptoes and glared up at him as if she could back him down.

Only Galene had those powers.

"Have you any idea what I'll do to you for this?" Malys raked a glower over his body. "You may delay my vengeance while you protect Braxen and his Andarion whore, but you haven't stayed my hand. When I get through with you, Hauk, you're going to wish to the gods that you were still in that hole Braxen dragged you out of!"

Fain duplicated her scowl. "What the hell are you talking about?"

"Don't you dare play stupid with me, you worthless bastard! You think I don't know what you're doing?"

"Yeah, not playing stupid. Apparently, I bathed in it completely, 'cause I have no idea what you're talking about."

She attempted to shove him back, only to learn he didn't budge unless he wanted to. "That Andarion whore who thinks she can have my male! I won't have it! I'll see them all dead first!"

Kareem finally found his voice again. "That's what I've been trying to tell her, Hauk. She thinks Galene is sleeping with my father."

Fain gaped at that unexpected bomb.

"I don't think anything," Malys growled. "I know it for fact! Just as I know you've been covering for them all these years!" She pulled back for the guards with her to step forward. "Arrest him!" She gestured at Fain.

Fain shook his head in warning. "Don't. First man to touch me draws back a bloody stump." He glared at Malys. "And are you insane? Galene isn't sleeping with Brax. Trust me. If he touched her, *I'd* kill him." He shoved his hand in her face to show her the tattoo he had that marked him, just as his son was marked with Felicia's name. And he pulled his sleeve back to show the rest of his markings. "Commander Batur is *my* wife. The only male she sleeps with is me."

Her jaw falling, Malys fingered his tattoos. "No . . . I don't understand. You married her after she had Braxen's son? Why? Did he make you?"

He curled his lip in disgust. "Hell no! Talyn's *my* son. I was pledged to Galene when we were children. And we conceived him before we graduated school." Pulling out his link,

444

he scrolled to a picture of the night before, where he stood with Talyn, Galene, and Dancer. "See for yourself. I assure you, those eyes don't lie. You know as well as I do that Ven's not stralen and only three bloodlines carry those genes. Venik isn't one of the lineages."

She scowled again. "Then why did Braxen override my orders and move her quarters from where I originally assigned them?"

Fain growled at her. "That was *you?*" He was still pissed about how they'd been greeted.

"Yes. I wanted to see how he'd treat her. If it was true that she was his pet."

Fain rolled his eyes at her petty jealousy and assumptions. "Yeah, well, Ven didn't do that. *I* did. I wasn't about to put my son and his mother in solitary slag cells. What in the Nine Worlds got into your head to make you think Galene was sleeping with Ven?"

"Eriadne. She bumped into us on Paraf Run and said it was why Braxen didn't kill Batur years ago when he led a strike team onto our base to capture her."

Morra scoffed. "Brax didn't kill us then because Ryn was with us and threatened to rain down Wasturnum hell if he harmed him."

Malys laughed bitterly. "You're lying. No Dane would risk clan war for some Andarion by-blow. We don't play those politics."

"You do when that Andarion is family." Fain swiped the photos to Jayne and Galene so that she could see how much they favored. "Jayne Erixour is Galene's cousin. She's of the Winged Batur bloodline and for Jayne and Talyn, Ryn would bust you and Ven wide open."

The color faded from Malys's face. "Oh dear gods . . ."

"Yeah. Eriadne played you. It's what she's best at. I can promise you that Galene has never touched Ven."

Malys returned his link to him. "Why did he allow the Alliance here?"

"To salvage the ships we take. It was the bargain he made. Plus he's more fortified than any other base and therefore safer. At least until the bombings started."

Malys staggered back to lean against the console. "Oh, Fain. I'm sorry."

He let out a relieved breath. "It's all right. You—"

"No, you don't understand," she breathed. "I had your son arrested, thinking he was Braxen's bastard. League assassins are waiting with a trap for him and Commander Batur."

For one heartbeat, Fain couldn't move as those words struck him like a blow to his stones. It was followed by a need to rip her heart out and feed it to her.

But he didn't have time for that.

"Where are they taking him?"

"The brig."

Turning around, he left the center and ran as fast as he could. Oblivious to everything and everyone, he snatched his link out and called for Talyn.

No one answered.

Terrified, he prayed and tore through the station, ignoring

all the beings who cursed him for his frenzied impatience. *Please be okay. Please, gods, don't do this!*

He called for Dancer.

"Hauk, go."

"Hey, *drey*." Fain tried to keep the panic out of his voice, but since he was running, there wasn't any way to sound as non-chalant as he wanted. "Are you on my ship?"

"Yeah. You okay?"

Panting, Fain cut around a group of Tavali, who shouted curses at him for almost slamming into them, and headed down the last hallway toward the brig. "Yeah." He didn't dare tell his brother what was going on. Not yet.

"Is Galene there?"

"Yeah. Why?"

"Nothing. Just make sure she doesn't leave the ship for a little while. Okay?"

"You're scaring me, Fain. What's going on?"

"Nothing," he repeated as he entered the main office for the Hadean Corps. Forgetting about his call, he rushed to the desk where their COD was entering data. "Where's Talyn Batur?"

The guard passed a bored look toward him. "You'll have to take a—"

"Don't fuck with me, you little *mogfart*! I'll rip out your min-sid spine and beat you with it!" He jerked the human up with one hand to show him just how easy it would be to do it. "Where's my son!"

"T-t-t-they're processing him. He's in Room One."

Fain dropped him straight to the floor. His heart pounding,

he rushed to the door and threw it open, terrified of what he'd find there.

The guards drew blasters on him. But he didn't care as he searched the area visually for any sign of an assassin.

For once, he relished the horrified expression on Talyn's face as he saw him.

Too grateful to find his son alive and in one piece to care about anything else, Fain grabbed him into a hug.

Talyn didn't return the gesture. He stood stiff and uncomfortable. "You've lost it, haven't you, Hauk?"

Laughing, Fain buried his hand in Talyn's braids and held him close. "No, thank the gods. I haven't lost a damn thing." He squeezed Talyn and kissed his cheek before he released him. Then he realized that the Hadean Corpsmen were still aiming for his head.

Fain cracked a smile at them. "There's been a little misunderstanding."

Talyn tilted his head. "Hear that?"

Fain caught the light snap a second later. "Trip wire." His only thought to protect his son, he grabbed Talyn and wrapped his body around him while trying to get him toward the reinforced inner hallways that were more sheltered.

Next thing he knew, everything exploded into flames and smoke.

CHAPTER 18

F ain came awake, coughing up blood. Every part of his body ached and hurt so much that he couldn't breathe. He couldn't move. Not a single part of his body. He was trapped beneath a crushing weight.

Please don't be my son's body.

All around, he heard screams and groans. The sounds of metal popping and fire. Alarms blaring.

But he didn't hear the one thing he wanted to hear most.

"Talyn?" Blinking, he wanted to brush the blood from his eyes to clear them. "Talyn?" he tried again, more desperate than before.

"I'm here." His voice was faint and pain-filled. But it was there. Just to Fain's left.

"Can you move at all?"

Talyn coughed, then groaned. "No. You?"

Growling, Fain pushed with every bit of his strength. But all it did was hurt him more. "No."

The lights went out, bathing them in complete darkness.

By sheer force of will, Fain dug his hand through the twisted debris until he found Talyn's arm. "I'm with you, *mi tana*. I'm going to get you out of this."

Talyn snorted. "Good luck, old man. But I don't believe in miracles." Yet even so, he squeezed Fain's hand back and then laced his fingers with his. "Can you reach your link?"

"No. It fell during the explosion. You?"

"No." Talyn cursed under his breath. "If I don't make it—"

"Don't talk like that. You're going to be fine. Just think about Felicia and that baby that needs a paka. You have a promise to keep."

"What promise?"

"To rip the body parts off any male who comes near her for unification."

Talyn laughed, then let out a fierce groan of agony.

Fain tightened his grip on Talyn's hand. "Squeeze as tight as you need to. I'm here for you."

His breathing ragged, Talyn's grip weakened.

That sent a wave of terror through Fain that made his own pain fade. "Stay with me, boy! Don't you dare break your mother's heart. You hear me? That's my job. Not yours."

"You trying to piss me off, Hauk?"

"I'm trying to make you fight."

Talyn let out a bellow of anguished rage. "Trust me, I'm fighting. I want the ass of everyone who had a hand in this." He paused his movements. "You knew, didn't you? It's why you came running in here like you did."

"I didn't know it was another IED. I just knew you'd been arrested and that you were being targeted by assassins."

"And you came running," Talyn repeated.

"It's what I would have been doing your whole life, had I known I had you. I'm . . . I'm sorry I failed you again."

Talyn coughed and wheezed for several minutes.

For a little while, they were quiet while they tried to dig themselves out, until Talyn finally spoke. "Can I tell you a secret I've never told anyone? Not even Licia?"

"Sure."

Panting, Talyn laid his head back to rest. "I only agreed to sign on with Erix Yetur as my Ring trainer because he'd been yours when you fought. It made me feel closer to you to be coached in the same gym where you'd trained. I used to imagine sometimes when I was a kid that he was you, and that you were the one teaching me."

Tears stung Fain's eyes at that confession. It was something he'd have never guessed, given Talyn's initial reaction to him, and it made him ache.

"Of course," Talyn continued, "I didn't know that until he took me to his office to show me his awards from his fights, and the trophies from the others he'd worked with. He wanted to impress me with his skills and their records. But it wasn't any of those that won me over. In that glass wall case hung a pair of red claw covers that he'd saved from his first award-winning fighter. From the first fight his protégé had won in record time against a much older and larger opponent. Erix kept talking, trying to convince me to let him take over my training,

451

but I didn't hear a word of it. I just kept staring at the name on those covers, and the picture of the young fighter that hung beside them."

"Venym Sting." Fain hadn't thought about that fight in years. Barely thirteen, he'd walked into that Ring so scared, he was still surprised he hadn't wet himself. He should never have been allowed to participate in a Vested title match at that age. It'd been criminal to throw him up against a title-holder, even in the Pinna Weight class. And he would never have done that to his son.

But his mother had demanded it.

Erix had held him back as long as he could. In the end, he'd been forced to do it or lose Fain as a client. Since he was Erix's first fighter, Erix had needed the creds too much to stop it.

To this day, Fain could see the stern resignation in Erix's eyes as the former Ring champion had clapped him on the shoulder. "I have faith in you, kid. You're fast. . . . You're tougher than any I've ever known. Just stay out of his reach. Remember, you don't have to win. You just have to stay alive. There's no dishonor in losing your first fight."

His mother had scoffed. "You lose this fight, you better not come home."

Positive they'd be pulling him out of the Ring in pieces, Fain had felt like total shit as he left the dressing room. Until he'd neared what he was sure would be his morgue.

Galene, who had told him she wouldn't be there to watch him bleed, was waiting for him. Her eyes filled with love, she'd smiled at him. "Kick his ass, Fain. Show them all the mighty

War Hauk you are. There's no one better than you. It's time they all knew it." She'd pressed her cheek to his. "And please don't get hurt. Every time he strikes you, I will feel it twice as much."

Those words were what had carried him to victory. They had fueled his need to end the match and make sure she didn't suffer a second longer than necessary. With one blinding punch, he'd laid that bastard out, and earned the name Venym Sting for it.

And his son—the son Galene had given him—had torn that record asunder the first time Talyn had stepped into the Vested Ring and made a mockery of Fain's abilities there. Damn, he loved them more than he could have ever imagined.

"I'm so proud of you, Talyn," he whispered.

Talyn swallowed and tightened his hold again on Fain's hand. "And that's the secret I never told anyone. It's why I fought like I did . . . why I chose red, gold, and white as my Ring colors."

The same colors as Venym Sting.

"All I ever wanted in my life was to be worthy of being my father's son. To do honor to you and your lineage, and not shame you or my mother."

A tear slid down Fain's cheek. "I love you, Talyn."

"I love you, Paka."

Fain bit back a sob as his son finally called him Dad. Not Father.

Dad.

"Fain! Talyn!"

His heart sped up at the sound of Galene's frantic voice cutting through the smoky darkness. "We're here!"

"Mom!"

"They're over there. Did you hear them?"

Through the darkness and debris, light danced from above. Yet Fain was none the better for it, as all it did was show him how bad off they both actually were. Talyn was pinned beneath half of a wall, and the debilitating pain in his own side came from a piece of beam that was buried in it. But the good news was it didn't appear it would take too much to dig Talyn out.

He, on the other hand, was going to be here for a bit.

"Fain?"

"He's by me, Mum." Talyn grimaced as he tried to rise up.

Something fluttered to the right of Fain, brushing against his arm. His breath caught the moment he realized what it was. "You're winged?"

Talyn flashed a bloody grin at him. "Yeah. It kind of popped out when the wall hit me. I take it Mum never showed you hers, then?"

"No, she kind of missed that. Hey, Storm! You've got some explaining to do about our boy, and another little secret you kept from me."

While workers and engineers helped survivors, Galene searched the snarled, smoldering wreckage with her heart in her throat. The only thing that kept her marginally calm was the fact that she could hear Talyn's and Fain's voices, and that Fain maintained a sense of humor as he continued calling out to her.

When Dancer had told her what had happened during his

call with his brother, she'd almost passed out from terror. It'd seemed like forever before she'd reached the site where the brig had gone up and she'd seen the damage caused. Fearing the worst, she'd recklessly started in even before the rescue teams and firefighters had shown up.

She hadn't cared. Not while her son and husband were trapped.

And as the light caught them in its beam and she saw how they were trapped in the gnarled mess, she had the same light-headed sensation again. Horror filled her as bile rose in her throat.

How could Fain even speak?

Choking on a sob, she fell to her knees and tried to pull some of the building off them.

Fain cried out.

Dancer pulled her back. "Give the engineers a few minutes to brace it. We can't start moving things around. The way they're in there . . . we could cause more damage and bring it down on top of them."

Galene bit her lip as the team set to work. He was right, and she hated that fact. Extracting them would be a scary game of weights and balance. "Fain? Talyn? Speak to me. Let me know you're all right."

"Not sure I'd classify this as all right. Definitely sucks to be here." Fain's voice faded. Then came back in a shout. "Talyn! Open your eyes, boy! Stay with me."

"Talyn!" Galene shouted. "What are you doing?"

"He's going into shock." Fain cried out as he struggled to

push against the beam that had him pinned. "Dancer! Get my son out of here. Now!"

Dancer squatted down by her side. "We're trying."

"Send me a lift. I can get to him and get it around him."

The engineer next to Dancer shook his head. "It'll crush Fain if we do that."

Dancer swallowed. "We can't do that, Fain."

"Yes. You can. Don't lip me. We're venting atmosphere. I can feel it. We need to isolate this section and we're going to have to make a hard decision soon, anyway."

Galene shook her head. "No! I'm not about to leave you down there with no ventilation."

"Yes!" Fain looked up and met her gaze. "Stormy, we both know I'm nothing but a worthless piece of shit. I've never done anything right in my life. Please, don't risk Talyn for me. We've got to get him out of here."

"He's right," another engineer chimed in. "We are venting atmosphere."

"Then work faster," she growled. "Get them out!"

"We don't know where the leak is. We could make it worse. Again, we might lose them both."

Galene broke on those words. "No!" She leaned over and tried to find them through the darkness. "Fain . . . please, don't do this."

"It's okay, Storm. I'll always be with you. You know that. Not even death will keep me from you."

Dancer met Galene's gaze with eyes filled by torment. "What do I do?"

"I don't know. I can't make this decision. I won't . . . I can't lose either of them. And I can't watch another brother die."

An aftershock shook the station, knocking the engineer from his feet. Dancer cursed as he went skidding sideways.

Galene barely caught herself before she fell, tumbling over the edge, down on top of Fain and Talyn.

Fain let out a roar of pain as more debris crashed on top of him and Talyn.

"Baby?" she called. "What's happening?"

"It went deeper. . . . I'm bleeding worse. You have to move fast. I'm not sure how much longer I can help Talyn. Send me the lift."

"No!" Talyn growled. "I'm not leaving you. We fell in together. We get out together."

Fain smiled at the son he didn't deserve. "You live. I live."

Talyn shifted and took Fain's hand in both of his. "There's only one thing in this life I want, Paka." He swallowed hard. "To hand my son to you for his naming. For him to carry on *your* name for another generation."

Closing his eyes, Fain savored those words. That was the highest honor any Andarion son could bestow on his father. While mothers chose the names of their daughters, the fathers picked the names of their sons. For a male to ask his father to name his son in his stead . . .

It was rarely done.

Normally, the birth father chose the names of family members he wanted to honor or impress. Friends who meant something special to him. Fain only had Dancer, but he wouldn't take the honor of Dancer being able to name his son after himself.

Besides, Dancer had *always* hated his name. And there was only one other Andarion Fain honestly treasured.

Fain blinked back his tears. "Then if it's a son Felicia honors us with, I would ask that he be called Talyn Aubrien of the Winged Blood Clan of Batur."

"Aubrien?"

He smiled sadly at his son. "The name I would have given you, after the War Hauk who gave his life to save his sisters. And Talyn for the greatest athlete and son Andaria has ever produced."

Talyn laughed, then groaned. His red eyes burned into Fain. "Love you, Paka."

"And I, you. Forever and beyond. With all I am, and all I hope to be."

The lift fell down by Fain's side, striking him so hard that for a moment, he thought he might lose consciousness. Only his sheer force of will and refusal to see his son perish kept him alert enough to pry it from the rubble and work it around Talyn. With the last of his strength, he pulled up on the beam that pinned Talyn's legs.

"Lift!"

They did. The moment Talyn began to rise, it shifted the weight of the beam that was piercing Fain and brought it down on him even harder. Fain bit his lip and tried to remain silent as pain ripped him apart. But he couldn't stand it. Crying out, he waited for death to stop the agony.

Suddenly, the pain lessened.

Not understanding the source, he looked up to see Nero and Hadrian through the breaks in the debris. With arms spread wide, they were using their Trisani powers to hold the rubble back from him while the engineers lifted Talyn out.

Galene pressed her hand to her lips and prayed beside Jayne as Talyn came free of the wreckage. Weeping silently, she ran to him. The medics placed him on the ground so that they could evaluate his condition. For once, he didn't fight them when they placed the mask over his face or even while they cut away his uniform.

That more than anything told her how bad his condition was. The only other time he'd not fought against medics had been after his last fighter crash.

Wanting to comfort him, but knowing she had to stay out of the medics' way, she squeezed his hand to let him know she was there and met his gaze.

She had half her heart safe.

The other part . . .

Galene glanced over to Hadrian and Nero. Both were sweating from the strain of holding up so much weight. Though to be honest, Nero looked *much* worse. Hadrian had always been the stronger of the two Trisani brothers. And that was the bad part about their exemplary mental powers. Too much, and they could give themselves brain damage.

Worse case, coma and death.

Jayne fretted by her side. "Hadrian can't do this much longer."

Galene ran to the side to see if there was any way to reach

Fain. Damn it! What good were wings when she couldn't even fly down to him? "Fain?"

"I'm here, love. I know they have to let go. Tell Nero and Hadrian it's okay. There's no need in them risking Jayne descending into hell to kill us all for them trying to do a good deed."

Hadrian snorted at his misplaced humor. "Not giving up yet, Hauk. Besides, you know how much I love to live dangerously. Why else would I share a domicile with Jayne? Risking her wrath is what I do for fun."

"You need to find a new hobby, my friend."

"How 'bout we get you out of that hole and you can teach me one?"

Fain coughed as his sight dimmed. Sadly, it wasn't going to happen. But he was glad that he wasn't alone. If he had to die, he wanted it to be with the sound of Galene's sweet voice ringing in his ears.

"We're losing oxygen. We've got to seal the area before we jeopardize more of the station."

Galene growled at the engineer. "Not until we get Commander Hauk out!"

Nero staggered and went down to one knee.

The moment he did, Hadrian's nose started bleeding. "I can't hold this alone. It's too heavy."

His breathing ragged, Nero tried to stand. "I . . . I can't." Anguish darkened his silvery blue eyes as he met Galene's gaze. "I'm so sorry, Galene."

Hadrian tried, but after a minute, he let out a fierce scream of agony before he fell.

And when he did, she knew it was over. Nothing but silence rang in her ears.

Cold. Dark.

Horrifying.

Fain was dead. For a full heartbeat, she couldn't breathe as that reality crashed down on her with the weight of the wreckage that had killed the only husband she'd ever have.

And out of the bitter, aching darkness, she heard a strange squealing sound. At first, she thought it was her soul screaming over the agony she felt.

But after a minute, she realized it was the sound of metal being bent and pulled apart.

Stunned, she looked from Hadrian to Nero, who wore shocked expressions similar to hers.

Hadrian shot to his feet. "There's another Trisani here."

Jayne drew her blaster. "Where?" She took aim at every shadow.

He glanced down at his wife and smirked. "Given the amount of power I'm sensing, that will only piss him or her off."

Suddenly, Galene saw where the help was coming from. On her right, Dancer, who had slipped away while she'd been preoccupied with Talyn's medical care, approached her with Syn, Caillen, Ushara, and Nykyrian. They flanked a tall, cloaked figure who had to be the unknown Trisani. By the height and broad shoulders, he was obviously male.

Without a word, he moved with the fluid grace of a wild hunting beast toward her.

When he came even with her, he stopped by her side, yet there was no trace of his features. The design of his clothes kept every part of his form hidden from sight. Only his accent gave any clue to his esoteric origins. Lilting and deep, it was as mysterious, gruff, and majestic as he was. "I swore to my blood oath brother that I would keep his family safe in his absence. And while I know you consider Jullien eton Anatole your bitter enemy, know that it is for him alone that I do this. I would never have exposed myself for anyone else."

With those words spoken, he spread his hand out and lifted Fain effortlessly from the depths of the debris. More than that, he bathed both Fain's and Talyn's bodies in a strange orange glow.

Uncertain, Galene met Jayne's shocked gape. "Is he healing them?"

She nodded wordlessly.

Unable to believe what was happening, Galene was torn between running to her son and to her husband. As if sensing that, the Tavali mystic lifted Fain's body with his thoughts and placed it beside Talyn's.

He gave her a harsh, red stare. "There. Now you can reach them both, Commander."

"Thank you," she breathed before she ran to them to make sure they were all right.

By the time she got to them, they were sitting upright and staring at each other and her, every bit as shocked as she was.

Laughing and crying, she grabbed Talyn and then Fain and rained kisses over both of them. "I swear the two of you are trying your best to shorten my life."

Fain couldn't speak as he held Galene against him and stared in amazement at being next to his son again. Unharmed and whole. "Are you all right, Talyn?"

"Yeah. Think so. You?"

"Aside from your mother choking the life out of me . . . yeah."

Galene nipped his chin before she pulled back. "You ever die on me again, Fain Hauk, and I'll kill you."

"Well okay, then. I'll keep that viable, sane threat in mind."

"Commander?" the engineer closest to them said insistently. "We've got to clear this area. We're still venting atmosphere!"

"All right. Clear it and seal it."

As they pulled out, she saw the looks on Hadrian's and Nero's faces as they gaped at the new Trisani. "Jayne?" she whispered. "What's going on?"

"I think they know him." Jayne slowed to wait on her husband. Galene stayed with her.

But it wasn't until they were clear that Nero grabbed the mysterious Tavali and slammed him against the wall so hard, Galene was surprised it didn't leave a dent in it.

When he went to hit him again, Hadrian caught him and held him back. "Stop it!"

"Stop it? Are you kidding? I haven't even begun the ass-kicking I have planned!" He glared at the Tavali newcomer. "How could you?"

The hood dissolved to show one of the most ruggedly handsome human faces Galene had ever seen. While Nero had dark blond hair and Hadrian brown, they were fair and angelic in appearance and features—similar in ways to Ushara.

But Trajen was as beautifully dark as an Andarion. With dark hair and eyes. He looked nothing like any Trisani Galene had ever heard of. "Don't you dare judge me, *brother*. You're lucky I haven't already killed you. Touch me again, and I promise you I will not show restraint."

Hadrian's jaw went slack. "He really is related to us?"

His breathing ragged, Nero nodded. "Yeah. You've always asked me what our brother was like. Hadrian meet Trajen." Nero's silvery blue eyes turned brittle. "How could you let me think you dead all these years? I have spent my entire life trying to find some trace of what happened to you and Julia. Wanting closure. Damn you for it!"

Bitterness curled Trajen's lips. "And I've spent my life trying my damndest to forget every moment of it all. Damn *you*." With those cold words spoken, he turned and left them.

When Nero started after him, Ushara cut him off. "Give him some space. Please."

He opened his mouth to speak, but she shook her head.

"Listen to me, Nero. I know him better than anyone. He didn't lash out at you. That's a good sign. Especially since you attacked him. Trust me. No one strikes him with immunity. No one."

Tears glistened in Nero's eyes. "What happened to him?"

Ushara hesitated before she answered. "When Trisa fell, your uncle sold him and your sister into slavery."

"He was supposed to protect them!"

"Yes, he was. Be glad you didn't make that last escape shuttle. Your mother was killed brutally in front of them as she sought to save their lives."

Hadrian winced.

"Thaumarturgus," Nero whispered. "I should have known the first time I heard his name."

Galene frowned at the word. "It's the name he uses. Does it have a special meaning?"

Hadrian nodded. "They were a sect of Trisani priests who voluntarily withdrew from the world. It was said that they were able to master their powers and do things with them that made a mockery of the rest of us." He looked at Fain and Talyn. "Apparently, it wasn't a myth."

Nero shook his head. "And here I just thought he took our term to use because he thought it was badass."

Hadrian snorted bitterly. "Well, a lot of people use it for that reason. Who would have thought?"

Sighing, Nero returned his attention to Ushara. "Is Julia a part of your Nation, too?"

Sympathy darkened her eyes. "No. I'm sorry. She died a long time ago from their cruelty. It left Trajen shattered and brittle. Completely mistrustful and withdrawn. Just be patient with him. He's harsh, but he is a good man."

Dancer scoffed. "Brothers, huh? What a minsid pain in the ass they are."

Fain draped his arm over Galene and laughed. "Tell me about it. You should have mine."

Hadrian flashed a grin at Talyn. "Feeling left out, little buddy?"

"Yeah, I got nothing to add to this. No ability to relate."

Jayne laughed. "You and Sway. My two lonely onlies."

"Ah, it's fine. I don't mind."

Hadrian sucked his breath in sharply. "Ooo, T. Have a care with that word. It always gives me chills."

Talyn frowned. "What word?"

"Fine. I hate it."

"Seriously?"

"Uh, yeah. Are you out of your mind? I live with Jayne and two daughters. The most terrifying four-lettered f-word a woman says in my house is 'fine.' I swear, every time I hear it, I cringe."

Nero laughed. "Jayne? What have you done to my brother?"

Kissing her cheek, Hadrian flashed a teasing grin. "Let me put it to you this way . . . God forbid anything should ever happen to her, but if it does I'm under orders to chain and lock her coffin shut during the middle of the funeral just to freak everyone out."

They all laughed.

Until the engineers sealed off the damaged part and cleared the brig.

"How many did we lose?" Galene asked.

The head engineer pulled his face mask off. "None this time, Commander. High Admiral Thaumarturgus saved the ones who were trapped. We were extremely lucky he was here."

"Yes, we were," she agreed. She gave Fain a hard stare. "We have to arrest Malys."

"I know. Believe me, I could kill her myself right now." Fain sank his hand in Talyn's braids. "No one threatens what I love."

This time, Talyn didn't protest when he hugged him. He actually hugged him back.

Galene choked on her tears as she watched Talyn and Fain embracing.

Jayne put her arms around her shoulders and hugged her. "It's so sweet I could barf."

Galene laughed. "You're awful."

"I know." She kissed Galene's head. "Now let's go kick some Tavali ass."

Together, they headed for Venik's quarters.

By the time they reached them, Ven was there with his oldest daughter, Circe.

Fain hesitated just inside the door. "Where's Malys?"

Ven swept his gaze over their group. "You know I can't let you arrest her."

Fain tsked at him. "Ven, she planted bombs on your station. She almost killed Hermione, thinking she was having an affair with you. She's plotted with Eriadne. You don't want the blowback from this to land on you, too."

"We've already banished her. Stain and Payne have taken her off-station where she can't cause any more trouble."

Galene gaped. "Are you serious?"

"She's my wife. I can't let you hurt her. Sorry." He passed a smug look to Fain. "I know *you* understand."

Fain slugged him.

Circe stepped forward, but Galene cut her off.

"Honey, you're not *that* big or tough. To get to him, you have to get through me."

The Tavali held her hands up and wisely stepped back.

Galene sighed. "Well . . . given everything that has transpired, I think you'll understand my next course of action." She tapped her link to an all-alert status. "Attention all troops and commanders, this is Prime Commander Galene Batur-Hauk. Effective immediately, we are pulling out of the Porturnum station. I want all gear packed and all ships capable of flight to be launched within the hour. I'll transmit our new base coordinates on a secure channel in twenty-three minutes. Prime Commander out."

Ven made a pain-filled noise. "You can't do that!"

"Oh yes, I can. We're not safe here. We can't trust you. Furthermore, I want the kill switch you have for Fain, or so help me gods, I'll shoot you myself."

"The who, what?" Dancer gasped as the others burst into similar exclamations.

Fain cringed as she exposed his secret. "Precious, you weren't supposed to talk about that."

"And I'm not leaving you at his mercy for another second." She faced Venik with steely determination. "Hand it over or your wife will never again have to worry about your pickle finding a new jar. I will take care of that for her. Permanently."

Ven glared at her. "Fine." He pulled the trigger out and held it up for her to see. "Take it. But before you do there's something you should know."

"What?"

He pressed it.

"No!"

Fain cringed and waited to die in a painful burst.

But nothing happened.

Nothing.

"What the hell, man?" It was his turn to glare at Ven.

Ven tossed the switch at Fain, who caught it in one hand. "When you became Rogue, it deactivated it."

Fain gaped at that. It actually made sense that the neuro-mapping might have bypassed the programming and deactivated the device, but . . . "You knew and you didn't tell me?"

"Of course not. I'm not stupid. You would have killed me without hesitation."

Fain digested that slowly. "Then out of curiosity, how did you find out it was no longer working?"

Ven turned sheepish. "Really rather not answer."

Rage exploded inside Fain. That could only mean the bastard had tried to use it to fry his brains. Furious, he grabbed him by the shirt. "I just might kill you yet!"

"You can't. You still owe me a tithe."

"You canceled my tithe."

"Did I?"

Fain narrowed his gaze. "Ven . . ."

He cracked an arrogant grin. "Just jerking on you, Hauk. Get a sense of humor." He broke Fain's hold. "Go on. I gave you your freedom. Now would you rather risk it by attacking me, or do something better with it?" He cut his gaze toward Galene.

Honestly? Fain wanted to beat the crap out of him until his fury was spent.

But . . .

Ven was right. He'd much rather let it go and be grateful he was alive and had his family with him. "You're fortunate I have to help my wife pack her gear, and mobilize an army. Otherwise, I'd be slipping on your entrails right now."

And with that, they left Ven to tend his own house. There was nothing more they could do here. It was time for Fain to put it all behind him, once and for all.

"Well," Caillen said with an amused grin, "we've destroyed half of Venik's base. I think our work here is done. Chayden will feel extremely vindicated when he sobers up. Anyone know how to fly his ship?"

Fain passed an amused stare to Galene. "Qory."

Talyn shook his head. "Nah, that's not a good idea. He was beyond past drunk when I left them. So much so, he couldn't even make confident obscene gestures at Venik."

Morra let out a tired laughing sigh. "I'll get them. I can trac-tor beam Chay's ship to mine. So long as someone covers me."

Nykyrian inclined his head to her. "We have your back, little sister. Always."

"Thanks, boss. So who wants the hernia that comes with helping Qory walk?"

Laughing, Talyn lifted his hand. "I'll take it. I already had one large object fall on me today. What's another?"

"Yeah, you should be careful," Nero warned. "We can't do another round yet to lift him off you. We have to have a good day of down time to nurse our head wounds, and I doubt Ushara can talk Tray into another heroic deed." He passed a questioning brow to the Fyreblood, who was being strangely quiet in their wake.

"Yeah, I'm not the safest bet on that. Jullien has much better luck when it comes to moving the immovable object known as Trajen, than I do." She screwed her face up into a becoming frown. "Not sure how he does it."

Nykyrian actually stumbled at that. "Really?"

Ushara nodded. "Your brother can be quite the diplomat when he wants to."

Nyk passed a frown to Dancer. "One day I hope to meet this Jullien *you* describe."

Dancer snorted. "Hope you're not disappointed by the little bastard when you do."

Jayne slapped him on the stomach. "Play nice."

Grimacing, Dancer rubbed his stomach and grumbled. "I was. That was actually the edited version of what went through my thoughts."

Laughing, Jayne rolled her eyes.

When they reached the landing bay, Galene stopped Nykyrian, Syn, Dancer, and Jayne. Ushara paused alongside them.

"So where do we set up now, Highness?" Galene asked.

Nykyrian swept his gaze around the bustling ground crews as they rushed to prepare the ships to launch. "My grandmother still holds Andaria. We can't go there."

"Lorens has taken Xera V back. For now, they're holding the outpost. I have reinforcements en route to them."

Nykyrian stroked his chin in thought. "Until this ends, I want our families secured and out of harm's way."

Ushara rubbed her stomach protectively as if she couldn't agree more. "I know a place, but you won't like it. And I will need assurances from you and your mother that my people will be granted amnesty from your troops and laws."

"We are not my grandmother. Neither my mother nor I bear any malice toward the Fyrebloods."

"Then I can offer you shelter in our lands. No one will find you there."

Nero exchanged a bitter grimace with Hadrian. "Won't Trajen protest?"

"Probably. But he needs his brothers. Sooner or later, his shell will crack and he'll let you in." She paused. "Or he'll kill you."

"Oh goody!" Hadrian said in a falsetto. "I can't wait! Jayne? Can we go get slaughtered by my brother I never knew I still had? Can we, please?"

She snorted at her husband. "Yeah, he has a head injury. And he's about to get another."

Nero ignored him. "Is Trajen married?" he asked Ushara. "Does he have kids?"

Ushara shook her head. "He's completely celibate. He claims it's how he maintains his wizard powers. As I said, he lets no one near him. Ever."

Nero scoffed. "He is Thaumarturgus. Old school."

While they fell silent, Saf came up to them to speak to Nykyrian. "Hey. I got Maris packed and stowed on Fain's ship.

I'll run point. I figured he'd be carrying Felicia, Galene, and Sumi?"

Fain inclined his head to him. "You know it, *drey*. Wouldn't trust anyone else. . . . Maybe Talyn. But he only has a fighter."

Saf saluted him. "All right. I'm on standby."

Ushara narrowed her gaze on him as Saf walked off.

Fain arched a brow at the odd light in her eyes. "What's wrong?"

"Are you sure we can trust him?"

"Yeah, why?"

"Strange feeling."

Syn glanced after Saf. "He is Kyr's brother, but there's no way he'd ever shit on us for Kyr. His loyalty has been tested and proven."

"And yet there is still someone on the inside feeding information to our enemies."

"We caught her," Fain reminded the Tavali vice admiral.

Ushara arched her brow. "You sure?"

"Well, not now. Thanks."

Ushara laughed. "Just doing my job, Commander." She glanced to Galene. "I'll send the specs to our base over to you as soon as I get on board." And with that, she headed off to prepare her own ship and crew.

Aggravated, Fain turned toward Nykyrian and Dancer. "I hate when they plant suspicion. Here I was all happy. Now . . ."

Nyk clapped him on the back. "Welcome to my world. I trust no one."

Talyn nodded in agreement. "I'll go pack up our gear while you prepare everything else."

"Be careful." Galene kissed his cheek.

Fain watched as they split up to make arrangements. Alone with his wife, he took her hand and kissed it. "What a day, huh?"

Galene walked into his arms and savored the warmth of his long, muscled body that was alive and restored. His clothes were still torn and bloody from his fall. She couldn't believe how close she'd come to losing him and Talyn only a short time ago. It terrified her. "I'm just glad you're still here and whole."

"Me, too, Stormy. Me, too."

"Don't you ever die on me again, Fain Hauk. I've lived too much of my life without you in it. You owe me at least sixty years."

"I don't know what you're talking about, Stormy. I'm planning on being immortal. So far, it's working."

Nero hesitated as he entered his brother's dark domain. The sleek, intergalactic class speed-cruiser was as black as the powers Trajen had mastered. There was something on the ship that seemed alive.

As if the walls themselves were a living, breathing creature.

"Why are you here?"

The disembodied voice might frighten a non-Tri, but Nero still remembered what it was like to live in a world where such things were common. "I wanted to talk to you alone."

"There's nothing to say. You chose the brother you wanted to save."

"That's not fair, Tray. I didn't choose Rian over you. He was seven months old. He could barely walk."

"Fine, then. You're sorry you left me behind. Blah, blah, blah. Apology accepted. Please leave." His tone was flat and emotionless.

"That's it?"

"That's it. I'm not a social creature. I crave solitude in all things. Especially in so-called family gatherings."

"Then I shall leave you to it. But I want you to know that though our blood family is fractured, we are here for you. Rian, Jayne. Me. Darling. Drake and Annalise. We are all that is left of the Scaleras." Nero hesitated, but when it became obvious that Trajen had withdrawn, he let his brother's bitterness hang between them as he made his way from Trajen's ship back to the exit.

But as he left the ship, he realized something. Trajen had fostered in the Tavali under Ryn's grandfather. . . .

In that moment, he wanted blood.

Furious, he went to Ryn's quarters and knocked hard on the door.

Ryn answered a few seconds later, completely disheveled and in a state that said he hadn't been packing. Rather, he'd been appreciating the fact that he had his wife with him. He pulled his shirt on to cover the scratches and teeth marks she'd left over his back. . . .

And other places.

"What is your problem?" Ryn demanded.

"Right now? *You*."

He widened his eyes. "What'd I do?"

"Did you know Trajen was my brother?"

The shocked expression on his face actually saved his life. "No. Honestly, I never thought about it. I guess I should have known if I had, but I never spent much time around him. He became Tavali when I was a baby and ran a crew for my granddad." He brushed his hand through his hair. "No offense, you guys are old. You don't age like we do. In fact, I don't even know how old you actually are. You're what? Nine thousand or something?"

Nero playfully slapped him. "I'm not that old, asshole. Barely three years older than your father. Who wasn't that old when he had *you*. And I'm younger than your mother."

"Now you're just being mean."

"Anyway," Nero said, trying to drag him back to the point. "I'm glad to know you didn't keep this a secret from me."

"No worries." Ryn scratched at the whiskers on his chin. "He's really your brother?"

"Yeah. I had no idea he was still alive." Nero cursed as his nose started bleeding again. He needed to rest. His head was killing him from what they'd done to save Fain and Talyn. After using that kind of power, he'd be weak for days. Rian would heal faster, but Nero had never been as strong as either of his brothers. "How did Trajen get to your grandfather, anyway?"

"He was cargo on a ship that my uncle raided. It was one of

Varys's first takes and Varys was the only one who survived it. When he came home, he had Trajen in tow. That's all anyone knows. Neither of them would ever talk about it. And all my mother's ever said is that Trajen was like a rabid animal in those days. He didn't even speak to anyone until after he'd earned his Canting. Only then, to issue orders. He worked for my grandfather long enough to earn his tithe, then he challenged for the command of the Gorturnum and became a hermit."

Nero winced at what had become of his brother. Having survived his own rounds of hell, he could only imagine how much worse it'd been on Trajen, who was much younger. And in the back of his mind, he saw that horrid night with crystal clarity.

"Where's the baby?" His mother had been frantic as Nero had come on board the shuttle with Trajen.

He'd glanced at his beautiful sister who'd been quietly sobbing, but trying her best to hold it together. Younger than Nero, but three years older than Trajen, she'd taken Trajen's hand to comfort him.

"I thought you had him already."

"I told you to get him! He was with Tray!"

"No. The nursery was empty." Frantic, Nero had cringed as more explosions had sounded from the fighting.

"It was Augustan you told, Mother," Julia said. "Not Nero."

"Where's Augustan?" She'd started for the ramp.

Nero had caught her. In her formal gown and heels, she wasn't dressed for searching and she couldn't run through the assassin squads who were looking for royal family members to slaughter. "Let me go get them. I'll be right back."

"No!" Trajen had screamed, running to latch on to Nero's leg. "You promised to stay with me!"

Nero had pried his brother's grip off and returned him to Julia's arms. "I know, sprout. But I'll be right back. I have to make sure that Auggie and Rian are safe, too."

Tears had welled in Trajen's eyes. "Don't leave me. I'm scared."

"We're all scared. But I won't let anyone hurt you. I swear it."

Sobbing, Trajen had stared up at him. "You promised to protect me, brother. Don't go."

"I have no choice." Nero had gone down that ramp and into a future that still haunted him.

Maybe Trajen was right. Maybe he had chosen one brother over another. But had he not gone back, Hadrian would have been slaughtered.

Just like Augustan. The assassins had been on top of his brother and were in the process of killing him when his older brother had used the last of his powers to teleport Hadrian to him.

Run!

And Nero had. With everything he had inside him. Only Hadrian had escaped the horrors of the downfall of their race intact. Too young to remember anything, he'd been hidden away and knew nothing of it.

Meanwhile, he and Trajen couldn't forget.

Nero had been there to see the death of their father and older brother. Trajen to see the death of their mother and Julia.

"You okay?" Ryn asked.

"Yeah." But that was a lie and he knew it. He hadn't been okay since the night his family had been brutally executed.

Trajen had been five. He'd been eleven.

And both of them had been lost ever since.

Nothing and no one would ever bring them home.

"You were harsh on your brothers, don't you think?"

Trajen paused as he heard Ushara enter the flight deck while he ran the last of his safety checks. "You're questioning me?"

"Always."

"Brazen, little girl. When did you become suicidal?"

"Your mistake for not killing me when you had the chance."

He didn't comment on that. It had been one of the very few acts of mercy he'd shown anyone in his lifetime, and he still didn't understand why she'd evoked that peculiar emotion from him when no one else ever had. "Shouldn't you be preparing for launch?"

"My crew's on it. I came to tell you where we're heading."

"I already know." He turned around in his chair to glower at her. "Another suicidal act of defiance on your part."

She approached him slowly. "Which is why I came in person. I knew it would anger you."

"Yet you didn't run from my wrath."

"It's not in me to do so."

One corner of his mouth lifted in bitter amusement. "No, it isn't." She was brazenly stupid with her courage. And that was what he admired most about her.

She paused to cock her head. "You're hiding something from me. What is it?"

And that was what he hated most. She, alone, could read his thoughts better than any Trisani ever born. He had no idea how, yet her powers were undeniable. "You will find out soon enough. For now, you need to focus on our evacuation."

Ushara frowned at him. She opened her mouth to speak at the same time his ship's security was breached.

Normally he'd have vaporized the miscreants. But the moment he started to attack them, he pulled back and opened the doors to give them unfettered access to his flight deck.

Instead of enemies, two adorable little girls came running in and jumped on him with giggles and hugs as they climbed up his body like feral monkeys. "Uncle Tray! Uncle Tray! Vasi said you were here!"

"Can I fly your ship?"

"No, I want to fly it!"

"Let me!"

"Let me!"

Smiling, he scooped the twins into his lap and held them. "I swear, I think you both grew a foot since you left home. What has your mother been feeding you? Fertilizer?"

Viv leaned into his chest and squeezed him tight.

Pressing his cheek against her hair, Trajen cupped her head in his hand and held her close.

Ushara felt her throat constrict at the sight of the dark, lethal Tavali lord holding her children with so much obvious affection. Only they were allowed to approach him.

No one else.

Trajen abhorred all physical contact. Of *any* kind. He normally kept an invisible force field around his body so that no one could even get near him. Yet from the moment the girls had first reached out to touch him as infants, he'd allowed them to so do.

It gave her hope that he wasn't as far gone as he liked to pretend. That inside the bitter darkness of his soul there was still a chance he could find a way back to humanity, and be a part of the world again.

"Have you two behaved for your mother?"

"We tried," Mira sighed. "Do we still get points?"

Trajen used reward points for them that they could use to pick things from his "treasure" room. They were items he bought for the girls and gave to Ushara. He spoiled them so much that she'd been forced to put a stop to it for fear he'd ruin them with it. Between him and Jullien, the girls were absolutely rotten.

He smiled. "You do, indeed. Now, if you don't mind, we need to leave and get you both home."

Gasping, they widened their eyes. "We're going home!" Viv turned toward her mother. "Can we ride with Uncle Tray? Please?" She folded her hands under her chin and begged in the cutest manner imaginable.

Damn, it was hard to say no to *that* face.

Yeah, okay, she was as responsible for ruining her daughters as they were.

But she couldn't give in on this. Trajen had a nasty tendency to pick fights, and she didn't want her daughters on board a ship that was likely to be in the middle of a bloody battle on the way back.

Ushara tsked at her. "It's probably best that you ride with me, precious. I would miss my girls."

They pouted in unison.

"Besides, if you stayed with me, I'd make you go to bed." Trajen wrinkled his nose playfully.

"No!" Mira jumped from his lap. "Love you, Uncle Tray!" She ran for the door.

Viv remained to stare up at him. "Why are you so sad, Uncle Tray? You look like you have a hurt in your heart."

He brushed the hair back from her cheek. "I'm fine, *mina yahee*. Never worry for me. Now go and catch up to your sister. I'll give you both bonus points for riding home with your mother." He kissed her head.

She scooted off his lap and ran after Mira.

Ushara paused as she noted the way Trajen stared after them. "Why did you really expose your powers to save Fain and Talyn?"

When his gaze met hers, the deep painful torment there seared her. "Because no one should have to hold the hand of their loved one and watch them die because of someone else's selfish cruelty."

Galene paused as she saw the expression on Fain's face as he stared out the window at the Porturnum station they were leaving. She couldn't quite read it, but then he was leaving a part of his life behind. While Venik might not have been the best to him, he had been the closest thing to family Fain had had for the last few decades.

"Are you okay?"

Fain startled at her voice. "Yeah. Just . . . thinking."

"About?"

"How glad I am Nyk's an asshole."

She frowned at his unexpected comment. "Pardon?"

Smiling, he turned and pulled her into his arms so that he could give her a scorching kiss that set her blood on fire. "If Nyk hadn't been an unreasonable asshole, I wouldn't have taken this assignment." He cupped her face in his hands. "I wouldn't have you now. Or Talyn. So I owe everything in this universe to my friend. The asshole."

"Maybe you shouldn't call him that, then." She rubbed her hand down his hard biceps. "And isn't he technically your brother?"

"Yeah, I guess he is."

Suddenly, a loud curse rang out.

Fain pulled back, expecting it to herald an attack of some kind. He gripped his blaster and went to check on Talyn in the corridor.

His expression horrified, his son stood by the equipment locker with Gavarian and Brach. But there was no sign of threat.

"What happened?"

Talyn slammed the door shut. "Um . . . nothing. Nothing at all."

All three of them appeared rattled.

Frowning, Fain exchanged a concerned look with Galene. "What is it?"

"Talyn?" Galene stepped over to him. "Should I be worried?"

He glanced from her to Fain, then cringed. "Um . . . probably."

"What do you mean?"

Sheepish, Talyn opened the locker and stepped back. "I'm not sure you want to see this, Mum. But I think Paka is one sick bastard."

She glanced inside at the same time Fain realized what Talyn had seen. Oh yeah. It was *that* bad.

Pressing the heels of his hands to his eyes, he cringed at the same time she looked inside. "I can explain."

She said nothing.

Terrified and dreading her reaction, he slowly lowered his hands to face her arch stare. She had her arms crossed over her chest as she waited. It was a pose Talyn duplicated with an annoying impatience.

With a sigh, Fain realized there was no way out of this, except to confess the truth. "Don't look at me like that. It's not like it's anatomically correct or anything. She's just the ship's mecha unit. That's all. . . . Storm? Animate."

A perfect duplicate of what Galene had looked like in school, the mecha blinked and stepped out of the locker. "May I be of assistance, Fain?"

Talyn screwed his face up. "Oh dear gods, it even sounds like Mum."

"I do not sound like a porn actress."

Talyn looked really uncomfortable as Gavarian and Brach burst into laughter. He glared at them. "You two hyenas better stow that."

They sobered instantly.

Fain growled at all of them. Then he gentled his voice for his ship. "Storm. Deactivate."

The unit returned to her locker and shut down.

Trying not to feed into their overreaction, Fain closed the door. He searched his mind for some explanation, then finally decided on just telling her the honest truth. "There was only ever you for me, Galene. And while she isn't you, I couldn't ever imagine a home without you in it. So there you have it. That's why she's here. I can't live without you. I never could."

Galene sniffed back tears.

Talyn grabbed Brach and Gavarian and hauled them away to give them privacy.

With a weepy expression on her face, Galene returned to Fain and pulled him close. "And may the gods grant that you never have to live without me again. For I know I cannot live without you either. All I can do is exist."

CHAPTER 19

Galene followed Fain off his ship with Sumi, Vega, War, and Felicia by her side. Ushara and the others had landed only a few minutes before them. But something wasn't right. The bay was too busy and everyone seemed to be in a tizzy of some sort. And there was a strange mood in the air. A deep sense of foreboding.

Confused, she headed to Nykyrian. "What's going on?"

"I'm not sure."

"Daddy!"

"Mama!"

"Dada!"

Suddenly, the whole place truly exploded with activity as Nykyrian's, Caillen's, Darling's, Syn's, and Maris's family ran out to greet them. Galene was completely overwhelmed by the sheer number of people.

Sumi laughed in her ear. "I know what you're feeling. It's scary. But believe it or not, you get used to it."

Kalea ran from Dancer's arms to embrace a little blond boy named Jayce while Darice greeted Nykyrian's eldest daughter, Thia. Then he took War and Vega around and made introductions between them and all the kids. Before long, they were mixing like old friends.

Galene swallowed. "How do you keep them all straight?" she asked Fain.

"It's not as hard as you think."

Relieved to see Jayne's familiar family, she headed for them.

But her joy was short-lived as she realized that Ushara wasn't sharing their happiness. In fact, she became more worried as each second went by. "Where's Jullien?" she asked Darling.

That sobered their group instantly.

Vasili came up to stand at his mother's back while Trajen picked up Mira and held Viv's hand. The look on his face as he stood behind Ushara said that he already knew the answer.

Cairistiona was the one who approached Ushara. "It's an honor to meet you, daughter. You are as beautiful as Jullien said you were."

Ushara swallowed hard. "Where is he?" she growled.

The tadara bit her lip as tears welled in her eyes.

"He's here . . . right?" Ushara looked past them. "Jullien! This isn't funny!" she snarled. "Show yourself! I mean it!"

Approaching them slowly, Aros cleared his throat. He tried to speak, but he couldn't.

It was Nykyrian's beautiful wife, Kiara, who took Ushara's hand. "He distracted our pursuers so that we could get safely away. He said to tell you not to worry. That he wouldn't break your heart."

Aros finally found his voice. "He saved Kiara's and Zarina's lives, Nykyrian. And mine. None of us would be here without him."

Nykyrian kissed Kiara's hand. Then stepped back. "Ready my fighter!" he announced to the nearest ground crew member.

Kiara visibly cringed at those words, but she didn't try to stop him.

Sumi let out a tired sigh as she turned to Dancer. "I know . . ." She kissed him. "Do *not* get hurt. If you do, I'm naming your son something awful in your absence."

He laughed.

Shahara handed her sleeping son to Ture and kissed his cheek. "We'll be back."

Syn kissed his son's head before he took Shahara's hand and headed after Nykyrian and Dancer.

Maris hesitated at the tormented look on Ture's face. "I'm sorry, baby."

Ture nodded. "I know. Be careful what you wish for. I wanted a soldier. I should have said I wanted an artist. Just remember, it's really hard to get blood out of your uniform."

Maris kissed him, then Devyn and Terek. "I'll be home soon. I promise."

"I know you will. Otherwise, I'll send Zarya after you and you won't like that."

Zarya kissed Maris's cheek before he left, too. She held

Darling's hand when he started to leave, keeping him there for a moment longer. "I hate for you to fight without me."

"I know. You're the better shot, but you haven't been cleared for battle yet. And you're still nursing. If I could feed Cezar in your stead, I'd let you go, but I think our son would be seriously pissed at us both if I tried to suckle him."

"You're not funny."

With one last kiss, Darling left them to join his brethren.

Desideria growled in equal frustration at her brother and husband. "It's not fair!"

Caillen kissed her and then his daughter and son. "Don't worry. Shahara will nag me to death before I ever get hurt. She still thinks I'm five years old."

Chayden gave Desideria a light hug. "I know, sis. Guard your man-meat from harm. Don't worry. If anyone kills Caillen, I want the honors."

Qory signed to her that he'd take care of them both.

"I love all of you!" Desideria called after them. "Come back soon!"

Hadrian began protesting like a champ, but Jayne forced him to stay with the kids so that she could leave with the others.

"Don't worry." Nero hugged his brother. "I've got her back for you. Nothing's getting through me."

Only then did Hadrian relent. Scooping his son up, he held Sway and watched as Nero and Jayne walked off and left him with his daughters and son.

Fain started after them, but Galene stopped him. "Not without me, Hauk."

He looked at the others who stood around them. "You have a base to set up, Commander. You're needed here."

She turned to Talyn. "Commander Batur? Take the camp and make sure everyone is safe and accounted for. You're OOD until my return."

Defiance blazed in his eyes, but her son was ever a military officer at heart. "Yes, ma'am."

Saf clapped him on the shoulder. "Don't worry, Talyn. I'll keep her safe. Besides, your father isn't about to let anyone get near her." He hugged Ture and kissed his nephew Terek, before he led Fain and Galene toward the others to mount a rescue for Jullien.

Talyn felt sick as he watched them launch. They all needed to sleep before they did something this dangerous. But at the end of the day, they were soldiers.

War was what they knew best.

Felicia took his hand in hers while Vega, War, and the rest of the kids played in their blissful ignorance of what was going on around them.

Savoring her touch, Talyn let it ground him so that he could focus on what needed to be done. He turned to issue orders, then stopped as he saw Ushara and her daughters. For the first time, the admiral appeared bewildered, and honestly, lost. The agony in her white eyes was searing and made his throat tighten.

Tylie and Cairistiona were trying to comfort her.

"Admiral?"

Ushara blinked before she met his gaze. "Yes?"

"We are guests in your home. And—"

"No," she said, cutting him off. Swallowing hard, she looked around at the ones who'd been left behind. And in particular at the children. "You are not guests. You're our family." She took her daughters' hands from Trajen and led them to Nykyrian's twin sons so that she could introduce them.

The two sets of twins who were the same age were amazed by each other, but within a few seconds they were old friends.

And as Ushara led them deeper into the Gorturnum base, and Sway came running up for Talyn to carry, Talyn realized that this base was *very* different from Venik's. The Tavali here, in spite of being mostly Fyrebloods, were much more open and friendly. Everything about it was family oriented.

This place felt like a home, a refuge, and not a sterile military base designed to rob and pillage.

As they walked toward their new quarters, Thia, Nykyrian's oldest daughter, came running up to them. Tall and blond, she was a beauty.

"So you're my new cousins. Oh my God! Felicia. I knew I loved you for a reason." Thia had been a frequent student at Kiara's dance studio where Felicia had taught part time, and had even assisted as an aide in some of Felicia's classes. "And you, T . . . Welcome to the family."

Thia laced her arms with them. "You do know that Hauk and Fain have always been counted among my favorites, right?" She squinted at Fain. "Now that I think about it, I should have realized how much you look like them. Why did I not see that before?"

"No idea."

Felicia winked at her. "Probably because you were afraid I'd hurt you for ogling my male?"

Thia laughed at Felicia. "There is that. And congratulations. I heard about your unification." Then she slowed as she saw Gavarian, and her eyes widened in appreciation of his handsome form.

Felicia passed a knowing smile to Talyn. "Tizirah? Have you met my nephew?"

It took Thia a moment to recover her voice. "Um . . . no. No, I have not."

"Gavarian ezul Terronova, may I present Thia of the Sovereign Blood Clan eton Anatole?"

He fell into a perfect courtly bow. "Tizirah. It is my honor and privilege."

"Is he married?" she whispered to Felicia.

"Widowed," she whispered back.

Thia let go of them to sidle up to Gavarian and take his arm that she squeezed. "I'm so sorry for your loss, Major. I hope it wasn't too recent?"

"No. It's been a couple of years."

"Still, it must hurt." Thia led him away.

Kiara groaned. "Thank goodness her father isn't here. Talyn, you should warn him before Nykyrian returns that he has no sense of humor about males courting his daughter."

Talyn let out an evil laugh. "Why should I? I look forward to the entertainment. Am thinking I should take odds on it."

Felicia rolled her eyes. "You're awful. . . . Don't worry, Highness, I shall warn him."

With that, Talyn left Gavarian and Brach in charge of seeing the staff and civilians quartered and housed while he went to monitor the others who'd gone to battle. It was something Ushara had left a short time ago to do herself.

As he located the Gorturnum command center and entered the room, Ushara looked away from her star charts and monitors with a frown. Unlike Venik's center, this one was open and airy. It felt as if it were actually free-floating in space. The view here was breathtaking and sweeping.

Two alien beings, Vasili and another Fyreblood, turned to stare at him curiously. The Fyreblood female with a good deal of suspicion.

"Relax, Captain. Commander Batur and the others here are at peace with us."

Only then did the female captain retreat to her chair.

Ushara returned to her monitoring. "What brings you here, Commander?"

"The same as you. I wanted to hear them and make sure you weren't left alone. After all, as you said, you're my family."

With a grateful smile, Ushara indicated the chair by her side. "There's really nothing to hear right now. They're flying dark through League space."

He sat down by her side. "Then it's going to be a long night." Reaching over, Talyn took her hand. "But we will see it through together."

No sooner had he spoken those words than the tadara, Sumi, Felicia, and Aros came through the door to stand vigil with them.

Within the hour, the room was filled to capacity.

Even Trajen came to sit in a corner, wordlessly observing them all while they waited for news.

"Jullien was taken by the tadara's forces."

Fain felt as sick as Nykyrian looked while the major made her report to them in the Alliance camp headquarters on the outpost base where they'd been hoping to meet up with Jullien and their remaining troops.

Aghast, Nykyrian stared at the woman. "And no one thought to help him?"

The major shrugged. "It was Tiziran Jullien."

So basically their allied forces had refused to fight with him and had allowed Eriadne's men take him without any backup whatsoever.

Fain cursed at what had been done to Jullien. After risking his life to save theirs, *all* of theirs, the prince had sent his own Tavali troops back with their family to protect and escort them through Gorturnum controlled space, thinking that his mother's royal guard would help him while he covered their escape. Instead, his mother's most trusted forces had literally thrown their hands up and left him to rot.

No, worse.

They'd hand-cuffed a wounded and bleeding Jullien, and handed him over to his enemies, gift-wrapped, so that they could walk away unscathed and "prove" their loyalty to Eriadne long enough to buy their own freedom.

Dancer shook his head. "I never thought I'd feel sorry for your brother, but damn, that was cold."

Darling sighed. "What do we do?"

Nykyrian pressed his gloved hand to the bridge of his nose and winced. "I don't know. We have no intel to work from. No idea where he is. If he's even alive at this point."

"Nyran hates him," Galene said. "Passionately. Since childhood. There's no telling what he'll do to him. And The League has a Thrill-Kill warrant issued for Jullien."

Which meant Jullien could be brutally tortured and killed with immunity from prosecution.

Nykyrian let out a long, slow breath. "This is not the news I wanted to take back to his wife. Not after everything they've done for us."

Syn scoffed. "No good deed goes unpunished."

Shahara popped him on the arm.

"It's the truth," he said defensively.

Dancer clapped Nykyrian on the back. "There's nothing we can do here. We can't mount a rescue when we don't know where to strike. If he's still alive, we'll find him."

Nykyrian turned toward Darling. "Please tell me he's still a rank bastard dog who deserves to be gutted."

"He's a bastard. But he took two shots for your wife and daughter, and another round in the back to save your father. That's something your father didn't want to say in front of Jullien's wife. When we left him, he was bleeding pretty badly." Darling shook his head. "He is not the same dickhead you went to school with. As much as I'd like to hate him, I have to say he earned my respect with what he did for us and the way he handled himself."

Shahara nodded in agreement. "There were glimpses of the old Jullien, but nothing like he used to be." She scowled. "Did you know that for a full two years after you were reported dead neither of your parents really spoke to him?"

"What?" Nykyrian asked in shock.

"Yeah," Darling concurred. "I heard your mom apologize to him for it while we were in hiding. Apparently, they got so caught up in their own grief they forgot they still had another son. Whenever he tried to see your mom, her secretary told him she was indisposed, and when he called the Triosan palace, they refused to put him through, as they didn't want to risk upsetting his father during his bereavement period. And your aunt apologized for throwing it in his face that his parents had no time for him."

"Who tended him, then?"

"Staff . . . your grandmother."

Nykyrian looked at Galene.

"I was banned from the palace then, too. But they're right. When I returned to duty, Jullien wasn't allowed to see her. Those were my orders. It always upset her too much. Whenever he came around her, she would only ask him about you. Most of the time, she'd attack him for keeping you from her. Blame him for your death."

Nykyrian cursed under his breath.

Fain sighed heavily. "Now that you mention it, I don't really remember his parents ever coming to school events for him.

Maybe a time or two, but rarely. He always had a reason why they couldn't be there."

"Yeah," Dancer said. "It was rare. I do remember how Merrell and Chrisen would mock him over the fact that his father would promise to visit and then back out at the last minute with some lame excuse. How often they all looked at him like he was shit. Of course, I thought he was shit, too, and deserved it. But he was just a kid, surrounded by selfish assholes who didn't give a minsid hell about him. It's why he was angry all the time. Why he lashed out."

Nykyrian's features turned to steel as he faced the Andarion guard. "I want this a priority. Find my brother."

"And your grandmother?"

"Kill the bitch."

Galene saluted him. "Yes, sir." Turning, she went to carry out her newest orders. And though she relished going after Eriadne, she couldn't believe how bad she felt for what had been done to Jullien. A male she'd wanted to kill herself just a short time ago.

But the more she remembered about how he'd been treated when they were kids, and what had been done to him while she'd been stationed at the palace, the more she realized that he'd been trying to survive his grandmother's cruel reign, too.

Royal politics were hell.

While they had reclaimed the Sentella's families, ferreted out the Porturnum traitor, and established a new Alliance base, there was still a war to be fought.

They had won part of it. But lost Andaria.

"What are you thinking?"

She paused at Fain's question. "I was thinking about what we lost this week. You?"

He pulled her against him. "What I gained that I never thought I'd have. You by my side. And the beautiful sons and daughters you've gifted me with."

Closing her eyes, she received his kiss and let those words wash over her. He was right. They had gained far more than they'd lost.

And it wasn't really lost. Only temporarily misplaced.

Come the morrow, they would evict the bitch and take Andaria back. Of that she had no doubt. And if Jullien still lived, they'd save him too.

After all, they were The Sentella. Impossible miracles were their specialty.

EPILOGUE

Fain frowned as he kissed Galene's hand. Gently, he brushed his fingers over her bruised and scuffed knuckles. "What happened?"

"Nothing."

He turned the lights up and saw that she had scratches and more bruises. Furious, he growled. "Who hurt you?"

"No one. Rather, I hurt someone else."

"Pardon?"

A becoming blush stained her nude body as she bit her lip in a way that never failed to make him hard. "I didn't really go shopping today."

Obviously. Unless there had been some massively discounted sale on female shoes guarded by a herd of rabid lorinas. "Where did you go?"

"To visit an old friend."

She was being purposefully vague and he didn't like it. "Stormy . . ."

Galene let out a long sigh. "I went to see Malys Venik."

Fain gaped at her. "What?"

Reaching up, she traced the line of his jaw with her fingers. "You didn't really think I'd let her get away with hurting you and Talyn, did you? I merely went to explain a few things to her."

"With your fists?"

She gave him a lop-sided grin. "I am Andarion, you know? You and Talyn don't have the marketshare on that. No one threatens what I love. I promise you, she won't be back again in our lives. And neither will Venik." She handed him her link. "I have your papers. He signed them."

Stunned disbelief filled him as he read through them. "I don't understand."

"He was with her while I was there."

Shocked, Fain gaped even more. "You fought Ven, too?"

"No. Him, I shot."

"Stormy! Are you serious?"

"It was just a flesh wound. I'd already cleared that possibility through Hermione."

Fain couldn't believe what he was hearing. "And she was all right with that?"

"Given that Malys almost killed her daughter-in-law with her betrayals and actions? Yes. Mack's pregnant, by the way. So Malys almost killed Hermione's daughter-in-law *and* grandbaby. I could have pretty much gutted them both and Hermione would have been okay with it."

With a nervous laugh, he brushed the braids back from her beautiful face. "You are insane, Galene Batur."

"Galene Hauk."

"Ger Tarra Hauk," he corrected with a smile.

Biting her lip seductively, she shifted her hips and ran her feet down his legs. "I like that even better."

His heart pounding, Fain stared down at her as he slowly slid himself inside her warm body. "And this?"

"Mmm. I definitely like this." With the tenderest expression, she ran her hand over the tattoo on his arm.

Fain savored that look and the feeling of her holding him. Of having her in his life. Forever. "Thank you."

"For what?"

"Bringing me home after I'd lost my way and forgot where it was."

"You don't have to thank me, Fain. I was out in the cold, too. Every bit as lost in the dark. And sadly, I didn't even know it. I thought I was all right alone. That I was happy and fine. But the truth is, every ship needs a hangar. And every heart needs a haven. You are that light that saves me from the darkness, and I don't want to dwell there ever again."

Cupping her cheek, he placed a gentle kiss on her lips. "My oath to you, Galene Hauk, you never will. For wherever you go, I will always follow. To hell and back. Forever and beyond."